This Time
Last Year

This Time Last Year

Jean Chapman

PIATKUS

First published in Great Britain in 1999 by
Judy Piatkus (Publishers) Ltd of
5 Windmill Street, London W1

This edition published 1999

The moral right of the author has been asserted.

A catalogue record for this book is available from the British Library.

ISBN 0 7499 0483 6

Set in 11/12pt Times by Action Publishing Technology, Gloucester
Printed and bound in Great Britain by Mackays of Chatham PLC

For my husband Alan, who lightens my life, journeys with me on my research trips and observes everything with a most professional and all-seeing eye.

My thanks are particularly due to Ruth Lunn, travel guide par excellence, who showed me the 'bories' of Southern France and went on researching in Paris for me when I had to come home.

'The heart has its reasons that the heart knows nothing of'

Pascal

Prologue

The taxi swept into the gravel semi-circle in front of the cemetery and before the taller of the two women could ask the driver called, '*J'attendrai*!'

'*Merci bien*,' Stella called, thinking she recognised him as a man who had probably brought them on this pilgrimage several times before. She was pleased to arrive; the tension inside the car was always unbearable the nearer Lucille came to this place.

Following her life-long friend through the huge wrought-iron gates, she reflected that cemeteries were like cities, which grew out of all recognition, so what had been the outskirts became the new centres. Fifty years ago the graves they came to visit had seemed to stand apart; now they were crowded in on all sides. She looked around philosophically. She and Lucille had reached an age when they were more at home with the names on these monuments than those who actually lived around them.

Lucille went ahead, as she always did, and Stella sat on the little bench she had paid to have put before the Cleauville family vault. It was with affection she read the names of Lucille's father and mother, Ernest Blair and Gabrielle.

'Gaby's' funeral had been the first she had attended here. She remembered how foreign these cemeteries had seemed to her. A graveyard then had meant green grassy mounds surrounding a Norman towered church. These French family vaults, often stacked one on another, had seemed like miniature skyscrapers, so the dead towered over you, rather than lay peacefully at your feet.

Though some dead always towered – or at least they threw very long shadows. She caught a glimpse of Lucille's slim trousered figure between the great sarcophagi as she went to her particular place. Stella always waited some time before she followed.

*

1

Lucille had to be alone when she came to this grave, alone and quiet to experience that wonderful moment of communication that had never in all these years failed to come.

Part of it came from a memory she had to reconstruct. A memory of a young man and a young woman totally in love, a moment when she had on the brink of lovemaking also felt she stood on a narrow band of time which ran back to man's dawn – and forward – she had not known for how long. But now she knew. Every time she visited his grave she knew. This secret was just hers and the man's whose name she traced with her finger.

It would have been difficult to pass on, hurtful to tell. She knew love conquered all time and that love was the only reality which ran from the beginning to eternity.

Chapter One

May 1940

'Be careful, Stella,' Will Hutton said again as he passed a case from platform to train, holding on to its handle to make his daughter pause. She squeezed his hand and leaned over to kiss him. This hastily arranged journey made them both feel there was too much to say and far too little time.

I must be mad, he thought, looking at his red-haired daughter and behind her at the pale blonde hair and paler face of her French friend, Lucille Blair. Letting them go to France with German troops already threatening to burst through Belgium on to French soil, the act of a man with more heart than sense. As Stella pulled the carriage door gently from his hand to close it and lean out of the window, he acknowledged her part in bullying him into agreeing. 'You'll make a good lawyer,' he said, 'argue the hind leg off a donkey.' She grinned at him and he shook his head.

He lifted a hand to Lucille. All he could do now was try to pull a few strings to help them on their way. 'I'll try to contact your brother, let him know you're coming.' He had to shout above the sudden roar of excess steam surging from under the train. 'And I'll call the French embassy – that may help. Ring me when you can!'

Lucille nodded dumbly. Ever since she'd heard in the morning of her mother's serious illness all her thoughts were focused on getting back to her home near Avignon to be at her mother's bedside.

'Goodbye, Dad,' Stella called as the train took up the slack, clanking the couplings between the carriages. 'God be with you ...' she called, but whispered the end of the line, 'till we meet again.'

''Ere you are love!' A couple of soldiers came pushing to the door with kitbags, packs and rifles to make a late departure from the overcrowded train. The men, who had obviously been asleep, caused a

3

diversion and a cheer as they and their kit hurtled from the moving carriage. They also left a welcome gap in the corridor as people moved up and others took the empty seats. The two girls were able to stand beneath a window, where there was a rail to grip. 'We'd better stay here for now,' Stella said.

'We can always sit on the cases,' Lucille said dismissively, then asked in serious confidential undertones, 'What do *you* think is wrong with Maman?'

Stella studied their hands, side by side, clinging white-knuckled to the window-rail as the train lurched forward ever faster. 'She wasn't herself in September, was she,' she said carefully; she wanted neither to alarm nor to raise false hopes. 'Tired, lethargic,' she added.

Lucille did not answer. She remembered that her mother had been dismissive of any enquiry, and they had all thought it was no more than a flu-like languor which would pass. She had certainly rested much more, on a bed settee downstairs some days, elegant, as French as ever. Lucille's father had hovered, concerned, taking her cooling drinks, calling the doctor, sitting by her, and when he thought no one saw, discreetly holding her hand. Ernest Blair in his bluff English way adored his French wife. Lucille knew he would be totally devastated if anything happened to her mother. She looked up at Stella. They must get to Cleauville.

Stella seemed to understand the unspoken appeal for she put a hand over her friend's. 'Don't worry,' she told her with steely determination, 'we'll make it. She's my *maman* too.'

Having no memory of her own mother, Gaby Blair held a very special place in Stella's heart. The families' friendship stemmed from the fact that the Blairs in France and the Huttons in England had sons and daughters the same age. So at the time Stella's brother Philip was at Stratford Preparatory School as a day pupil, Jacques Blair was sent over to board at *his* father's old school. Philip and Jacques had become soul-mates, Jacques came regularly to their home, and eventually Jacques had taken Philip to France for a holiday. His little sister, Lucille, had begged for Stella to go and be her friend. The first time the girls had been eight, their brothers eleven. Every year since, twice, even three times some years, Cleauville Farm had been their second home, and Gaby Blair their French *maman*.

Stella watched the English countryside streaming past, green and wet, the lanes deserted, the smaller railway stations passing in a blur of milk churns and baggage trolleys. She felt her heart yearn for the full happy days at the French farm: the laughter, the picnics; helping with the harvests; the quiet blissfully warm evenings when sometimes Gaby would sing, Jacques and Lucille too, for they all had tuneful

4

voices, and when their three voices rose together, the more reserved English, Ernest Blair, Philip and herself, had joined in, times sweet enough to bring tears. Surely they were not gone forever?

They had been on holiday there when France and England had declared war on Germany last September, just eight short months ago. The four had been together again at the Huttons' family home of Avonside last Christmas, when the war had seemed to be in suspension. Men had come home in new uniforms and evacuees had made their way back to London and other big cities with their belongings and gas masks, all eager to celebrate the seasonal festivities in their own homes when the expected air attacks had not come.

Stella remembered the excitement when she and her father learned that Jacques, Philip and Lucille would all be there, the preparations, the huge Christmas tree from the garden, the fun after church on Christmas morning, opening presents. It had seemed such enormous luck. Philip on leave from the army, Jacques from his new-found role as war correspondent for his Parisian newspaper.

After lunch they had put on coats, scarves and gloves, muffled up against the bitter wind and the four of them paired up to walk by the river; not as they used to do girl with girl, boy with boy. Philip had been with Lucille, fooling about, Philip trailing a willow stem in the icy river and splashing her. Stella had advised pushing him in, offered to help. Jacques had caught her hand, jokingly, as if to restrain her and help his friend. The two in front had been too intent on their game to notice that the contact had brought other consequences. She had turned to Jacques to protest and found herself staring at him with the sudden realisation that he was absolutely no relation to her, that the stupid kind of electric shock running through her arm was something quite other than the feeling one had for an adoptive brother. Until that moment there had been odd times when Jacques's smile had seemed deeper, his gaze had held hers longer than usual, but she had always shrugged him off, twirled away. Maybe the war, the threat of more permanent partings, a passing regret for times gone, had triggered this deeper reaction. Was that what it had been?

For Christmas he had given her a heart-shaped pendant with a new moon in tiny seed pearls and a star of a tiny ruby. 'Wear it for me,' he had said and as he and Philip had left, he had kissed her cheek and whispered, exaggerating his French accent, which always made her giggle, 'it is my 'eart.'

'Fool!' she had said, but felt her gift of a new Swan fountain pen and propelling pencil left something to be desired, though he had immediately clipped them into his top pocket and patted them as if they held much future worth.

5

She glanced down to the sweetheart neckline of her summer dress, which provided a perfect complement for the pendant. She thought of the pictures inside, the two of them cut out from a springtime snap taken at Cleauville in 1939. Only last year, but the young man and woman in the pictures already seemed so much older.

So many taken out of their ordinary lives. Her glance took in the crowded corridor, men and women swaying together to the erratic movements of the train, speeding to places and futures undreamed of this time last year. People swapping stories, perhaps talking to each other as never before, the war their mutual topic.

She wondered if wanting to see Jacques again so much was love? He could make her laugh and she remembered his ability to let her cry. He had been with her holding her hand, after their old spaniel had died; helping her father dig his grave, then taking her to pick long-stemmed buttercups from the field old Jasper had most loved to be in. She remembered how bright they had looked laid on the new-turned earth.

A movement at her side broke the memory as Lucille released the window-rail and sank down to balance on the end of her suitcase, head in hands. Stella sat down beside her, precariously on the edge of her own case. 'When we stop at the next station, I'll jump out and see if I can get us a drink ...'

'Please don't, I couldn't bear it if you were left behind.'

'You could hold the door open ...' she said but Lucille gripped her arm.

'It can only be another couple of hours to London.'

It seemed longer, though they did get seats opposite each other after several stops and they were able to relax a little, though not talk so privately. Instead Stella listened idly to a nervous-sounding girl telling an older woman that she was 'going *all the way* to London' to meet her boyfriend. 'I've never been to London before! But my Tom's promised he'll be there to meet me. He sent me the fare and everything. He's an officer, you see!'

Stella smiled obligingly as the girl's triumphant glance came her way, and hoped 'her Tom' wouldn't let her down – ever. She wondered what her own reunion with Jacques would be like? She looked up, speculating, and caught the girl's gaze on her again, saw her blush and looked quickly away. Said too much, revealed too much perhaps, though Stella would have liked to know more. How long was it since she had seen Tom? How tremendous was this reunion going to be?

She looked across at Lucille. Her eyes were closed but she seemed to sit forward in her seat as if willing the train to go ever faster. With

6

the end of the journey so ardently wished for it was going to be a long, long few days. The one thing she took comfort in was that her father would be hard at work pulling as many strings as he could, and being a barrister he did have contacts through friends in the London Inns of Court, who might in turn, she supposed, have friends at the French embassy.

Friends in the right places, people in the know, that was what they needed at this time. Jacques had used his contacts as a journalist to reach them via a friend in Fleet Street; now he was on the way to his mother.

Stella was gazing out at the last watery glimmer of sunlight on the horizon as the guard came into the compartment to pull down the blinds. 'Sorry, miss, regulations,' he said as he reached over her, 'but we won't be long now.'

The girl opposite wriggled in agitation as they drew into Euston station – and Tom was there standing under one of the dim shaded lights. Stella saw her run to his open arms through the press of people as they heaved their belongings out of the train. She laughed aloud as the sailor whirled the girl around regardless of passersby, who had to dodge flying legs, retrieve a lost shoe. She was so involved in their joy she just stood in the doorway holding her case. 'Come on, m'dear, m'country needs me if not you!' A venerable old gentleman with a white Kitchener-style moustache stood above her waiting to get off.

'Sorry,' she said and stepped smartly out of his way, smiling as she realised Tom was not an officer after all, just an ordinary seaman in bell-bottoms. So what if she loves him; but why tell fibs?

So many arriving, departing, meeting, separating, milling around. Stella and Lucille were pleased just to follow Will's detailed instructions, taking a taxi from the station straight to the Cumberland Hotel. They arrived to find he had telephoned and booked for them. It was a comfort to have this tangible evidence of parental caring. The porter organised soup and rolls from the kitchen as it was way past the dinner hour. Neither of them unpacked more than their night clothes, as they had determined to be at the French embassy as soon as it opened.

They took their cases with them the next morning, merging into the early rush hour of workers and a multifarious parade of uniforms of all services and nations. Some buildings looked as they always had, while others had doors and windows sand-bagged and bastioned. Stella wondered if the French embassy would be recognisable.

They stopped aghast when they reached its vicinity. There were so many people at its doors it looked like an impending siege. 'Surely they cannot all have family emergencies!' Lucille gasped.

Once inside their names were taken, added to a lengthy list and they were directed to spare seats on a bench next to an anxious-looking elderly woman. Looking round it was possible to say everyone looked anxious, if not in many cases distraught. One or two were crying, even an elderly man quite openly weeping and using an enormous spotted handkerchief to mop his face.

'I need to travel to Paris immediately,' the woman seated next to them announced as if stating her prior claim. 'My granddaughter will be waiting for me.'

Stella nodded sympathetically, feeling Lucille tense and unhappy by her side.

'You see my daughter married a Belgian.' The woman checked her bags as she spoke, valise at her feet, handbag clutched on her lap as if her departure was imminent. 'And my granddaughter's school has been bombed, many of the boarders have been killed. My daughter is sending Zeta to me for the duration. She has been put on a train by herself, a label around her neck.' The woman's voice rose in alarm. 'The child will be terrified.'

'How old is your granddaughter?' Stella asked.

'Just twelve years old.' The woman's eyes grew large. 'You cannot travel across the Continent at twelve!'

'We did, madame,' Lucille said and as they waited they swapped more of their experiences, pausing mid-sentence to watch intently as officials moved around and people were summoned to different desks and offices. There was plenty of time and they overheard much, but nothing heartening or reassuring.

'Everything in France is confusion.'

'No one knows what they are doing,' and more sinisterly, and subversive whispered in such a place, 'No one knows what the government is doing.'

They eventually told their story to a harassed official behind a huge ornate desk overflowing with papers. Finally as the two of them stood together, their pieces of paper with names, addresses, reasons in his hand hovering above a pile of seemingly similar pieces of paper, Lucille gave a cry, 'Please, if we do not go at once it will be too late. I may not see my mother ever again.'

'There should have been a telephone call about us from ... Paris,' Stella added with reckless invention.

Tired dark eyes met hers and with a sigh he rose and went to study a further list on another table. For what seemed an eternity his finger ran down the sheet, turned a page, then paused, changed direction and ran along a line. He referred to their papers for what seemed like an eternity.

'*Oui*,' he said to himself, but shook his head at them as he came and placed their papers in a space near his stamp-pad, applied the magic rubber stamp and handed them over. 'Go to the south as quickly as possible,' he advised wearily.

'*Merci*,' Stella said quickly, as Lucille looked likely to ask some of the questions his advice raised. She did not want to be involved in any further business with the officials in case he asked about *her* relationship to Madame Blair near Avignon.

'I must telephone Dad.' She led the way to the nearest booth, leaving Lucille with the cases while she tried first her father's office, then home.

'Stella! Thank goodness!'

For the first time she thought her father sounded old and tired, all pretence of the cold legalistic approach gone as he heard his daughter's voice.

'M'dear, have you been to the embassy?' Listening briefly he went quickly on. 'You must go to Waterloo Station and travel to Southampton. The SS *Hantonia* is still sailing between there and St Malo, but no one is sure how long the service will last.' He paused to ask, 'Lucille, how is she bearing up?'

'So terribly anxious to be home.'

He thought his daughter would have made a good lawyer, keeping her aims well to the fore all the time. 'One more thing, remember when you reach Paris that Jacques's concierge will always let you into his apartment if the need arises.'

'We don't mean to stay overnight, we'll sleep on the trains. I'll let you have progress reports as I can. 'Bye, Dad.'

'*Au revoir*, m'dear.'

'*Au revoir*,' she repeated feeling corrected, instructed to be sure to return.

They made their way immediately towards Waterloo station, determined to board the next possible boat train. They were passed by units of soldiers marching with packs and rifles, and from a corner a newspaper seller shouted the latest headlines. 'Holland surrendered. Belgium fights on!'

'I wonder if that woman ...' Stella realised they had not even glanced her way once their own papers had been stamped, just hurried away.

Lucille shook her head, 'I don't know.'

As they joined the queue to buy tickets she tried to grasp what this latest news might mean, tried to assemble a clear map of France and its neighbours in her mind. Belgium she could picture top northeast, Holland a series of broken fingers of land north of that, both

9

countries with Germany on their eastern borders.

They moved slowly forward in the line. No one talked much in this queue and everyone arriving at the window seemed to take a very long time, faces pushed close to the opening, conversations urgent, then appealing, finally accepting. But most turned away with tickets and change, so some it seemed would definitely be travelling. She comforted herself with the thought that while Paris was very much north of centre, France was a big country.

'Mademoiselle?'

She looked at him sharply. Was everyone trying to travel French? She urged Lucille forward to make their request as if even here they must be cautious.

'St Malo?' He glanced at the clock in his office. 'Via Southampton, train in forty-seven minutes.' She gave Lucille a nudge and a nod. The money was paid, the tickets flipped from one of many racks.

'Southampton to St Malo, it'll be days before I get to my mother,' Lucille complained as if she had only just realised the extent of this longer route.

Stella drew her away. 'I think perhaps we're lucky to be able to go at all.' As they stood looking and listening to the men crowding the station, added to the underlying roll and rumble of boots on platforms came the heavy crunching rhythm of yet another column marching in. Once broken from their formal ranks, the men were animated, calling to each other, joking, waving to the girls, who waved back.

'Do you think Philip is in France?' Lucille wondered, looking around as if scanning the crowds.

'Dad's sure he is,' Stella answered, 'and I'll be happier once we're the other side of the Channel, then we won't be so easy to stop.'

'Shipping, it is being sunk in the Channel?' The question and the precise clipped French accent made them turn to see a children's nurse, a French La Bonne in uniform, in charge of two small children, a girl and a boy, in coats and berets in spite of the warm May day. 'I 'ave *mes enfants* to think of.'

'I think not,' Stella said reassuringly as the children's dark eyes focused on her. 'I've heard of none that have left from Southampton. You are going there? If we can help.'

'You are kind.' The nurse inclined her head but moved decorously away.

'Diplomat's children, do you think?' Stella speculated as they watched the nurse glide off like a black ship with two little boats in tow. 'Wonder why they're travelling back to France now?' She thought what a lot of children Hitler was uprooting, evacuees, children of mixed parentage, small displaced persons wandering about

Europe with labels around their necks.

'I feel as if I have spent all my life away from my mother.'

'Oh, no!' Stella gave a brief laugh at the idea. 'You will feel better when we're on the move again. You never really left home until last year – and she's always been there – for us all really.' She stopped, feeling every remark made about Gaby fraught with implication and unconscious double entendre.

'It will be good to see Jacques again too.'

'Yes,' Stella agreed, feeling a strange kind of yearning, her heart opening out, listening for echoes of experiences past and the boundless expanse of those yet to be. Jacques was a different journey.

The train drew into the docks and the SS *Hantonia* lay waiting alongside the quay, gangplank down, its discharged cargo of early French vegetables and fruit stacked ready for collection. So much seemed the same, trade going on, a steady trickle of people climbing the gangplank, a crowd to see them off. But there was a difference. The old excitement of departure was replaced by a tension. Hands were clung to in the last moment before sailing, some turned back for second, third, embraces; so much they had to say to each other, instructions, promises; some it seemed were still being implored not to go, tearing themselves away to mount the gangway.

A weary-looking stewardess pointed out their double cabin, while further along the corridor they saw La Bonne and her charges being shown into a *cabine-de-luxe*. The departure bell rang; passengers could hardly be all aboard. 'That's very quick, what time do we sail?'

'The captain is taking the boat backwards and forwards as quickly as he can.' The stewardess smiled bleakly. 'It's been pandemonium in all the Channel ports, St Malo gets worse each time we go back. Trainloads of people in the sidings waiting for a boat to England, or Jersey, anywhere. So many people are wanting to leave France.' Her quizzical glance posed the question as to whether they were doing the right thing travelling in the opposite direction. She shrugged when neither spoke. 'The last sitting for dinner will be eight thirty,' she said, adding as if an afterthought, 'Please do not bolt your cabin door through the night, it could be dangerous if we had to abandon ship.'

Later they wondered if they should undress after her remark, but decided they would keep their underwear on and have their outer clothes and handbags where they could easily find them even in the dark. Alongside these they placed the two cork lifejackets that were in the cabin.

They lay on their bunks talking a little at first then lapsing into silence as they felt the roll of the ship increase. They had left the shelter of Southampton waters, the Solent, slipped past the Isle of

11

Wight and well out into a choppy English Channel. Occasionally a larger wave hit the side with a resounding echoing thud. Stella thought fearfully of mines and torpedoes, and how far they had to go, all around the Cherbourg peninsula; then thinking of Gaby and Lucille she rejoiced in the fact that they had got away.

They woke to find breakfast nearly over, but the croissants, jams and cheese made them feel better, and gave the air of being somewhat nearer their destination. Afterwards they went right to the prow of the boat and were amazed to see how quickly they were cutting through the waves. Lucille stared straight ahead as if straining for the first glimpse of France. Speeding home, towards her French *maman*, Stella mused, watching the water surging and breaking in white foam high up the bow.

The sun and the wind whipped their cheeks to bright colour, and the sea breezes were refreshing after the night in the stuffy cabin. They walked the deck and saw the nurse with her two charges installed in deck chairs under a canvas awning. The children were busy with small notebooks and pencils, but La Bonne was being harangued by an elderly Frenchman wearing his bulky cork lifejacket.

'Marshal Pétain, *eighty-three*, madame!' He shook his finger in her face to emphasise the folly, 'summoned to Paris, asked to take over the army, while it is the mistress of Premier Reynaud who is making the decisions for the country! And,' he confided to the increasingly stony-faced nurse, 'we all know it is a woman's privilege always to change her mind!' The nurse gathered up her charges and bags and left the comfort of the deck chairs. 'France,' he called after her, 'does not know what she wants! But Germany knows exactly what Herr Hitler wants! France, Europe and Scandinavia under the jackboot, crushed by the panzers and the Stukas. That's what he wants for his master race!'

They wondered if he was not just inflamed with anger against the disarray of his fellow countrymen, full of concern for his country, or maybe drunk as he immediately swung round to find a new passenger to lecture. Before they could escape he pointed and almost ran on his neat little gaitered feet at Stella. 'You're English,' he shouted. 'There's a lot of anti-British feeling been stirred up.' He raised his arms above his head and made wild circling, mixing gestures. 'There's no firm lead from the French government, and people are listening to Herr Goebbels because he's gushing out anti-Communist propaganda!' He lectured the two of them now as if he were on some formal podium. 'They fear the Communists more than the German fascists! *Les imbéciles*! My son, he is a socialist worker in Lyons and they have arrested him! They think he is a Communist! I ask you, mademoiselle!' He appealed first directly to Stella then more widely to the audience of passengers who were listening intently all around, but who averted their eyes immediately the man's gaze swept over them. 'Ah!' he accused them, 'look away! What Christians! I tell you be careful, my friends, Germany is purging everyone who does not look like an Aryan, and France is interning all those who act like human beings! There is no hope for the world!'

Out of the corner of her eye Stella saw La Bonne appear briefly and point towards the orator. The finger was followed by a steward who came to ask monsieur to please go to his cabin. The monsieur shrugged off the steward's hand and said with some dignity, 'I 'ave finished, said all I wanted to say.' He closed his mouth very firmly and went to sit in a deck chair. 'You may bring me a coffee,' he told the steward.

That was the way to do it, Stella thought, boldly! If you dared to speak out, be bold and unrepentant. Many cast anxious glances at the dapper little man in his black business suit and his huge cork lifesaver, sipping his *café au lait*, but for the rest of the voyage he kept his own counsel. Even so it was quite a relief to see St Malo's rocky islet protruding way beyond its huge river estuary and to see the ancient ramparts of the old town beyond.

As they docked they could see that the building of the Southern Railway was packed with people and luggage waiting to board. When they in turn learned that there was a train leaving shortly, they ran with their cases to buy tickets. This train travelling towards the capital was only sparsely occupied, but it certainly smelt as if it had been lived and slept in for several days. They opened as many windows as they could and stood or sat in the sweeter air flow.

They arrived in Paris at midday on Thursday 16 May, having left Stratford station nearly forty-three hours before. They alighted into chaos. The station was a seething mass of desperate older men, women, children all laden with bulging bags, cases and as many worldly goods as they could carry. What was happening? Had all Paris, all France, gone mad? Stella glimpsed panic on Lucille's face; they appeared likely to lose each other in the crush as the two of them were buffeted and bumped. The noise was horrendous as the excitable mass bellowed and screamed to each other.

Stella gestured towards the pillar of an archway and the two dragged themselves and their cases through a sea of panic-stricken Parisians. Protected somewhat from the tide of people, Stella raised her voice to ask what was happening.

'The tickets for Biarritz are all sold out,' a flustered woman, her magnificent feathered hat askew, answered, 'and the trains to the

13

Riviera are jammed. You have to go where you can!' She pulled two other hat boxes close to her and launched herself back into the crowd.

'The rich, mademoiselle, are running,' was the sardonic comment of a long-faced railway official as he tried to force his way out of the station against the throng.

'But from what?' Lucille asked clutching his sleeve.

'Not so much from what, mademoiselle,' he told her 'but with – with the government. The ministers are burning their papers in their courtyards, people have seen the bonfires this morning. That is enough for those with money. They have all packed and are leaving Paris. If our government is going, well . . .' The shrug said as much as the words. 'All very well for them as can!'

'We have to get to Avignon,' she told him and he pulled down the corners of his mouth. 'Try tomorrow,' he said, throwing a thumb over his shoulder at the frantic would-be travellers.

'Follow him!' Stella said. 'Let's get out of this station.'

The two kept in his wake, Lucille gripping Stella's coat until they were across the street and could look back at the crowd, like outsized, burden-toting ants all scurrying for cover. 'Hopeless.'

'Jacques's apartment,' Lucille suggested.

'I think we must.'

They made their way by metro to Place de la République knowing that however much they wanted to reach Cleauville, they had to assess this new situation, plan the next stage, perhaps just stand still for an hour or two. On the underground they heard the same story repeated, wheelbarrows being used at embassies to throw their archives on hastily lit bonfires. *'Tout est perdu!'* Everything is lost. 'Or being thrown away!' the voice of contempt came from further along the carriage. 'They are making a gift of France to the Fatherland.'

The concierge of the apartment had known both of them ever since Jacques had come to Paris as a journalist in 1937. 'How rich do you think Madame Astier is?' Stella asked as they carried the cases along the avenue of four- and five-storey houses. 'Do you think she will have run?'

'I think she has too much respect for all her apartments.'

Lucille was right. Even as they approached her property, they could see the tall gaunt figure of Madame Astier standing arms akimbo on top of her front flight of steps, seemingly defying the world to do its worst. For a moment she paid them no regard, but then as they paused below her steps her jaw dropped with astonishment. *'Mon Dieu!'* she breathed, 'how can it be?'

They kissed the gaunt old proprietress's cheeks and she drew them inside almost conspiratorially.

14

'You know about my mother?' Lucille asked.

'I am so sorry, Jacques told me before he left.' She paused to push the coffee can over the heat. 'But when you see him you must tell him not to come back here.' She shook her head at them indicating they must drink their coffee first. 'Then I will show you.'

Wonderingly they followed her up the stairs to Jacques's apartment on the third floor. 'The gendarmes came yesterday looking for Communists.'

'But Jacques is not a Communist! He is fighting for his country as well as being a war correspondent!' Stella felt suddenly ashamed that they had let the dapper little man on the steamer be ignored, like some screwy old idiot, for the rest of the crossing.

'He has friends who have friends who are!' Madame turned on the stairs above them to nod, emphasise the certainty. 'It is enough. For twelve months it has been enough, for French boys with what they call "a social conscience" to be interned!'

When they reached the door she handed Lucille the key. 'They said it was "a purge" and I should be careful who I relet my apartments to. They took away boxes of things.' She shrugged and spread her hands, 'Evidence, they said.'

'Oh!' they both exclaimed as they saw the devastation inside. The flat had been very thoroughly ransacked, drawers emptied out, book-cases emptied, with the books strewn, lying pages fanned as if each and every one had been leafed through then thrown down. Stella remembered newsreels showing bonfires of books in Germany and Jacques using that same word 'purge'. Two years ago, perhaps longer, he had said Hitler was planning to purge Germany of everything and everyone he saw as less than a perfect Teutonic specimen: gypsies; the Jews; the sub-normal; the crippled. She in her comfortable world near the heart of England had wondered if this talk wasn't just his new wild, journalistic exaggeration.

When Madame Astier left them to rest and decide on their next action, they found instead they were tidying and restoring the room. Lucille folded and put back sweaters and socks into drawers, while Stella picked up the books, closing them carefully so pages should not be doubled over. One had a bookmark of green silk, shot through with a gold thread. She tried to tidy it into the pages but it was too long, then it fell out altogether and she knelt quite motionless for some seconds before retrieving it. She recognised it as one of her own hair ribbons.

She remembered it well enough, for it had been the last hair ribbon she had ever worn. Her brother had pulled it from her hair, flourished it around, out of her reach, called it childish. She had smarted under

15

his teasing, humiliated by the presence of Lucille and nineteen-year-old Jacques. Jacques had retrieved it, handed it back, but she had snatched it and thrown it down on the grass, stormed off unseeing. Tears flooded her eyes again as she put it back into its folds and replaced it in the book, an anthology of English poetry. She wasn't sure she hadn't stamped on it for good measure! She must have seemed so gauche, so naive, so childlike – but Jacques had kept the ribbon.

Lucille went from bedroom to kitchen and began to tidy and sweep in there. When finally Stella had replaced all the scattered books on the bookshelves, and she could remember the proper places for many, there were huge gaps. What could the gendarmes have taken? Then she realised it was all the works of Gorki, Chekhov, Tolstoy, all the Russian authors. 'For God's sake!' she exclaimed. 'It would be laughable if it wasn't so pathetic.' Then she was silent, kneeling with her hands thrust into the empty spaces on the shelves, suddenly believing in the German purges, in all that the intellectual writers, and journalists like Jacques, and passionate old Frenchmen, had warned of. She was bitterly ashamed of being one of the many who had ignored or doubted – of being one of the grasshoppers who had chosen to play uncaring, unheeding, all through the summers.

The next moment she was on her feet, heart pounding as she heard Madame Astier's voice raised, footsteps on the stairs and then an imperative hammering on the door.

Chapter Two

Lucille reacted first, rushing to close the kitchen and bedroom doors. She swept a tide of magazines into a rough pile on a table, then sitting down in an easy chair, picked up one of them and nodded her readiness. Stella automatically straightened her own dress and hair as she crossed the room. It felt like their first steps into the realms of international conspiracy. She thought how easily they fell into the roles.

She opened the door to find a soldier, a French officer, knuckles at face height ready to repeat the pounding on the door. 'Lucille? Lucille Blair?' he enquired, surprising her by snatching off his cap.

'I am Lucille Blair.' She came forward, magazine in hand.

'Of course!' His nod was almost a bow. 'I remember.'

Stella gestured him inside. He glanced back down the flight of stairs before stepping into the apartment. He was black-haired, very tall, six foot three or four, skin taut over high cheekbones. She thought he only needed a ruff around his neck to make a good model for some French family's aristocratic ancestor.

'You remember?' Lucille queried.

'It is a long time ago. I came to Cleauville when you were just a girl – long hair and long brown legs, I remember, on a swing.'

She seemed struck to surprised silence by the description.

'You are a friend of Jacques?' Stella asked.

'And I recognise you!' he added enthusiastically. 'Jacques has shown me your photograph. Stratford. On a river, in a punt.' His face seemed to become more animated, less severely aristocratic, with each addition to the recollection. 'Stella,' he finished triumphantly, nodding his head, encouraging her acquiescence.

'That's right,' she said smiling, relaxing, in spite of the circumstances, 'and you are?'

'My name is Jean-Paul Bisset. I know Jacques very well.' He paused and looked around again. 'Madame Astier said there had been

17

a raid? They usually leave chaos. You have tidied up, or ...?' Then he saw the bookcases. 'What did they take?' Then blew out his lips in disgust. 'I can guess. *Les imbéciles*!'

Stella remembered the landlady's words. 'Are you a Communist?' she asked.

'That,' he shook his head at her, 'is not a question you should ask, labels are dangerous these days, but ...' he waved a derogatory hand at the spaces in the bookshelves, 'I will never acquiesce to fascist principles.'

'But Jacques's friends are your friends,' Stella persisted.

'Of course! This is why I am here.' He threw out his arms expansively, including them. 'I'm on my way through Paris with a convoy for the front. I was going to leave a message with Madame Astier, but she told me you were here.' From his pocket he pulled out a small ring of keys. 'I heard about Madame Blair, and I am so very, very sorry.'

'Jacques has already gone to Cleauville,' Lucille told him.

'He was fortunate – to get away, I mean – even a day later and ...' He pushed out his bottom lip and shook his head. He repeated the shrug before tossing the keys in his hand. 'But I have a car. My darling!'

Neither answered, diverted by the 'darling', not quite sure if he referred to the car.

'The address is on the key ring. If neither of you can drive I am sure you'll find someone very willing to do so in exchange for a lift south.'

'I can drive,' Stella told him.

He dropped the keys into her hand, adding, his manner now crisp, businesslike: 'There are two spare cans of petrol in the left-hand corner of the garage, take those with you. Something's triggered a flood of people to try to leave Paris today, and the roads are already crowded with Belgians.' He paused, tutted. 'There's a Michelin guide in the car; if I had a map I could show you.'

Stella ran over to where she had replaced Jacques's world atlas. 'This any use?'

'Sure, you can look up the details later in my guide.' He hastily found the map of France. They all bent close over the table as his finger located the Ardennes. 'Many panzer divisions have pushed through the Ardennes, coming around the north end of the Maginot Line.' His finger moved from Belgium into French territory. 'They've smashed through fifty miles of our defences at the River Meuse, and are advancing steadily.' He slowly drew his finger east across towards Paris.

18

'Paris! Surely not! Paris will never fall!'

Stella was too appalled even to echo Lucille's shock. For the first time the war was more than reports and talk, more than people panicking and running away. She had a vivid recollection of going into court to hear her father prosecuting a young man who had attacked an older man. 'Why did you think the man had a walking stick?' The young man had shrugged. 'The man had a stick because he was in pain, the stick was to help keep the weight from his painful leg. You kicked it away.' The populations of Belgium and France were running because the stick they had leaned on, the Maginot Line, had been kicked away – useless – and because they were afraid, terrified of Hitler and the evil he stood for. She thought of her brother fighting on that same front Jean-Paul's finger indicated as crumbling away before the forces of the Fatherland.

'So you see everyone from the north and east wants to get away as quickly as possible.'

She had difficulty bringing herself back to concentrate on what he was telling them.

'This is the way I would advise you to go.' Again his finger moved across the outline of France, this time south and west out of Paris towards Tours, Poitiers, Limoges, Tulle, approaching the area of Cleauville and Avignon more from the west.

'That will surely take us days longer,' Lucille wailed.

'You may take much, much longer the more direct way. There are Belgians driving cattle, walking with goats and dogs on leashes – believe me – and there will be more dive-bombing or machine-gunning on those roads. On this route, as yet, it is not so effective for the Stukas to inflict so many casualties.'

They digested all the implications of his advice in silence. He straightened and looked solemnly from one to the other and added almost apologetically, 'You must know what you face. But now I must go. I wish you both God speed, and that you find Madame Blair is not so ill as you fear.'

'We are in your debt,' Lucille began hastily as he moved towards the door.

'For ever I should think.' Stella gave the keys a grateful flourish.

'It is nothing.' He shook his head, smiling, as they followed him. 'Jacques's always been a good friend. We met at a lot of parties, mutual friends you see. He always told me all about his family, and his English family. I felt included.'

'Jacques does include people,' Stella heard herself say.

'Makes everyone listen to his ideas you mean, goes on and on!' Lucille gave an apologetic shrug for her brother, but Jean-Paul shook his head and smiled down at her as she hurried forward to open the apartment door for him.

'No,' he said. 'I have no close relatives, so to listen was a privilege.' He bowed to them both, one hand on the banister rail. 'My regards to Jacques,' he said as he smiled broadly adding, 'and if the car reaches Cleauville intact tell him to look after it for me. *Au revoir*. My convoy awaits.'

He inclined his head and turned to begin his descent. Instinctively both girls raised their hands, still feeling the departure too soon, their expressions of gratitude so incomplete. Stella was aware that even as the keys dropped into her hand there had been no contact, no touch of hands. Lucille murmured that she was pleased he *had* listened to her brother, put her hand on his arm and strained upwards to kiss his cheek. 'I think we must make a proper goodbye, even if we have not met before.'

'Ah! But I saw your hair and ...' he paused to describe the high sweeps of a swing, 'flying against an oak tree and a blue sky!'

Lucille reddened, Stella laughed as she clasped and shook his hand and he stooped to kiss her cheeks.

They were all three aware that this was stolen time, a last flirtation with the moment, poised there at the top of the stairs. There was an army vehicle, a convoy, waiting somewhere for its officer. Stella clasped the keys tighter, thinking of the urgency of their personal journey, with war scurrying at their heels. It made the etiquette, the kissing of each cheek, the social ceremony, all the more important.

'Till we meet again,' he said. With a wave he was away, calling back, 'As your Stratford guy says, "Parting is such sweet sorrow."'

'That,' Stella concluded quietly, 'is also quite a guy.'

Lucille stood leaning over the banisters listening to the sound of his footsteps running down, out into the avenue. '*Sacré coeur*!! Do you know what that all makes me want to do?'

'Go straight off to find this car?'

'No! I want to ... I want to destroy something, kick something to bits, like this bloody war is kicking my life, your life, his life, all to bits – to tiny pieces!'

'*Non*!' Madame Astier's voice came sternly from the stairs. 'That is what Paris is doing, France too for all I know, tearing itself to bits. You must do good things ...' She paused as she reached the doorway of the tidied flat. 'Like this! Put things right again.'

'How can he make so very little of going to the front?' Lucille asked.

'It's how some men have to deal with things, make light, make jokes,' Madame Astier assured her, adding more briskly, 'Jean-Paul

20

told me what he had in mind, so I'm packing food for you, it will see you through until tomorrow. You will not want to stop too often searching for places to eat.'

'How well do you know Jean-Paul?'

'Know! I know him. He is a cheeky rogue!' She turned on her heel and clattered down the stairs laughing to herself, then called back, 'He should never be going to war.' She roared with laughter again. 'He should be on the stage!'

'I don't remember him coming to Cleauville,' Lucille murmured.

'Or throwing up your "long brown legs" on the swing!' Stella teased.

'*Non*,' she replied with utter seriousness, then smiled ruefully and asked, '*Pardon*. I have lost my sense of humour, I think.' She walked back into the apartment, to the table. Stella too came to look again at the atlas. Lucille's eyes were fixed on the way the Germans had smashed through the forests of the Ardennes. Somewhere Jean-Paul Bisset had to go with his convoy. Somewhere there Philip was fighting. After a moment Stella reached forward and traced a finger towards Tours and the hundreds of miles they had to go.

Downstairs they found Madame Astier had prepared them omelettes and coffee, and as they ate she folded bread, cheese and sliced cold meat into cloths, and began to put fruit into a bag.

'Madame, won't you come with us?' Lucille asked. 'I know my father would be pleased...'

'Leave Paris! Never! I shall be here waiting for you all to come back.' She nodded, so certain of herself, as she waved them back to their meal and diverted them with stories of Jean-Paul's ability as a mimic and '... dressing-up! *Mon Dieu*!' she remembered, 'the fancy dress parties they had! You'd not believe!' It was strangely sobering to find she had helped with Jacques's parties for his journalist, writer and artist friends. This was an aspect of his life they had known nothing about.

They left Madame Astier with regret and new affection. She had it seemed thought of and done everything in her power that might help them, insisting at the last moment they take her street guide of Paris. Never had she been so informal before as she confided, 'My name is Madeleine, call me Madeleine.'

They found Jean-Paul's address and that the largest key fitted a pair of wooden doors beneath his rooms, and inside a small arched cell of a garage they found a large Wolseley car.

'How strange,' Stella exclaimed, 'I'd expected, well I suppose I'd expected the French equivalent of an open-top, something sporty.'

'Perhaps this says something more about Jean-Paul,' Lucille said.

21

'That he's a joker!' Stella suggested as she struggled past the car to check the whereabouts of the petrol cans he had said were there.

'Perhaps more that he needs security,' Lucille said thoughtfully, 'as well as the good times.'

'Can you see a light switch?'

'If Jacques is his friend he probably has a serious side.'

Stella was concerned about the proportions of his car and its narrow clearance of the walls. 'If it gets to Cleauville intact,' Jean-Paul had said.

'Can you drive this?' Lucille asked, watching her squeeze through into the driver's door.

'No problem,' she answered, neither admitting her reservations nor the fact that she had no licence. Her 'driving' had been restricted to taking an old Model T Ford around the garden and down the lane to the paddock where she had 'passed' a series of obstacle tests set up by Philip, who had bellowed instructions at her most of the time, mostly she felt because she performed better than he did. There had been plans for her own car – well, she had made plans for her own car – then the war had come. She was *au fait* with the mechanics, having pored over various engines as her brother took them to bits and rebuilt them. It was the city streets and the coming encounter with Parisian traffic that concerned her.

She touched the wall getting the big car out and round but nothing serious. 'I think it'll polish over,' Lucille reported as they loaded the heavy jerry-cans and their suitcases into the boot, and the food on to the back seats.

Stella felt that remark was a little like telling the condemned man to avoid a puddle on the way to the gallows, but said nothing as the pragmatic Lucille was already examining the street guide and announcing, 'We have to turn right, across the Place de la Concorde.'

'OK!' Cautiously Stella kept to the right but was appalled when she reached the broad expanse of city road, then the Place de la Concorde, so quickly. Five or six lanes of traffic streamed either side of the fountain marking the site where Louis XVI was guillotined. *In 1793,* she silently reminded herself, *and Stella Hutton and Lucille Blair in 1940 unless I can relax my grip on this steering wheel.* She tried, noted without turning her head that they had passed the American Embassy, but her hands remained white-knuckled. Perhaps they would laugh about this sometime.

She gritted her teeth and ignored Lucille's tense comments, until she suddenly cried, '*À droite*! To the right! We turn right here!'

Stella did, there was a screech of brakes and someone shouting. 'Keep going!' Lucille advised, 'we didn't hit anything.'

22

'I have to stop and sort this all out,' Stella announced, her heart banging like an extra piston.

They reached a quieter avenue lined with chestnut trees in full flower and she drew in to the kerb and stopped. Then with the engine off she depressed the clutch and practised moving around the gears. She rolled up a coat to sit on and another to put behind her back. Lucille consulted the road map and the Michelin guide from the glove compartment and wrote down a list of roads and towns. The two of them compared the list, the map, then set off with a little more caution.

'If you drive like that they'll think we're kerb crawling,' Lucille complained as they went along at walking pace.

'You want to drive?' Stella asked ungraciously and made a show of readjusting the coats on her seat, then risked depressing the accelerator a little more.

It took some half an hour of very careful driving, having to reverse once when they passed a vital turn for Tours, before an increase in speed did not mean a fiercer grip on the steering wheel.

Beyond the city they both relaxed. 'Thank goodness,' Lucille breathed and offered conciliation. 'This is a terrible big car to handle.'

'Like a bus!' Stella replied with feeling, but with growing confidence overtook a car with a mattress strapped to the roof. Shortly afterwards they passed another car with two mattresses roped on its roof, the car itself packed to the gunnels with children. Fortunately the traffic coming the other way, towards Paris, was light, so they made good time, their powerful car easily able to overtake the monstrously loaded cars, lorries and trucks which regularly appeared on the way before them.

'Do you think they're from Belgium?'

Stella didn't answer that question, having suddenly realised the real reason for the mattresses. 'Look!' She jerked her head at a truck they were passing which had a mattress strapped over its cab. 'It's in case they're ... we're ... attacked from the air, machine-gunned!'

In the ensuing silence inside the Wolseley the noise of the engine seemed louder – and the roof very thin. Stella resisted an urge to crouch over the wheel, make her body area less. Lucille was struck silent for several minutes, then in a voice several tense tones above normal, asked, 'Would you like something to eat as you drive?'

'Good idea. I'm certainly not thinking of stopping.'

Their burst of laughter was ragged with anxiety, but helped. They ate cheese and bread and apples as they drove, and as the evening came they began to pass many who were beginning to pull off the road for the night. 'Jean-Paul was right,' Stella reflected, 'the roads more directly south from Paris must be packed solid.'

As evening became night, the road ahead of them shone starkly white under a rising moon and thankfully the draught of air from the side window was cooler. Only a few others were still travelling, while on the verges they passed a succession of miniature camp sites: tents and tarpaulins set up next to cars and trucks, some of which had off-loaded tables and chairs, while dejected displaced dogs sat tethered to familiar objects in strange places, and babies cried.

It was late into the night, with Tours behind them, when a violent bump and a lurch from side to middle of the road had them both crying out in alarm. Stella slammed on the brakes but the car had already stalled.

'What's happened?' Lucille cried. 'What is it?'

'I think I hit something,' Stella said, leaping from the car, dreading what it might be. But the road ahead was empty. Nothing lay prostrate on the road, and only a pair of huge boulders marked a field gateway. 'I must have hit one of those. I ... was asleep,' she admitted, her confidence shaken that she could have allowed such a thing to happen. 'I'm sorry! You all right?'

'Just hit the side window I think,' Lucille said, rubbing her head, 'but I was fast asleep too. We have to stop! You need a rest in a proper bed.'

Stella peered at the luminous hands of her watch. 'It's half past three in the morning.'

'Stretch out on the back seat then, have an hour or two really resting. There's mineral water and bread and ...'

'No, nothing to eat,' Stella said as she bent to look at the nearside wheel. 'Wonder we've not got a puncture, it felt like a good bang.'

Lucille, who was leaning into the back seat to move the food while fretting about her own inability to drive, to take over, called urgently, 'Quick! Get the car to the side of the road! Something's coming up behind us – fast – at least a couple of cars, or trucks or something.'

Stella gasped and was more startled because as she straightened she could see lights approaching from in front – and the Wolseley was in the middle of the road. Jean-Paul's car was about to be sandwiched if it did not respond to the turn of the key and the ignition button at first go. 'Get on the grass verge,' she shouted to Lucille. 'Stand well back!'

Glancing in her mirror as she wrestled with the choke and ignition, she knew that whatever was approaching from the rear was doing so at reckless speed, and there was more than one vehicle. The engine whirred but refused to turn; there was no time for either of them to swing the starting handle. The headlights were high on the vehicles coming the other way, trucks or lorries she guessed, travelling at a more reasonable speed, but those behind were almost upon them. She saw Lucille start towards her from the verge.

'Get back!' she screamed. 'Keep back!' Her voice was lost as two sleek black limousines swept in a tight, klaxon-blaring swerve around their vehicle. The second one, which only saw them at the last moment, clipped the Wolseley's front bumper as it passed. Stella felt the car wrenched to one side, and saw Lucille, who had been on her way across the front of the Wolseley, fall.

She screamed Lucille's name but it was lost in the hooting and screeching of brakes as the approaching vehicles met the speeding limousines. Before she could jump out the first lorry had come to a jolting halt half on the grass verge alongside the Wolseley. For a second Stella saw the pale, horrified face of a young soldier standing up in his seat as he applied the brakes. The lorries behind came to an equally rapid stop but remained on the road.

Almost immediately there were several soldiers out of the lorries running towards the front of the car.

'Lucille!'

She was pushing her way forward. It was such a relief to hear her talking. 'No, it just threw me off balance, just grazes and bruises I think.' She saw Stella and reached out a reassuring hand. 'I'm all right!'

'Thank God!' Stella said a sob in her throat. 'It would have been my fault ...'

They heard orders being shouted and realised that the lorries were full of soldiers, who were being told to stay where they were. It did not prevent those nearest the back of each lorry leaning out and demanding to know what was happening.

'Those cars,' the driver who had reached Lucille first muttered, 'they had diplomatic flags. They're not going to the front line!'

'No, the opposite way! Fast!' an older man put in, spitting heartily into the night.

A burly sergeant came hurrying over to hear their story. 'You've broken down?' he asked, his gesture querying their position in the middle of the road.

'I think we ran out of petrol,' Lucille said before Stella could confess, 'that's all.'

'You have petrol?' the sergeant asked.

'We won't have enough, but we're hoping to buy more when our cans run out.'

'There's a lot of traffic ahead of you running the pumps dry,' he said, rubbing his hand up his well-bristled cheek. He turned to the driver and muttered something. In seconds a jerry-can of petrol was being discreetly emptied into their tank.

'*Merci, monsieur, merci, je vous remercie beaucoup*!'

The convoy moved slowly off; as the second lorry passed the two girls a small package was thrown to them. Chocolate.

'It's us who should be giving them something,' Stella noted.

The two stood and waved, calling their thanks and '*Bonne chance*!' Then the men began singing the song popular all over France, '*J'attendrai*'. It was taken up loudly all along the convoy, but as the two stood watching and listening, and the distance between them grew, only the yearning seductive tune came back to them in dwindling waves of sound.

They stood with their arms about each other. '*J'attendrai toujours*,' Lucille murmured.

Stella found herself praying that Jacques was still in Cleauville, would be there when they arrived – safe at least for now – then felt ravaged by concern for her brother.

'Jean-Paul Bisset taking medical supplies, followed by the ones who'll need them.' Lucille's voice was hard. 'Such long hours of pain, such anguish to come for so many, such madness!' She paused, then added, 'I should be at a hospital, helping.'

The car started at the first touch on the silent, empty road. They pulled on to the verge and collapsed on front and back seats.

It was only other refugees moving past them the following morning that roused them. Stella found a stream and after rinsing her face, hands and arms sent Lucille to bathe the grazes she had on her knees and elbow, while she prepared a breakfast of the last of the food Madame Astier had provided.

'Perhaps we might stop for coffee when we buy more food later,' Lucille suggested as they finished the bottle of tepid mineral water.

They realised how fortunate the incident had turned out to be for them when they saw the queues of cars at petrol stations in Poitiers. 'It was worth a few bruises,' Lucille said as they passed a garage owner who was just waving a stream of cars away, arms raised in apology.

'What about stopping for a proper meal?' Stella suggested.

'*Oui!* Look, there's a side turn, if we get out of this traffic ...'

They took the turn, which they found led to the town's station and were soon involved in a different kind of jam. A train had obviously just arrived and they found themselves not hindered by cars but by people coming from the station in a flood, again with unwieldy loads of belongings no normal travellers ever carried. Both car and crowd came to an enforced stop, and Stella asked a woman forced tight against her window where they had all come from.

'Belgium, we are overrun,' she answered despairingly as she leaned forward and with her free hand grabbed the shoulder of a boy of about nine who was with some determination still trying to push through the static crowd.

'Why come to Poitiers?' Lucille leaned across to ask.

'My husband works for the government and the rumour was they were coming to Poitiers – so we knew our country was finished. He insisted I got away with our son.'

The two exchanged glances. Did this explain the speeding limousines?

Lucille reached to where they still had half the bar of chocolate from the soldiers. She passed it to Stella who handed it to the mother for her boy.

For a moment they thought the little unlooked-for kindness was going to overwhelm the woman, but there was no time, as the crowd ahead moved again and willy-nilly everyone was taken on. She waved the chocolate back over her shoulder and nodded her thanks.

It was too much, too many traumas, too many individual sorrows. 'Let's get out of the town, shall we,' Stella decided.

They did not stop until they reached a village where Lucille glimpsed white cloths and bentwood chairs under a striped awning. They ate their first hot meal since the omelettes at Madame Astier's: meat and vegetables, followed by a plum tart and wonderful coffee. There was they found a *boucherie chevaline* next door, then a hardware shop, then a *pâtisserie* where they were able to buy both savoury and sweet pastries. Before they moved on again Stella emptied one of Jean-Paul's cans of petrol into the tank.

The final can was put into the tank during late afternoon, and Lucille insisted it was time they looked for a place to sleep that night. 'It is important you rest properly tonight, then surely we'll reach home tomorrow!' Stella was finding the continual linking of the need for her to rest, with the urgent need to arrive at Cleauville as soon as possible, wearing to say the least.

'There is also the need to buy more petrol from somewhere – and we have no coupons.'

'I'll offer twice the proper price,' Lucille said. 'Anything to get home now we are getting near.'

'Near' was not quite how Stella saw it. She would have preferred to reach Tulle, or beyond, but knew by the growing sense of irritation she felt with everything that her companion said, that they should stop, sleep, and then tomorrow she would be able to drive as never before.

They found a tiny hotel in the next sizeable place, and stopped immediately to ask for a room. When they entered the small foyer an elderly, tiny, stick-thin Frenchwoman was listening to a wireless set with such intensity they stood back and waited until the confused babble of sound was switched off with an exclamation of disgust.

'They think everyone is an idiot! They tell us what they think we want to know, not what is really happening. They say they will defend every yard, every street, every house from the Boche. Are you from Paris? Do you know what is happening?'

They explained both where they were from, what they had seen, and where they were going and why, Lucille adding a tentative statement that they needed more fuel.

'Ah!' she exclaimed. 'So! The governments will be safe! Our rich will be on the Riviera, but *our* men! Taken from their farms at a moment's notice. Marched away! *La mobilisation générale*! Men who had no more idea how to go to war, than to sew a shirt! And us women left to struggle, left to do every little thing. My sons! *Zut*!' She snatched a key from a rack. 'You look exhausted! Follow me.'

She showed them to a bedroom at the back of the hotel, overlooking a river. The room itself was spotless, with well-scrubbed floorboards, bright woven mats and counterpanes, and a washstand with jug and basin for which they were promised immediate hot water. Stella ached to just throw herself on to one of the beds.

The busy little woman was more than true to all her words. They ate well, slept wonderfully and breakfasted on the freshest bread ever dipped into bowls of café-au-lait.

'Also mesdemoiselles,' the proprietress told them, 'the tank of your car is full, plus a little more in a can.'

Lucille jumped up and took her hands, kissed her cheeks. 'I will never forget you, madame, never!'

'It will be on your bill,' she answered with a wink. 'I wish you good speed to your *maman*.'

Good speed they did make. Stella drove much faster than on the previous day and Lucille lapsed into silence as if preparing herself for what they might find had happened at Cleauville.

The countryside changed: dark looming shoulders of hills interspersed with agricultural tracts, vineyards, olive groves, all was becoming more like the land of their happy times. Jacques and Philip, Lucille and herself. She had worried for a time that she had not tried to contact her father again, but, as is the way with travellers, as the gap widens, home concerns are left behind, largely forgotten in anticipation of arrival.

Would Jacques still be there? She could not imagine compassionate

28

leave being very prolonged with the Germans advancing so rapidly; and if Gaby was better – which she wanted with all her heart – then Jacques would probably be gone. Even to think so gave her a bleak feeling, as if all her hopes for the future had been swept away.

How was Ernest Blair coping with his invalid wife? She knew he would be devastated if anything happened to Gaby. What she as a visitor had always seen was the absolute adoration of Lucille's English father for his French wife. Lucille would be both a comfort and a great asset, even with her curtailed nurse's training. While she? She would do every little thing she could to help, to make matters as right and normal as possible.

Her resolve was adamant, but by the time she began to recognise the road north of Cleauville she was driving in a kind of stupor, and Lucille sat fast asleep. The car spluttered, stalled and stopped. This time the fuel was at an end. She used the last bit of momentum to get them well into the side of the road.

'That's it,' she said, leaning her head on her arms.

The sun was risen and the car already stiflingly hot when Lucille awoke. Stella lay with her face pressed against the rim of the steering wheel and for a second Lucille wondered if they had crashed. She got out of the car cautiously and stared around. They were nearly at Cleauville, just a few more kilometres, seven, eight at the most. A groan from the car sent her back to find Stella holding her neck and with the mark of the steering wheel across one cheek.

'We've really run out of petrol now.'

'I'll take one of the cans. There's a garage not far, you remember! You stretch out on the back seat. I shouldn't be long.'

Stella did not remember but watched Lucille set off at a run with the can, then getting out of the car she stretched out on the grass in the shade of the car, drifting into a half-sleep. She wondered whether their luck could possibly hold and Lucille would return with another gallon or so, or whether it would not have been better just to take their cases and start walking, hoping for a lift as the morning drew on. Her daydream was full of images of arriving at the white farmhouse with the mellow orange tiled roof, the green shutters at the windows, the different smells, of the river, of the fields dry but burgeoning in spring and if you lifted your head high the hot true Mediterranean smell of herbs and pines, the land of lizards and cicadas.

She awoke to find Lucille squeezing her shoulder and softly calling her name. 'I have bicycles,' she said.

Stella blinked, not quite awake. 'Bicycles? Oh, bicycles!'

She struggled up to find that Lucille had ridden back on one bicycle pushing another. Both were men's models and one had a delivery carrier on the front.

'Where?'

'Pas de Crédit!' Lucille gave the name they used for the owner of a tiny garage her father used for metalwork repairs. Stella remembered him now, morose by nature, a fat greasy becapped man who advertised his business only by a huge sign refusing any credit to anyone. 'He had no petrol, his regular delivery has not come, but he recognised me and offered the loan of the bikes.'

Stella hesitated about taking the cases, but Lucille, in no mood for any dithering, produced two pieces of rope from the front carrier, tied one case on that and the other on the smaller flat carrier on the rear of the second bicycle.

Straddling the crossbars, they pushed off cautiously, finding their balance. Stella found it more difficult than driving the car; it certainly made her realise just how exhausted she was.

'Half an hour,' Lucille called over her shoulder. 'We should be there in half an hour.'

Chapter Three

Ernest Blair stood at the bedroom window, while behind him Gaby slept. He knew she slept because the grip on his hand had relaxed, her fingers falling away. Each day there were fewer signs by which he could tell the difference between sleep and drugged wakefulness. To stop the pain, the doctor had said, she will not be so much with us.

He knew this could not go on, should not go on for her sake, but he clung to her, and Gaby knew his needs too well. The good doctor, who had become part of their daily lives, had told him to go away for a time. 'She needs a rest from you my friend.' He had laid a hand on his shoulder and turned him from the room. 'The nurse is capable, have no fear.'

It wasn't fear he felt, it was more the sensation of being butchered, his heart ripped out, his ribs splayed, chopped through, halved. He had an image of things halved. Even, he thought, apples, the fruit that had brought him to France as a buyer in the first place, even they withered. This is what he would be, a withering half of a whole. But not yet, he thought, gritting his teeth until they hurt, not yet, even lying there she was with him, part of him.

'The other half.' He knew the English colloquialism, now he knew why it was so apt. He heard a deeper breath, a sigh, from the bed and wondered if his will for her to remain disturbed her even through the drugs. In truth he felt it did. He made an effort of will to let the high flood of his emotions ease, drain away. He made himself look through the window he stood at. He could see as far as the end of his drive and Hector's cottage with the *tricolore* flying on the old man's home-made flagpole, a flick of red white and blue stripes against blue-green pines.

Hector was two things passionately; the first was a patriot. He had fought in the 1914–18 war and lost a leg at the Battle of the Somme. The second was his fervour as *décanteur extraordinaire* for Ernest's

31

household. The old man had a nose for the best wine vintages, and even if he did nothing else but help bottle the farm's wine, Ernest considered he well earned his rent-free cottage.

Scowling and leaning nearer to the window he realised that for some time he must have had in his view two figures, cycling, coming on past Hector's cottage. He immediately thought of his son. All the news Jacques gleaned from his newspaper friends in Paris was of defeat and retreat. Now there was someone cycling here, undoubtedly with an urgent message of recall.

But why two, he wondered as they came so urgently on; so confidently, as if they knew every metre of the way. They were almost at the house before it struck him that they were girls, and then it was Stella's red hair he recognised first. He felt a different pang to his heart as he realised his daughter and his English daughter were here, they had come.

He went immediately to the bed, knelt by it, took the inert hand. 'They've come!' he whispered to her. 'The gang's here, Gaby, the house is no longer ours! Take cover!' It was an old joke, always delivered when the gang of four had arrived for holidays. 'They've come,' he repeated and was startled as her fingers curled around his.

'Huh!' The sound that escaped his lips was not relief but the end of one tiny agony. Days ago after Jacques had arrived she had murmured Lucille's name and he had told her that he had sent a message. For the past three days he had hung tortured on the horns of a tender dilemma, as he wondered if Gaby was waiting for Lucille, hanging on. He had heard desperately ill people could do this, spin out their lives to achieve a last ambition, to see a loved one. He had been agonising, as another day dawned, whether to say he did not think Lucille would be able to leave England. Now she was here! Stella too. Soon they would be here in this room. 'Any minute now, Gaby Blair, and your daughters will be with you. Lucille and our English daughter.' He bent to kiss her fingers. 'We'll just wait here,' he told her, 'they'll find us here together.'

Jacques heard the clatter, then the voices in the hall. He rushed from the kitchen, angry that anyone should be so thoughtless, and desperate that neither his mother nor his father should be disturbed. He burst silent but aggressive into the hall – shaggy-haired, dishevelled, glowering – then it was as if the puppeteer dropped the strings. His mouth fell open in disbelief, and animation and joy followed.

'It is you! Both of you!' he gasped as both girls fell upon him.

Stella felt his arm hard about her waist as briefly she leaned her head on his shoulder. It seemed like the only meaningful thing in all the world. He kissed them alternately, and they clung to him, then as

32

the questions began to come, he signalled up towards the closed bedroom door and drew them back into the kitchen. There was so much to ask and tell, but as he poured them wine there came an instant of awkwardness; suddenly normal exchanges were of no more concern and world matters of no importance.

'So?' Lucille asked. The word came awkwardly, sharply. 'Tell us, Jacques.'

'You have to be ready to comfort Papa.' He paused as his sister lowered her head, but knew he must leave no doubt, no room for unreasoned hope. 'You have to be brave for his sake. There is ...' But this was not possible to say. 'It is only a matter of time.'

She stood up suddenly, rejecting, wanting away, but she remained very upright, very still. Stella, watching, felt the rebound of emotion from brother to sister. She admired Lucille's control as she asked the other thing they had to know, uttered the words if ever spoken, then whispered. 'Is it cancer?'

She felt the blow as Jacques inclined his head, the moment when there is no escape, when dread becomes a confirmed reality.

'I must go up to see her.'

'Pa's there,' he went on, unable to hide the other concern that was now more and more on his mind. 'He's with her nearly all the time. It is difficult to make him leave her, and rest himself. I worry what will happen.'

Lucille looked to Stella.

'Perhaps it's best one at a time,' he suggested, wanting to spare Stella longer, knowing her impulsive response to every situation, perhaps even wanting her to himself just for a selfish moment.

'Stella's driven here, days and nights. It's her mother too.'

'I won't stay long, just say hello and come down again.'

'I'll wait in here for you.' He listened to them go upstairs, the door open, the muted voices. He could imagine the scene, imagine the shock of Gaby. His mother had gone from being attractively slim to being skeletal. 'Nothing to fall back on,' he had heard the doctor say, 'no reserves.' That had been the truth, no reserves, his mother had burned out so quickly. In the spring she had seemed to be convalescent, in the summer wavering between health one day and utter weariness the next. Then the continual exhaustion and the irrefutable symptoms had brought a diagnosis – confirmed after Christmas – and for a time his father had carried the burden alone.

The door opened very slowly and Stella came back into the room, leaned on the closed door. He gave her time but as she looked up at him he was unprepared for the bereft look of anger.

'We should have come before.'

33

He spread his hands to explain but she interrupted.

'Now is too late!' Her voice sank low both with regret and accusation. 'You should have sent for us before.'

'No,' he protested, but she turned away. 'No, listen to me Stella, listen.'

There was no neutrality in how she felt, no image but that of the gaunt face on the white lace-edged pillow. She agonised that the bedroom was still so elegant; Gaby's touches were everywhere, dried lavender and flounces, while the person ... And surely it was not fair! She had already lost one mother.

'I have been here five days,' Jacques began.

She walked away from him, to the window, stood arms folded tight over her chest, shoulders hunched and taut. Perhaps she had been so busy just getting here she had not really prepared herself for the situation. All she felt like doing was launching an attack on Jacques, pummelling his chest with her fists. Couldn't he see what he had done? Denied them a decent goodbye.

'The day I arrived.' He paused and would not hurt her with the memory of his mother's greeting. 'Jacques!' she had breathed through a beaming twisted smile. No more, just his name. He began again. 'The first day Maman did not seem in too much discomfort, except when she needed to be tended, lifted, washed. The third day it was obvious she needed more drugs to allay the worst ... I felt the doctor was only waiting for our lead. Pa agreed with me, and when we mentioned it the doctor acted immediately, only saying it would take her slightly further away from us.'

Stella bit her lip as hard as she could, tasting bitter hot blood in her mouth. Wasn't this what she had said! They were too late! Wasn't it nearly over? All their good times, all the love in the world she had received here, the pain was all that was left.

'But she knows when we are there,' he continued quietly.

She swung round, challenging. 'How can you say that! How can you know?'

'I do know because this morning she played a game with me, a game she used to play in church, when I was small, and restive to be outside. She used to hold my hand and draw her thumb across my palm, a kind of secret sign that she knew how I felt. This morning she did that to me, twice, as if to say that you might think once was an accident, but twice and you will know.'

Stella had walked to stand in the open doorway. Outside a skylark burbled on and on, high in the sky, on the edge of hearing.

The bubble of her anger burst; she had been letting her own grief come before that of Gaby's real children, before Jacques as a little boy, years before she had come into their lives. 'I'm sorry,' she said. 'I'm so sorry, Jacques. Please forgive me. It must have been ...'

'Electrifying, I think is the word.' He laughed briefly. 'I've been needing to tell someone ever since it happened. I rushed out of the room and I've been unable to do anything since. I thought I might have to resort to old Hector! It shook me to the core of my being. I wanted to dash around shouting, She is there! She does know!'

In this new silence the tiny bird in the vast sky seemed more audible, more sweet.

'You always were the one I learned from,' she said feeling instinctively this was a lesson of the most profound wisdom, one she must take to heart. 'But why does it have to be the good people?' Echoed in her mind she remembered her own Irish grandmother saying the same thing about her own mother. 'Why, Jacques?'

He shook his head at her as she turned. 'I thought my mother would live for ever,' he said quietly.

'So did I,' she whispered, wanting to tell him how much her heart yearned for it to have been true.

'But time overtakes us all.'

'Jacques?'

'My leave ends the day after tomorrow.' He led the way from the kitchen into the tree-shaded black courtyard, with its ancient archway through to the orchard.

'What would happen if you didn't go back? I mean the country's in such a state!'

'I'd be a deserter.' He shook his head at her.

She felt suddenly angry with him for even thinking of conforming, when so much they had seen and heard convinced her that those in authority were certainly running, sending men to the front, yes, but running themselves! 'Not playing the game as your public school taught you to!' she said ironically, 'not English!'

'Not even half-English.' He raised his eyebrows quizzically, as if he had expected she should know him better. 'I'm a journalist, as well as a soldier, it's part of the job to be where the action is.' He stepped closer to her, lowered his voice, 'Don't think it hasn't crossed my mind, but I know I have to go, to be able to live with myself I have to go. It tears me in two with Maman as she is.'

She ached to take him into her arms with the same selfless caring as she might have Lucille, or Philip, comfort him as sister to brother, but that relationship she knew had gone for ever. She just felt ashamed, regretted the stupid jibe, felt she must make amends, at least make her own decision quite clear. 'I shall stay you know, just as long as I'm needed. I've only been helping out in Daddy's office until I was called up for proper war work, so even if Lucille has to go back to her nurse's training, I can stay.'

He shook his head. 'If the war goes against us, if France is overrun, you and my father are one hundred per cent English, so you would be interned immediately.'

She looked to protest but he took her hand and gripped it, as one would a child who wants to run away, dodge consequences, but must be made to listen. He quietly passed on the information he had gleaned from his journalist friend in Paris the evening before. 'The Germans have defeated the French Ninth Army, they've swept all across the old battlefields of the First World War from Mons to Arras. They're rapidly encircling the First French Army, the Belgian Army and the British Expeditionary Force. They were on the outskirts of Nouvelles yesterday, and there's little to stop them attacking back along the Channel coast towards Boulogne, Calais, Dunkirk – closing the trap.'

'Philip's with the BEF,' she interrupted, 'but the last we heard they were having to make the men listen to lectures on "Why We Are Fighting", while they were really all wondering why they weren't.'

He swore profanely under his breath. 'People are not being told how serious it is.'

'I should think a lot of them can guess now, at least those watching the refugees pouring through their towns and villages.' She paused as their eyes met, then had to concentrate to finish her thought. 'And in any case your father won't go!'

'No, and never willingly even after Mother ...'

'But there will be a respite for us here.' Impulsively she took his other hand and shook them both in her own, reassuring. 'There's Paris! That will be defended! You do think that?'

'Yes.' He pulled her closer so she felt her hair brush his shirt. 'There are posters going up everywhere telling Parisians to fight for every street, every building. "To arms," they say.'

The 'Marseillaise', the most patriotic song in the world, rang with splendid echoes in her mind that had nothing to do with love of either country. 'Your flat had been raided did you know?' she asked breathlessly.

'I heard,' he said briefly. 'It seems of little importance now.'

'No,' she agreed, then suddenly grinned at him, 'but we tidied it, Lucille and I.'

He regarded her smile. 'Stella,' he said and it was neither question nor opening gambit.

Her heart answered, yes, and it was as if she suddenly knew herself for the first time. Stella. Red hair, speaks too readily, like her Irish grandmother, brilliant father; sister to Philip, adopted sister of

36

Lucille; belonging to Jacques. 'Yes,' she said gently, 'that's me.' She felt her commitment was biblical in its greatness and rightness. Suffer me not to leave you.

'This is not the time, but after the war, after ... all this ... when we can think straight ...' There was a noise in the doorway and his father stood there.

'Stella,' he said gently and reached out a hand. 'Let me look at you properly. My dear, thank you for coming, for getting Lucille here.' She thought he looked like a blind man feeling the way, and she forgave him his interruption, as he reached out his hand and arm shaking with weariness. She ran to him, kissed his cheeks, agonised again over his ravaged appearance and drew him to the table.

'You are not to be on your own again,' she told him.

He smiled at her bleakly, grateful for the words, but his eyes told her he would always be alone once Gaby had gone. Always. She glanced at Jacques and understood his concern.

'They will stay when I have to go,' Jacques reassured him.

'You're all very good, Gaby has many who love her.' It was a statement, and it was true. 'Lucille is talking to her now. I'm to have breakfast, I'm told.'

'Yes, and you and Lucille must rest,' Jacques told her.

Stella awoke feeling quite strange; a sensation of light-headed well-being made her reluctant to open her eyes. She floated in a kind of strange liquid light, and realised that what she felt was truly rested for the first time in days. She had the impression that she must have lain quite unmoving for some hours stretched between the cool lavender-perfumed sheets. She moved and still felt a hint of cramped painful muscles from driving for so long. Ah! She remembered everything, and stretched groaning a little as full wakefulness came – and she was hungry, really hungry.

She rose and listened intently as if trying to gauge the mood of the house, the latest turn of events. She looked at the clock. Seven. Seven at night? She had been persuaded to go to bed at about four in the afternoon. Had she slept for three hours or fifteen? She went to the window, to where the sun was beginning its long hot climb. It was morning. Fifteen? An awful sense of loss came with the knowledge. This was the second day. Tomorrow Jacques had to leave.

As she left her bedroom Jacques was coming from his mother's room. He waited; she took his hand as they went silently downstairs.

'Have you been with your mother all night?'

He nodded, but she saw his jaw flex, as if holding back that experience as he asked, 'Do you feel better?'

'Except for all the hours I've lost.'

'Lucille and Papa have just taken over from me, and I'd like to get out into the air for a bit. I wondered if when you've eaten, we could take the cycles back to old Pas de Crédit then walk on and pick up Jean-Paul's car. It can go in one of the stables here, I'd like to save it for him if we can. I've found a can of petrol.'

It seemed Lucille and Jacques must have talked for hours after she was asleep, for he knew all that had happened. 'I've telephoned my contact in Paris again, hoping he'll be able to relay another message to your father to let him know you've arrived,' he paused and grinned, 'I didn't mention that you had *driven* here!'

'He'd have me on trial! In his head anyway.'

Briefly, wearily, he smiled recognition of that fact about her father. '*You* should sleep.'

'Later,' he said. 'Let's not waste the cool of the morning.'

It felt intrusive busying herself in Gaby's kitchen, making coffee, sandwiches, taking a bottle of the farm's own wine. 'I must sit with your mother for a time when we get back.' Jacques left a note on the table to say where they had gone.

It would have been difficult to remember that there was a war as they cycled along the tree- and bush-lined lanes, passing from shade to sun, shade to sun with mesmeric regularity, except that Jacques insisted on talking about it.

'I've given it much thought and I want you to promise that if the Germans do get south of Paris you and Lucille will try to persuade Father to go down to Marseilles, or one of the small seaside villages, and take a boat to North Africa. From there you should sooner or later be able to get back to England.'

Stella did not answer, her mind full of the wearisome hours, days, nights it had taken to get from England to Cleauville.

'Do you promise?' he asked and when she still did not reply his hand came out and authoritatively gripped the middle of her handle-bars, bringing both bicycles to a stop. 'Have you been listening to me? You've not answered once.'

'It's all so ... so ... speculative! All if, if, if.'

'But it's all I can do,' he said urgently. 'All I can think of before I have to leave.'

'Jacques, I'm sorry.' She bent her head repentantly over his hand, so that her hair brushed his fingers. 'I do promise, of course I do. But your father, he won't want to leave even ...' She shook her head at him.

'He won't want to be imprisoned either, you must persuade him – when everything is done.'

She could not bear the agony on his face. To have to speak of the death of a mother they both loved so much was a needle-sharp torment. She reminded him of her pledge to do as much as she could.

'Don't worry about afterwards. We've all been to Marseilles lots of times and we know a lot of men with boats along the coast, we'd quickly find where to go, what to do.'

He nodded his acceptance of what she said, but she saw it was more resignation than satisfaction that he had done as much as he could.

'We'll all make it,' she urged on him. 'All of us.'

'Not all of us,' he said quietly.

'I didn't ... I ... meant the four of us I suppose, you and Philip, and ...' She broke off. 'You must think I'm an uncaring fool.'

'No, never that. It's just that I can't get my mother out of my mind for more than a moment.' He released her bicycle. 'I willed her to die last night.'

She stood quite motionless, not shocked so much by the statement, more stricken by the torment that had created the wish.

'It would have been best,' he went on, 'just she and I holding hands, the tremors that shook her body and brain would have eased, ceased. I willed her to let go, that Papa would not come and see her like that – then suddenly she *was* still – and I – but she was just quiet.' He was silent for a moment then asked, 'Do you hate me?'

'No, no, of course not. Never! But there are so many things I am only just beginning to understand.' She stood on a pedal and led the way on again. 'The trouble is they are all rushing at me so quickly. Things like ... well, I never really understood when people talked about it being "a blessing" if people could die. I couldn't imagine it would ever be good – but I understand that now. I didn't know what heart-sick meant, though I do now, I didn't know what real yearning meant until now.' She knew she had switched to her own personal problems and she fell silent as she saw the garage looming up before them. Then as they drew near, the old garage mechanic came out and before he was in earshot she added, 'I think as well I've been an awful selfish snob. I didn't appreciate how kind people could be, people like Madame Astier, Madeleine. I used to think she was just a joke.'

'As we used to Pas de Crédit,' he whispered. 'The terrible thing is I can never remember his real name!'

'Butterflies have to settle sooner or later.' The phrase Gaby had once used about the four of them all flitting about and having a good time came readily to mind – but she did not speak it.

The old garage proprietor was carrying welding equipment and loading it into a disreputable-looking trailer. His overalls, baggy, greasy, hung indifferently from his shoulders, straps looped around a variety of buttons he had undoubtedly stitched on himself.

He raised his hand in greeting. 'Young man,' he said, then in his usual gruff manner enquired about Madame Blair. He listened attentively, and when Jacques added that he had no extension of leave and had to go the next day, the old mechanic said, 'I shall look in on Hector and your father's place every couple of weeks to make sure everything is OK. He must not neglect ...' he frowned as if he found himself on too personal ground and pushing at an acetylene torch ended with '... his machinery.'

'Thank you so much, so very much, monsieur!' Jacques gripped his hand, surprised and touched by the man's practical thoughtfulness. 'It will give me comfort to know this.'

'It seems I am not the only one who has been making plans,' Jacques said as they walked away.

Stella was feeling desperately that she had to try to telescope several years' worth of living into a few hours, but as they walked on, Jacques carrying the petrol can, Stella their food, the burden of too much to say, too much to explore, overwhelmed her. She was silent until the car loomed into sight.

'I was amazed when it was an English Wolseley. He seemed the wrong kind of man to have such a car ... somehow.'

'He won it from an English milord,' Jacques told her, 'in a card game at a party! I doubt he's ever driven it more than once!'

'Oh!' Unconsciously she ran her hand over the dusty scratched wing and wondered what that did to Lucille's philosophy that it was a symbol of Jean-Paul's need for stability in his life. She looked up to find Jacques gazing at her quizzically. 'Getting it out of the garage,' she added, explaining the deep scratch.

'No.' He dismissed the damage. 'You're wearing the pendant. I noticed of course when you arrived.'

'I wear it always.' Her hand covered the heart protectively.

'That makes me very happy,' he said with a new note of humility in his voice. 'You're the one bright thing in life.'

'Then I would have travelled twice as far to be here.'

'Stella,' he breathed, as if uttering her name in a thanksgiving, then leaned back on the wing of the car, head bowed; for once his powers of words and reasoning failed – or were held back.

She felt she stood on the brink of some experience, whose floodgate should and must open now. 'When we tidied the flat,' she said, 'I found my very last hair ribbon folded into a book of poetry. You've kept it all this time.'

He nodded. 'You were so beautiful, so distressed; your red hair and

40

pale, pale face. It captured a moment for me, a moment perhaps when I stopped thinking about you as some other little sister.'

'Oh! As long ago as that!'

'So,' he said, pushing himself upright, coming close, anxious to make his own discovery, 'when was it for you?'

'At Christmas on the river bank, when Philip was splashing Lucille.'

'Oh!' He made his exclamation, his astonishment greater than hers. 'As late as that!'

She laughed and allowed herself to fall gently forward on to his chest. He folded her in his arms, as if it was what he had been aching to do for a very long time.

'Please kiss me, Jacques, properly. Really properly.'

'I feel I am doing wrong,' he murmured, 'it is not the time.'

'If not now, when?' she demanded earnestly. 'Perhaps never. It feels as right as anything to me.'

'It feels wonderful to me, but is it fair to you?' He tipped her chin up to look into her eyes and she saw her effect on him. 'Soldiers have a saying, love and leave behind.'

'There's another,' she told him, feeling almost coquettish and brazen as she sidled her head. 'Better to have loved and lost, than never to have loved at all.' She dropped her head suddenly.

'What is it?' he asked.

'No, nothing.' She remembered her father saying it once when he had been telling her about her own mother. 'And you,' Will Hutton had ended, 'are living proof of that love. So it never will be lost.'

'Come on.' He suddenly made a move and picked up the food bag, adding as an afterthought, 'And perhaps we should put the can over the hedge too, in the shade and out of sight – *l'essence* is getting scarce and valuable.'

He led the way over a ramshackle wall into an olive grove which edged an expanse of vines. He carried the bag and led her along to where a dip between trees and vines made a shady private place. He reclined against the slope of grass and held out his hand to her; for a moment she stood beyond his grasp, looking at him, this man, she thought, who had quite suddenly emerged from the boy she had always known. Then she took his hand and fell to her knees before him, leaning her head into his shoulder. His hands slipped under her armpits as if he might lift her bodily, but he guided her into his side, burying his face into her hair.

'My English ...' he whispered as his hands pushed up the white Aertex top, but the appropriate noun eluded him. He ended 'girl' – but it was not a girl who responded, who as she felt the dry grass

41

rough under her shoulders sensed his moral hesitancy, and recklessly stripped off her own top, undid her own bra.

He thought she lay like some Pre-Raphaelite beauty, hair autumnal red in the shade; skin milky white; a dappling of sun through long slender leaves broke ripples across her flesh as if she moved in green waters. He reached out to her, catching his breath, but all other resolves escaped him.

Most of what she saw was his face, his eyes, his black hair framed by olive-green leaves and ageless cordlike twists of trunks, hard, timeless symbols. So this was the watershed she had been anxious not to miss – and quite right too, she thought, if this was what he wished, then so did she.

It was only afterwards, when he was asleep, that she was suddenly embarrassed by their mutual nudity; looking down at the first male she had seen since Philip at bathtimes, and that before he went away to his first boarding school. She calculated that Jacques was better blessed, and on the thought sprang to her feet lightly, not disturbing him. The breeze caught her hot skin and she lifted her arms to it. What freedom, what beauty – us and Provence. She took an experimental few steps out into the sun and felt vine tendrils brush her thighs, then her waist. She was surprised how cool, even cold they felt, how sensual, how aware she was of every tiny contact.

'I love him,' she began – then far off she could see a figure, a farmer probably walking his crop, looking down, occasionally bending. She crouched and breathed into the very depths of the man's vines, 'I love him, I love him – remember.' Then she crept back and slipped on her shorts and top.

She had been reluctant to wake him, had lain back by his side, close enough to touch if she spread her fingers, but not intruding on his rest. There was so much still to face, he had the trek back to the war zone and before that there would be the moment of parting. She gave a little gasp as if of pain, screwed her eyes tight against threatening tears and prayed.

'*Sacré Dieu!*' The initial shout had her springing to her feet, but she understood no more of the guttural verbal attack being made on them. The farmer she had seen far off in his fields now stood above them like the angel of retribution discovering the devil.

Jacques woke and scrambled to retrieve underpants and trousers, hopping about on one foot as the man gesticulated and stabbed the air with fingers like gnarled twigs. 'No good,' the old man screamed, 'no good comes of such things. You will see.' He pointed dramatically heavenwards. 'The good God sees!'

Jacques, now decent, held his arms up in a gesture of appeal.

42

'Monsieur, we are young – and there is a war – I must leave tomorrow!'

'Leaving your sins behind you! Go! Off my land.'

'Oh!' Jacques threw out an impatient, dismissive hand. 'You are too old, my friend.'

They began to walk with some dignity away from the still-muttering farmer, but a kind of mutual excitement built up as Jacques caught her hand. 'Come on, you sinner!' he said and they began to run. They reached the road, then Jacques had to go back to retrieve the petrol. Stella leaned on the bonnet of the car waiting for him. He put down the can and took her into his arms, he pushed his face down, muzzling into the base of her neck and she heard him laugh briefly. She wasn't sure whether the noise *she* made was laughter. Then both froze in disbelief as the man's voice again harangued them. They turned to find he had followed.

'How is it that such as you have fuel for pleasure outings!'

'I do not believe this man!' Jacques said quietly. 'I may have to help him on his way.'

'No,' she pleaded as he clenched his fists. 'It will only take more of our time.'

'Ah!' He turned swiftly on his heel, agreeing. '*Oui!*' He stooped swiftly to pick up the fuel can again. The old man misunderstood Jacques's intention, and perhaps also understood he had pursued them too far. He stepped quickly back, staggered and fell. Jacques shook his head, then went over and offered the man a hand. He did not take it, but struggled to his feet and hobbled away, still muttering savagely.

The man's pursuit, then his fall, had swept away their last capacity to see any vestige of humour in the incident. Instead in the stoop of Jacques's shoulders she glimpsed an extra weariness. She took the can from his hands and emptied it expertly into the tank. 'I'm an old hand at this.' He ran his hand up her arm and touched her hair as she put the empty can in the boot and she added, 'But quite new at other things.' He grinned, momentarily easing out the new grim lines in his cheeks.

Chapter Four

They did not sleep again but kept a vigil at Gaby's bedside all the last night of his leave. The hours had slipped by slowly at first in the agony of watching, the feeling of hopelessness, yet they knew they were right to be there. Stella held Jacques's hand sometimes, and sometimes they sat either side of Gaby and included her, made a circle of their hands, their own joining lightly above the still and silent patient.

Then after the sun made a first magnificent slit of light on the horizon how quickly the hours sped by. Day came too soon; the time of Jacques's departure loomed like a dread appointment beyond which it was impossible to see. Pas de Crédit had volunteered to give a lift to the station in his old lorry; it seemed to Stella like waiting for the tumbril – and it came, on time if not before, chugging and rattling past Hector's cottage, where she knew the old campaigner would wait to give Jacques a send-off.

All the goodbyes were painful – Lucille; his father; his mother; Stella walked part way along the drive to make her own goodbyes. She heard the lorry come slowly up behind her. Jacques held out a hand. 'Ride a short way,' he said.

They made a slow solemn progress to the end of the drive to where Hector stood outside his cottage, wearing an old army peaked shako and his medals. The *tricolore* flying behind him, he stood to attention and saluted. Jacques jumped down and stood to attention before him and solemnly returned the salute, then they shook hands and embraced. '*Bonne chance! Bonne chance!*'

He got back into the cab and sat squeezing Stella's hand. 'At the next bend, I think,' he said huskily. She was not sure whether he spoke to her or their driver. She turned to look at him, tears, panic, love overwhelming her. He put his hand under her chin and lifted it, nodding his total belief in her.

44

'*Au revoir, ma belle amie,*' he whispered.

'Come back to me.'

'Be sure of it,' he answered and as the lorry stopped at the corner he handed her down. 'Now my family needs you,' he said and indicated to where Lucille had walked to stand by Hector.

The lorry drew away, his arm lifted high out of the window, then came the curve in the road and he was out of sight. She felt bereft, even now with the sound of the engine still in her ears, even while she still had the feel of his hand cupped under her chin, she felt truly dispossessed.

She heard someone calling and lifting her head at last saw Lucille had come quite near to her, arms outstretched. As they met, Lucille held her close and tight, with such a new intensity she knew something had happened.

'What is it?'

Lucille immediately understood and reassured her. 'No, no, it was Jacques. He watched you walking away from the house then asked us all to go back into Maman's room. He made a formal kind of announcement, as much to Maman as anyone,' she paused to keep control, 'he told us all he loved you not as a sister any more, but as much as any man can love a woman he wants to spend the rest of his life with. As much as Papa loved Maman. He ...'

'Oh!' Stella turned to look the way he had gone. The new joy brought a new agony, and a rising surge of will that against whatever odds he should return – or she would go to him, wherever he was, she'd go. 'Sod Hitler!' she said vehemently.

Lucille took her arm to walk back to the house. 'Of course I knew really.'

The letter arrived the day after Jacques had left. The envelope had been double-franked, the second time from Lyons, that date clearly showing as five days after the enclosed notice of recall. Stella kept the envelope as evidence, and showed it to Hector, should there ever be any charge for Jacques to answer.

'I can witness the day it came, mademoiselle, do not fear!'

Their days and nights at the farm fell into a pattern, a routine of caring, so Gaby with the help of a part-time nurse was never alone. Stella saw Hector most mornings as she walked to fortify herself for the day, a kind of spiritual renewing before returning to the quiet house, where the irrefutable end stalked and laid tender traps. She found Lucille shedding tears over a note found in a kitchen drawer, a message her mother had written years ago ordering special pastries for when 'the gang' arrived. There was a jumble of earrings in the bathroom cabinet, which no one had the heart to remove. For Stella there was the danger of unwittingly quoting one of Gaby's many apt sayings.

Stella saw a lot of magnificent and lonely sunrises, often from the spot where she had alighted from the lorry; it was the only tryst she could make. Often as she walked back she saw Hector raise his flag to the coming day and would stop to listen to him grow indignant as he repeated the confused mass of conflicting information coming from the radio.

With infinite patience Stella managed to find a station which occasionally broadcast short news bulletins in English. When this source reported that French and English forces had tried to break through to each other near Arras and failed, this was a big blow to Hector, who knew the old battlefield. The news of a mass evacuation of troops at Dunkirk, and then that Calais had surrendered, was a blow to Stella, for she knew the port so well. She also knew that had the reports been in French she might well have doubted the truth of them.

The following morning the sunrise was peppered with small clouds taking war colours from the sun and as she walked back towards the farm she remembered how Jean-Paul's finger had swept over the atlas, the pincer movements he anticipated the Germans would make. She remembered the more eastern ports being cut off even when they had landed at St Malo – and there was her promise to Jacques – if things became worse then they should all make for the coast and North Africa.

Deep in thought she was almost at Hector's cottage before she was brought to a standstill by the new chilling symbol that flew from his flagpole. It was a black flag that lifted and fell in the morning breeze. She found herself breathless on his threshold. 'Hector! What is it? Has Paris fallen?'

He rose slowly from his kitchen table, covered with the war maps and homemade flags he had his meals over and around. 'Dr Chabrol was called and I have just come from the house. It is all over. Madame no longer suffers.'

'Ah!' It was both anguish and relief. 'But I should have been there.' She ran back to the house. Only last evening she and Lucille had taken Ernest's hunting guns and hidden them inside Jean-Paul's tarpaulin-covered car.

Lucille was still by her mother's bedside. Stella went quietly to her side and found herself letting out her breath in controlled wonder, for Gaby looked peaceful at last. The tensions were gone and her face looked younger, just as people said sometimes happened. The nurse came into the room carrying bowls and towels; she nodded

46

meaningfully at Stella, asking her to take Lucille and Ernest away.

'The nurse just needs time alone.' Stella shepherded the two to the kitchen. Ernest was certainly not distraught. He was controlled, but would not be comforted – he would not be touched – and moved away as they tried to put their arms around him.

'She is to be buried in her wedding gown,' he said. 'She was proud that it fitted her still – and so was I. I know where it is.'

He startled them by having so many things already fixed in his mind, knew exactly the arrangements that must immediately be made, supervising, going back upstairs to find and lay out the dress. He soon made both girls feel useless and in the way, though with his consent they wrote a joint letter to Jacques.

They moved through the days in an agony of knowing all must be done, but knowing also he should not be doing it all. 'There will be reaction sooner or later,' Lucille predicted, 'there has to be.'

The activity was followed by inertia, by a bent, old, exhausted man who once the funeral was over sat in the kitchen, or the farm office – and did nothing. Doctor Chabrol said to give him time – but time seemed to be something they were soon to run out of.

On 11 June they called on Hector to find him savagely pinning a line of swastikas all along France's border with Italy, from Switzerland to Monaco. 'Mussolini has made a "Pact of Steel" with Germany,' the old man told them, and his suppressed anger was such that they did not question the meaning of the phrase, the implications of his black symbols inked on pieces of paper bags and pierced with dressmaking pins from the farm, were all too ominous. Italy was not like the battle lines drawing in around Paris, hundreds and hundreds of kilometres from Avignon. Italy was near – a hundred kilometres or so – nothing for tanks and armoured vehicles.

'We have to decide what we will do,' Lucille urged as they left Hector savagely creasing and cutting up a further paper bag with a huge razor-sharp butcher's knife. 'I should be nursing, helping somewhere.'

'Jacques made me promise we would all make for Africa if other ways were blocked, go from there to England. Then we could do our bit!'

They found Ernest in his office, his hands resting on a pile of unopened letters. They told him of the latest development, but as he showed no response they emphasised the nearness of the Italian border, the real danger of internment. 'Avignon housed the Italian popes,' Lucille added with a degree of desperation, but the seeming irrelevance of the remark at last roused her father.

'Yes,' he said like a man making an effort to drag his mind back from some great distance, 'that is what you should do.'

His firm intention to remain, no matter what, was quickly clear. They must go, but he would stay. 'Why?' Lucille sprang up from her chair, paced the kitchen, exasperated, frustrated. 'You've never even been back to Mother's grave!'

He looked briefly at his daughter, then about him, lifting his head, as if he saw beyond the walls of that room to the whole house. 'Your mother's here,' he said quietly.

'Yes. Sorry, we're sorry,' Stella heard herself mumbling as if it had been her accusation, then she rose quickly, took her friend's hand and added encouragingly, 'We're taking flowers today.' They waited, breath held, for a response, an offer to go with them. They watched his head lower, saw him slip back into his state of apathy.

'You should go, think of your own father,' Lucille said as they left the silent motionless man. 'I can't leave him.'

'My father's pretty self-sufficient – he's had to be over the years. And how would I feel if I left you? No. I couldn't do that. It's either all of us, or we stay, do what we can here, even if it's only to keep your father and the farm going.'

'If the Italians and Germans close in none of us will have any chance. We'd all be interned, everyone knows we're English, part English.'

'We would have to hide.' Her mind ran a gamut of possible hiding places, pictured Hector keeping watch at the end of the drive. She felt her skin rise and prickle as, for the first time, she accepted the real possibility that France could be overrun, defeated.

On their way to the cemetery they called on Hector, asked him to walk up to the house and eat lunch with Ernest.

The Cleauville family graves formed an impressive block to one side of the burial ground. Stella always felt it was like walking in miniature streets between windowless stone buildings, though many of the sarcophagi had carved frames along their sides in which were named all the members of the family inside each massive stone box.

They arranged the long-stemmed Madonna lilies in the deep stone container with meticulous care.

'It's all we can do for Maman now,' Lucille said as she finally rose from her knees.

'Yes,' Stella reluctantly agreed, swallowing hard. It was not her place to weep first, hers to keep her vow to help in every way. 'Perhaps we should try to help your father in a different way, try to interest him in the farm, in his vines. Perhaps cut a sample of the green grapes, take it and ask his opinion.' She warmed to the idea. 'I mean the vines will be here no matter what happens, whatever Hitler does.'

The vines, yes, and the olives. Stella sat back on her heels as her senses recreated every moment of their lovemaking, so when Lucille answered, 'We could I suppose,' she was not sure what she was talking about.

Stella half rose, then lowered herself slowly down again and said quietly, 'Don't look round but I think there's a man lying behind the grave with the angel near the gate.'

'What's he doing?'

'Hiding, or watching us, I'm not sure.'

'We'll find out,' Lucille said as they walked slowly towards the gates. They exchanged glances as the legs they had glimpsed during their approach were pulled in. Stella gestured that she would go one way and Lucille should go the other, giving no chance of escape.

There was a scuffle as they simultaneously rounded the tomb. Not a village youth as Stella had supposed, but two men: tramps were her first judgement. One scrambled to his feet, while the other remained with his legs outstretched in front of him, head down, but aware, for she saw his cheek muscles flex and unflex.

The one on his feet ran a hand through his matted hair, pulled at his jacket, standing almost at attention though he, like his companion, looked ill, hollow-cheeked, and ashen with fatigue.

There was something incongruous about the two men, the polite way one tried to stand straight, almost appeasing, while the one on the ground by his very unresponsiveness suggested a stark aggression. Both were obviously wearing someone else's clothes. The one standing had old corduroy trousers and a frayed-edged jacket with torn pockets. The one propped against the tomb had on workman's blues, but beneath the trousers they could see army puttees, though by the dark blood stains they might be thought more bandages than uniform.

The word deserters sprang to Stella's mind.

'Are you injured?' Lucille stooped to ask the man on the ground.

He did not answer, but the other nodded. 'He took an ankle injury before we started walking.'

'How long have you been walking?' Stella asked.

'Two weeks. We are French soldiers, mesdemoiselles, we were overrun. If you could give us somewhere to sleep for the night, something to eat, then we could be on our way.'

'Where to?' Stella asked.

'Home!' the man on the floor exclaimed. 'You have any other ideas for us?'

For a moment no one spoke. Accusation trembled on Stella's lips but a glance from Lucille plus their abject condition silenced her, for the time being.

49

'Could you walk about another half kilometre?' Lucille asked.

'I've made a crutch,' the other man said. 'We'll get there if there's something to eat at the end of it.'

'But of course,' Lucille replied.

'Then you can tell us your story,' Stella added, but though the man on his feet nodded, neither spoke.

The crutch was a piece of a branch, with a 'v' for under the arm. It was a clumsy aid and progress was slow. Watching the effort it took Stella remembered how as children they had paired up to make seats for each other. Holding crossed clasped hands, the passenger's arms around the carriers' necks. Philip and Jacques had run outrageously fast with each of them in turn, while the girls had collapsed, or pretended to, under the weight of Jacques or Philip.

She assessed the taciturn man and his struggles with the crutch. They could carry him like that, arms around their necks – a deserter's arms, while Jacques and Philip were fighting. It became a moral dilemma as the man stumbled and her anger against him became more intense.

What seemed like a choice between evils was banished as they heard the sound of an engine and a farm tractor with a trailer came into view. Lucille waved but the man was already stopping. 'Can you help us?' she asked. 'Give us a lift to Cleauville?'

He grimaced his willingness and jerked his thumb towards the trailer. 'You've found some strange fellows.' He made no further comment as the two men were helped aboard; the girls sat on the sides of the trailer holding on tight as they moved jerkily off.

When he reached the farm drive he turned and drove right to the kitchen door, where Hector appeared holding a wine bottle and glass, while behind him Ernest sat on at the table.

Hector stood back watching critically as the men were offloaded and the driver greeted him by name. 'Hector! Don't say too much old man, I've heard of a lot such as these coming.' Hector mumbled some unintelligible comment and waved a dismissive hand as the tractor drove away, the driver calling back, presumably to the strangers, '*Ne vous en faites pas*!' Don't worry.

The questions in everyone's minds were not to be answered quickly. The men were beckoned to the table, where they cleared the remains of the meal laid: bread, cheese, sausage, fruit pie, everything put before them, they ate ravenously. They drank copiously of the wine Hector had brought to the kitchen – and then were so very obviously nearly falling asleep it would have been inhuman to try to find out anything from them.

'Let me dress your ankles and feet,' Lucille said. 'I am a nurse. Then we'll find you a place to sleep.'

'There's plenty of fresh straw in the barn,' Hector said, 'and blankets'.

'Horse blankets!' Lucille protested.

'Good enough as we are, mademoiselle.' He attempted a smile, a joke. 'If we ever get clean again it might be another matter.'

'What are your names?' Lucille asked.

'Victor Nodier, at your service.' He bowed his head almost as if he were used to being in service.

'And you?' she asked kneeling before the man in blues as she began to roll up his trousers, then carefully to unwind the knee-length puttees. 'Yours is?'

'Pierre, call me Pierre,' he said, his eyes intent on the lengthening strip of khaki in her hands.

'How long since you had these off?' she asked.

'About a week,' he said and when she tutted he added, 'We had nothing clean to put on, so there was no point.'

'They're mine,' Victor nodded at the puttees, 'we had no proper dressings left.'

'We never had any proper dressings,' Pierre growled.

As she reached the ankle the material was stuck. Stella was quick to bring a bowl of warm water with disinfectant and a cloth. 'Papa, could you fetch me the first-aid box from your study? Papa!'

Hector, who had gone in and out replenishing the wine racks in the pantry while the men ate, now bent and touched Ernest, repeating the request.

'Who are these men?' they heard Ernest ask as Hector followed him. The mumbled reply did not sound flattering.

'The old man,' Pierre asked, 'he would have fought in the first war?'

'He lost his leg on the Somme. He hero-worships his old fighting officer de Gaulle.'

'He's right,' Pierre grudgingly approved. 'Lost a leg, good God!' he added. There the conversation ended as the seriousness of his ankle injury became apparent.

'How did this happen?' Lucille went on soaking the khaki strip until she could pull the last section away.

'A shot,' he said, drawing in his breath, 'German panzers.'

'I think you've lost a bit of ankle bone,' she said, drawing in her own breath as the full extent of the raw wound was exposed. Stella bit her lip and closed her eyes until Lucille ordered, 'More lint, and more clean water.'

'It'll take a lot of washings before your feet are clean,' she told him as she worked, so gently it seemed to Stella, so efficiently. 'The good thing is perhaps that some of your blisters in fact look more infected

51

and inflamed than your ankle, but we'll see how everything looks in the morning. You need sleep.'

The other man's feet were worse. He had obviously helped Pierre to his own detriment. His feet were rubbed raw all around both heels and over his insteps which were high, and had obviously caught most severely on his boots.

When both men were installed in the barn and asleep before the doors were closed, the debate began. Stella seriously thought they should be reported to the authorities. 'If everyone deserts where will we be!'

'What authorities! You are not in England now,' Lucille said in weary frustration. 'You know what it's like here! Give them a chance, let's hear their story properly in the morning.'

'You don't worry, they won't be here in the morning,' Hector prophesied. 'They'll be long gone before any cock crows!'

'I don't think so,' Lucille said, 'not if I am any judge of people. Those men are so weary they'll sleep until well into the morning.'

'I'll come and see then,' Hector said belligerently, 'come and see what they have to say for themselves. What excuses!'

But the first person to arrive the next morning was the doctor. Lucille greeted him and poured him coffee. 'Papa is not up yet,' she told him.

Dr Chabrol sipped his coffee in silence, emptied his cup and accepted more. 'This is more a ... a social call,' he said. 'I'd like to talk to you all.' Stella thought he was pale and unlike his urbane self, so much so she wondered if somehow he knew of the two men in the barn and they were already in trouble for harbouring them; she had heard of similar things in Britain.

'I'll go and tell my father you're here.'

Lucille was about to leave the kitchen as Stella asked, 'Is it about the soldiers in the barn?'

'We found two men in the graveyard yesterday. One had been shot in the ankle.'

'Deserters, we think,' Stella added.

Dr Chabrol looked startled at the word, then put his hand to his forehead and rubbed his forefinger backwards and forwards across his brow, as if it might erase some crease or problem that lay there.

Ernest came into the kitchen, the two men shook hands. 'My friend, I've come on a strange errand, but first I should like to see the men you have sheltered in your barn and hear their stories.'

'Hector says they should be shot and that's all I know about them,' Ernest replied with a shrug which seemed to indicate he cared neither one way nor the other.

52

'And what do you say, sir?' Pierre stood in the doorway on his crutch, Victor behind him, and addressed the doctor directly.

'What I might have said has changed radically in the last twenty-four hours,' he answered, getting up. 'Come in my boy, let's have a look at that ankle.'

'First eat,' Lucille declared, bringing to the table a tray of milky coffee and croissants. The men's faces brightened so much, suddenly and briefly they looked young – boys – heartrendingly vulnerable.

'Tell me where you came from,' Dr Chabrol said.

'We were taken prisoner at Crécy, then there was a push back by our tanks and we escaped – but then . . . ' Pierre shrugged, pausing as if trying to make sense of his own experiences, his croissant dripping back into his bowl. 'We were so mixed up with the enemy we didn't know where our lines were, and the Germans . . . ' He shook his head as if this part of the story he could hardly believe himself. 'They came on and on, always another line, always more . . . '

'Coming on and on as if they were going to summer parties in well-pressed trousers, short-sleeved shirts, well-fed, well equipped, while . . . ' Dr Chabrol took up the story as if he had been there.

'While we ran out of ammunition,' Victor put in, 'after we'd spent nights hiding under broken-down lorries, in ditches, with no food.'

'And the Germans looked as if they had spent the night in first-class hotels.'

Everyone in the kitchen was now watching and listening to the doctor. 'We started in Flanders with horse- and mule-drawn cannon, which ran amok as the Stukas flew in. We are ending in Burgundy with men equipped with 1914 helmets and no ammunition. We are retreating river by river . . . '

'Yes! Yes!' Victor interrupted. 'We thought we would make a stand at the Oise, then we thought it would be the Marne, then the Seine!'

'But we just kept on retreating,' Pierre said grimly, 'and we'll soon all be in the Mediterranean, up to our backsides in blue sea – and where were the bloody officers?'

'I know where one was,' the doctor said quietly, 'my son arrived home in the middle of last night. He had travelled home from south of Paris – by bus and bicycle.'

The good doctor lifted his head then as if to receive sentence on behalf of his son. No one spoke for some moments, then surprisingly it was Pierre who said, 'No one should make judgements. Until you have seen the efficiency of the Nazis, ever coming on, stepping over, singing over their own dead as they advance with their shiny tanks, followed by their shiny kitchens – and their shiny mobile crematoriums.'

53

'Edmund, my son, says France has been trying to refight the last war, treating Hitler like some latterday Kaiser, when they should be treating him like Genghis Khan.'

'Your son is right,' Pierre agreed. 'I was a language student at Berlin University in the thirties, saw some of his cleansing policies – the gipsies, the defectives, the Jews – interned, then God knows what exterminations or atrocities took place.'

'This, my friends, is the real reason for my visit. Edmund is convinced France will fall. He says German planes have been showering down pamphlets for days now saying "Frenchmen, prepare your coffins! Frenchwomen, get out your ball dresses! We're going to dance the soles off your shoes ... "' He faltered, turning to Ernest as he drew a pamphlet from his inside pocket and laid it on the table for them all to see. 'As an Englishman you should take your daughter and her friend back to your own country as quickly as possible.'

Everyone in the kitchen had been so riveted by so many revelations it startled them all as Hector appeared at the doorway and announced, 'Paris has been declared an open city.'

Stella's gaze was attracted by Ernest as he suddenly and violently flung down the glass he was holding and snatched up the pamphlet, his eyes ablaze with anger.

Chapter Five

Jacques plucked a pamphlet from the bushes as he left the stricken train south of Paris.

Midway on the slope of the embankment he paused and glanced at the paper. That it offered Frenchmen death was no surprise – but the message to the women to prepare their dancing shoes enraged him. Goebbels with his war propaganda machine had successfully terrified the French into believing the Communists would invade from Russia so fast they would have snow on their boots; now they were trying to divide Frenchmen from Frenchwomen!

He trudged on remembering his mother dancing at village fetes in the village square; the harvest celebrations. How his father loved the dance too, or more accurately how he loved to dance with his Gaby, becoming more exuberant than any Frenchman as the evenings had worn on. He remembered overhearing his father repentant and apologetic one 'morning after', and his mother laughing. The thought that *any* Frenchwoman would fraternise with the enemy was appalling to him. He had left his mother's bedside – her death bed – and Stella and his sister unsupported to scrabble back into this futile chaos.

He looked towards Paris, to the rail lines splayed and lifted heavenwards, cratered fields, all liberally strewn with copies of the pamphlet he held, like confetti at a demonic battlefield wedding. He looked over the nearest highway, which from a distance was so crowded with refugees it looked like a black river running sluggishly but irrevocably south. He pushed the screwed paper into his pocket. It would serve as a reminder of the power of the printed word, the power of persuasion. It served as a reminder of what he might do if he could not reach his army unit.

He had thought the railway line would be a better option for walking than the road, but the bomb craters were too many and extensive. He paid a silent tribute to the accuracy of the German bombers.

On the road, moving against a tide relentlessly trying to make headway in the opposite direction, he found himself helping to push cars from ditches; he secured a collapsing wheel on a laden pram for distraught grandparents, who in the mêlée had lost their daughter-in-law; but was unable to answer any of the questions two society ladies in a high-powered sportscar laden with huge strapped trunks asked. They obviously thought he was an idiot. The comment was made, as some called to him to turn around, or asked did he know where he was going? *'C'est un imbécile!'*

At first he had singled out any man in uniform, but he soon realised the futility of trying to waylay and question the odd ones, or the straggling ranks, of retreating men. There were many with injuries supported along by their fellows – they had neither ammunition, field dressings, nor leaders. Many looked sadly at him, others regarded him with enmity and growled, answering question with question, 'Where have *you* been?' But it was a shock, when as the troops became greater in numbers, the words 'a defeated army' came to his mind.

As the afternoon wore on he was aware that his once-upright walk was becoming the same round-shouldered trudge of those going the other way, and in his mind he began to write a news report:

I had begun to meet a defeated army, retreating with the people they should have been defending.

The displaced men and women walked as in a nightmare, moving on as fast as they might from what they feared and yet with hearts full of regret for what they left behind.

I saw people manhandle a broken-down car from where it blocked their way, leaving it and its occupants, a woman with two small children, abandoned and stranded. The picture of her sitting, head in hands on the running board of her car, a tot by either side each with a hand on her knee will be a permanent image in my mind.

The nearer I came to Paris the more tense and silent were the travellers and if a new noise came from the engine of any of the cars trapped in their crocodile, eyes immediately went to the skies, hands tightening on children and bundles, ready to throw themselves to the ground.

When the Stuka did come, roaring like an express train low along the road, we flung ourselves to the verges and ditches, but this time it didn't fire on us. I found myself nearly lying across an old woman who shook her fist at the sky. 'Playing with us!' she shouted. 'Playing!' It was the only act of aggression I saw – towards the

56

enemy. The old lady sat on the ground, legs straight in front of her, her body shaking with sobs. I saw how everyone ignored her, walked on, each one's eyes shuttered to their own concerns. As I lifted her to her feet, placed her bundle back in her hand, she turned on me and said, 'They machine-gunned my husband's cows in our fields! Why? Why!' She was still repeating her question as I gave her a little push on her way. She seemed to be alone.

Like me, he thought, alone, struggling back, one man against a sea of refugees to find a unit that probably no longer exists. What good was he doing? Shouldn't he turn round, throw his fate in with the rest, make his way back to Cleauville, look after his own women? Keep his head down, be blind to the confusion around him? He knew he could not, it was not the way he could ever be. He knew what he should be doing. His hand balled the paper in his pocket; he should be writing, distributing the facts, the truth – not merely composing things in his head.

So many people composed letters of complaint, harangues exposing injustices, but never got them on paper. What good did that do, except dissipate the personal passion? He should be showing the world the truth of what was happening to France and its people, painting the pictures with his words – and in Paris he knew the newspaper offices, had the contacts.

He resolved to head for his flat and his old office, although he was not sure quite in which order. There would surely be people in both places who would be able to tell him what was happening. Madame Astier most certainly would. He felt a little lift of the heart at the thought of the old stoic. He was quite, quite sure she was not heading south!

Just as Jean-Paul had advised south and west to Stella and Lucille, Jacques headed west and north into Paris, walking on as evening deepened to night. What seemed extraordinary was that while he could hear gunfire in the distance, there were no soldiers here. So where was the enemy they were all fleeing from? He reached boulevards he had never before seen free of traffic. Once he heard the steady roar of approaching engines and at a distant intersection saw first the shuttered headlights, then the rear lights of what looked like a troop of men on motorcycles. There was something chilling in the regular spacings of the lights, the controlled roar of the cruising cycles; he felt instinctively they must be Germans. But if that were so, it would mean the Germans were south of Paris and surely that could not be. He must remember the day and date, the thirteenth he thought, the evening of Thursday 13 June 1940.

Jacques came into the centre of his capital, eerily silent, no traffic, no people, no distant deep rumble of the underground trains, nothing moved. Overwhelmed by the atmosphere, he too stood still, he was in a city keeping some terrifying vigil, a city sensing the hand of death already poised above its shoulder. It reminded him of the vigil he and Stella had kept through his last night. He swallowed hard, pushing away the personal, that would be too much at this time. In its place came the anger. Where, he silently protested, were the citizens of Paris? The citizens of the republic? Where were they, armed with whatever they could put hand to? Where were the barricades?

'My God!' he breathed as he recalled the routed troops he had met, and realisation of the truth came. 'They have abandoned Paris!'

'*Parlez-vous anglais*?'

He started, his hand raised to defend himself as a man spoke almost at his elbow; emerging from the darkness of a doorway the man switched on a small torch which he shone on Jacques's uniform, then his face.

'*Mon ami*,' he said urgently, 'I really need help if you can speak English.'

'*Oui*,' Jacques acknowledged.

The man turned back into the doorway and Jacques heard the rattle of a key in a lock, then a metal grille was pulled back and an inner door unlocked. 'Come in,' the man instructed.

Jacques found himself inside a chemist's shop with the man talking rapidly to him as he led the way through to the dispensary and across that to a small door which he opened to reveal a flight of bare ladder-like stairs. 'I can't make him understand. He's in my stockroom, and now the Germans are so near I must ask him to go. I understand the first thing the Boche do is to hunt for the English, for those in hiding – and now they are ...' The sentence trailed away but by the light of the torch Jacques saw his shoulders rise in apology. 'I cannot afford to draw attention to my family, my wife's people are Jewish.'

He led the way calling to whoever waited above. Jacques followed and as the light was switched on in a tiny windowless room, all shelves and boxes, he saw a man propped in the far corner, a blanket tucked up over his shoulders. The man struggled to his feet revealing a brown leather flying jacket and blue Royal Air Force uniform.

If it were not for his height he would have looked like a boy, the epitome of the English 'Just William', Jacques thought, freckled to a fault, red-haired and grinning, holding out his hand. 'Lennie Forryan, shot down at Dunkirk,' he explained. 'Some French chappies hid me in a barn, then passed me on in a cart until I reached Paris. Now I seem to be stuck. Can't make head or tail of this johnnie.'

The chemist was apologetic, shrugging his shoulders continually as he conveyed through Jacques his personal situation – and that of 'Paris, abandoned.'

'Was that official? Was there an announcement?' Jacques demanded.

'First they tell us to fight, for every street and every house, but,' the chemist shrugged again, 'I have a friend who is a Parisian policeman ... our government has fled, the general who remains, my friends says, is talking to the enemy. At first, I did not believe, but now ... now we just wait for the Germans, hold our breath and wait.'

'I have things I must do – a lot to do before daylight. I'll take the pilot to my apartment, I have civilian clothes there.'

'*Mais non!*' The chemist was badly alarmed. 'You could be shot as spies! As uniformed combatants you would only be taken prisoner.'

He translated for Lennie who with youthful enthusiasm scoffed, 'Only! No fear! If you can kit me up with civvies I'm with you.'

Before they left Jacques told of seeing the motorcyclists. 'So it is possible the city is already surrounded.'

'Cities are big places to hide in,' Lennie declared optimistically.

'I should have taken my family away before,' the shopkeeper mused with a bleak look in his eyes, as if he already saw his own end as well as that of others of his family, 'but I did not want to leave my business, and I did not believe it would happen – not to Paris.'

No, not to Paris. Jacques too felt the enormity of the blow, to forsake one's capital city without a single shot in its streets – it was contrary to all their traditions. We should have fought for Paris *quartier* by *quartier*, he thought, for the sake of our country, our revolutionary ancestors, our honour!

The three parted solemnly, aware their paths were never likely to cross again; the chemist full of apology and pessimism; the young airman eagerly, happy at last to be able to move on, to communicate. 'But no talking until we reach my flat,' Jacques warned him. No sense in moving under cover of night if his companion started talking in 'jolly' English slang expressions.

They walked quickly, but there were distractions. As their eyes grew accustomed to the dark Jacques became aware of the number of dogs wandering the streets. Some of these sidled hopefully towards them, trying to placate with lowered heads and wagging tails, but receiving no return greeting they slunk off, to go on waiting, their canine vigil in stark contrast to the retreating human flood. He noticed too many cats on walls. There had been stories weeks ago of long queues at vets' surgeries waiting to have animals put down – perhaps that had been kinder. He tried not to look at the animals, not to think of the years of devotion they had probably given to their fleeing owners. He remembered Stella's old spaniel, the buttercups on the grave. He tutted and immediately the young airman's hand was on his arm. 'You OK?'

Jacques nodded.

'It's the dogs, isn't it?'

Jacques nodded again.

French flags flew on some of the main hotels, but they were shuttered, silent and dark. Occasionally the distant night sky was lit by a flash of gunfire giving it all a strange kind of stage quality, as if the playscript said 'sound of distant gunfire off set'. The Stars and Stripes fluttered above the American embassy in the Place de la Concorde and there were lights and activity behind the gates. If only the Yanks would decide to come into the war, he thought, for England's sake now if not for France's.

In the quarter near his flat the blocks of apartment houses were like dark canyons and utterly silent. He felt the pilot's hesitation as he quickened his own pace, but he made no sign, only plunged ever more rapidly onwards now the first of his goals was so near.

He found the outer door of the apartments bolted, the windows shuttered. 'Stay here,' he whispered, but even as he spoke a voice demanded '*Qui est là?*'

Paris, he thought, does not sleep, only waits. 'Madame Astier, it is Jacques Blair.'

There was some muffled exclamation and a rattle of bolts as the door swung open. The hall and staircase were in darkness, but in the meagre light from her own apartment Madame surveyed the two, her jaw dropping, mouth growing wide in astonishment; then she lifted her hands as if in prayer, but swore as roundly as she could. Then to the surprise of both men she leaned forward, grasped them each by the front of their jackets and pulled them inside, making them feel like small naughty boys.

'*Mon Dieu*!' She allowed Jacques to embrace her but then she pushed him away. 'Only you – *only you* – could do this! Is it fancy dress?' Even as she asked the question she was shaking her head. 'The Germans are all around Paris, we are being occupied any hour and you come here dressed in ...' her hand described his uniform, 'with an English ...' she peered closely at Lennie and flicked open his jacket, 'airman.'

'Pilot,' Lennie said, 'would she understand pilot?'

'Yes, she would understand pilot,' Madame Astier told him. 'Do you understand fool! Idiot!'

Jacques took her hand and led her back into her apartment. 'If you

60

want us to go at once, then we will,' he told her.

'Idiot!' she repeated gently. She waved the airman in and plumped up the cushion of her easy chair for him. She poured coffee from the can on the stove as Jacques told how they both came to be there, how he had left matters at Cleauville.

'Your family should leave France,' she said gravely, tutting as she added, 'and the English mademoiselle. You should have gone back sooner, taken them all away.' As she spoke she took from one side table a notice which she placed before Jacques. 'These,' she said, 'have been left pasted on the walls of our city,' she stabbed it with her finger, 'from the man who was in charge of the *Parisian* army!'

General Hering, having been called away to command an army, is placing the military government in the hands of General Dentz. Paris is declared an open city. Every step has been taken to ensure in all circumstances the safety and provisioning of the inhabitants.

'Called away to command an army!' Jacques quoted in disgust. 'Why isn't his bloody army here? Where did you get this?'

'Verit, the old caretaker at your newspaper, called with it earlier, he saw them being posted up.'

'Verit! Ah! I want to go to the office, I want to know what is happening to the newspapers.'

'Nothing!' Madame said. 'They are finished, like everything else!'

He looked at her, speculating more than listening. 'We need civilian clothes. I should have some that will fit our friend here.'

Madame Astier accompanied them upstairs as if unwilling to be left on her own again, so soon. She recounted how Stella and Lucille had tidied his rooms, then how Jean-Paul had come. 'Is his beloved car safe?' she asked. Then she tutted at herself, 'As if a car matters when all France is in peril!'

'We've hidden it in a barn, and ...' He paused, recollecting how they had taken the can of petrol to collect the Wolseley, and their lovemaking under the fig trees ...

'And?'

He tried to pick up the threads of what he had been saying. 'And I hope they do as I told them and escape down to the coast and across to Africa.'

While Lennie was trying on clothes, Jacques went to his bookshelf and finding the book of poetry, let it lie in his palm. It fell open where the ribbon was. He touched it gently then took it and put it into his wallet, looking up to find Madame Astier regarding him. 'Oh! And!' she said, nodding.

61

'It was her last hair ribbon – Philip pulled it off and she wouldn't have it back.'

'A child no longer.'

'No,' he agreed, then grinned.

'*Oh là, là!*' she cried with an excited laugh, like a young woman herself, then her face changed. 'I did not expect to laugh at anything this night. Whatever you need me to do I will do, I will be here, whatever happens.'

'*Merci*, Madeleine!' But he wondered how far she might take her promise? He picked up the notice Verit had torn from the wall. 'We need something like this, posters and an underground newspaper that will let the people of Paris and France know what is really happening. There may be someone at the office who can help. There would surely be some kind of printer, and materials.'

'In the middle of the night?' Lennie asked, coming into the room.

'Yes!' Madeleine agreed with an iron-willed certainty and ignoring the pilot. 'Bring whatever you need here.'

He questioned her with a long look. Did she know what she risked, what it would entail? She nodded slowly several times.

He had never seen his newspaper building in complete darkness before, the long ranks of tall windows, the arched doorways, the garages at the far end. All the places he knew took on new proportions, unlit black shapes etched on blackness under a paler sky. The silence was eerie. He had never heard it this quiet before; ordinarily there was always bustle, always someone whistling as they bundled parcels of newspapers into the delivery vans, or stocked a street seller's barrow. He thought of the revolver he had seen Lennie transfer from his uniform to the civilian jacket, and wished he had the same protection.

The main doors were locked but he led the way down a short alleyway to where a small side door led into the back offices for the commercial section, where small advertisements were taken over front counters. The editorial department, the hangout of the reporters and sub-editors, was upstairs. He listened and was sure in the distant reaches of the first floor there was someone moving about. He beckoned the pilot after him and was about to mount the metal-edged stairs quietly – for the first time ever – when a light went on at the far end of the downstairs corridor.

'Who's there?'

'Verit?' Jacques went forward. '*Mon vieux ami!* What are you doing here?'

'What I always do, monsieur.' He held up the broom.

'You should be with your wife, my old friend.'

He shrugged. 'She is with her mother. Sometimes the Germans seem a better choice!'

The two younger men laughed briefly, then Jacques nodded towards the light from upstairs. 'Is anyone else here?'

He rolled his eyes upwards. 'Monsieur Bayland,' he said, 'came about an hour ago.'

'Bayland!' Jacques led the way at a run, his feet clattering as of old on the thick metal stair treads.

A figure appeared at the far door. 'Bayland! My old friend.'

'Jacques? Where the devil have you sprung from ...' The old chief reporter staggered even as he spoke and the two younger men rushed to support him.

'What is it?' Jacques asked when they had helped him to the news editor's comfortable armchair, but Bayland grinned at them.

'I,' he told them, 'have just defaced every single piece of type in this building. There is no way any German will print a newspaper here in a hurry.'

'You can't have ... surely.' Jacques doubted the capacity of anyone to deface so much.

'You'd better believe it,' he said giving a satisfied jerk of his chin. 'I'll sleep better tonight now. I'm bloody exhausted anyway!'

'Your friend has destroyed what you needed?' Lennie asked.

'Who's *your* friend?' Bayland asked.

Jacques explained the English pilot's presence and his own mission. Bayland looked at them calculatingly. 'What you want is one of the mimeograph machines out of the downstair's office, that and a pile of stencils.'

'Yes!' Jacques said with enthusiasm, leading the way, 'and as much paper as we can carry.'

'What about one of the old hand barrows from the warehouse?' Bayland suggested.

Jacques clapped him on the shoulder. 'A genius!'

The noise of the barrow in the silent street was appalling, like a tumbril over cobbles. 'Keep going,' Lennie urged.

Jacques broke into a run, but had no doubt that behind the closed shutters many were listening in fear, thinking their passing heralded the beginning of German rule in Paris.

Chapter Six

On the morning of Friday 14 June 1940 Paris held its breath and waited. No sound of doors opening and closing was heard, no clatter of carts or bicycles as their owners jolted them out into the early morning streets, no cries of greeting, no hooting scurrying traffic – nothing. For a time silence reigned.

Then on the edge of hearing came a faint noise, a buzz like a single bee, which grew in volume to sound like the whole swarm – a purposeful mass heading, or so it seemed to every listener, their way. It grew louder to a recognisable growl of cruising motorbikes, scouts and outriders for those who followed. For then closer came the sinister rumble and hiss of big-tyred vehicles, lorries, infantry trucks. Finally, with a slick but chilling metallic rattle, came the caterpillar-tracked army vehicles, and the tanks.

The sinister ribbons of sound threaded, pushed, flooded through main squares, thoroughfares, cobbled streets. Residents sat on in their homes, not wishing to see from their windows these first moments of occupation, to witness German troops roll unopposed into their city.

Jacques, Lennie and Madeleine had not slept. They had spent the night carrying up to a back attic all that might be needed to make a place to hide in and to print a news-sheet. They moved in a single bed, mattress, blankets, a set of shelves, a table and bentwood chair, candles, a small supply of tinned food, plus everything they had hauled from the newspaper offices.

It was Lennie who showed them how a huge pine cupboard which stood in the adjoining attic could be fixed over the door to the back room, which was windowless except for a skylight. This cupboard, he explained, could be altered so that one of its back panels opened to allow them through into the further room, and only the most assiduous searcher with an eye for comparing external and internal measurements would even suspect a second room.

'Well it sounds wonderful, but ...' Jacques began.

'If you've tools I can do it, no problem,' he told them. 'My grandfather was a master cabinet-maker. It was what I wanted to do actually, but ...' he shrugged, 'my father's in banking.'

In his civilian trousers, shirt sleeves and a pencil stuck behind his ear, Lennie was transformed from a boy looking as if he was playing at being a pilot into what looked very much like a man following his trade. Jacques was also much impressed by his skill as his ideas began to take shape. The back panels were skilfully removed from the cupboard, remade and reassembled with a sliding end panel. 'Not the one directly facing the cupboard door, that might be too obvious,' he said as he worked. 'Then with some clothes hung in it ...'

Madeleine and Jacques exchanged appreciative nods. Jacques watched Lennie's hands as they moved over the wood, seeming to caress, assess, and find new value in the pieces; and the inelegant workaday tools Madeleine had found were not clumsy in his hands.

'We need to do two other things,' Jacques said. 'One is to find out how much noise you can hear when this is all shut up and we're typing or working the mimeograph machine, and the other is to have some kind of warning system for if the Germans ever come looking.'

'I can do that,' Lennie said. 'What you need is a light to come on in the attic, with the switch somewhere near the front door. But we'd need a good length of wire.'

'I'll get it,' Jacques promised.

'I'll get it,' Madeleine corrected. 'You two had better keep off the streets until we know exactly what is happening.'

It was mid-morning when Madame finally ventured out. She had wanted the other two to go to bed in her apartment rather than Jacques's own, but he was convinced there would be no kind of raids or searches so early. 'There will,' Jacques hazarded, 'be plenty the Germans have to take control of first.'

They woke to her knock in the early afternoon. She carried up to them soup and bread – and her frustrations. 'Eat, while I tell you,' she said.

'Did you get the wire?' Lennie asked.

She nodded. 'I stole it,' she said.

'You?' Jacques choked. 'I don't believe it!'

'Listen,' she said peremptorily as she sat at the table with them, 'then you will.' But before she began to speak she contemplated her hands on the table before her and for a moment Jacques wondered if she was praying.

'I saw Verit, your caretaker, again. He was waiting for me, did not want to come to the house again in case it compromised us.'

65

Jacques's spoon slowed on the way to his mouth, then returned laden to his bowl. 'What is it?' he asked watching her face carefully, sensing she had news of real moment to impart.

'Verit saw the liftman at *Paris-Soir* leave during the night, Verit called out goodbye, said he thought it was very strange that this man who was a speaking acquaintance did not reply. Today he saw that same man come back, but now he has taken over. He is not only a lieutenant in the German army but is rumoured to be a member of a wealthy German publishing family. He has already begun to plan a Nazi version of *Paris-Soir* for tomorrow!'

'But I know the man, Joseph something, he's been there for years!'

'Even so.' She shrugged away Jacques's surprise. 'Listen! I also talked to my friends who own Le Petit Chat, and they have heard from a baker that in the big restaurants favoured by our *revered* politicians, waiters who have stood and listened to careless chatter for years are welcoming the first Germans as old friends. More! In a bistro behind the Place du Palais Bourbon a nun who has made regular charity collections from customers has emerged as a man, a German spy.'

Lennie spluttered and laughed in disbelief. 'Well! I say! A difficult thing to do, unfrock a nun!'

Jacques looked over to his depleted bookshelves and shook his head at Lennie's incredulity. 'Even though bakers are notorious gossips, I begin to believe it. Nuns are everywhere, *go* everywhere, we hardly notice them. The fascists have been planning this a long time – and they're so damned efficient and organised.'

'*Oui*!' Madeleine rose abruptly and went over to turn on the wireless. A German voice announced music by Wagner. She flicked the knob off again with theatrical dislike. 'They say they have taken over everything. They came with uniformed engineers and took over the telephone exchange, they have trained announcers on that.' She flapped a hand towards the set. 'And I've no doubt everything else is under their control. There are swastikas everywhere, and loudspeaker cars shouting out that no demonstrations are allowed and,' she paused, 'any hostile act will be punishable by death.'

She sat down again, heavily, shaking her head in disbelief at all she'd seen. 'And they look as if they're setting up band stands, wiring up loudspeakers – that's where I stole the spool of wire.'

They regarded this stiff-backed, black-clad old Frenchwoman with much respect in view of the words she had just repeated. 'Hostile acts will be punishable by death.'

Jacques was determined to go and look around for himself. There was news, history, to be reported. Lennie said he would go on with the carpentry and the wiring of the alarm light.

Jacques pulled a workman's cap well over his eyes and walked with shoulders hunched like a man older than his years. Reaching the vicinity of the Étoile he could hear military bands, began to see the loudspeakers set up as Madeleine had reported, but the sound of the music as any kind of celebration for the French was quickly contradicted by the sight of machine-gun batteries, or gun-carriers, on every corner.

For one heart-stopping moment Jacques found himself confronted by a German soldier, who halted millimetres before him with an air of mocking menace. Then the man grinned, obscenely, showing an extraordinary number of solid white teeth. His breath smelt of garlic. From the satchel on his shoulder he produced yet another leaflet which he thrust into Jacques's hand. He clapped him on the back and went away laughing. Jacques glanced at the paper to find he was advised among other things to think of his poor children and his lonely wife and demand that his government stopped the fight.

He walked on, witnessing for himself the overwhelming efficiency of the Third Reich, as storm troopers tore down French warbond posters proclaiming that France would win. Behind the troopers came a band of men with ladders pasting up new posters showing a soldier holding a radiant French child stuffing his face with a piece of well-buttered bread, while two more waifs looked enviously up. '*Populations abandonnées, faites confiance au soldat allemand!*' Abandoned people, put your trust in the German soldier.

With ever-increasing nausea in the pit of his stomach he came to what he thought of as the heart of his city. Here above the martial music came the unmistakable thudding march of hundreds of jack-boots; he imagined the very pavement trembled beneath his feet. He was appalled as he came within sight of the Arc de Triomphe, where hundreds of soldiers, thousands even, column upon column, goose-stepped past the sacred place, past the flame on the grave of the unknown soldier. Everything gleamed in the sun: bayonets flashed, buttons glinted and the military music came from no fewer than five bands, one on every corner. The beat of the music and the boots felt like blows. He glanced at the faces of the few civilians who stood watching with him and saw his own stunned disbelief mirrored on each one.

'The Germans march on our grave,' a woman's voice said nearby.

'The Boche always go too far,' an elderly man muttered as the bands took up another march, 'always overdo it.'

Then when finally, finally, all the troops had passed, immediately in their wake came buses loaded with off-duty soldiers carrying cameras instead of rifles. They began photographing each other in their thousands before the Arc de Triomphe. They fooled about, posing in ridiculous ways before the sacred place; Jacques's stunned mind began to wake to a cold anger at these 'tourists'. How he despised them; without the whip of authority they were no more than louts. Yet louts which had flooded his city with troops and decorated every high and sacred place with their blood-red flags with that ugly black symbol like a spider crawling over everything.

He began to understand what it meant for a country to be 'occupied'. He truly felt taken over, so swamped by these totalitarian victors that he must fight against a feeling of overwhelming inertia. He must get to his typewriter, struggle to put feelings on paper, but what he needed was to find just some sign of resistance, something more than the man with his face puckered in tears as he watched the parade, something more than his own revulsion. News was what he needed, hard facts on which to hang the emotional appeal.

Near the Eiffel Tower he found French Algerians cashing in, selling their goods to this great influx of new customers, who were buying everything: oranges, nuts, chocolate, even slabs of butter, and eating, chewing and licking, throwing their litter down. He remembered Goebbels had promised the Germans guns before butter – now they seemed to have both.

Then he found his story. The Tower was decorated by another blood-red German flag with its harsh black symbol, but he overheard that the lift had been sabotaged and that German soldiers had had to walk up its 1671 steps, *and* the operation had to be repeated because the first flag was so enormous it tore in the wind.

He wrote his headline and named his publication as he turned away. It would be *Frère Jacques*, and its first headline would read: 'Shame! Our resistance was blowing in the wind!' It would be a scathing story, it would reflect the scorn he saw in the faces of the German officers and the ordinary soldier. Then he would tell them of these other ranks who fooled about and took photographs of each other in front of the sacred flame. He would tell them to look up to the skyline they had surrendered to the black crosses on blood-red fields, to where only the wind had shown the courage to tear the conqueror's symbol.

But he must not forget the work of the lift saboteur, and there were others; he thought of his old chief reporter scoring and rendering useless all the lead print of the newspaper. At least no one would walk in there and try to produce a newspaper the next day! These stories must inspire similar acts without endangering the perpetrators.

He found himself wandering like a refugee in familiar streets, noting hotels and banks being taken over by officers who marched in followed by uniformed secretaries carrying document cases.

As the June evening began to soften the colours of those harsh red flags, he saw that some restaurants were reopening – and the Germans were flooding in. He saw enormous plates of food coming to the tables and the customers demolishing heaped meals with the same all-consuming efficiency as they had consumed Paris.

He arrived back at the apartment and went straight up to the attic and wrote his first article, ending with a stinging call to undercover resistance. 'Sabotage! It is the way to ensure the Third Reich reaps the whirlwind of its gluttonous appetite. It is the only way to regain our honour!'

It was late when he came down to his apartment. Cutting an accurate stencil had taken a lot longer than rattling out a report for sub-editors. He appreciated that maintaining their supply of stencil correction fluid might present a problem in future. Lennie sat at the table cleaning an ancient electric plug. Jacques turned on the radio to hear the news from the BBC. He wondered what Britain would say about its ally's surrender of its capital? They would be right to condemn.

Instead of the usual precise tones of the newsreader there was a woman speaking. In slow careful French she pronounced each word like a schoolgirl, but with great warmth and sincerity. It was only as he listened that he realised it was the Queen of England. 'A few days ago,' she said, 'I was visiting in our hospitals the French wounded from Dunkirk. To each of them I spoke in French and asked how they were getting on. All of them, even the most seriously wounded, answered cheerfully with one short phrase: "*Ça va!*"' There was a pause, then the Queen took up her theme again. 'I believe whole-heartedly that after these bad days the time will come when our two peoples will, by their endurance and hard work, have made good our armaments deficiencies, and will also be able to say to each other: "*Maintenant, ça va*".'

'Now things are all right.' Jacques repeated the words and stood rigid with emotion as the 'Marseillaise' was followed by 'God Save the King'. Lennie also stood to attention and Jacques saw his lip quiver before he said huskily, 'I have to get back to England. They'll need pilots.'

Chapter Seven

If any of them had made any judgements about Dr Chabrol's son the reality of the man who came to the farm with his father was hardly what any of them expected. He came not as a defeated officer who had abandoned his command, as Stella had judged, but as a man with a new assignment and a tight time schedule.

He was small, pale, black-haired and had the air of a man smouldering, prepared to burn himself out to fulfil his mission. 'We need organisation, and we need to begin now.'

'What are we talking about?' Stella asked. 'Evacuees ... or ...'

'Yes, soldiers, anyone running before the Germans.' As if to reinforce his words he pushed a fist across the table in her direction. 'Babies are dying on our roads south – not just because the Germans are machine-gunning but because they have no milk! No food! For God's sake, no one seems to realise. There are thousands upon thousands of people moving before a rolling steel tide of Germans. They have eaten out the food in the places they have passed through, like locusts in the desert. And this is the summer! Think about it! What will happen if the rout goes on into the winter? I hate to think. I hate ...' He stopped, shaking his head, wiping his brow. Stella glanced at his father, wondering if the doctor too suspected his son might be less than well.

For a few seconds the only sound in the kitchen was the deep tick of the pendulum wall clock. All eyes focused on the intense young man. Then Ernest pushed his hand into his pocket and drew out the pamphlet Dr Chabrol had brought, which Stella remembered had stirred him to his first spontaneous reaction since Gaby's death.

'After France the Germans believe it will take them a couple of months to finish England off,' Edmund commented as he watched the message from the Third Reich being smoothed out on the table.

Ernest looked up and said, a waver of anger in his voice. 'Then they do not know English men, and they certainly do not understand

70

French women. What do you want us to do?'

Stella and Lucille exchanged glances, then simultaneously rose to go to Ernest's side. Stella put her arm tentatively over his shoulders and felt how the bones had rounded these past months under the burden of Gaby's illness and death. Lucille stooped to kiss his cheek and the dam of grief gave way as tears sprang from his eyes, overflowing, overwhelming. Lucille gave a great sigh as at last he allowed her to take him into her arms and they shared their mutual loss.

'I'm sorry girls,' he whispered, reaching to hold Stella's hand, 'I couldn't bear anyone else near me.'

'We know,' Lucille reassured him, 'we understand.'

Stella became aware of the embarrassment of the three younger men, strangers still, and tried to persuade Ernest to take a few private moments, but he shook his head, wiped his eyes. 'I've recently lost my wife, I do not intend to lose her land without a fight.' He pressed his hands down flat on the table either side of the German missive. 'It seems to me we haven't much time,' he said. 'If a country abandons its capital then it is surely as good as finished!'

Stella bit her lip. What he said had to be true. She tried to imagine Churchill giving up London – and could not. Instead there came sharp images of Jacques waving from Pas de Crédit's lorry, of Philip in the hall at home surrounded by his kit, tennis-racket on top of his bag, as if he was going on holiday. Lucille was full of hope that Philip might have been evacuated from Dunkirk, but Jacques had seemingly gone back straight into the hands of the enemy.

'*Oui*.' Dr Chabrol's agreement was low, grim, ashamed, determined to do better than their government. 'There is much to be done. Food, milk for babies, medical supplies, blankets.'

'Safe hiding places, safe houses,' Stella said, remembering the panic at Jacques's flat when Jean-Paul had arrived. 'We'll need to know who we can trust.'

'And more. I want to organise much more,' Edmund interrupted. 'We must organise an underground force to fight, to sabotage the Germans' ambition to rule the continent of Europe.' He paused. 'The more trouble we cause the better for our ally's efforts.'

'England will go on fighting,' Lucille stated, patting her father's shoulder.

'Give us the lead!' Pierre leaned forward and spoke quickly. 'Keep us out of the prison camps and we'll fight.' He looked around the table. 'We already have a doctor, two nurses, an officer and two soldiers.' He grinned. 'That's a good beginning.'

Stella felt that a smile lit up most faces, but it transformed Pierre's. 'I'm no nurse,' she protested.

71

'You'll learn,' he said and laughed as she replied, 'I'm just afraid I might!'

'So we know each other, this house, this family,' Edmund Chabrol ventured. 'We could do no better than begin from here.'

'Yes.' It was Ernest's acquiescence which made it a positive decision.

'We'll be the first group to organise here,' Edmund declared, 'but there'll be others, many others. We must link up, make a network of resistance all across France, all across Europe.'

'Guerrilla warfare.' It was his father who named and defined their intentions. 'War carried on by small bodies of men acting independently.'

'But with more idea of what we're supposed to be doing than the armies of France have had,' Pierre stated.

'And better equipped!' Victor declared, the irony echoed in Edmund's hollow laugh.

They began immediately. Dr Chabrol and Ernest left together to approach people they knew well, those they felt would be with them. The three younger men began to talk of maps, targets, information on rail movements. Doing was a relief which helped lift the awful feeling of doom as with every news broadcast the shadow of the Axis fell further over France.

A system evolved whereby once the approach was made Lucille and Stella followed up with calls on the women. They began organising bedding, mattresses in rows in attics, barns, outhouses, they took stock of their food supplies, became parsimonious with everything. Fruit and vegetables were garnered and stored against future shortages.

The next day, every day from then on, in two or threes at first, then in family groups and in small crowds the refugees, the weary, the hungry and the fearful came, and it seemed to Stella that each group of arrivals were more needy than the ones who had travelled before them. The rows of mattresses began to fill with those who needed more than a bed for a night, some at the end of their mental and physical tether, some injured, all exhausted. The yards around the farm filled too, with handcarts, boxes on bicycle wheels, prams, the belongings they brought with them. Many were still hopeful of reaching Marseilles, or one of the lesser ports, and escaping to Africa.

Lucille said she had tended every size and shape of foot in France, Stella said more grimly she felt she'd washed them all. 'The secret,' Pierre said as he began a self-inflicted task of washing and rinsing a pile of blood- and sweat-stained socks, 'is not to think of how many more are on the way!' He hobbled around like a man possessed, trying to fulfil every need that came under his eye. He persuaded Ernest that the women really needed somewhere they could do their own laundry. Between them they repositioned an ancient wine vat near the well.

Even in the confusion of arrivals a camaraderie grew and they began to impose a kind of pattern, a system of need and expediency. Those who had relations or any kind of acquaintance in the area were helped, or taken by Pas de Crédit, to find them; all able-bodied Jews were moved on coastwards as fast as Ernest and Victor could establish links. The old, the sick, the ailing children were billetted at Cleauville where Lucille and the doctor could more closely keep an eye on them and Pierre find innovations to make their miserable lives a bit easier.

It was only a week since the fall of Paris, but the search for supplies, particularly bedding and blankets, was taking them ever further afield. Stella trudged wearily back to the farm carrying two blankets, all she had managed to secure from a neighbouring farmer. She reckoned she had become an expert cadger, but had not stayed to try for more when she had recognised the man who had caught her and Jacques in his field. His wife too had seemed anxious for him not to see she had parted with anything, and had ushered Stella out of the front door of the house as her husband drove his tractor around to the yard.

She wished she could tell Jacques of her near encounter, and hoped that *he* would somehow have been stopped from getting into Paris, that he too would be forced back south to his home. Here they could organise and fight together, side by side, which would make it all more bearable.

Lost in thought she did not see Hector at his cottage door until he spoke.

'So!' he called, 'we have come to this!'

She supposed she did look a bit of a sight, dragging along with two heavy blankets. She looked up and was startled to see the old man balanced in his doorway, his peg leg raised into the air, so the material of his trousers hung on it, like cloth on an airer. He spread his arms to balance, a fearsome character actor in a weird ballet.

'This I gave last time,' he shouted at her. 'But now they have no spirit for the fight. France! France?' He repeated the word as if he did not know what to make of it, then he shook his fists and spat into the dust. 'Capitulated! That is the word. Capitulated!'

She stepped back automatically as he lurched forward.

'What about you?' he demanded. 'What about England? We're allies. Shoulder to shoulder.'

She saw the little ring of wine bottles near the doorstep.

'I'll tell you! Disgraced! They should have listened to de Gaulle. But no, they fetched back Pétain, another useless old man!' He stood balanced again, demonstrated his wooden leg, slapped a gnarled hand over his heart, and fell.

She rushed to him, helped him sit straight, but he did not heed her questions as to whether he had hurt himself.

'De Gaulle was the man! He wanted to build an army of tanks and planes, a mobile force, he wrote a book telling them how. But nobody bought it except the Germans! And me!' He prodded at her with a punishingly hard finger and added reprovingly, as if condemning her absence at such a time, 'It was on the wireless. Pétain has talked to the Germans "soldier to soldier" he says and when the fighting stops it will be all honour! They'll see! They'll see,' his voice rose to choking fury, 'when they're under the heel of the jackboot, they'll see!'

So it had come. What it really meant she could not begin to realise, she was too concerned about Hector to begin to think. 'Monsieur, please, calm yourself a little.'

'Mademoiselle, I am ashamed! England, the world, should never forgive us. We have given in.' He slumped down and closed his eyes.

She went into his cottage to fetch cushions from his old rocking chair and saw that he had swept every pin from his maps and every map lay torn into many, many pieces. 'They should've let you take charge,' she told him as she heaped the cushions alongside his head and shoulders then slewed him carefully round, having to take hold of both the real and the wooden ankle to make sure he was straight. He groaned as she did so and she cringed, holding her breath, wondering if his stump still hurt him. 'Some nurse I'll make.' When she was convinced he was as comfortable as she could make him she left him to sleep off his binge.

She heaved up the heavy blankets on to her shoulder once more and drew a deep breath of the dry, aromatic, musky aroma of the fields. What was going to happen to this country? What was going to happen to her, Lucille, Ernest? Was internment now imminent? Just what did 'capitulation' mean? Would all the fighting stop on French soil, and the Germans walk into the whole country as they had into Paris? Would Germany be in control of France as it was in control of Belgium, Austria, Holland? Italy was on their side, but whether Norway was still fighting she was not sure. The thought of Britain's isolation made her heart beat faster.

Two months, Edmund had said the Germans thought it would take to finish Great Britain. She knew that could never be true, and better to escape and fight than be interned, she was sure. But the last news from their contact at Marseilles was that the port, the whole coast, was completely overrun with people trying to reach Africa. She paused to hitch up the blankets and to wonder about all those they had taken in at Cleauville. Lucille would not abandon the sick, she knew that.

How would things work? Would the French police have to carry out German orders? The local gendarmerie would know all about Ernest, Lucille and herself. Should they go into hiding now, or try to make a run to the Spanish border? Stella was reminded of Jean-Paul's graphic pincer movements over the northern and eastern parts of the map of France. They all lay within the grasp of those greedy jaws now.

She carried the blankets up to one of the smaller farm attics. This had been given over to two venerable old Jews, one of whom, Franz Speidel, had been a concert violinist, who with his brother Zachary, an even frailer old man, had been feeling the worst of the cool nights. As she climbed the last of the stairs she could hear the radio. Someone had found the six o'clock news on the BBC. 'Mademoiselle, listen and tell us!' Franz cried out.

Stella listened, shocked to hear not just confirmation of what Hector had told her, but a translation of the speech made earlier in the day by Pétain to the French people. France, he said, was overwhelmed by superior forces. The French army was instructed to lay down their arms. An armistice was to be signed with Germany.

'An armistice! *Mais ce n'est pas vrai!*'

She covered them both with the extra blankets, but Franz, who had a bad chest, threw it off in his distress as if nothing could comfort him. 'Never! Never would our armies give in. Find out more, mademoiselle, please let us know.' She left the old men furiously reassuring each other that it was just German propaganda.

In the kitchen, which had become unofficial headquarters, Dr Chabrol stood as if struck quite rigid looking at his son. 'Then it is true,' she said.

'Yes, our senile Marshal Pétain has announced that he has assumed the direction of the government, and,' his voice deepened to sarcasm, 'thinking of the unhappy refugees that clog our roads, and though it breaks his heart, he tells us it is necessary to stop fighting.'

'We have been betrayed!' Edmund said, staggering as if under a physical attack. He sat down quickly and gripped his head between white-knuckled hands.

The news spread to the refugees, all of whom were stunned, stricken, appalled. They seemed to draw into themselves, as if they must each come to terms with this new equation in their lives. Then a curious feeling of inevitability came over many, and the next morning some were already talking of going back to their homes. 'If

75

the war is over for us, then we may as well. We only cause problems here.' Others felt more openly relieved. 'At least the fighting is over for us, no more bloodshed!' It became a kind of palliative they spoke to each other, for there was little else to say. It was not even quite true, for news came that there were still pockets of men who fought on, particularly dug deep in the huge emblematic Maginot Line, beyond the news of the armistice terms.

Germany, they learned, would occupy all French territory north of Tours from the west coast to the east, plus a strip down the western coast to the border of Spain, so neutralising their Atlantic seaboard. France must pay the total cost of the occupying German forces and administration. The French fleet would be collected and disarmed. While French prisoners of war would remain in Germany, France must immediately hand over all German subjects in France – names to be supplied by the Gestapo.

As each batch of news came through Stella as promised conveyed the news to those who were still bedridden. They had tried to persuade the two elderly brothers to take one of the proper bedrooms in the farm, but they refused, and remained in the attic. Stella was unprepared for the shock they showed when she told them of the German subjects who had to go back.

'This, mademoiselle, will include us,' Franz told her. 'I played with the Berlin Orchestra until 1933, then we left Germany and came to live in Paris, but we were born in Germany. We are the people Herr Hitler hates most, Jews who have slipped out of his clutches.'

'This is the plot to take us back,' Zachary whispered fearfully, 'so they can destroy us.'

'Don't worry, we won't let them take you,' Stella reassured him. 'We'll get you away.' She nearly added 'quite soon', but there were no guarantees.

'There are younger than us to worry about,' Franz said, 'more arriving all the time.'

'We can cope,' she told him, aware that another group of men had been approaching as she climbed to the attic. They would have reached the front door by now, while Ernest and Lucille laboured at the back.

'Like a communion,' she heard Franz comment to his brother as she left them with their supper of bread, wine and a little cheese.

She paused on the first-floor landing looking down on the ragged disparate group. Since the ceasefire the families of civilian refugees had dwindled, replaced by men – husbands, sons – struggling home. Abandoned by the army, they returned demoralised more than defeated. Lacking any leadership they obeyed all that remained, their individual homing instinct.

She watched as the men sought to put themselves in some kind of order. They were self-conscious, returning to areas where they were known; caring what people thought they were straightening their collars, patting and brushing the dust away, running fingers through their hair. She hurried down as if to save them some of their efforts, to show it did not matter. As she opened the front door, a very pale young man who was using a bundle of twigs to go over his clothes, grinned. 'I don't want to be a disgrace when my mother sees me,' he said.

This teenager was not far from his home and wanted no more than a rest, a drink and whatever they could spare to eat; then he was determined to finish his return on foot. 'It is the way I left,' he said.

The older men were in worse shape with wounds, ulcers, bad blisters. It was becoming difficult to find anything more they could tear into bandages. Stella, always hoping to leave the dressing of wounds to Lucille, had become adept at making a comfortable bed out of a clean sack stuffed with straw, plus a blanket or coat. Their main trouble was that in each group there would be one or two who ought to have gone to a hospital, 'long-stayers' Lucille called them, so beds and proper mattresses were at a premium.

Stella told Lucille and Ernest of the fears of the two Jewish brothers.

'It's Zachary, he's so fragile. I think his brother has looked after him all his life,' Lucille said.

'We could encourage them to try to walk a little more every day, build up their strength,' Stella suggested.

'I'll go and have a word with them,' Ernest decided, getting up from the table. 'Victor came back today. He'd cycled into Spain near Cerbère *and* back again, *and* established a link in an escape route over the Pyrenees!'

'That's great,' Stella said. 'That's something really positive! Tell the brothers, that should cheer them up.' She watched him go then returned to Lucille. '*We* might need to go over the mountains before long. I don't mean to be interned if I can help it.'

Lucille did not answer. Though her father was throwing himself into every aspect of resisting the Germans, it was still a moot point whether he would ever leave the farm. Then before she could speak they heard him coming back quickly, almost running.

'They've gone,' he said.

'Gone? They can't be.' Stella shook her head.

'Come and look.' Ernest led the way.

'I wouldn't have thought they could,' Lucille said as they followed her father. She spoke quietly, feeling the two brothers might well be somewhere in earshot.

'Not without us hearing or seeing,' Stella agreed.

Ernest displayed the room as he had found it. The men's black hats and coats hung on the back of the door, the blankets Stella had so recently carried to them were folded neatly on the homemade palliasses.

'I don't like this,' Lucille said.

'No.' There was such a weight of grim agreement in the one word she turned to her father.

'What is it?' she demanded. 'What do you know?'

'Victor's heard that since the armistice there've already been many suicides by Jews. Now these terms have been broadcast there will be more who can't face being sent back to Germany.'

'Oh! no, you don't think ...'

'I don't know. We'd better search. They can't have gone far.'

'Hector would have seen if they had gone his way,' Stella said hurrying off to check that possibility.

Lucille and Ernest searched the outbuildings, orchards, roads and lanes south towards the village, but without any result and darkness finally forced them back into the house.

'We'll look again and enquire around tomorrow morning,' Ernest decided. 'I think that is all we can do. It's possible they found a lift.'

The next morning Ernest and Stella asked everyone as they made their rounds. It was Lucille who went to the orchard again. Stella saw her coming back towards the house, hand clamped over her mouth, and ran to her. 'What is it?' she asked.

'They are at the far end of the orchard behind the apple trees,' she gasped. 'They've slashed their wrists.'

'Are they ...?'

'Yes, now, but last night when we were searching and calling they must have been there then, just hiding, just keeping quiet – just dying.'

'Just choosing to die.' Neither of them had seen Edmund, with Ernest, come from the kitchen.

'They were holding hands,' Lucille said, and burst into tears.

Ernest took his daughter into his arms, shushing her as if she were a small hurt child. 'I was talking to Franz the other day,' he told her, 'he said he and his brother had good lives until Hitler came – but everything had gone from them now. It happens, m'dear, as people get older.'

Lucille put her arms around him and held him very tight. Stella agonised silently, wondering if she had spoken out about the hope of getting them away quickly, or if they had known about the escape link Victor had forged, they would have been more confident and waited.

'Another funeral,' Ernest said later after Edmund's father had confirmed death, and the two bodies had been tidied and laid out in one of the small outhouses. Stella brought down the black homburg hats and coats from the attic. She gave the hats to Ernest and watched as he reverently placed one on each man's chest. It gave a military air to the slight black-suited figures, she thought, a touch of dignity, a final worldly salute. The coats would be passed on to the needy.

It was a very sober trio who at the tail end of the evening collected wearily back in the kitchen, then exchanged questioning glances as they heard a vehicle approaching. They listened, holding their breaths – everyone was waiting for the first move the Germans might make. Was this it? Then they heard the vehicle cough, stutter, come to a stop with a bang. 'Pas de Crédit!' Lucille breathed, half relieved, half annoyed with this late visit. Had he brought someone seriously hurt, incapable of walking? She thought ruefully of the two spare straw sacks Stella had put in their sitting room and wondered if their home would ever be just that again.

They listened as footsteps approached briskly through the archway from orchard to courtyard. Stella felt her heart begin to thump. These were not the shuffling weary steps of refugees. This was one man coming quickly, breezily – officially. No one moved, but their gaze was fixed on the doorway, in which quite quickly a man's figure appeared. 'Hello there,' he called heartily, but no one moved, or answered.

He stood in the doorway, filling it, beaming down at them. Not a refugee, or a homing soldier, but a very tall, very stout middle-aged man, dressed in a salt-and-pepper suit and waistcoat, a thick gold watchchain looped across his ample stomach.

'Let me introduce myself,' he said stepping over the threshold, 'Claude Rennie at your service.' Still no one stirred. 'And my business, you ask. I am here as a buyer for a group of fruit juice manufacturers.' Still he evoked no response. 'Business – life – has to go on, you know.'

'Who says?' Ernest asked.

'Oh my dear sir, Herr Führer says so. France has to pay for the privilege of having German troops occupying half its territory. Are you not aware of the terms of the armistice?'

'Oh! yes.' Lucille leapt to her feet. 'We are aware. Very aware. I don't think we have any fruit we want to sell, do we Father?'

'You mean to tell me I have come all the way from Paris to this place, and there is no business!' His voice seemed to rise almost in comic imitation of Hitler's hysteria at a pre-war Nuremberg Youth Rally. 'No, no, *fräulein* of the long brown legs and flying hair, that cannot be!'

For a moment there was silence. Had they really heard what he said correctly? Lucille had gone very pale and taken a step further away.

Stella suddenly realised, his tallness giving him away, though her mouth still sagged open in disbelief. Madame Astier had said he was a joker, should have been on the stage – but this – and coming at this time, talking about the armistice terms! She glanced at Lucille to see if she too knew who he really was.

Lucille's mind was still overwhelmed by the suicides, the tragedy, the appalling thought of the Jews lying quietly bleeding to death as they searched, rather than have to go back to Germany. She looked at him, frowning, this man who had come here on *business*? It was too much, and what was he doing now? She stepped further away from him as he reached up and pulled off his hair, a wig. Then he held his hand to his mouth and the full cheeks disappeared.

He laughed and gave his false belly a good shake, up and down, but Lucille seemed trapped in some awful nightmare she could not wake from. Stella watched her closely. 'It's Jean-Paul,' she told her. 'Jean-Paul who lent us the car.'

'No, no, no!' Lucille backed away and around Jean-Paul, who came forward as if to embrace her, and ran from the kitchen.

'What have I done?' Jean-Paul asked. 'This is terrible.'

'I'll go after her,' Stella said.

She saw Lucille's pale dress near the archway through to the orchard. 'He couldn't know what had happened,' Stella said gently, reaching to touch her shoulder. Lucille spun round to throw her off, then turning to the wall she beat at it with the flat of her hand. 'I hate him!' she sobbed. 'How could he do this to me?'

'What do you mean?'

'Make me feel like this!'

Stella was astonished, though she remembered Lucille's passionate outburst when Jean-Paul had left them in Paris. 'I want to destroy something,' she had said, 'kick something to bits, like this war is kicking my life, your life, his life, all to bits ... ' Stella never remembered anyone else ever having such a startling effect on Lucille.

Stella caught her arm as she would have thudded her hand at the wall again. 'You feel like this because of Franz and Zachary. It's not Jean-Paul's fault. He just came with his comic act at the wrong moment.'

'An actor! Is that all he is?' Lucille demanded. 'Someone playing a part?'

'No, I hope not.' Jean-Paul's deep resonant voice startled both of them. 'Your father has just told me about the Jews. I am so distressed to have caused this.' There was no response. 'One of the reasons I am here is to help people like that escape,' he paused, 'and the other is to bring you greetings from Jacques.'

'Jacques!' Stella exclaimed. 'Jacques?'

'*Oui*, I met up with him three days ago in Paris at his apartment. He sends his love, I'll tell you all when ... ' he broke off as Lucille suddenly turned and ran away, through the arch towards the orchard. Stella made to follow, but Jean-Paul caught her arm. 'I'll go,' he said, 'you reassure her father and tell him about Jacques.'

Stella stood for a moment uncertain, then could hear Jean-Paul speaking not very far away, his tones dropping from coaxing to a deeper, more personal, more confidential note. She felt herself breathing faster and thinking of Jacques. Jacques in Paris, she could hardly wait to hear more and hoped Lucille would soon feel able to come back to the kitchen.

She stood and listened a moment longer, and while Jean-Paul's words were inaudible, the tender caring tone made her unexpectedly think, 'Poor Philip.'

Chapter Eight

Lucille had never stopped thinking of this man who had run from her brother's apartment with such seeming indifference. She had hardly been able to contain her anger at the thought of his energy and wit being lost, his life wasted. Then perversely she had been just as overwhelmed when she had finally realised he had returned. From an active resentment of the 'buyer' tactlessly ignoring all the problems around him, to the realisation that it was Jean-Paul had been too much.

She had rushed away and when he had followed the only way to escape was into the orchard. She had not gone many steps before she was trembling as if with ague, feeling she would fall, but the next moment Jean-Paul was there, supporting her. He leaned down speaking low, comforting and apologetic words.

She shook uncontrollably as he tried to hold her. He became more and more concerned. 'Shall I carry you back inside?' he asked. She drew in her breath, felt her stomach quake as if with laughter verging on hysteria. She thought of him carrying her inside – over the threshold like a bride – and the laugh escaped, shaky, half inclined to tears.

'I never much liked people dressing up,' she said. It wasn't even true.

'But I couldn't have got here without dressing-up, pretending,' he said earnestly, 'so I'm not sorry for that. But for carrying on the deception when I reached here! Imbecile! How could I! I thought it would be a joke.'

'At any other time it would have been.' She found she had stopped shivering so uncontrollably as she reassured him.

'You forgive me?' he asked anxiously.

'If you forgive my stupid reaction.'

'Ah!' She felt his arm leave her waist and gesture out into the soft warm darkness, but she anticipated its return. The next moment he was before her, stooping to kiss her on both cheeks. 'A proper hello,' he said, 'and one for luck as they say.' He stooped again and kissed her lips swiftly.

This third light touch was so unexpected it took her breath, seemed as magical as his metamorphosis, only much more charming. She was sure she would just have stood entranced, had he not taken her hand and gently led her back.

She was aware of Stella's searching look, but did not meet it, as she reassured her father she was all right. The shakiness was certainly gone, but she felt so different: weak, drained and yet fired by a new consciousness. It was, she thought, as if someone had opened a window in her mind she had not known existed. She needed time to explore before she could share.

Her father was asking after her brother, wanted to know how he had met up with Jacques again? Jean-Paul was now the one to be disconcerted. He clenched his fists and drummed them once on the table and gave a deep ragged sigh. The others exchanged glances. They had seen this same sense of confusion, of puzzling where to begin, many times.

'I rejoined my unit,' he began, then stopped. He shook his head before looking up with a glance so direct and frank it was a challenge that demanded total belief. 'If only someone had said to us ... ' he made an extravagant gesture with his arm, '"defend this gatepost with your lives" we would have known where we were, but ... ' He shook his head. 'We milled about, with little food and eventually no ammunition. I sent a despatch rider out into the blue,' he lifted his hand as if releasing a bird, 'a bit like the dove from the Ark, to find someone, somewhere, in command. The man rode twice round the nearest town centre before realising the Germans were there, then rode out again before anyone realised who he was. We were routed and overrun the next morning, massacred by very accurate mortar fire. My despatch rider didn't escape this time. But it was the sense of being let down by your own side that was the worst.' He paused as if trying again to come to terms with it all. 'Then the Germans made loudspeaker announcements to say that Paris was in their hands, France would follow in days, Britain in weeks.'

In the silence that followed he absentmindedly picked up a piece of a notepad left lying on the table and carefully made it into a tiny boat. 'We did not know how true, or how close to being true, the first two were.'

'But Jacques?' Stella prompted him, aware this must have happened days, many days, ago. 'How did you meet?'

'Several of us escaped ... that is hardly the word either ... it was just chance I suppose. No one found us after the battle, and we came across no one. The others decided they would try to make their way back to their homes. I headed back to Paris. I couldn't believe all opposition had really stopped.'

'You saw Jacques in Paris?'

He nodded. 'I bartered some clothes, civvies for uniform, bits and pieces from villagers as I headed towards the city, hiding by day, walking by night. I slunk like a stray dog to his apartment, but Madame Astier gave me a great welcome, couldn't wait to show me where Jacques and an Englishman, a pilot, are setting up an activist newspaper.'

'Jacques is setting up a newspaper,' Lucille corrected.

Jean-Paul acquiesced with a regal nod, then looked up and grinned. 'Madeleine and a chap named Verit, a cleaner from Jacques's newspaper offices, are acting as newshounds and distribution. The pilot just wants to get back to England to carry on fighting.'

'Perhaps we can help him,' Ernest said. 'We're establishing links in an escape route over the Pyrenees.'

'This is what we need to do.' Jean-Paul leaned urgently across the table. 'Establish and keep open lines of communication and escape routes. I came because we heard that the demarcation line between occupied and unoccupied France is to be strictly regulated and there will be "punishments" for those who try to cross without the necessary visa.' Any tone of levity left his voice as he added, 'We need to be able to cross and recross that line.'

'So were *you* stopped?' Ernest asked.

'Oh yes, just as we intended. My business credentials are masterpieces – another aspect of the Parisian group that is forming, we have experts at most things. I was given my pass, and,' he pushed his hand deep inside his shirt, 'I stole a few more.'

'Oh!' Lucille gasped, awed and appalled by his audacity.

'I sat down, woomph, pushed my case on his desk, everything was scattered! A clumsy great oaf of a Frenchman. Then I helped the Herr Inspector pick everything up, that made it all worse. These Germans do like things just so, order in everything, their desks ...' Jean-Paul gave a cameo of his performance only thrusting his hand back into his shirt and pulsing it in and out, a perfect mime of inner fear.

Lucille could picture it all so vividly: the actor, the official; the crime, the possible punishment. You fool, she thought. You dear stupid fool. 'What if you'd been caught? Are they worth the risk?' she asked, looking at the forms he had stolen.

'Of course!' Stella intervened passionately. 'Don't you see how important it can be to be able to go to Paris, or bring this pilot over to the farm?'

'I can,' she answered, giving her friend a look which said she quite understood she wanted to go to Jacques.

Stella's chin and her colour rose. 'I'll go and start preparing Jean-Paul a bed. In your room, Ernest, is that OK?'

'Before you go, Jacques made me promise to say something to you all.' Jean-Paul's seriousness now had everyone's attention. 'Stella, Ernest, you're English, Lucille half-English. Jacques – and I – think you should all immediately move south to the coast, take a fishing boat over to Africa, or go through Spain to Gibraltar.'

No one answered. 'You all risk internment if you stay here. The Germans are nothing if not efficient, and the local police will have to co-operate or risk imprisonment or death themselves. It is only a matter of time, days, hours even. I promised to help you escape.'

'You're going over old ground, old chap,' Ernest told him. 'I don't intend to leave, neither do I intend to be interned, not easily anyway. I've a few hiding places organised for myself – and the girls if they still insist on staying.'

Jean-Paul turned to Stella. 'Jacques said you had promised.'

'I don't feel held to the promise if Lucille and her father want to stay here. As long as such as you and Jacques are staying, I shall stay and do whatever I can to help.'

'With more wounded coming south I shall nurse,' Lucille said. 'Dr Chabrol is planning to open the old church hall as a hospital. I shall work there.'

'Jacques said you were all self-willed.'

Ernest laughed. 'He should talk.'

'It might be prudent to dye your hair,' he said looking at Stella, 'and for both of you to dress more like the French peasant girls. You should all have papers which show you as pure French.'

'Edmund Chabrol will help there,' Ernest said, 'he has such things in hand.'

'I could be Hector's granddaughter,' Stella exclaimed. 'He'd love to deceive the Germans.'

'There'll be serious risks for anyone who hides you – concentration camp at best I would have thought.'

'I was joking,' she said.

'Even so,' he shrugged, 'if you could depend on Hector ...'

'With our lives,' Ernest affirmed.

'It might be your lives,' Jean-Paul stressed, 'and his – many have already died for less.'

In the silence that followed Lucille remembered the brothers united in death as in life, holding hands, supporting each other as they had always done. She glanced at Jean-Paul and found he was looking her way. She wondered how often he had thought of her since that brief meeting in Paris.

'Someone has to stop this monster, or he'll rule the world by fear.' Ernest picked up a bottle of the wine Hector had just bottled, automatically reviewed its colour against the light, then leaned forward to refill the glasses. 'Drink up! Jean-Paul has brought us news of Jacques, he's alive, well, helping the cause. We must learn to celebrate the good when we can, otherwise we may not survive.'

Later, when she could tell by Stella's even breathing she was asleep, Lucille quietly sat up and placed the tiny paper boat Jean-Paul had made on the bedside table. Seeing it in danger of being swept into the rubbish she had slipped it into her dress pocket. The breeze moved the light curtains fitfully and sometimes the boat was in moonlight which made it look like creamy ivory, other times it was like a pale ghost floating on a flat dark sea.

She felt it was meaningful. A boat meant another journey, a journey she had begun in her brother's apartment, when she had risen from her chair with the magazine she had been holding upside down. She wondered if Jean-Paul could possibly feel the same. Had he any real feeling for her, true feelings, or was he just a flirt? A fun man, fun to everyone?

But there was more to him than that. He had valued hearing about their extended English family, Stella and Philip. She thought of her mother and felt a pang of loss, keen and sharp as new. How she would have loved to know what her mother thought of Jean-Paul – and what of her daughter literally mooning about, unable to sleep on the strength of what? A small extra kiss.

But Gaby had always said it was her father who was the romantic. He had first seen Gaby in the orchard out there helping pick the apple crop and had loved her from that moment – and forever. Then she remembered how her father had always said he had fallen in love with her mother the first time he had come to Cleauville as a *buyer for a firm making apple and grape juice drinks*. How strange a coincidence – or perhaps more realistic to think that Jacques had suggested playing 'the buyer' as a good reason for travelling, the perfect disguise for Jean-Paul?

Maybe then she took after her father, because it didn't matter how Jean-Paul came there. 'I just know I love him,' she whispered to the night and the pale little boat on the dark sea, 'just as my father was so sure all those years ago.'

It gave her such a strange premonition as an extra gust of wind set the tiny model moving, sailing towards the edge of the table. She reached out to save it.

Chapter Nine

When Stella awoke the next morning Lucille's bed was empty. She went to push open the shutters and stepped out on to the tiny balcony, leaning over the black wrought-iron balustrade. The air had that balmy quality, just enough movement to say there was a breeze, just enough dawn heat to be pleasant, and there was no sound other than birdsong, twitterings in dense conifers. It felt like a pause, the world taking time to breathe. A moment of calm, perhaps before the moment of truth.

Into the peaceful green arena she saw Lucille and Jean-Paul emerge from the shadow of the house and walk towards the huge oak tree which had years ago supported the long-roped swing. Together already, this early, she thought. She watched Lucille run to peer up into the branches of the oak and point something out to Jean-Paul. Then Stella half gasped, half laughed, as Jean-Paul, obviously to Lucille's surprise, took her waist and raised her right up into the branches, pushing his arms up ever straighter, until at full stretch. She could vaguely catch their laughter and the tone of Jean-Paul's instruction to hurry up.

In a few moments Lucille was pulling down a rope which must have been caught up or wound around the branches. Then the two of them just stood, side by side, lolling together hanging on to the single rope. She could not hear their words now.

She knew that because she loved Jacques, the same did not have to be true of the other brother and sister, and she recognised, with a sinking heart, her brother had no chance. 'She's found someone who really suits her,' she whispered. The other had been just a cosy thought, a double wedding after the war, brothers and sisters marrying. A pipe dream. But remembering how Philip had been last Christmas, fooling about in a paper hat as they cleared the dinner table, chasing Lucille with a sprig of mistletoe, she knew he too had made assumptions.

Below Jean-Paul pulled the rope away to its fullest extent, ran and swung out forwards, backwards. Lucille squealed a warning – but too late – the old rope gave way right above her head, snaked down around her and the swinger landed in an untidy heap of long legs on the bank. Each was up in seconds, rushing to see if the other was hurt. The incident, Stella noted, gave them freedom to wrap their arms around each other. Then as if sensing they were being watched Lucille looked up, waved and they walked towards the house. Her free arm remained around Jean-Paul's waist.

Stella leaned out. 'Trying to break your neck?' she called.

Jean-Paul waved her to come down. 'We're going to take the car out of wraps.'

'Oh!' She made a quick review of the scratches and dents as Jean-Paul added, 'I have coupons for *l'essence*.'

'I'm sure! Stolen of course!' she called back, but was full of admiration both for his theatrical bowing acknowledgement and for his audacity. She hoped to get him to tell in more detail about crossing the demarcation line. She wanted to know every detail of the procedure, for given the opportunity she was going to Jacques. In precarious times people should be close to those they love, she thought, as if justifying the idea to a third party, *and* she could help with the underground newspaper.

In the house and the outbuildings there was an extra quietness that morning; even in the yard the collection of trucks, prams, carts was less. Most of the refugees unhampered by the really sick were moving on, to contacts or relatives further south, or back, retracing their steps, hoping to find their homes intact. She could just glimpse the major road around the shoulder of the nearest hill. It was already busy with vehicles and groups of people making their way north to the uncertainties of living under German rule.

She silently wished them *bon voyage*, but knew that as the tide of strangers in the area retreated it would leave them more exposed. Pétain's new fascist State Police would be more able to ferret out those who were ordered to return to Germany and to intern foreign nationals. She suddenly remembered Nadia, daughter of the Blairs' old housekeeper and expert on all things worldly and medical. She wondered if Nadia could get her some hair dye? Nadia must have bleached her ends for years, so no one would question her buying such a thing.

By the time she reached the barn Jean-Paul was leaning nonchalantly on the dented wing of his Wolseley. When he frowned and looked down at his feet as she approached, scenes with Philip berating her for scratching his beloved Morris did come into her mind. She was quite prepared to defend herself – 'extenuating circumstances' her father would have advised pleading.

But he began more in the manner of one about to confess than accuse. 'You know I mentioned the pilot who's at Jacques's apartment.' He glanced at Stella. 'He has not just red hair – but freckles! He could not be more English. He's been helpful *they say*, but he endangers everyone every moment he is there. And he wants home, wants back in the fight. We've established a link to slip him east of the demarcation line at Tours, then he will be transferred to a base near Clermont-Ferrand. I've arranged to pick him up there. I thought I might have to bribe someone with petrol coupons for the use of a car, but thanks to you two I can use my own.' He paused. 'The other thing is since Ernest said he's establishing a escape link down through Spain, I want to ask if I can bring him here?'

'Why not?' Stella asked.

'Two reasons. Ernest, Lucille, all of you, there's been so much trauma, personal trauma. It puts you all in added danger, and ...'

'And?' Lucille prompted quietly.

'If successful he may be only the first of many such escapees.'

'Great! Case proved I would say, no need for more argument.'

'My father will risk anything to help the fight,' Lucille added quietly. 'It gives him a reason for living ...' She cut the sentence off, merely adding, 'He needs to be busy.'

'We all want to do our bit,' Stella said, then floated the idea, 'I'd like to go to Paris.'

Jean-Paul pushed out his bottom lip to an exaggerated degree. 'Paris is like a city with the lid clamped tight, but it could boil over any second.'

'But *you'll* go back?' Lucille asked.

He nodded. 'It's necessary. I came to establish contacts, links in escape routes – so I do have to return.' He paused to lift an arm to Ernest who appeared briefly in the doorway of the main outbuilding. 'So I'll approach your father.' He sighed as if that was one weight from his mind, then smiled at them both. 'My disguise'll help me move around. I have "official" papers to show the authorities, but I wouldn't mind having a passenger to help me navigate there and back.'

'I could do that,' Lucille began eagerly, 'I know the area so well. I could navigate.' Then she stopped. 'Oh! But I'm sort of committed to helping Dr Chabrol establish his hospital in the church hall.'

Stella leaned forward on the bonnet of the Wolseley and ran her hands over the paintwork. It was quite warm already and smooth, dustfree, wiped clean after its interment in the barn. It reminded her how she and Jacques had ridden the bicycles back to Pas de Crédit, then carried the petrol can and retrieved the car. She glanced at her friend's face, wistful, wishful. 'OK,' she said, pushing herself upright. 'I hate people's feet and nursing, and making beds, but I guess I can make myself useful to Dr Chabrol and his merry band of helpers. You go with Jean-Paul.'

She turned and walked briskly away but Lucille ran after her and caught her arm. 'Thanks,' she said, 'I thought you would be ...'

'Thinking of Philip,' Stella added quietly and her friend nodded.

'I was, I am, but ...'

'This is different,' Lucille said with quiet intensity.

'I can see that.' She mimicked one of Jean-Paul's shrugs. 'Go on,' she said, 'there may not be much time.' Today may be all you have, she thought, remembering the feeling of that day being a pause, the calm perhaps in the eye of the storm. She watched Lucille go back to Jean-Paul, then was overwhelmed by a sense of desolation as they stood by the car just talking, just looking at each other. She hurried back to the house, to things to be done to help ease her yearning for Jacques. Keep busy, that's the secret; she'd heard the old adage many times from her father.

She met Ernest and Edmund coming out of the barn. 'I'm just going to introduce our "fruit buyer",' Ernest said.

'He's got news that will please both of you,' she told them.

When Edmund met the tall aristocratic Jean-Paul it was like the meeting of opposite poles, the small, dark and dour meeting the tall, handsome and witty, but once they began to talk there was no difference in their aims.

Lucille trailed behind the two men as they returned to the house, and was afraid for Jean-Paul, as they planned. He was so confident, so casual as he told Edmund of his current missions. One of their number, he said, was secretly crossing the channel to visit General Charles de Gaulle who was organising the Free French forces in England. He was sure help, radios, money would come from England. 'We have one Parisian who's broadcasting coded messages regularly to England, so if you have information to send let me know. I can justify being in this area for about two weeks.'

Two weeks. Lucille felt herself colour as he looked straight at her, two weeks, so short a time.

'I have arranged to go to Clermont-Ferrand tomorrow,' Edmund was saying. 'There's a huge Michelin tyre plant there with thousands of militant Socialist and Communist workers. There's a group forming there, and contact with a technician who's going to help us build our own short-wave radio sets.'

'Ah!' Jean-Paul's arm went around the other man's shoulders and they stood talking in low tones for some time. Then there was much slapping of backs and joining of hands, the handshake fierce and long, accompanied by smiles and nods. '*Vive la belle France!*' Edmund proclaimed. '*Vive l'Angleterre!*'

Ernest came hurrying back as Stella was dishing out breakfast for their remaining refugees. 'Come on, young Stella,' he said briskly, 'no time to waste. I want you *au fait* with all the escape routes, the hidey-holes and the warning signals Hector and Pierre have concocted.'

'And all that before you go off to screw bedsteads together,' Edmund called over to her.

'I really get the glamour jobs!' she groaned but somehow there was a difference, an excitement – the energy of the whole group had lifted. However dire the situation they at least now knew where they stood. The French government was in disarray and had capitulated, but there was a pattern of resistance forming, a knowledge of other centres, and the beginnings of webs of communications. There was motivation as they saw clear ways they could carry on fighting.

'Perhaps you won't recognise me when you come back.' Stella touched her hair meaningfully as they said goodbye later that morning.

Lucille thought what a crime to cut and colour that beautiful auburn hair, but then she suppressed a smile as her gaze turned to the 'businessman' seated next to her.

'You will please,' he said as they drove away, 'not look at me like that or I shall stop this car immediately and throw off the disguise. I am not supposed to be a figure of fun.'

Lucille heard herself giggle. For goodness' sake, this was a serious mission which could mean a young man's life if they failed – and she was giggling! 'No, sorry – it's just that everything is so unexpected. I wonder if anything will ever be the same again?'

'Not after coming here, finding the two of you again, my life definitely will never be the same.'

She did not answer immediately, telling herself not to read too much into a casual kiss and an arm around her waist. She turned to the window to watch the last slopes of her father's vines disappearing behind them. She thought of their first encounter in Paris, that had been earth-shattering because she had never believed in anything so impractical as love at first sight. The shock when he had first emerged from his disguise had been traumatising. One moment she was detesting a stranger walking so blithely into their tragedy, the next ... 'Are you an actor?' she asked.

He roared with laughter. 'No! I belonged to an amateur group, and the newspaper people always get together, used to get together, and put on a pantomime, or sometimes a review. I used to be involved because I was a friend of Jacques.'

She remembered Madeleine talking of the wild theatrical parties at the apartment. 'An amateur group?' she queried.

'Yes, at the museum. I'm an archivist, I worked in the dusty bowels of the humanities department before I was mobilised.'

'No! I would never have guessed. Never! If you had told me you were a rich aristocrat's son, a playboy, I would have believed that without question.'

'You think I am an extrovert,' he said with a rueful laugh. 'I am when I'm with people, acting out a role. It is the escape of a very shy man.'

She was not sure whether to believe him or not. Shyness was the last trait she would have imagined he possessed. 'So how will I know when it is the real you?' she asked.

'Oh! you'll know,' he said with such quiet certainty she felt a kind of thud at the bottom of her spine, and every nerve in her body seemed to vibrate and tingle as if some vital heartstring had been plucked.

'And you?'

She realised he was repeating the question.

'What do you do?'

'I'm training to be a nurse, or I was, in England.'

'I *would* have guessed that,' he said, 'you're caring, comforting, yet practical.'

'Makes me sound a bit stuffy, like an old comfy cardigan.'

Ahead of them a party of refugees was straggling across the road: a woman struggling with a pramload of children and a man, with what looked like a handcart of old people. Jean-Paul slowed, but as he did he sang quietly in an American accent, 'Wrap yourself around me honey, hold me tight.' Then, tutting, he shook his head. 'We can't just drive by this lot, can we?'

They found the pathetic party were near the end of their resources of strength and money. They were returning to Poitiers, having run before the German advance. The old man on the cart waved his walking stick. 'I said we should stay put, but no one ever listens to me.'

Jean-Paul fetched the map as Lucille drew Jean-Paul's attention to the old lady who, head bowed, was overtaken by uncontrollable shuddering fits. 'I could take some of you as far as Langogne if it would help.' He showed the younger man, who must have been in his late

92

fifties, the place some halfway between Avignon and Poitiers. He nodded eagerly. 'If you could take my father and my aunt, I can manage my grandchildren, and we'll travel much quicker.'

The idea caused some consternation on the part of the grandfather, but once they had settled on a meeting place at the main post office the old people were helped into the back of the Wolseley with their personal bundles. The son was dividing a handful of coin, obviously all he had, when Jean-Paul pressed him to put it back in his pocket. 'I'll see they're provided for,' he said. The man dropped his head, frowning, too overcome to voice his thanks. Jean-Paul gripped his forearm. 'Bear up, you'll soon be home.'

Lucille packed rugs and coats around the old lady in the back of the car. The shuddering eased but she began to rock gently, ceaselessly, as they travelled, reminding Lucille of a zoo near Stratford Stella's father had taken them all to – and a bear silently weaving and grieving in the middle of its pit.

The old man was garrulous enough for them both. They learned the children's father had been called up in the general mobilisation, while their mother, who had ailed for some time, had died in the New Year.

It was a relief finally to deposit the old couple in a small hotel near the main post office. Jean-Paul in his role as businessman made an impressive show of paying for the care of 'these valuable citizens'. Lucille could see the hotelier did not quite know whether Jean-Paul was a German or French official, but the effect of obtaining what they needed was the same. They bought a meal and the old folk were given a good room, which Jean-Paul inspected; he paid for two nights' board plus meals.

After the old man's constant chatter it was pleasant to be silent as they left Langogne. Dusk fell and the countryside took on new aspects as the setting sun made long templates of the tree-shadows. It gave an air of beautiful melancholy, the day slipping away. Time, like the night, seemed to be closing in on them. The pilot was to be at the rendezvous from midnight that night onwards for twenty-four hours. After that the contact who had delivered him would return to check he had been picked up. If not he would be taken back along the escape line and the process repeated on another date.

Whatever happened by the time they got back to Cleauville, two days of Jean-Paul's stay would have gone. She moved restlessly, then reminded herself of her duty. She was navigating.

'If Stella had ...' she began.

'I don't want ...' he said at the same moment.

They both laughed. 'You first,' she said.

'I was going to say I don't want to be too late and leave that

Englishman hanging around. He speaks French as if he's reading from a school primer – and his English is worse! All "wizard prang" and "what-ho". He wouldn't fool a German for two minutes.' He accelerated as if to divert the impending disaster. 'What were you going to say?'

'That if Stella had come instead of me, she could have shared the driving.'

He turned to her and smiled. 'I'm very happy with this arrangement.'

Me too, her heart answered.

'And,' he went on, 'Jacques wouldn't thank me for dragging Stella away from Cleauville. He pictures her there, talks about her in particular places – in the courtyard, at old Hector's cottage, under olive trees.'

'No, I'm sure he'd prefer it was his sister!'

'Dragging you out here into the wilds of the Auvergne? Now I feel guilty.'

'Don't worry,' she interrupted, 'I really wanted to come.'

It was, she felt, like a first date, their silences full of floating questions, difficult to frame within the bounds of brief acquaintanceship. She watched their dimmed headlights pick out the little campsites that had been so familiar on the way south with Stella. At least the danger of bombing and strafing was over; for families travelling back to their homes that must mean a lot.

'Jacques didn't talk too much about his life in Paris,' she said after a time. 'I suppose we were going our separate ways in separate countries.'

'Why did you decide to nurse in England?'

'I felt I would get better training in London and be near to Stella and . . .'

'Philip.' He picked up the name she was hesitating on.

'Yes, Philip and Stella are like brother and sister to me.'

'But not Jacques and Stella?'

'No,' she admitted, 'the kind of separations the war was bringing seemed to make them realise their feelings towards each other had changed.'

'To love,' he said as if to himself. 'Yes, we value what we have much more when someone threatens to take it away from us.'

'Stella is all but officially my sister-in-law. Jacques has told us all that he intends to marry her. He told our mother before she died.'

'Jacques has a gift for words.' He spoke gently over the catch in her voice. 'I tell him he should write a book, a novel. He has the imagination. Create his own world.'

94

She laughed. 'He'd be in complete control. Yes, he'd like that! He's a great organiser of everyone, given the chance.'

'He's even pinpointed the place where we have to rendezvous.' He paused to lean forward, peering ahead over the steering wheel as their dimmed headlights picked out a section of badly churned up road. 'Quite literally I mean. There's a flashlight in the glove compartment; if you shine it under this map he's drawn you'll see.'

'Sounds like my brother!' She took the piece of paper and checked the rather cryptic initials of places and the tiny pin hole, and added, 'You really did need a navigator!'

They began to encounter more areas of the road that had been bombed. Several times they had to make detours because of craters. It was obvious they were going to arrive way past the first appointed hour. She could feel Jean-Paul's tension as he concentrated hard on the road ahead and she began to hold her breath every time other headlights loomed. The danger of being stopped and picked up was much greater as they neared the industrial town. Her mind ran wild as she imagined what would happen should the Germans frisk Jean-Paul. They would immediately discover the padded waistcoat – after that ... She forced herself to concentrate on the road, to remember the layout of the road on the map.

Luck seemed to be with them. The roads were quiet as they neared the rendezvous west of Clermont-Ferrand, an ambulance and a solitary car all they encountered in the last kilometre. The pinprick identified a narrow turnoff into woodland. Jean-Paul slowed to allow her to look for the turn, until she saw a gap and ordered, 'Right here, it's only a tiny, tiny turn.' She was not at all sure she was correct as they found themselves on a steep stony path which wound up away from them in the darkness.

They had hardly left the road proper when another vehicle swept in behind them. '*Nom de Dieu*! Where did he come from?' Jean-Paul breathed in surprise. 'He must have been parked with his lights off.'

'Watching for us?'

The headlights behind them glared bright enough now as they switched up and down demanding they stop. He swore under his breath.

'What do we do?' she asked, though unless they left the car and made a run for it in the woods there was no choice.

Jean-Paul slowed the car and stopped. 'Stay in the car, don't speak,' he hissed as he got out and went blustering forward to meet the policeman who came officiously towards them.

'What is this?' the man questioned. 'Who are you? Where are you going?'

Half turning in her seat she could just make out that Jean-Paul answered first in German, then as if accommodating the official switched to French, volunteered papers. Her heart beat louder as another uniformed officer got out of the vehicle, a burly man who shouldered in close to Jean-Paul. Then the next moment the group seemed to relax, step back, she thought she heard a laugh, then arms were raised as if in recognition of a favour. The men got back into their vehicle, laughing, reversed rapidly back to the road and were soon out of sight.

'What did you tell them?'

'A middle-aged German businessman with a young French girl, plus a little bribe, is the same all over the world.'

'No surely . . .' she said, unconvinced. 'I'm surprised they let it go at that – and a bribe!'

'Not money. I told them that you were from the village the other side of Clermont-Ferrand and your name was Claudette and that you would be back there in about an hour if they wanted you.'

She gasped, spluttered with laughter. 'You're terrible!' She turned and leaned towards him.

'I know.' Suddenly their faces were very close. 'I just hope our pilot is not late,' he added in a whisper, then he kissed her on the lips, a light brushing touch. When she did not move away he put his arm around her shoulder and held her so his next kiss was firmer and there was no possibility of retreat.

'Oh! I don't know though, perhaps just a little late would do,' he whispered, cupping her face with his hands. 'But close your eyes so you can't see Monsieur Claude Rennie. This is the real man who kisses you, who loves you. This is a man who fell in love with you long before the war began, and will love you when the war has finished, for ever.'

He paused, held himself and her quite motionless so she felt suspended in time, as he waited for her to answer. It had taken her breath. She had hardly hoped for so much; her heart hesitated, then flew with its answer, with a love that was full of images of coming home after eons of time waiting for this moment, and this man.

'And I love you,' she said. 'I loved you the moment you clattered down Madame Astier's stairs.' She remembered the anger that had come over her, the anger that comes with bereavement, his going had been such a separation.

She drew in a ragged breath through her mouth and he stooped and kissed her lightly, but this time his tongue came to taste her lips, touch inside over her teeth and back. Primitive sensations obliterated all reservations, all logic, as she leaned nearer to him, felt that ridiculous

96

businessman's suit and didn't care. She knew the real man, wanted to give to him, to be all his.

Love had always been the centre of her life, her home, her father's life, her dear, dear mother, and now she had found the man she wanted to centre her life around. She lifted her tongue and gently touched his. It was a sweet, tender, melting moment – and then there was time for no more, for his fingers became still and rigid on her cheeks.

'There's someone coming,' he said. By the light of their still-burning headlights she could see that the bushes ahead were moving to a far greater extent than anything else touched by the evening breeze.

His hands dropped to his lap and they sat and waited, tense, expectant, as the movements became more vigorous and before long a tall slim figure emerged. They saw a hand go up and give them a very English-looking salute.

He sipped her lips once more. 'It will be the sweeter for waiting,' he said.

Chapter Ten

'The switch of language from German to French was masterly,' Lucille enthused, 'a touch of genius!'

From the moment they had brought Lennie Forryan exhausted but smiling into the farmhouse everything Stella thought had taken on new aspects. She wondered if Lucille knew how radiant she looked, how at every opportunity she and Jean-Paul stood close, held hands? Ernest observed with an air of speculation before quietly voicing his conclusion to Stella. 'They remind me of myself and Gaby, our first summer here.' Stella suppressed the 'Oh dear' which sprang to her lips.

It was not just this new relationship which honed a new edge to their sensibilities. Making contact with Nadia about hair dye had brought the tall sexy, gossipy girl back into their lives at Cleauville. Nadia not only agreed to get and apply the hair dye but volunteered to cut Stella's springy mop to a style closer to her skull. 'Less English!' While she worked on her hair she told Stella a sinister story giving a foretaste of what life might be like under the heel of the German jackboot.

Nadia had news from a friend who lived in Luray. An old lady there had actively objected to having her house requisitioned. For her protest she was tied to a tree in her front garden and shot. Her daughter was forced to leave her mother's body tied where it was for twenty-four hours, as a warning to anyone who tried to resist German 'requests'.

'Is it true?' Stella asked.

'Oh! yes, my husband Claude, you haven't met my husband – he is ...' She paused to make a noise like a powerful motorbike starting up. 'He witnessed it before he escaped from the Germans and walked home. Like all these people you have helped!' she enthused, the scissors scything through the red hair. 'Everyone knows what you have done and anything me or my Claude can do to help here at Cleauville you've only to ask. Madame Blair was so good to my mother when she worked here. She went almost at the same time as Madame, did you know? We say she went to look after Madame Gaby.'

Later Edmund confirmed the story of the old lady in Luray, adding another account of a young man who could not bear to see the Germans take over his land without protest. Étienne Achavanne had cut the telephone lines between a German field commander and the airfield at Boos, making it impossible to warn the airfield of an impending RAF raid. An act of solitary sabotage, it resulted in eighteen German planes being destroyed on the ground. Étienne was arrested and executed. 'Our first martyr,' Edmund firmly proclaimed. 'We must be proud, his name must never be forgotten.'

Edmund managed to find satisfaction in many things that might otherwise have depressed them. When French radio announced that Marshal Pétain was leaving Clermont-Ferrand for Vichy, where the empty, well-equipped hotels of the famous spa offered more salubrious quarters for the ancient leader, he declared, 'That gets that old fool out of the way! His entourage, and manipulator Laval, could have been a nuisance at Clermont-Ferrand.'

Plans to move Lennie on the next leg of his escape were being completed when Hector, expert now at tuning into the BBC broadcasts, heard that the British had boarded all the French vessels in Plymouth harbour – two battleships, four light cruisers, eight destroyers, several submarines and a number of smaller craft had been secured. The French crews totalling twenty thousand had been told that they could return to their homes in France, or join the Free French forces to carry on the fight. 'They think most will return to their homes,' Hector ended quietly.

Stella watched him carefully, no histrionics this time, but his eyes were full of impotent anger.

'Given such a chance in the middle of a war I should think every man would choose to go home,' Jean-Paul remarked lightly.

'Not all!' Hector denied.

Edmund laid a hand on his shoulder. 'They're not all readers like us, my friend. If they'd studied Hitler's raving in *Mein Kampf* they would not be so eager to rush home and bury their heads in the sand.'

'They will wake up with their arses on fire,' Hector concluded.

'Some will go to de Gaulle,' Ernest mused, 'and Churchill could hardly let the French fleet be used against us.'

But Victor was clearly worried. He explained that the very first 'safe house' on the escape route was one where both sons were in the French navy. 'I was shown photographs, the father is so proud of them.'

99

'Then they will fight on!' Hector said, 'not come running home!'

'That's right!' Lennie looped an arm around the old Frenchman's shoulders. 'But I need to run home to get back *into* the fight!'

'That's different,' Hector growled giving him an approving cuff. 'I wish you God speed.' They both lifted their free hands to each other as if raising glasses. The disparate pair had struck up a rapport from the first moment of meeting, as if each recognised in the other the desperate urgency to resist the enemy, to be in the fight.

'We're off tomorrow, y'know!' Lennie confirmed. It had been decided because of the pilot's background he and Victor should travel as jobbing carpenters and that evening Edmund had brought the necessary papers, another bicycle and workmen's blues. 'Everything is spot on!'

Stella half expected him to add 'tickety-boo'.

She did not see Victor and the pilot the next morning, as they left before daybreak, but she saw Lucille and Jean-Paul holding hands rather wistfully later in the day. She knew he too would soon be leaving. He had information he felt vital for the Parisian Resistance groups to know and pass on: sites for possible air drops; contacts with sympathisers willing to be agents at Clermont-Ferrand and another moving to Vichy with the French government – sensitive, urgent information. How Stella ached to have an active part in that organisation, instead of just being a kind of nursing ancillary.

It was Ernest who called them to hear the news at midday. They grouped around the radio to listen to the French newscaster, in damning, sombre tones, announce that on the same day as the British took over the French warships in Plymouth they had attacked the French naval base at Mers-el-Kebir in Algeria. 'Four French battleships have been sunk and over one thousand two hundred French sailors killed.' The announcer went on to give the names of the ships which had been destroyed.

'*Mon Dieu*!' Jean-Paul breathed, the continuing details from the radio lost as their minds tried to encompass the outrage.

'And the nearer Victor and Lennie get to the coast, the more likely they are to be involved with people with naval connections,' Ernest mused. 'And there is nothing we can do but wait.'

The evening was softening to night as a solitary familiar figure came pedalling furiously along the drive. They hurried to meet him. 'I told you about the sons,' Victor gasped as he half fell from the bike. 'There's been an attack in Algeria. They're waiting for news. Their ships were two of those attacked. The *Mogador* and the *Provence*.'

'And the pilot?' Ernest asked.

100

'They're ... holding him ... like a hostage. I tried reasoning, but the father's beside himself, he came out with his gun. He took Lennie and locked him in his cellar, then sent me back to tell you that all help is finished if the British have killed his sons. I didn't know what else to do. He fired a shot over my head, then at the ground. I thought he'd punctured my tyres.' He turned to make an appeal to Jean-Paul. 'You might be able to make him listen.'

'The pilot is our responsibility.' Jean-Paul's manner was businesslike now as he swept a hand to include the whole group. 'We've failed to move our first escapee on safely. It won't do. He must be recovered ... but the information I have for Paris is also important.'

Ernest quietly growled his agreement to both statements.

'I'll go to Paris,' Stella volunteered at once. 'Come on, don't look doubtful, just let me go. I know the city, the language.'

There was a silence into which Victor carefully launched the idea that what they needed was for someone who could really persuade people that it was right to resist, to travel along the line of safe houses. 'Hopefully taking Lennie with him. It would make it a much more reliable escape route for others. Otherwise we're always going to have doubts.'

Jean-Paul looked at Ernest, who sighed, expelling the breath quickly with the air of a man knowing there was no perfect solution. 'We are responsible for that young pilot. I'm also responsible for ...'

'I really want to go.' Stella reacted quickly to his glance. 'To help of course, but I also want to be with Jacques, you must understand how I feel.' She saw immediately that she had said the one thing that would convince his father – love had always motivated Ernest's life. Her heart raced with mounting excitement as she realised she might really be allowed to go. 'I've a good memory for detail – and maps and things could be put on a piece of silk and sewn into my coat under the lining.'

'I know where there is a piece,' Lucille said.

'Anyone would think you two had been spies all your life!' Jean-Paul said.

'But what we'll need is another bicycle,' Victor added.

'Bicycle!' Jean-Paul pretended horror. 'Claude Rennie travels by car.'

Two days later Stella was on the train waiting for her papers to be checked. She had wanted to travel so much she had not anticipated just how much her heart would pound, how dry her throat would become, as she heard doors being slid back along the corridor, then with a startling crash the Nazi official entered her compartment. His

101

voice was impatient, sharp, as he moved between the crowded seats, his manner curt, unbending – papers were snatched and shoved back sharply under people's noses. He reached a couple next to her and there was trouble.

'What's this!' the officer demanded.

She did not hear what the man mumbled as the Nazi bent over him threateningly, and questioned him sharply. 'So when did you come to France? Did you not know that all Jews are ordered back to Germany? Why have you not done so?'

'I am doing so now,' the man said with dignity.

'It is,' the soldier's spittle reached the man's face, 'too late. You have broken the law.'

'I do not see how that can be ...'

The officer waited to hear no more. He leaned out of the compartment, made a signal down the corridor and immediately two soldiers (bully boys Stella immediately thought) rushed in and the two were pulled up to their feet. The woman stooped to pick up her bag and stumbled; as Stella reached over to grasp her arm and steady her, their eyes met. Never had she seen such bleak despair in anyone's eyes. It reminded her of an injured fox her father had once shot out of pity. The fox too had known its end had come; it had made no sound as the gun had rung out. These two were silent, unprotesting, as they were harried and hustled to their fate.

Stella was so busy watching out of the window to where others taken from the train were being loaded into closed lorries that she did not see the outstretched hand until she felt her own papers snatched from her grasp. Before she had time to worry about them, they were pushed back at her without a word and the man was gone.

Before the train moved away she saw the couple again, being hauled up into the back of the lorry. A soldier impatiently jerked the woman's bag from her hand then hurled it in after her. They had not, she thought, looked at all like Jews, just as she with black hair and some of Nadia's black clothes presumably did not look English. She remembered the Jewish brothers, hands joined in death. She remembered the quiet dignified funeral she had attended in the Cleauville cemetery. She wondered briefly if after all they had not been right to take their own lives? A wave of nausea swept over her, though she was surprised to realise she really was going to be sick. She rose hurriedly, flung open the compartment door and ran with one hand over her mouth, the other grabbing wildly at window rails and frames for support in the swaying corridor. She reached the toilet compartment just in time and was violently ill.

She grasped the handbowl and peered at the pale-faced black-haired

102

woman. 'Not like me to be sick,' she breathed, then studying her reflection wondered if Jacques would know her. She didn't want him to see her looking so dreadful, but the nausea passed as quickly as it had come and by the time she had reapplied makeup and brushed her short hair up to the top of her head she felt fit to face the Parisian streets. In fact, she thought with satisfaction, she looked Parisian.

Walking to the métro she finally altered her wristwatch forward one hour. The announcement that all clocks in the occupied zone had been adjusted to German time she had ignored until she acknowledged that life might be complicated enough without trying to live one hour behind everyone else.

She almost resented that Paris should appear so much the same, the buildings, the trees, the squares, the gardens, the river, but enemy uniforms were everywhere. It seemed Paris was now *the* place for German troops to spend their furloughs. Every one of them seemed to be carrying a camera and snapping away like mad. Paris, its famous streets, statues and arches, was being subjugated in a more insidious way than by battle. Rape of a fair city, Stella thought, and hurried to reach Jacques's apartment.

As she neared the square her heart began to race again. Would Jacques actually be there? She had to resist the temptation to run as she came in sight of the building. She half expected Madame Astier would again be at the top of her steps. But the area was very quiet, abnormally empty. She saw a woman cradling a tabby cat looking from her window, but as she glanced that way the woman retreated immediately. It seemed no one casually sat in doorways, took constitutional walks, or risked being seen unnecessarily any more.

She ran lightly up the steps and rang the bell. There was no answer. She gave the bell a longer pull, turning back to look around. If it had not been for the woman at the window she might have thought the whole area had been evacuated. She turned back to the door and held her breath as it began to open, quite slowly. One thing was certain, she knew that it was not Madame who was the other side. The figure revealed was a small stooped old man she had never seen before. He had very black piercing eyes and just stood in the doorway silently waiting for her to speak.

'*Bonjour, Madame Astier, s'il vous plaît.*'

'*Non!*'

'She is not here?' Stella queried. She was unsure whether to ask for anyone else. 'Could I come in? I've come specially from Cleauville to see her.'

He signalled for her to wait where she was, but closed the door on her.

He was back in a few moments. 'Who sent you from Cleauville?' he asked.

'Jean-Paul,' she ventured. The door immediately opened a little wider and Madame Astier stood there, aggressive, eyes shuttered.

'*C'est moi, Stella*,' she breathed.

Madame Astier expelled her breath in a trumpeting of surprised relief. 'Ha! I should know! From Jean-Paul!' She lifted her arms from the elbow and made circling motions. Once inside, the door was closed and she embraced her, kissed both cheeks, exclaimed, 'Look at you! Your hair!'

Stella looked pointedly at the old man.

'Oh! this is Verit, he and I ... well never mind, you can hear all that later. How are Lucille and her father – and mad Jean-Paul?'

Stella grinned. 'All fine! All busy. I'll tell you all that later too. Is Jacques ...?'

'Ah! yes, of course.' She gestured for Verit to stay where he was and without another word led the way upstairs, but beyond Jacques's apartment, up another flight into an empty attic. Stella noticed that Madeleine clicked the light switch though nothing appeared to happen. Then she led the way across to a wall, empty except for a large wardrobe. She opened the door, reached inside, gave a rap on the back, then gestured for Stella to precede her. Stella was not sure she would have stepped into the huge closet if anyone other than Madame Astier had invited her to do so. '*À gauche*,' Madame instructed.

In the dimness inside she turned left and as she did so a panel moved under her hand and she found herself facing Jacques.

He looked at her and frowned, half lifting a hand.

'*C'est moi*,' she repeated her own introduction, 'Stella.'

'Stella!' He made a little jump of surprise, his face a kaleidoscope of disbelief, astonishment, joy. 'Stella!' He caught her to him, held her away, laughed again, then held her very close, very tight, very still for a long, long moment.

When he pushed her away his face had changed. 'Did my father let you come?' he questioned, frowning. 'How did you get over the demarcation line? Have you papers? Where's Jean-Paul? Nothing's happened to him, has it?'

She shook her head, said 'yes' and 'no' in rapid succession, told him quickly about Lennie and Jean-Paul and why she had come, that she had information in her head 'and maps in my coat.'

'*Mon Dieu*!' he murmured and she could see him clenching his teeth. 'It is too much, this risk for you.'

'And you!' She indicated the secret door behind them. 'Oh Jacques, I don't care if I'm with you.'

104

'But I care,' he said huskily and pulled her back into his arms, holding her tight. 'I care. And look at this stupid hair you have got!'

She laughed into his shoulder. 'Hector says it is just right for a French girl working in the fields.'

'Hector! Dear old soldier, I want to know so much.' He stepped back and looked at her in the dull little attic space. 'You are like a gift from the angels. I'm still not sure I believe you're real.'

'But I am,' she said, stepping to him and lifting her hands up to his face. 'You sent Jean-Paul to Lucille in disguise, now I have come to you the same way.'

He did not question her link of his sister and Jean-Paul as he very gently held her close and kissed her with a passion which both knew must be reserved for later as the light above them flickered on and off again.

It was much later before they were alone without fear of interruption. Stella had sat for some time at Jacques's desk passing on all the information she had memorised. Madeleine had unstitched her coat, and it was obvious from their mutual excitement that the intelligence she had brought was important. 'Tomorrow I must pass all this on, Jean-Paul gave me an address,' he said. 'And I can tell Paris what's happening in the unoccupied south, that there is resistance there!'

Stella was exhausted, but did not protest when Jacques refused to leave the workroom and go downstairs for a meal. She saw it as a means of being alone at long last as Madeleine offered to bring them up a supper tray.

While they waited she told him about Jean-Paul and Lucille. To her amazement he was not surprised and did not mention Philip. 'It was just waiting to happen, he was always enamoured of her from the time she was a schoolgirl, and once they met properly, pphut! Away they would go.'

She nodded. 'It is like that. It is frightening, I think, so much love at such a time, and already they are parted again. He has gone with Victor to try and free your pilot and see him on his way. Lucille looked devastated when they were planning to go.'

'Sounds like my little sister, she's always needed something or someone to care for, love, fuss over.'

'She's nursing. Dr Chabrol's set up a hospital ward in the old hall next to his home.'

'So there are still refugees?'

'A lot of soldiers struggling home with wounds, and quite a few elderly refugees, plus one or two babies, who are needing longer care.' She told Nadia's story of the old lady of Luray.

'There are rumours of people being forced out of their homes in

Alsace and Lorraine,' he told her. 'The Germans are coming over the border and just seizing French property, anything and everything that takes their fancy.'

'So they're just pillaging! But I thought an armistice meant ...'

'Peace, an honourable settlement! So did most, but now we know it will be at a price. I'm waiting for some more definite details, then I shall write an electrifying article in our newspaper. People must know the truth.'

'I want to help, I'm not a bad two-finger typist.'

He looked at her solemnly as the light again flickered above their heads and Madame returned with their supper. He took the tray. '*Bonne nuit*,' he said with a bow. '*Bonne nuit*, Stella,' Madame Astier called.

'Shall we take it down to my apartment?' he asked. 'Make ourselves comfortable.'

She followed him down and as they entered *now* she felt she had arrived, here was the familiar. Her eyes sought the slim volume of poetry with the ribbon. He placed the tray on a small table and turned to her. 'Welcome to perilous Paris,' he said.

'But not here, not this moment.' She put her arms around his neck.

'No, some moments must still be for lovers,' he whispered, his lips on the base of her neck, his hands running from her back to her waist and up to her breasts. 'You are my reason for fighting, for living, for being.'

And suddenly for no reason she could think of, she began to tell him of the two Jews in the orchard, then the man and woman in the train. He listened as his hands comforted and explored, undid and took off her blouse, carried her to his bed.

Then as quickly and unexpectedly as she had begun talking, she stopped. There was no more to say as she clung to his neck for a moment then helped him take off his clothes, kissing his shoulders and chest as he did so.

She heard him sigh and found she was crying, not consciously, tears just seemed to be running of their own will from her eyes. He saw and kissed them away. She tasted salt as he kissed her lips, then her neck, her breasts, her navel.

'Forget,' he breathed, his head resting lightly at the bottom of her ribs. 'Forget.'

She felt her body, self-willed as her tears, arch to his lips, respond to his every touch, until they reached the climax of all forgetfulness, and then slept.

They ate supper at four in the morning, made love again with the tender knowledge of a journey already travelled, and slept again.

Chapter Eleven

In the weeks that followed Stella became part of the strange world of subterfuge. In an extraordinary way the war in occupied Paris seemed more remote than in unoccupied Avignon. There she had helped deal with refugees, distressed families, people. In the attic room she typed stencils, set up the mimeograph machine and ran off the news-sheets.

When she mentioned this to Madeleine she raised her eyebrows. 'It is a honeymoon I think you and Jacques have!' Stella felt her cheeks burn, but the older woman went on with the air of one issuing an order. 'Make the most of it! In the streets there is fear, disaster, I think, waiting to happen. Pray to God it does not happen to us.'

She began truly to understand the risks they ran when the next news-sheet was ready for distribution. For the first time she and Jacques were to work together outside, though as they left the deserted square for the busier streets, he said, 'Just follow me, don't make it obvious. I'll let you know when you're to join up with me again – and if you lose me make your own way back to the apartment.'

She thought it was as if they both became different people as, hands in pockets, head down, he led her through streets busy with workers on lunch breaks; across the Place de la Concorde she had last negotiated in Jean-Paul's Wolseley. She had trouble following without appearing to do so, but it became easier with practice. She learned to cross roads keeping him in the corner of her eye, to slow and quicken her pace making it seem as if it was other pedestrians who caused her to do so. She was grateful for the efficiency of her disguise, for the new supply of hair dye Madeleine had bought for her. Red hair and a gingham print dress would not have been so easy to make anonymous.

Their way became quieter, the streets narrower, the buildings so high either side the sun did not penetrate the depths, only slanted geometrical patterns at corners. The properties were deserted: small

107

businesses, she guessed, closed and abandoned. She noticed foreign names, many Jewish names, above the shuttered workshops and warehouses. It made her feel more anxious not to be left behind, certain it would be difficult to find her way back unaided. Ahead of her Jacques turned yet another corner and she was overwhelmed by a desire to run, but she did not do so, though as she turned the corner she was biting her lip and her heart was pounding with anxiety.

He was waiting the other side. 'Well done,' he said.

'Well done?' she questioned. 'What do you mean?'

'You followed me well, didn't panic when I got out of sight.'

'Did you do that on purpose?'

'Sort of, a sort of test, see what your nerve was like.'

'Do you know what I want to do?' she asked, confronting him closely as her heart slowed its pumping panic. He shook his head. 'Kick your bloody shin!'

He gave a quiet laugh. 'Sorry, but it was necessary, through the city anyway.'

'But not that last corner! I wanted to run like mad to catch you up.'

'But you didn't.' He took her arm, his tone approving. 'You didn't. Lives, yours, mine, may depend on that ability to control what you really feel.'

She still felt aggrieved and slightly patronised as she assured him, 'Don't ever think I'll let you down.'

He dropped a kiss on her cheek. '*Pardon*,' he breathed, then took her arm and led her to the far end of the street, where, after checking there was no one in sight, he produced a key, opened the gates and led the way inside, closing but not locking the gates. He did the same with the double doors into the warehouse proper.

Inside it was dim, with a lingering smell she knew but for a moment could not name. She sniffed – like paper being pressed with a hot iron. It was the kind of smell the village shop had back in England when the newspapers were first delivered. Newsprint, but apart from a few filthy well-trodden pages the place was empty. 'What have we come here to do exactly?'

'I don't know if you realise, but every afternoon Verit calls on his way from home and takes a bundle of our news-sheets hidden under his shirt to the newspaper offices where he cleans. During the night, when there's only one duty reporter and cleaning staff on duty he hides these in a certain driver's lorry. When we have finished printing an edition and Verit has taken them all to the offices we meet Maxim here. Maxim drives a newspaper lorry during the afternoon, but works at the Humanities Museum during the morning.'

'He comes here with the ...'

'Newspapers tied in bundles and our news-sheets hidden in his lorry.'

'So there's no chance of putting the sheets in the newspapers before they are bundled up?'

'No, too dangerous, too many people around in the daytime, and as you'll see it's quite time-consuming.'

'And your newspaper is still allowed to print.'

'Because it has become a collaborationist newspaper, with a top German editor brought in from Berlin.' He broke off to listen. 'But those who buy the later evening editions get more than they pay for.' He grinned at her. 'Come and help me open the gates.'

A medium-sized covered delivery truck was waiting at the gates and drove quickly inside right through into the building. This time Jacques locked both gates and doors behind himself. Once inside a big cheerful-looking blond man jumped down from the cab and was introduced.

'Maxim Gapon, may I introduce my fiancée, Stella Hutton.'

Maxim bowed low. 'Most charmed.'

Stella shook his hand warmly. 'But you are not French.'

'A quarter, three-quarters Russian.' He bowed again. 'A rebel Russian, from a rebel Russian background,' he said. 'We make it our second profession.'

He laughed continually and seemed to make little effort to keep his voice down as he swung bundle after bundle of tightly bound newspapers from the lorry to a raised loading bay. She could imagine him in Cossack dress twirling to the beat of a sabre dance and shouting out in wild abandon.

'I wouldn't have believed how satisfying this could be,' Stella said. 'Every Parisian who buys their evening news gets ...' She rehearsed how the sheet fell into her hands on opening the newspaper.

Maxim gave one of his great laughs. 'I know, some of the museum staff are having more fun than they have ever had in their dusty academic lives!'

'Though they do risk imprisonment, torture and death,' Jacques added.

'Only if they're caught!' Maxim roared with laughter again, but while he talked and laughed he worked at a furious pace. His role was carefully undoing the thick hairy string and once a bundle had been propagandised he used his weight and strength to retie the bundles with the same length of string. Stella felt his fingers and hands must be raw with the effort.

'An hour and twenty minutes,' Jacques announced when they had finished. 'OK?'

'I'll make most of it up,' Maxim answered as he climbed into the cab, 'but they just think I'm a lazy Russian bastard!'

'*Bonne chance*!' Stella raised a hand as he prepared to leave and Jacques went to open the doors and gates. She followed intending to help close and lock up but as Jacques was pulling the first street gate to, someone called out. Stella froze, her brain trying to categorise the call – warning, enquiry, appeal? She heard Jacques mutter something under his breath and try to close the gates more quickly. There was the sound of running and her heart was in her mouth; she half expected the sound of shots after the lorry, or at Jacques. She ran to be at his side. She was just in time to see a petite young woman portering a small black suitcase push by Jacques into the yard.

'Close the gates,' she begged, her voice shaking with anxiety. 'Please! I'm from the museum. I tried to reach Maxim before he drove away.'

At these words Jacques drew her inside, locked the gates and gestured towards the open doors of the warehouse. Once inside she begged them to be quiet. Outside they could hear what sounded like Maxim returning with the lorry. Jacques lifted his hand to the door again but the woman shook her head vigorously and stayed his hand. Stella too had assumed it was Maxim come back. Then the outside gates were rattled with a startling ferocity and a voice called out in German. Further along the street they heard other gates being given similar treatment. Another call, and an answering voice replied '*Nein*!' There was more conversation then the vehicle engine revved up and they heard it go away.

They waited in breath-held silence until the engine was out of earshot, then the girl sagged, at last putting down the case. Stella shared her relief as she fought down a sudden wave of nausea. She gritted her teeth and hoped this was not the way she was going to react to dangerous situations. It really would not do.

'How did you know Maxim would be here?' Jacques questioned sharply now.

'Only because other days when I've been out at midday I've seen the lorry coming from this way, and I do know why he makes the diversion.'

Jacques glanced at Stella giving a minimal shake of his head as if to say give nothing away, as the girl paused to take a deep shuddering breath. 'Today,' she went on, 'I saw him come out of these gates, but he drove the other way, so I couldn't catch him.'

Jacques looked at her with suspicion and then down to her case.

'It's a short-wave radio,' she said and as Jacques bent quickly to examine and open the case she went on. 'My boss at the museum was just setting it up for a midday call to London when the Germans

110

arrived for "a tour" of the museum. But they were searching for someone ...'

She paused to hold her mouth, then her heart as Jacques replaced the long wire aerials more tidily over the set. 'What happened?' he asked more gently now.

'They came into the outer office, then walked past me unannounced into my boss's office. Today he had set the radio up in his private washroom. Every day he calls from a different place. We're four large museums in one, so it's a big area,' she explained. 'I pretended to go all coy and embarrassed and rushed to knock at the toilet door calling out that he had important German visitors, then fussed around to find them chairs they obviously did not want! He came out putting on his coat, and then took them off on a guided tour. As soon as they had gone I went and repacked the radio, climbed out of the toilet window and began to walk around the streets, thinking I would just wait around until the Germans had left the museum. Then I began to feel selfconscious, it was like ...' She paused to shake her head as if at her own inadequacy. 'It was like striking poses in front of a camera. I felt sure I was attracting attention.'

Stella wondered as she often did at the ability French women had to look chic in the dullest black. This girl had enlivened her outfit with just a touch of red scarf at the neck and a small Art Nouveau dancer on her lapel.

'I walked well away from the museums. Then one of their street patrols drew alongside me. They drove along at a snail's pace, the soldiers just leering, grinning. I've seen them do it before, trying to pick up or intimidate girls, but I suppose because I knew I had the radio, and would incriminate the whole museum network if I was stopped, I began to panic. I waited until their jeep was just ahead of me at a corner, then turned quickly, left, right. When I saw Maxim in his lorry it felt like a lifeline. Here was my chance of getting a lift and escaping. I ran after him.' She paused and leaned back on the stone loading bay. 'You know the rest – except,' she paused and looked up at Stella then across to Jacques, 'I am sure I recognise you. You are a friend of Jean-Paul. I have been to your apartment to a party. *Oui*?'

She had their undivided attention but Jacques did not confirm anything, only questioned, 'And you?'

'I am an archivist, though because everyone is pinched trying to subsidise the German occupation, I do a secretarial job as well.'

'So did you work with ...?'

'Jean-Paul!' She nodded enthusiastically. 'He's a dear, dear man, we all love him, but we need to warn him not to return to Paris.'

111

They both automatically stepped closer to her as her voice dropped and she continued in hardly more than a whisper. 'There have been a series of raids on clandestine groups. Jean-Paul has been acting as a go-between, collecting information, making new contacts, recruiting. A dangerous role.'

'He's gone south,' Jacques said as she paused.

'Look! If you know where he is he *must* be contacted. There've been arrests, and someone must have named Jean-Paul. The police have been to his lodging and this morning,' she paused as if making some quick mental review, 'I think they were looking for him at the museum. The Germans were polite, very respectful to our Director. Perhaps there is no real suspicion that the museums are the centre of a resistance movement. We shall see. But Jean-Paul must be told. Will you warn him?'

'We could telephone,' Stella suggested.

They both looked at her in horror. 'People do not trust telephone calls any more,' the girl said grimly. 'There have been many arrests after such calls.'

'But ...' she began, then felt an icy thrill run up her spine as she realised *she* would have to go back.

'We'll see to it,' Jacques reassured the girl from the museum, 'and perhaps it would be as well if we hid the radio here for the time being, let Maxim pick it up on his next trip.'

'No, that won't do. We make regular calls to London and listen out at special times for messages. I must take it back, my boss built it.' She patted the case. 'It's his baby! But it's all getting more dangerous. The Germans, who began as gentlemen, are becoming less so day by day.'

At the moment of parting they shook hands. 'I did not introduce myself,' she said with a wry smile. 'I think it is better that way.'

They left the warehouse together, discreetly, making sure the street was deserted. They all split up before they reached the busier streets, the girl leaving first, walking more purposefully on a route she had predetermined to take her past the museum so she could see if the Germans had left. She then planned to return the radio through the toilet window and herself through the front door.

'Now we must separate,' Jacques said to Stella.

I know, her heart answered. I know.

'I have to go and see contacts about more stencils and paper. We're getting very short. The Germans are beginning to keep a very close watch on stationary stocks.' He stopped and kissed her cheek. 'You all right?'

She smiled bleakly and shook her head.

112

He touched her hair with such tenderness it destroyed her heart. 'But what else can we do? Who else could we send?'

'No one,' she admitted, 'no one.' She forced an image of a brave face which made him smile.

'Grazed knees and lost tennis matches,' he said, 'you never let anyone see it hurt. But I knew.'

'And when Philip teased.' She remembered the ribbon. 'But off you go, see you later.' Later, she thought, for their last night together. Their last night *this visit*, she corrected herself.

She reached the apartment just before five o'clock, Madeleine came immediately to their special short, long, short, ring, '*Qu'est-ce que c'est que ça*? What has happened, you look dreadful.'

To her mortification Stella went to answer and then had to rush past her and head for the kitchen sink, where she was very, very sick. Madeleine pushed a towel into her hand and supported her, arm around her waist, until the worst was over.

'Sorry ... ' Stella began, 'I ... '

Madeleine passed a damp flannel to her, and as she wiped her face asked, 'When are you going to tell him?'

Stella stared at her blankly for a few seconds, then realisation came to both women at once.

'You didn't know?' Madeleine waved a dismissive unbelieving hand. 'It has been so obvious, toying with food, not drinking the tea I bought specially now the sickness '

'I'm ... pregnant,' Stella said with disbelief. 'Is that what it means? I thought I was just scared of the Germans.' The idea sounded comic said aloud and she giggled inanely, briefly.

'And Jacques has no idea either?'

'No, of course not.' She wanted to deny that it could possibly be so, but she could hardly be as illogical as that. It surely was the worst possible time. 'I can't be,' she stated; if she denied it vehemently enough it might not be true. 'I can't be.'

'The honeymoon comes to an end,' Madeleine said quietly, then seeing the girl's distress, she took her into her arms. 'It is the gift of love, this is what my mama used to say.'

It is not what my father would say, she thought, grimly remembering his judgement of a system where families lived in constant penury because of having unplanned children one after the other. 'Lack of decent education,' he averred. She could hardly plead that, or ignorance. 'You mustn't tell Jacques,' she told Madeleine. 'I have to go back across the demarcation line again.' She went on to explain all that had happened and the peril Jean-Paul was in if he returned to Paris. 'But I shall come back.'

113

Madeleine listened gravely.

'It will be bad enough – if he thinks I am pregnant, and I may not be – he'll only worry more.'

'When was your last period?' Madeleine asked, her manner dismissing any possibilities.

Stella hesitated. 'I've never been regular,' she said, 'I've never worried about it.'

'Evidently, but now you should. Think.'

'April time I suppose, but ... ' She stopped, unable to say that they did not make love until May. Surely it could not have happened then, the very first time. That seemed unfair.

'So you could be four months.'

'I'm ... ' Whatever she was going to say, was swamped by the thought that in five months' time she could have a baby, she could be a mother. For goodness' sake, surely not – and Jacques could be a father! She gave a gasp of astonishment. 'I can't believe it.'

'Sit down,' Madeleine ordered, 'we must be practical. If you have to return to Cleauville, it is best you stay there.'

'People have babies in Paris.'

'Lucille would be good to have around.'

Stella rose quickly and paced around the kitchen. 'Look, do you mind if we don't talk about it any more just now. I ... need to come to terms.' The full implication of the situation was still only just beginning to occur to her. Lucille, Jacques's father – and old Hector for some reason came censoriously into her mind's eye. It was the wrong time, that was for sure.

In the silence the front door bell made them both start as it again gave their signal.

As Madeleine rose Stella said urgently, 'You mustn't tell *anyone*. Certainly not Jacques at the moment.' When the older woman made no answer she begged. 'Promise, please? It is my news, isn't it.'

'Your news.' Madeleine turned back, nodded and promised.

Jacques came in, businesslike, helped himself to coffee from the can on the stove, then turned and looked at the two women. 'You've told Madeleine,' he stated. For a moment Stella was startled until he added, 'about Jean-Paul. It's obvious Stella should go back.' He looked at Madeleine for support.

'It is,' she said, 'as quickly as possible and this time carrying nothing that'll incriminate her. She must run no unnecessary risks.'

Stella felt the words had extra meaning, that somehow Jacques would guess. She found herself clasping her hands in front of her stomach, then hastily let them fall to her sides.

'I must contact some of our people ... ' He trailed off looking from

114

one to the other as if he sensed there was more he was not being told.

'So I must go,' Stella said, defensive, caught between something she did not want told and something she did not want to do. She saw him believe the atmosphere was her reluctance to go.

'Yes, as soon as possible. Tomorrow. Even then,' he paused and began to pace up and down, 'it's possible Jean-Paul is already on his way back. So,' he spread his hands as if to calm the moment, 'we have to be practical.'

Stella did not look at Madeleine as for the second time she was told they must 'be practical'. It was a cold, clinical word, and did not begin to meet how she felt.

'I must do two things. Set up some kind of watch to intercept him if he does return in the next twenty-four hours, and,' he looked back at Stella, 'make full use of your trip. Collect any requests or information from London for those organising in the south. There's a lot to do.'

Thought of things to do made her feel better. If baby there was, it would be in the future, a long time ahead. She should feel proud to be the associate of such as Jean-Paul who risked everything to organise and spread the network of the Resistance, and Jacques who for years before the war began had done his best to spread the truth of the Hitlerite regime. His mission to tell the people of France the truth was sacred to him.

He kissed both of them, Madeleine making shrugging protest, before he left again, within minutes really of coming in, but not before, with a slight shame-faced grin, he had asked if she would begin cutting the stencils for his next news-sheet.

'Of course,' she said, 'we must be practical.'

Madeleine and he both laughed, but for different reasons.

Bravado was all very well, Stella thought as she sat alone in the attic carefully typing his latest disclosure about evictions of French citizens, but was it true that *'Man's love is of man's life a thing apart. 'Tis woman's whole existence.'* I mean, she argued with herself in time to the tap of the typewriter's keys, while women have to have the babies it has to be true. Another inner, coarser, voice seemed to chip in with *'It's always the girls who bring the trouble home.'* She remembered a disgraced girl in the village and how she herself had defied the prejudice and spoken to her at the bus-stop. Only, she remembered, pausing to disentangle a bundle of key levers, to be brought up short by a passerby who had destroyed both the girl and the good intention by informing her aloud that the girl was *'not yet married'*.

She was checking the last page of stencil before taking it out of the typewriter when the light above her head flickered. She rose to open the panel. Jacques stepped inside saying, 'The English need all the information they can get about safe houses in Clermont-Ferrand, Vichy and Marseilles. I've lots of other things for you to memorise.'

She was diverted by the darting thought: *'The father of my child.'*

'There are one or two specific areas,' he told her. 'I'll help you memorise the map references, some code names and transmission times. You won't have any problem with those.'

'He seemed like another brother until last Christmas.'

'You look pale,' he said, taking her confidently into his arms. 'Pale but interesting.'

'I feel pale,' she said, unmollified, ungeared to the new mood.

'Come, my love,' he began almost as if he too were falling into the Byronic mood.

She scowled at him, thinking she could blame him, it was his fault, his act. *'Takes two to tango,'* the coarser voice reminded her.

'Let's go to bed, shall we.'

It was not even a question, she thought, it was an assumption. 'Let's go to bed,' she repeated, then added, 'I haven't even got a bed of my own to go to.'

He unclasped his hands slowly. 'What is it?' he asked quietly. 'I felt something was wrong earlier this afternoon, when I first came back.'

'No! Nothing!' she turned away, gritting her teeth so she did not dissolve into tears. 'Nothing!' she repeated vehemently. Was part of all this going to be losing control over her own body? *'Sure!'*

'Sounds like something,' he muttered, 'sounds like very much something.'

'Oh no!' She felt a terrible inner battle going on and rounded on him. 'Nothing! I'm not going away. Nothing will ever come between us. I'll just be able to trip back here whenever I like. There's no war, no danger, no Germans, no ...'

He tried to take her into his arms, but she resisted him, whirled away. 'What can I do to change any of that?' he asked. 'Tell me, and if I can I'll do it.'

'You've already done it, haven't you!' The coarse voice surfaced. She was appalled by the sound of her own crudeness and diverted into another attack. 'You've set up a news-sheet, involved all kinds of people, Madeleine, Verit – do *they* know the risks of being arrested, probably tortured ... it's happening, isn't it?'

'Some sacrifices have to be made if there's to be a free future.'

'Some *people* you mean!'

'Yes.' His voice too changed to that of the formal language of one

116

who works with words. 'People must live free, unthreatened, unmolested lives. I'm looking to the future!'

'So am I,' she said *sotto voce*, 'and I can't see the way.'

'What!' He drew nearer again. 'This is the way, what we are doing. You have to believe that! Helping England to win the war, to come back and drive the Nazis from every metre of French soil.' The voice of the orator dropped to personal appeal. 'It's our country, Stella, our land, our vineyards, our future.'

He grasped her hands, trying to convince her with more arguments, overpowering her with words, as was his way.

'There is a double watch on Jean-Paul's flat. The Germans already have it staked out, but now so have his colleagues from the museum. The one motivated by true affection will be more efficient,' he told her as he led her by the hand out of their secret attic.

'You really believe that don't you?'

'Of course! True love can move mountains, it is the greatest force in this world and the next.'

'Jacques ...' She stopped as they reached the apartment door.

He put his finger on her lips, then opening the door drew her inside. 'We don't want to shock Madame,' he said then added with a grin, 'yet again.'

'Madame is ...'

'Is?'

'A constant surprise. She reminds me of an ornament my father has in his study, three monkeys, one with its hand over its eyes, one covering its ears and one its mouth. "Hear all, see all and say nothing" he used to call it.'

He nodded agreement. 'I would trust her with my life.'

'Me too,' she breathed then reached up to kiss him on the lips. Perhaps it was time to stop talking.

He let her hang around his neck as he pulled her blouse loose from her skirt and pushed his hands up to her breasts.

She was stirred to the depths of her being by his caresses and walking backwards pulled him towards the bed, where she stood while he undid the back zip of her skirt, let it fall to the ground, then unbuttoned her French knickers, while she undid the buttons of his trousers, first the waist, then the flies. This is why I am pregnant, she thought, and did not care.

Chapter Twelve

The farm, the kitchen, the sitting room, upstairs was completely deserted, and as Stella roamed the empty rooms she felt there was an air of abandonment, as if the exodus had been sudden.

Ernest's room looked kind of ransacked, yet there were clothes she had never seen before strewn about on the bed and chair. Had they been taken over, the property seized? Had the words she cut into the stencils in the Parisian attic become reality here?

The room she had shared with Lucille looked the same, but the sitting room was 'disturbed'. It was the only word Stella could think fitted the strange disarrangement of the furniture, the cushions tossed into crushed piles. The kitchen was strange too, there was a loaf savagely hacked about, a sausage roughly cut, standing aslant on a newspaper, dirty glasses, half-consumed bottles of wine. Gaby would have been appalled.

There was no sign that Jean-Paul was still there, no padded businessman's waistcoat, no hat or jacket in the hall. Was her return for nothing – or were they not back from the Spanish border? She was about to go and look at the room above the stables where Victor slept when she heard a noise outside, a pebble rolled under a shoe, the sound of someone approaching through the courtyard to the kitchen.

She stepped quickly back into the shadow of the hallway and waited. She heard a light step, a tut and then the sound of glasses being collected and taken to the sink. She stepped forward. 'Lucille!'

'*Mon Dieu*!' Lucille started then cried out in relief and joy. 'Stella! It's you!'

They ran to each other, clung hard, embraced for long, long, moments. They separated slowly, almost selfconsciously, searching each other's faces as if trying to divine answers to questions they hardly dare broach.

'Where's everyone? Where's Jean-Paul?'

118

'We thought you might stay with Jacques ... longer.'

'I've come to ...' She paused, caught her friend's hand. 'Jean-Paul's not gone back to Paris has he – not likely to set out while we talk or anything?'

'No! No, he won't be going anywhere for a time,' Lucille reassured her.

'But where is he? What's happened here? Something has.'

'He's with my father, the two of them are hiding out between Hector's cottage and the old bories. There was a police swoop, Pétain's new State Police.' She paused to register distaste, hatred. 'All English nationals are being rounded up and interned. Hector was at the farm alone when they arrived, and he told them you and Ernest had already gone back to England and he was caretaker.'

'Brilliant!' Stella exclaimed. It also explained the state of the house. 'And you?'

'I was with Dr Chabrol at the hospital when they came there later the same day. Our local officer was with them, so he knew me anyway.' She shook her head as if to shake off remembered fear. 'When they walked down the ward towards me I was sure I was going to be arrested, but our man made some remark as they reached me, and they all paused to watch me rebinding an old lady's leg ulcers, then moved on.'

'So the local policeman's on our side, that'll be ...' she bit off the word 'lifesaver' as too near the truth, 'useful. But Jean-Paul?'

'Luck was with us that day, Hector being here, then Victor driving Jean-Paul to the hospital ...'

'Hospital?'

Lucille nodded but continued, '... sees the German staff cars and does a swift u-turn to the farm. Hector and Victor made him as comfortable as they could in the sitting room until they could get Dr Chabrol – and of course I came once we knew.'

Jean-Paul lay in the dark cottage and realised if he kept perfectly still nothing hurt, which must mean a slight improvement. He fretted when he was all alone; he should be in Paris fostering his new contacts. He had been away too long. He should not be dallying here. His mouth twitched, he breathed in a little too sharply, and groaned; hardly the right word but when Lucille was around it felt exactly like 'dallying'.

If he could fill his mind with nothing but Lucille, then it would be bliss, but always his mind went back to the Resistance, the colleagues he should be supporting, drawing the nets of the organisation ever tighter. He wondered if his protracted absence had caused difficulties, gaps in logistics – or worse, any loss of valuable contacts?

Lucille argued that he could not possibly return until he was fully recovered, and in his heart he wanted to roll over as a puppy might, have its tummy tickled and stay for ever at her feet.

He saw the sense of her argument that he could not afford to draw too much attention to himself, and a heavily padded fruit buyer who had to be pulled and lifted to his feet all the time was taking too many risks. He could *perhaps* make up some kind of story, instead of the truth, which was that he had nearly been caught with an English airman crossing the Spanish border.

There had been joy and success in the mission, but there were images, faces, that haunted him in the quiet cottage room. The man who had lost both his sons, killed by British attacks on the French navy. The danger of extricating the pilot from the farm cellar, the white face with freckles, the red hair, emerging from the gloom. Victor snatching the man's shotgun and threatening not the man, for he was obviously beyond caring what happened to him, but his poor traumatised wife. He could remember their faces, one wiped out with shock, the other demonised by the anger of a double bereavement.

Then there was the lamb-to-the-slaughter look of that pilot, Lennie Forryan. Released from the cellar he had been overcome with pity for the couple, had talked about them at every opportunity as they travelled. Jean-Paul felt he had an unworldly quality, perhaps a shyness like his own concealed beneath his chatter and his flyer's slang. He hoped Lennie never got near enough to an enemy plane to see his opposite number clearly, or he'd be letting the enemy off – and getting shot down himself.

They had parted company to divert a border patrol they had almost walked into. In the scramble that followed Jean-Paul had shown himself and headed back along the track, while Victor and Lennie had gone on to rendezvous with the partisans on the Spanish side. He had felt more like the boy's grandfather than a near contemporary, as even *then* Lennie had turned momentarily to him with goodbyes and thanks, while he urged the boy away after Victor.

There had been shots as he scrambled off-track to escape. After some hectic crouching runs and jumps he had fallen, between fierce rocks. In agony, unable to move, he had bitten into his lip to keep quiet as he heard the patrol pass by. The rocks had held him like great scissors; he had been trapped with no proper purchase for hands or feet. He had wondered if it was the end of his career in the Resistance – and of his life, as the icy cold night passed and no one, friend or enemy, came his way. He had thought a lot about Lucille, was so grateful for the knowledge that she loved him with it seemed the same passion he felt for her. If there was no more, there was that, and it meant more than anything else in his life.

At midday when the sun and a high circling eagle had become his tormentors, the faithful Victor's face appeared over the rockface. It was like relief from some endless mythological punishment. His own call, his attempted cheer, had been a rusty croak. Then being told Lennie was safely over the border, on his way home, had made it seem a triumphal release, but his wounds had a keen soreness and began to bleed again as he was eased from his stone cleft and placed on a litter by two silent sturdy mountain farmers.

He remembered no more until he had come to in the farm sitting room where Dr Chabrol knelt on the floor to stitch and bind him up, refusing to let him be moved again for a couple of days.

For the last three days he had lain in this tiny dim bedroom. He glanced at the luminous hands of his watch. Lucille should soon be here. She was working long hours every day, for news that there was real medical help to be had at Cleauville had quickly spread. There were, she said, all hospital departments, from surgical to maternity, crammed into one church hall.

He wanted to be free of this wearisome role of patient, wanted to be by her side while he was here, not lying down, wasting time. He wondered if he dared get to his feet and try walking? The idea was abandoned as he heard something, someone approaching, talking – more than one. He held his breath, listened intently, his hand moving to the revolver tucked under his uninjured side. Then came the prearranged tap on the door and Lucille was there, her fair hair in a businesslike pleat framed by light, as if it brought in some of the sun with it.

'I've a visitor for you,' she said coming over to the bed, kissing him briefly on the forehead, then standing back so he could see who followed.

'Stella?' He questioned her presence. 'This is a surprise – but – there is a but.'

She nodded, went over to kiss him gently on both cheeks, then sitting by his bed she gave him the warnings from Paris.

He tutted, exasperated, as he explained. 'I've set up a centre for falsifying identity cards, and another producing demob papers. I'm the organiser, the go-between – and I'm banished! I don't think so!'

Stella could appreciate his frustration. 'Jacques says there's a real flood of escaping English and French soldiers from detention centres, hundreds are finding it easy to walk out, getting away before guards and trains can be organised to take them to proper POW camps in Germany. There is no time to ...' She broke off as Lucille stirred irritably, defensively putting herself between Stella and Jean-Paul.

121

'There has to be time to heal,' she said meaningfully. 'Dr Chabrol said he had never seen bruises like those on Jean-Paul's ribcage. It was only the pressure of the rock on his open wounds that stemmed what might have been fatal bleeding. Imagine that!'

Stella had a graphic mental picture of exactly what she meant, and felt the stupid nausea sweeping over her again. She turned and ran from the cottage. Outside she was violently sick and was leaning back on the wall, exhausted, when Lucille came to her.

'You all right?' she asked. 'Not like you.'

Stella walked away from the cottage and its gently soughing shade of pines, out towards the vines.

'You're tired, overstretched. You'll be better after a proper night's sleep.' Lucille walked after her, stood by her side, and when she did not answer, did not look up, she said, 'There's something else, something you've not told me. Something's happened?'

'In a way,' she said and blew out her breath noisily like one preparing to take a plunge. 'But you must swear not to tell anyone else.' There was no reply. 'Otherwise I don't tell you.'

'I swear,' Lucille said, reminding Stella that even as a twelve-year-old her promises were never given lightly, but once given never broken.

'I think I'm pregnant.' She saw her friend's lips part in shock.

'Is it Jacques's?'

'Of course! Whose else would it be?'

'We've had several rape victims come to us, so thank God it's not that. Does Jacques know?'

Stella shook her head. 'And he mustn't, not yet. I mean I *may* be wrong, I've heard of morning sickness, but ...'

'Oh! It can be other times. Have you any other symptoms? I presume your periods have stopped.'

It began to feel like an official consultation, or Madame Astier all over again. She nodded. 'I've gone off tea, can't face it.' Stella looked appealingly at Lucille as if for friendship's sake she might be able to come up with a different verdict.

'You're pregnant,' Lucille said with certainty, but as if to soften the diagnosis put an arm around Stella's waist and added in a tone of some wonder, 'Good gracious, I shall be an aunt!'

'What's this then?' a male voice called. 'Stella!'

Lucille's father emerged from the trees at the far side of the cottage, carrying a sack.

The two separated as if the words implied they had been caught, as years ago, in some mutual mischief. 'The unsuspecting grandfather,' Stella whispered before running to greet him. She heard Lucille giggle before commenting as if to remind them both, 'These are desperate times.'

They retold their stories clustered around the invalid's bed, with the extra information Ernest brought that two more English soldiers were now hidden at the bories, a well-concealed group of medieval stone shelters, used by shepherds long ago, overgrown and abandoned until now. The sack contained their worn-out boots which would be passed on to the cobbler in the village to repair as best he could before Victor set off once more to pass them on to their new first safe house.

'Victor's the real hero,' Jean-Paul added with conviction.

'He's certainly the work horse at the moment,' Ernest agreed. 'We can't spare anyone else to see these people along the line. He's gone back again today, a French airman desperate to join de Gaulle and fight on. Every one we can get out now is one more trained man back in to fight the ...'

'Buggers!' Stella supplied.

Jean-Paul laughed, then groaned.

'Good to have you back, Stella!' Ernest said.

'There's no reason why I shouldn't help is there?' There was a silence but she pressed on. 'I'll go with Victor next time, then I could go alone, take turns with him.'

'I still feel responsible to your father, you know,' Ernest said quietly. 'Perhaps they would be glad of you at the hospital?'

Stella's heart lurched at the mention of her father, who felt long-lost to her. Then her stomach went queasy again at the idea of being at the hospital. She gritted her teeth and silently blessed Lucille when she said, 'I think Stella's best out in the field. We have Nadia as a regular ancillary now, and her husband Claude, he's home and ...'

Stella interrupted with a noise like a motorbike roaring away. 'Well, that's how Nadia described him.'

'Anyone less r...r...r... rumph would be hard to imagine,' Lucille said. 'He's big, ambling, amiable.'

'He's a good husband for her. Her mother loved him too I think.' Ernest's remark held a wistful quality and she guessed he was thinking of the time when Nadia's mother had been Gaby's permanent help, confidante, friend. Ernest, in his determination to help France fight on, sometimes forgot his grief; at other times, like now, it overwhelmed him, so intense for a time it seemed to paralyse them all. Stella, watching the passing emotions of loss and tenderness on his face, felt a sharp physical pang of grief herself as she thought of the grandchild Gaby would never see. But it was Ernest who recovered first. 'Come on, m'dear, let's leave these two love-birds together.' He held out an arm to shepherd her away.

'I don't know about that,' Lucille said, 'the good doctor is coming soon to examine and rebandage the patient.' Jean-Paul groaned.

Ernest and Stella walked companionably together to the house. 'You must tell me all about Jacques's news-sheets and about Paris. How is the city bearing up? I want to hear everything, and,' he paused to nod towards Pas de Crédit's lorry just passing the top of the farm drive, 'there's something to tell you about. There goes our short-wave radio!'

Stella looked at him, then after the disreputable lorry with its normal load of welding tools and farm machinery either being returned or collected for repair. 'You mean it's on that lorry?'

'Yes, our own mobile radio station! Edmund brought a radio back from Clermont-Ferrand. We have a contact there and in Vichy.'

'And in Paris, I've brought you a call sign and times from Jean-Paul's contacts at the museum.' She tapped her temple. 'It's all in here. It'll be quite good to offload it.'

'That's wonderful.' He took her hand. 'As you say we'll beat the buggers.'

The hand that took hers was broad, rougher, but walking by Ernest's side did remind her of walking with Jacques. They were of like height and build, his manner so similar, bending his head slightly her way when he spoke in easy conversation. Yet Jacques was like his mother too. His Frenchness showed in his dark eyes, his deep passions for the history of this land, his mother's land and family, his ability to be upset – or soothed – his intensity.

'You're very quiet,' Ernest said.

'I think I'm looking at everything with new eyes,' she said with complete honesty. 'The vines, the melons, your patch of experimental apple-trees behind the house, the olive-trees, ageless, beautiful, biblical.'

'It will be here for you when I've gone,' he said quietly. 'The land is a timeless trust. You and Jacques must look after it for me – and for Gaby.'

It seemed to her that Jacques had said much the same thing on her last night in Paris. There had been an esoteric layer to her conversation then.

'For you, Gaby, Jacques,' she promised, 'and those to come.'

Chapter Thirteen

The behaviour of the German troops in Paris had not been too repressive through the long hot summer of 1940. Citizens generally had been careful to avoid confrontation, but the posters announcing the pernicious law which made *any acts judged against the interests of the new regime punishable by death* made French hackles rise.

Students and activists who had begun in small ways to harass the occupying forces, with pinholes in fuel pipes, grit in tanks, or stickers proclaiming 'Back off from the Germans' on bumpers, stepped up their acts of disobedience. Telephone calls became a lottery as cables were continually being cut; a warehouse full of German military equipment was fired.

The Germans now used the law issued by the Pétain government to back up their thinning patience, and citizens were arrested for things as petty as voicing an opinion about the mannerless way some soldiers demanded goods in short supply from the shops. Each arrest brought more recruits to the underground army: injustice was hardening attitudes into resolution.

Madame Astier heard about the latest arrests while she was sipping an early lemonade outside the Café d'Hortense on the Boulevard Saint-Michel. The undercurrent of gossip at nearby tables of this busy café was of nothing else. She listened, and with a black shopping bag at her feet she looked what she was, an average elderly Parisian. She was even so on a mission, waiting patiently for the time when someone would join her at the table near the long container of box hedge. After exactly five minutes by the huge café clock, the person would depart, leaving a folded newspaper carelessly lying on the chair. She had carried out the routine several times and now no longer looked at the person who took the vacant chair, her eyes going only to the clock. Five minutes exactly passed, and on cue the woman left. Madeleine slid the newspaper from the chair on to her lap without

125

looking down, then finishing her lemonade she pushed the newspaper into her bag and began to make her way home.

She wondered what extra items of news this particular paper would have meticulously typed in down the central fold, or in the late news section. These reports came from pre-war newspaper contacts, retired journalists, who now reported on any German misfortunes, the successes of the Resistance and the Free French, all untold by the official Nazi-run newspapers.

She hoped however they were not too lengthy. Jacques was missing his girl in more ways than one. The number of times he swore and cursed as he typed each issue had certainly grown and the smell of correction fluid was strong in the attic workroom.

She shook her head as she thought of Stella. So clever they thought themselves and still got into trouble. She hoped the girl would have sense enough to stay in the Unoccupied Zone, she would be better there, with Lucille being a nurse ... and Jacques's father ... a child would help fill a gap in his life. '*Qu'est-ce que c'est que ça?*' she cried out, her thoughts violently broken into as she placed a foot on the steps of her apartment house. 'What's this?' She was alarmed to find her arm taken in a fierce, desperate grip. She turned sharply expecting to see a uniform, a Nazi about to sweep his hand into her bag and retrieve the newspaper. Instead her assailant was an old woman, not nearly so tall as herself, but obviously in a far more extreme state of anxiety.

'Please take me inside,' she said.

'Why? What is this? Who are you?'

'Inside madame, for pity's sake.' The old woman looked distraught, though not disreputable.

Madeleine gave the special ring on her own door bell. If this was a trick at least Jacques would be warned, the attic room would be closed, all noise stilled. 'This is your house, but we wait outside,' the woman noted suspiciously.

'I thought I had forgotten my key,' she said brusquely, recovering it from her pocket. 'And how do you know this is my house?'

'I know all about you Madame Astier, that is my problem.' The woman was enigmatic, and closed her mouth into a thin tight line. She obviously intended to say no more until they were inside.

'It will be both of you I want to see,' the woman said, as Madeleine ushered her across the hallway into her apartment. Madeleine paused to put her bag carefully away into a closet.

'I knew it would all come to no good.' The manner and voice of the woman changed as she sat down uninvited and began to rock in the manner of one in extreme pain or mental anguish. 'Away from

126

home all hours. He was an old man, a stupid old man. Worshipping the ground those journalists trod! Not normal.'

'Who are you talking about, madame?' Jacques asked from the doorway. 'What is your name?'

'*Why* have you come here?' Madeleine asked, automatically going to stand by Jacques's side.

'Because you must know what has happened! Because it is your fault!'

'Fault? What, madame? Do we know you?'

'You know my husband. You know Verit!'

'Verit?' Jacques queried, alarm on his face. He and Madeleine exchanged glances. They had been expecting Verit that morning but he had not come.

'*Oui*! *Oui*! Verit! My husband!' The old woman picked up her handbag from her lap and shook it as if it were to blame. 'He was arrested last night.'

'*Mon Dieu*!' Madeleine gasped. 'What happened? What did they do?'

'What did they not do.' Madame Verit gave a short humourless laugh.

'The police?' Jacques asked, 'not the Nazis?'

'What is the difference now! They are like snakes, sidling into the house, asking polite questions, then ...' she arched her hand into the shape of a snake's head and darted it forward in a sudden strike. 'The next moment they break up our home searching, then they grab ...' she paused as if seeing it all again, 'and his shirt comes open and all these sheets of paper come falling out.'

Madeleine pushed a can of coffee into her hands and urged her to sip it before she went on. 'They thought that was a great joke. They turned to me as they bustled him out and said, "Say goodbye to your husband" as they dragged him away and wouldn't tell me where he was being taken.'

There was silence, the wall clock loud, the coffee smell suddenly metallic, cankerous. 'I'll find out,' Jacques said, his voice low, tense.

'There has to be a trial,' Madeleine said.

'I've heard of these trials.' Madame Verit shook her head.

'How did they get on to Verit?' Jacques pondered. 'And if Verit have there been others?'

'The café was full of talk of arrests,' Madeleine remembered.

'Could you have been followed here?' Jacques asked.

She shook her head. 'No, I went to my granddaughter last night, she is at the Sorbonne. Her friends made sure I was not followed. I do not think the police suspected me. It must have been obvious I did not know about ... ' She opened her handbag and pulled out some creased copies of the news-sheet. 'My granddaughter said it had been written by a professional journalist.'

Jacques took them from her. 'What made you so certain it was me?'

'Oh! for years he'd always walked along this street to work, and when you started at his newspaper he pointed out where you lived. He adored you reporters, did you know that?' She nodded at Jacques. 'He came home full of your exploits, your jokes – you were like gods to him.' Anger filled her voice again as she pushed out a bony clenched fist at Jacques. 'Ahh! I've no patience ... you men, one bangs a drum, holds up a flag, the other rushes to follow!'

'Madame,' Jacques persisted. 'I think you too have our cause at heart, or you would not be here warning us.'

She shook her head at him. 'I hate waste! I don't want my Verit to *suffer* for nothing.' The word made her sigh again. 'I don't think he'll tell them anything, but then ... I do not know what they'll do to him.'

The ticking of the clock was again loud in the silence.

'You see my old man really would die to help you! He'd rather be at that newspaper office cleaning the latrines than at home. Imagine! The old fool, I told him so often enough. But I care about him, he is my life – now it may be over, I know he is my life. I don't care too much what happens to me if he is not coming back.'

'Have you no other family, madame?'

'Our daughter died fifteen years ago, and our son-in-law who is Dutch moved back to Holland in 1936.' She clucked at the uselessness of that, then pushed herself wearily to her feet again. 'But I must go. I promised my granddaughter I would not be too long. I don't want her to do anything wild! These students, they think they can stop the world if they will it.'

'I'll escort you,' Jacques said. 'I need to make calls, find out where Verit is, and I'd like to meet your granddaughter.' He took her hand between both of his. 'I can't tell you how sorry I am, I'm really fond of Verit, the affection is not all one way.' He kissed her hand.

The old head bent very low and for a moment the kind words threatened to do what the police could not, reduce her to tears. Jacques, still squeezing her hand, saw the jaw muscles work, the chin tighten. 'So,' she said quietly, 'that's how it all is.'

'I wish I had a car,' he said as they walked, his arm supporting hers.

'Don't worry, I'm stronger than I look,' she said, adding as they passed a group of soldiers, 'I have my anger and my hatred to keep me going now.'

When they arrived at the blocks of student lodgings, Jacques noticed that a young man leaning near a corner pushed himself up and followed them. When they arrived at Number 3, and the old lady produced a key and let herself in, the young man walked closely past, paused, then raised a hand to someone who came forward to meet Madame Verit. The red-haired girl inside raised an answering salute.

'You are well looked after, mademoiselle,' he said as he was introduced to Marie Weilburg.

'There is need, is there not.' The words had sting and he bowed his head in acknowledgement. The fire ran in the family it seemed. 'I shall keep my grandmother here as long as she will stay.' The tone was dismissive.

Jacques found himself wondering if all redheads were so outspoken. He bowed his head again, then felt a bit of a fool and thought he saw contempt in the girl's eyes. He held her gaze and said quietly, 'Your grandfather has helped the fight for freedom – my conscience tells me I have to go on no matter what the price we all have to pay.'

'Of course!' She took a step towards him now. 'We ... I feel the same. It's upsetting when it ...'

'Gets personal,' he supplied.

'It's someone you love.'

He bowed his leave; he had much to do. The parting was formal; he still felt both women put much of the blame for the old man's fate on his head and he knew he was guilty of taking old Verit's help for granted. But as he left the building Marie stepped outside with him, pulled the door to.

'I'll let you know immediately I have any news – and if you hear ...'

'Yes, of course. What do you expect for him?'

The news-sheets on her grandfather's person shot the legal phrase *in flagrante delicto* into his mind. Faced with this other redhead it also disarmed him with the memory of Stella hurtling the Latin phrase at him as he and Philip had been caught red-handed 'fixing' a game of cards. 'At best a prison sentence,' he said, forcing his mind back to her question.

She nodded, dropping her head momentarily as her grandmother had done, then she asked, 'Could I do the work he was doing? Take his place?'

He shook his head. 'I think not.'

Her voice was low as she went on. 'I know he was helping you distribute your news-sheets, somehow you were getting them put into the Nazi-run press, but we, the students, have ways. We know kiosk and shop owners. We could get them distributed in other ways if you need us.'

129

'And I,' the door opened behind Marie, and Madame Verit was there, 'will pick them up from your address and bring them here.'

He felt both humility and anguish as he left the two women, but before he tried to establish where Verit had been taken, he must contact Maxim Gapon.

He made his way quickly to the central museum. He was careful; he did not want to draw any more attention to the museum, its group of Resistance workers and its secret radio.

There was no evidence of a German presence either outside or inside the museum portals, but he still hesitated to make an immediate open enquiry. Jean-Paul had been the go-between, but Maxim must be told what had happened to Verit. Maxim said the newspaper people did not know his real name, but if his lorry had been searched and the Gestapo were waiting for the driver, whatever name he had assumed, with forged papers to match, would not save him.

He glanced at his watch. It was nearly midday; he could not afford to let Maxim leave the museum. He decided he must make some approach to someone but now could see no official anywhere. Quickly he found his way to the humanities department, to a desk surrounded by card index cabinets and huge shelves of bound copies of newspapers.

The girl behind the desk ignored him. He coughed loudly. She looked up, eyebrows raised. 'I am looking for Maxim,' he said, 'a message from a sick relation for him.'

'Oh he's probably left, he finished at noon,' she glanced at her watch, 'and he's always away on time.'

'It is important. Where would I catch him if he has not left?'

'Staff exit, he usually leaves that way. Out of the front door, turn left twice.' Her gazed dropped to the papers on her desk.

He turned away without speaking. '*Merci*!' she said to remind him of his manners. He spat back a word of such rudeness she gasped.

He was striding out through the foyer when there was the sound of footsteps hurrying after him and a hand caught his arm. 'Can I help you?' a woman asked.

'No,' he said without looking, or pausing. 'I am in a hurry.' Then he saw it was the girl of the radio set and stopped. 'I have to contact Maxim at once!'

'Come with me.' She spun on her heel and led the way rapidly back through the foyer and a door marked 'No admittance'. A corridor, another door and the street was visible. 'He may have gone,' she said and hurried to look up and down outside. Shaking her head, she came back, then he saw her smile briefly and nod to someone behind him. He turned and there was Maxim pulling on his jacket. 'This way,' she

130

said briefly to both of them, and led the way back through the first door, but diverted into a small room where old volumes lay on tiers of shelves and a long bench held all the materials for renovating the old books.

Jacques quickly told of Verit. Maxim sat down carefully as the story unfolded. 'I do not think you can risk going back to the newspaper,' Jacques ended.

'*Non* ...' he agreed, then looked up and smiled bleakly at the two of them. 'I have been thinking for some time that I should go to England, find de Gaulle and be one of his freedom fighters. Perhaps now is the time.'

They both made assenting noises. 'Go to the room,' the girl said, 'stay there out of sight until the next radio call, we can perhaps make arrangements.'

'I need to go back to my own place first,' he said.

'*Écoutez bien*!' The petite woman wagged her finger at him. 'First Jean-Paul, now Verit, next you! Go to our room and wait!'

'It is ...' He gave his broad lazy-looking smile. 'I have two parakeets.'

'*Sacré Dieu*!' She lifted her hand in impatient astonishment. 'I will see they are rehoused! Will tomorrow do?'

He nodded, then held out his hand to Jacques. 'We have worked well together. I wish you luck – and I hope we all meet again – someday!'

'Wait for me here, it is important,' she told Jacques. 'I have literally to unlock a few doors, we have a secret chamber in the museums for such emergencies.'

Many times footsteps approached the door, but always went past. It seemed an endless twenty minutes, but then suddenly the door opened and she was back without him hearing her approach at all.

'Sorry I've been so long, but Maxim has gone – left – on his way. I was in time to catch the end of the midday calls. We can do things quickly when we have to.' She paused and smiled. 'My boss – you know, the radio operator, would like to meet you. And I think after all you should know my name is Claudette Maine.' They shook hands formally and then he followed her to a large office near the front foyer. 'Professor Thierry.' A tall aesthetic-looking man in his early sixties rose from behind his desk, Jacques felt his manner looked relaxed, almost casual, but the glint of the eyes behind the gold-rimmed spectacles was calculating, shrewd.

'Jacques Blair, yes.' He nodded, adding the code name sent south with Stella. 'Frère Jacques. I hear of you from many sources.'

'You surprise me.'

'It should not. Radio sources from the south and from England know of your existence, Paris certainly does – and are you still going to be able to distribute the pamphlets I find in my official newspaper?'

Jacques was surprised at the ease with which the man chatted of such things. It seemed strange to be talking here openly in a bright, airy, magnificent office, after his own activities enclosed in a secret attic.

'I believe I shall,' he said. 'Verit's granddaughter is a student at the Sorbonne ...'

'Ah!' the professor interrupted, as if satisfied his visitor had an answer to the problem, so he did not want to hear more. 'Youth and energy, reckless daring.' He leaned back in his chair, his eyes half closed but on his young assistant.

Jacques remembered Maxim's words about the academics having a more exciting time than they had ever had in their lives. He glanced at Claudette and saw as she looked at the professor there was hero-worship and admiration in her regard. She would, he thought, climb out of any number of closet windows to save his skin.

'It can be an explosive mixture,' the professor added, 'but not as treacherous as the collaborators who work on the Nazi press.'

Jacques glanced at him sharply. 'Is this how Verit was picked up?'

'I believe so.' The man's mouth pressed into a thin line. 'It is how we lost the services of Jean-Paul, those trying to curry favour with the new regime.'

'A message has been taken to Jean-Paul ...'

'Indeed,' the man agreed as he took on his most professorial aspect, the teacher pleased with his best pupil, 'and received. The radio codes you sent south have been in action today, which is another reason I wished to meet you. "Frère Jacques is thanked for his message courtesy of Pas de Crédit." You will know what they mean? Your smile tells me so.'

The pleasantries seemed over then and Claudette was sent as a kind of sentry to the outer office. Jacques was fast forming the impression of a man whose mind was as orderly as any card index. He obviously kept all the information about the Resistance in his head and only pulled out the cards it was necessary for any one person to know.

'We are at a critical crossroads in this war, *mon ami*,' he began, scooting his wheeled office chair round so he sat at the front corner of his desk next to his guest. 'Britain stands alone, Hitler fully expects it to capitulate. He does not know Churchill!'

'Or the English,' Jacques agreed.

'Göring advises him that the Luftwaffe will bomb them into submission, and destroy their fighter squadrons so that an invasion can be made *should* that prove necessary. Göring personally does not think it will be.'

Jacques raised his eyebrows in surprise at both the information and the presumption. 'Your information must come from very high sources.'

'It does,' the professor said with the certainty that needed no emphasis. 'It also tells us that anything we can do to hamper the German efforts on this side of the Channel must be done, and done quickly. I have taken the opportunity to despatch Maxim to the coast. He is skilled in map-making, his services detailing the fortifications and stockpiling of resources by the enemy on the coast will be invaluable. He is then under instructions to go to Brittany where we have a fisherman of extraordinary foolhardiness, who keeps managing to cross and recross the Channel.' He leaned back in his chair, linked his fingers behind his head and smiled, his countenance full of the utmost content. 'Doesn't it give you pleasure to know such things?'

Jacques shook his head, not in disagreement but in amazement at the man's coolness.

'But I badly need a replacement for Jean-Paul. I would like to ask you to give over much of your work on your individual news-sheet to your student friends and be that replacement.'

'I feel my efforts to inform, to spread the true stories, are valuable.'

'*Pardonnez-moi,*' the professor asked with the air of one about to give greater offence, 'but there are other underground presses operating. I have a need of special importance, work I cannot do myself. Unfortunately I am too "public" to disappear for days at a time. Whereas ...'

'No one would miss me,' Jacques supplied his added qualification for the post, 'but I could never give up my writing. This is what I feel I was put on this earth to do, and now it is more important than ever to inform. The Germans only report their bombing raids on London, they are not reporting the losses the Luftwaffe are suffering at the hands of the English Spitfires.'

'Hmm! Could you do both?' Professor Thierry leaned back but was already nodding his head at his guest.

'What would that involve?'

'Most times being away from Paris for three or four days, perhaps a week. Making hazardous approaches to people who could be Nazi sympathisers.' He paused, watching Jacques closely. 'Rewards? Imprisonment, torture, death if you get it wrong.'

Jacques shrugged. 'The same for all of us if we get it wrong. Little different to lying injured on the field of battle.'

133

'Would you be happy to go south almost immediately, to Clermont-Ferrand first, then Vichy?'

His heart leapt stupidly at the chance of going south, and the thought of real activity after the days and weeks he had spent in his attic was appealing. 'I would have a lot to arrange,' he said thinking of Verit's granddaughter, 'some delegating to do.'

Professor Thierry chuckled. 'I knew you were my man as soon as you walked into my office.'

'And Verit?'

'There I am sure I can achieve more than you. I'll learn what I can, I have the contacts.'

'When do you want me to leave?'

'Tomorrow.'

Chapter Fourteen

They rounded the shoulder of the hill, and though Lucille had not previously planned this meeting at the end of the day in detail, she knew now exactly where she wanted to take Jean-Paul. This slope pushed up not to a peak but to a circle with a hollow in the middle, like a miniature green volcano. She had named it La Tasse, as a child, and the name had stuck, a cup on the top of her father's land.

'What have you brought?' Jean-Paul asked, reaching to take the bag from her, but she swung it beyond his reach.

'Wait and see.'

He laughed and did not argue, but when he reached the rim of the cup he stopped and looked back, watching the smoke from the fires of vine stems drifting in long smudgy grey lines away from them, floating across the irregular rectangles and triangles of fields up over the hills southwest towards the watery Camargue, home of white horses, black bulls and pink flamingoes, then up to the dark blue Mediterranean sky.

She walked on to the centre of the hollow, took a small yellow check cloth from her bag and laid out bread, cheese, wheat cakes, apples, fresh figs from the farm courtyard and wine. She sat and watched him taking in the view, flexing his shoulders and back to relieve the aches and strains of the day. She had overseen his convalescence with the same observant care, helping him when reluctantly he had to face the fact that his injuries had been serious, that recovery was to take weeks, not days.

'It is too much. It overwhelms me.' He swept an expressive arm over the landscape. 'I see all this, and I have you. We're together. It feels like a miracle.' He thought it was like tempting fate even as he voiced it aloud. When the war was taking so much from so many millions of people, why should it give to him all he had ever wanted? Since he had begun to feel better he spent his days torn between

135

wanting this idyll to go on for ever, and impatient for his recall from his mentor, Professor Thierry. 'In peacetime it would be the most wonderful holiday, the most ...' He turned and looked at her. 'It could have been our honeymoon.'

'I wanted to bring you here. This was my special place as a child, my retreat from trouble. It's just far enough away from home to think, but not be afraid. And better still, Jacques never liked it up here, he said you couldn't *see* anything, which of course,' she patted the grass by her side, 'you can't in the hollow. And no one can see you.'

She could smell the smoke on his clothes and in his hair as he folded his length down carefully beside her. It had been his first full day in the fields striving to regain his strength. She had been surprised when she returned from her nursing to find he was still working. 'Pushing himself too hard,' her father had said, nodding approval as she had quickly packed the bag.

'You've found it hard work, digging out gnarled old vine roots.'

'Your father didn't let me do too much of that. He had me stoking the fires more than anything else,' he said, but still arched his back and neck muscles again.

'Good. You must be careful, not damage any of the tissues and muscles that are still healing.' She pushed a hand up inside his loose blue workman's shirt, massaging his shoulders, then as he gave a low groan of satisfaction she knelt beside him, urged him out of the shirt and continued to knead the shoulder muscles with gentle effectiveness.

'Stella should be back tomorrow,' he said as she worked, 'and Victor probably.'

'From points north and south, yes.'

'You should have a medal for extreme valour,' he said.

'Why? What are you talking about? Some nonsense ...'

'You are on dangerous territory here. A massage, she offers.'

She slapped him lightly on his uninjured side.

'Ouch,' he obliged.

'I'm not worried. I've dealt with patients like you before.' Gently she let her fingers fall down with the lightest of passes over the jagged scar running from the middle of his back across to his left hip.

She was in a tender dilemma. She wanted him healed, but she wanted him to stay with her while she helped nurse the many in need of care at Cleauville – and she knew she could not have both.

Only when her fingers came to rest where the scar ran below his trouser belt did he ask, 'What do you do with such patients?'

She leaned her head on his back and laughed. 'You don't really want to know.'

'I want to know everything you've ever done,' he answered.

'Does that hurt?' she asked, testing the tightness of the belt over his injury with one finger.

He drew in his breath and bent lower over his knees and for a moment she wondered if her touch had pained him.

'I think you should look,' he said and the belt slackened over her finger, 'give me a full examination.'

'Oh!' she said; her voice held a tremor which did not match the words. 'This would be where in London we would have fetched matron, who must have weighed sixteen, seventeen stones, and she ...'

'Non!' he protested. 'Horrors! Tell me no more.' He turned and pulled her round and down into his lap and stooped to kiss her. 'I can feel your lips smiling,' he said, moving his own on hers.

In exchange she turned her head a little sideways and brushed his cheek with her eyelashes. 'That is a butterfly kiss,' she said, blinking against his face.

'Butterfly Blair,' he whispered, 'do you know what I'd like to do?' His fierce growl made her squirm like a child listening to a grim fairystory. 'I'd like to pin you in my collection. "Butterfly Blair" I would write underneath. A unique specimen, but does not like other specimens displaying false colours.'

She could chuckle now as she remembered her own reaction to Jean-Paul's sudden appearance as Monsieur Claude Rennie. 'Another characteristic,' she interrupted, 'is that it mates for life.'

'Does it?' he asked carefully, 'and has this ... unique, magnificent, specimen found its mate?'

'Oh yes, it's on its honeymoon.'

He stooped and flicked his eyelash on her cheek. 'The butterfly summer,' he breathed.

She remembered that some butterflies only lived for a day, emerged from their cocoon, flew a brief time in all their splendour, mated, then died. She turned to him, the agony already in her heart. 'You'll go back, won't you?' she stated flatly, 'as soon as the message comes.'

'Oui. We can't stop fighting until the war is won.' Then as if he saw the protest coming he kissed her gently, sipping the words from her lips, stopping her ever practical objections. 'Be a butterfly my love,' he whispered, 'live for now, bask in today's sun, take no need for the morrow.'

'As you do?'

'Touché.' He breathed into her neck.

'I remember Stella's father having a gardener who used to say, "Do as I say not as I do."'

'Such hypocrisy,' he said, but the words sounded like an endearment as his hand stroked the length of her bare arm.

She reached up and touched his shoulder. 'Your skin is still warm from the sun.'

He bent close over her. There were so many glib, amusing answers he could make. Until Lucille his encounters with women had been mostly after parties, usually in his wild Parisian days costume parties, where it was easy to play the role of Casanova. He knew this girl was his true love because for once in his life he did not want to disappear behind a façade, he wanted to be himself. He looked down into the lucid straightforward honesty of her eyes. 'I love you Lucille,' he said, 'with all my heart, mind and being.'

'And I love you,' she said.

He stooped to kiss her gently, but the touch of their lips burned between them with a tender intensity. He drew away very very slowly as if the separation might be painful.

She looked up at him with adoring wonder in her eyes. 'You always make me want to say stupid things, not like me ...'

'Like?'

'Come fly with me,' she ventured.

'Promise always to say stupid things like that – but only to me.'

'I promise,' she said and knew they had entered the special time when words were just like actors covering the exploratory movements of the love game. They had made love before; each time seemed a greater miracle to him. Gently he undid the buttons of her dress – she sat up, helped pull it over her head. All she knew for certain as they took off their clothes was that she loved him more than she loved herself, more than anyone else in the world, more than life. She could, she told herself, certainly die for him without a second thought.

Together they were cupped in this green Eden and as she selflessly gave and he carefully took, they did fly, wonderfully, amazingly together.

'*Mon Dieu!*' he said, awe-struck as he looked at her, '*je t'adore, toujours*, for ever.'

'And ever,' she added. 'Jean, I ...' She reached up, languid now, and touched his lips. 'Do you remember making that little paper boat?' she asked suddenly wanting to tell him of the stupid way her heart had leapt in alarm when it had nearly been swept from the table – wanting to tell him to take more care.

He shook his head, looked puzzled, then both heard someone calling their names, someone not far away.

'It's Stella,' she said, 'and *she'll* know where we are.'

'You shared a lot, you two,' he said almost wistfully.

'Not as much as we're going to share,' she told him. Then it was a bit of a scramble putting on clothes and repacking the uneaten supper. They hurried to the top of La Tasse and there was Stella waving and coming smiling towards them.

'She seems excited,' he said.

'Welcome back!' he called when they were in range. 'Successful mission?'

'Yes, no problems at all,' she said as she hurried to be by their side, 'but I've just heard a message I'm sure is from my father!'

Lucille stopped and gasped in joyful astonishment, waiting for an explanation.

'I called to see Pas de Crédit on the way back – for more petrol if he had it – and he and Edmund were making their eight o'clock call. There was some routine stuff, then a message came relayed from England. The operator's code name was "Redhead" and the message spoke of knowing that one brother was safe by the river, and hoped everything was fine for the other three.' Stella paused then exclaimed, 'It could only have been my father, don't you think?'

'I do,' Lucille agreed thoughtfully, then the next moment realising how wonderful that really was, the two of them wrapped their arms around each other and did a little jig down the path in front of Jean-Paul. Even as they rejoiced Lucille was aware that Stella would not be able to keep her condition secret much longer. 'Were you able to send a message back?'

'Yes, old Pas de Crédit's a real expert, he's got an old tarpaulin over some terrible old machinery, and hidden inside a threshing drum thing which opens up, there's a spiffing short-wave radio! It's amazing, and of course it's mobile, so there's not so much chance of it being picked up. He can transmit from a different place every time!'

'We know! While you and Victor are gadding around everyone else has been working on it!' Lucille exclaimed. 'So what did you send back?'

'Something stupid like "Redhead One, this is Redhead Two, all well in the south."' She laughed, full of the pleasure of the tenuous contact. 'Wasn't it lucky I was there just at that moment? And you see what it means?'

'That Philip's safe,' Lucille said. 'He must have got out at Dunkirk.'

'And that my father must be working with the Free French in London!' Stella stopped and beamed at both of them. 'Don't you think?'

'It does look like it,' Jean-Paul confirmed. Forming a fist to give the air an uppercut he enthused, 'Resistance is growing!'

'Then the line began to break up,' Stella said, 'and Pas de Crédit signed off, but he was so pleased, I gave him a hug and he blushed! Right down to the roots of his overalls.'

'You're top of the world then,' Lucille said nodding, posing the tacit question about her afternoon sickness.

'I feel wonderful! A good mission, we got six out over the demarcation line and they're on the way to Spain, then the radio. This makes it today I am going to tell Ernest and everyone my news.'

'It is time,' Lucille agreed, linking arms with her.

'What's this?' Jean-Paul asked, but both girls shook their heads at him. He pretended to sulk, kicking a stone ahead of himself, making them laugh as Jean-Paul became a moody, scowling schoolboy.

Stella, who for the past week had suddenly and unexpectedly stopped feeling queasy at inconvenient times and had begun to feel physically well and mentally uplifted by the news of her father and brother, had started to think the telling of her condition would be nothing, or at least easier because of the good news.

Later in the farm kitchen the radio message was discussed from every angle. Then they speculated about Victor's return, which should be on the following day, and about Pierre's decision to leave them and make his way on to his own home. Then the level of chatter fell – and she felt Lucille's gaze on her.

Ernest was replenishing glasses. Stella frowned. It was always easy for other people to push you to face unpleasant decisions, like rushing you to the doctors when they would never be so keen to go themselves. She *had been* waiting her opportunity, watching Ernest as he played host to them all – he appeared at ease – and now she was about to bring him another problem.

She remembered the whispered stories about unmarried mothers. Some girls, sent on protracted holidays, later came back alone, sad and languid. Others were sent to some aunt or other, and the babies were farmed out to suitable couples, or the family moved at the appropriate time and returned with a baby to be brought up as a younger brother or sister to their real mother. It was always the girl's fault.

She could return to Paris, even though Madeleine had obviously thought it was better for her to stay in the country. Wherever she ended up, she wasn't going to make an invalid of herself ... she would not be a burden.

Ernest rose and went to the door. 'This is a bit of an occasion, we'll try some of the new wine, Hector, drink young Philip's health.' But he refused the old soldier's help as he picked up a bottle crate and left the kitchen.

Ernest on his own suddenly seemed a much better option. Stella jumped up and went to the door, startling Hector who half rose to his feet. 'You heard something outside?'

'No, no,' she told him, putting her hand on his shoulder. 'I have something I want to talk to Ernest about, and Lucille has something to tell you both while I've gone.'

'Have I?' Lucille asked and Stella nodded firmly to her. 'Please. Then I won't put this off again.'

Ernest consciously kept his shoulders square and his bearing upright until he was out of sight, then his stride shortened and slowed. By the time he reached the doors of the huge barn he had to make a real effort of will to pull open the heavy door.

He walked into the dimness and stood for a moment closing his eyes, fighting for self control. He had watched Lucille laughing, saw her glances at this man Jean-Paul, and had felt Gaby so close, he believed he only need have stretched out his hand and she would have taken it.

Come to me now, he yearned. These youngsters, Gaby, they don't know how quickly time goes, they think it will all last for ever. They think I'm coping. He wasn't sure whether the anguished laughter was aloud or in his head. 'Help me, Gaby,' he whispered as he went to the bench near the door where Hector did the bottling.

His thoughts were broken into as he heard a discreet shuffle of a foot and a cough.

'I didn't want to make you jump,' Stella said as she came slowly into the barn, 'you looked so thoughtful.'

'Searching for the matches,' he said, wondering and a little irritated that she had followed him. 'Lose my head if it were loose.'

She watched Ernest as he found the matches in his pocket and lit first a lantern, then a candle. He lifted a bottle from a group at one end of the bench and held it before the candle flame, looking at the wine's clarity and colour. She knew even then – had she been able – she would have chickened out, but already Lucille would be breaking her news in the kitchen.

'You should learn about the wines we make, Jacques was never much interested. Unless it was written in a book I don't think he believed it!'

'I'd like to learn,' she said, 'but I need to talk to you – about something else.'

'Good! Good!' He heard himself picking up the strings of normality, giving out the right messages, while inwardly he recognised the true meaning of being heartsick. 'You must learn all I know, but more importantly you must learn from old Hector. What he doesn't know about wine ...'

141

She dropped her head as he enthused, feeling that not telling him immediately amounted to deception. She guessed that in peacetime, and certainly if either she or Lucille had a mother between them, the wedding ceremony would have been brought forward with great haste. She would have been a bride in no time. The one thing she was grateful for was that Jacques had told his family that he did intend to marry her.

Ernest lowered the bottle to the table, and for the first time since she had appeared in the barn really looked at this English girl with the cropped dyed black hair. 'What is it?' he asked. 'My dear girl ... is Jacques all right? You've not had bad news?'

She shook her head. 'No, nothing like that. Jacques is fine as far as I know.'

'He's such an eager fool for anything he believes in, I always feel he'll be martyred in the end!'

'That wasn't quite the way I was thinking of him.' She paused, took an involuntary step towards Jacques's father and went on quickly. 'To be honest I'm expecting his baby.'

There was silence; the flame of the candle wavered in the draught of Ernest's hand as it fell to the bench. 'Good God!' he breathed.

Stella watched him for some further reaction, wondering quite what else she could say. She wondered if she should apologise, half opened her lips to do so, but he truly did seem speechless at the news.

Ernest was listening to a inner voice. 'Show her you care. Look at the girl, she's terrified of what you are going to say, what you are going to do.'

'Yes,' he said as if in answer to a question Stella had asked.

'I'm sorry,' she said, 'sorry it's such a shock.'

'Seems old Hector's going to have a busy time teaching everyone about our wine!'

He held out his arms and she ran to him. 'You're so like Jacques,' she said gratefully.

'Don't think he'd thank you for saying that.' He kissed her on both cheeks. 'So we have more planning to do,' he said and a huge involuntary sigh overtook him, 'but then there's Lucille, Nadia, Jeannette Chabrol – plenty of women to call on.'

'So you don't mind if I stay and the baby's born here?'

He was surprised at the question. 'Where else?' he asked, 'and if we can get Jacques here we might manage to arrange the wedding first!' He regretted the light-hearted, if true, remark as Stella's face clouded over.

'If,' she repeated, 'but he doesn't even know about the baby yet. I

142

kind of didn't really know myself until I got back here.'

'Well, well, I reckon it does these journalists good to be on the receiving end of the news sometimes. Look, my dear, you go back and tell the others, because I'm going to bring some special wine in to celebrate the advent of my grandchild.'

Stella let him go, carrying the crate and the lantern down to where a shallow cellar led off midway between wine-vats and bottling bench. It felt like a major hurdle overcome.

Ernest felt more as if he was going to ground, running away to hide, than fetching wine to celebrate – celebrate a grandchild without his Gaby!

'Why are you not with me when I need you?' he whispered and the anger of his loss made him want to throw the lantern into a pile of old wicker baskets and burn the whole place down. He talked of teaching an unborn grandchild about the wine but he could not envisage that future, any future. He wanted to break and crash about, as the finality of his loss overwhelmed him.

He sat on the brick thrall, put his head in his hands and gripped his hair, threatening to pull it from his scalp. 'Gaby!' The name echoed around the cellar, but there was no answer, no hand on his shoulder, no murmur he could catch.

They'll miss you soon.

'I know,' he answered the thought.

The wine. You laid some down the day Jacques was born.

He nodded. 'So I did.'

Six bottles.

'Yes.' He rose and found the rack with the date on it.

Just two now.

He acknowledged Gaby's good common sense. 'Just two,' he agreed.

Chapter Fifteen

Madam Verit always managed to produce a glass of wine for Jacques when he visited her at her granddaughter's flat. If anything the immediate hospitality added to his sense of guilt about Verit himself.

All he had learned was that the newspaper where he and Verit had worked was riddled with informers and collaborators. Professor Thierry had found out Verit had been taken to the Cherche-Midi prison to await trial, that the interrogating officer was a German who spoke perfect French, and Verit had been 'interviewed' on numerous occasions. Madame Verit had been allowed to hand in clothes with food and notes hidden inside, but on the last occasion the bundle had been pushed back at her and she had been told not to come again.

Madame Verit was totally sure only of one thing, which she emphasised to Jacques whenever her husband was mentioned. 'He would never have given you away, old fool that he was.' He raised the glass to her and to Verit, never commenting on her use of the past tense.

She had been as good as her word, picking up the news-sheets Jacques produced every fortnight. Always she had a cabbage, or a loaf, on top of her roomy old shopping bag as she portered the weighty ream of printed pages across Paris under the noses of the Germans. Her worst moment had been when a young German soldier had stooped to lift her bag on to a bus. 'Look after your own grandmother!' she had abruptly told him, sweeping the bag from under his hand.

Marie, her granddaughter, had organised teams of fellow students who took a few news-sheets each and pushed them through letter-boxes, slipped them into magazines on news stands, left them on café tables, even pushed them into people's pockets. Jacques sat sipping his wine, thinking how much contact with Marie and her friends, only some four, five or six years younger than himself, had helped not just his Resistance work, but the gap in his life after Stella had gone south.

The constant flow of ideas – practical and wild – that came from the university commune sharpened his wits, kept him going at this time when his immediate friends and loved ones were no longer around.

Going more often to the museum he had access to the new radio links. The messages received from the Cleauville frequency reassured him that their work was going well. He knew of 'Redhead' and 'Redhead Two', knew Jean-Paul had been asked to stay on the unoccupied side of the demarcation line to supervise the movement of British, French, Dutch and Polish soldiers through France, to Spain, Portugal and on to England to rejoin the fight. With the death sentence now mandatory for anyone sheltering such men it had become more urgent to move them out of the city.

October in Paris had been a month of rising tension. German posters threatening punishments and death multiplied, but nothing stopped the telephone cables being cut, or the rise in the number of tracts, pamphlets and clandestine newspapers that were distributed.

By the end of October when Pétain announced a need for 'genuine collaboration with Hitler' there were few Frenchmen unaware of the duplicity of the terms accepted on their behalf. The Latin Quarter of the Sorbonne and the students' lodgings were beginning to seethe. More and more de Gaulle stickers and graffiti contradicting the official German posters were appearing, and petrol bombs were being dropped from rooftops on to German vehicles.

Madame Verit had been alone when Jacques had arrived, but soon Marie and a laughing group of young men and women came tumbling into the apartment. They greeted Jacques with enthusiasm, patting him on the back, filling up his glass, while Jacques wanted to know what this particular celebration was about. 'Have you shot Hitler?' he asked.

'No,' one called, 'not us, *you*. You've shot him in the foot!' They all roared with laughter again, and André Tillon who Jacques had first seen watching over Marie and her grandmother the first time he had come to the apartment exclaimed, 'Between us we've made Hitler a laughing stock. Everyone is repeating the story you printed about Moses' stick.' He collapsed into a chair and pulled Marie on to his knee. 'We have just made sure the Germans know the joke, that is all. We've posted up large print versions all over Paris!'

Jacques was guilty of a twinge of jealousy seeing the two together. He had been as far south as Clermont-Ferrand and longed for the day when he could walk into his father's house again. He smiled as he thought of the surprise he would give them.

'It was wonderful!' Marie was enthusing. 'People stopped to read it looking all serious, probably thinking it was another German

145

regulation! Then their faces would change, their shoulders relax. It's like giving someone a tonic making them laugh!'

Andre slapped Marie playfully on the thigh. She swiped him back, then stood up, and with one finger across her top lip to represent the moustache and the other in the Hitlerite salute she pronounced the joke for the assembly.

'Herr Hitler has consulted all the cleverest men he can find. Engineers, mariners, even astrologers. He is desperate to find a way to cross the Channel and conquer the pig-headed English who refuse to surrender. All summer he's tried to find ships to carry his army across the water – and failed. But then someone told him the story of Moses parting the Red Sea, and the people of Israel walking between the waves dry-footed. Hitler demanded to know how it was done, and being told that God provided Moses with a special staff, he said he *must* have it! He *demanded* to know where the rod was. The crowd of wise men fell silent as Hitler raged at them to tell him its whereabouts. Eventually one brave soul replied, "The rod is in the British Museum."'

Marie dropped her pose and added, 'It is what the English call a shaggy dog story.'

They all erupted into laughter again. Jacques shook his head at them, they were in the mood to laugh at anything and everything. Then one of the young men began to tap out the rhythm of the 'Marseillaise' with his fingernails on the table. Immediately there was silence, then one by one, phrase after phrase, others joined in. It was obviously a practised piece. The growing resonance of the beat was at once sinister and inspiring, like threat and promise.

On 28 October London radio added to the feeling of defiance by reminding the French people that Armistice Day would soon be coming. Traditionally the holiday commemorated the victory of France and the Allies over Germany in World War One. London suggested that people should remember the day by laying flowers at the Arc de Triomphe, on the Tomb of the Unknown Soldier and at the foot of the statue of Clémenceau, the 'Tiger of France', in the Champs-Élysées.

The students of the Sorbonne were already making plans to be visible, but confrontation was assured when on 10 November the Paris newspapers carried the announcement: 'Public administration offices and all private establishments will work normally on 11 November in Paris and in the department of the Seine. Commemorative ceremonies will not take place. No public demonstration will be tolerated.' Students received orders to attend their classes all day.

The plans to make sure there was a large but peaceful demonstration

146

of unity against the occupying forces began to feel feeble and inappropriate as the blanket bans became known.

Jacques felt he was regarded as some kind of benevolent uncle figure, when he was primed by André 'not to get involved' but to witness and report on the students' first defiant act of the day.

At first light on 11 November 1940 Jacques was in place as instructed. The city was very quiet, with that special feeling Paris always has in the early mornings, like an elegant lady of uncertain age who has washed, dressed and presented herself as exquisitely as care, and a pink and gold dawn, can make her.

The noise of a lorry coming from the direction of the Place de la Concorde seemed an outrage. Jacques caught his breath as the Citroen truck swung from the Place de la Concorde and up the Champs-Élysées to stop next to Clémenceau's statue. From the back students carried a gigantic wreath with an enormous visiting card a metre or so in length decorated with blue, white and red ribbons. The card bore the name in thick capital letters of its supposed donor 'Le Général de Gaulle'.

The truck left and Jacques moved closer; there were few Parisians about this early but the huge card and wreath drew everyone who glanced that way to it. An elderly man and women approached uncertainly, read the card, then gripped each other in a spontaneous embrace. The man then stood and saluted while the woman put her hands together and bowed her head in prayer. Jacques had the theme and headline for his next article: 'Her Prayer For It To Be True.'

Another woman walked hesitantly to the statue. She looked like a concierge on the way to her duties. She stood a long time soaking in the message on the card, the wreath, then turned away clasping her tattered old bag to herself as if she hugged some joyful secret. He watched while a man with two schoolchildren came to the statue. He flung his arms into the air and waved a thankyou to the heavens, while the children covered their mouths and giggled – but they would remember.

There were others, but then he watched as the police came, quite soon – too soon. They took away the card but left the wreath intact, even so they were too late. The act had been witnessed, approved and the news of it would travel all Paris and France – and the world – that was part of his job. He also ensured that the huge wreath was pointed out and the message of the confiscated visiting card was passed from person to person as the hours went by. The flow of Parisians bearing flowers to the statue of their 'Tiger' grew ever larger, ever more heartwarming. If Jacques had ever doubted the patriotism of the French, ever cursed because he thought people were settling down

147

under the yoke of occupation, he repented now, his heart full of pride and compassion for the many he saw in tears for their country's present state.

Thousands brought their tributes all day long. The air was heavy with the scent of lilies, roses, every kind of flower from the exotically nurtured to the humble garden chrysanthemum. A huge circlet of colour spread like a carpet around Clémenceau, celebrating 'the Tiger', nicknamed for his ferocious attacks on all he found dishonourable and equally savage defence of all he knew to be good.

Madeleine had declared her intention of going to the Tomb of the Unknown Soldier later in the day and Jacques, seeing the ever-growing crowds – and the unease of the police, though they made no attempt to interfere, rushed back to the apartments, wrote his first report while the emotion was high and the impressions sharp, then accompanied Madeleine to the Arc de Triomphe in the afternoon.

They stood for some time watching the crowds milling all around the triumphal archway, symbol of past French triumphs. Madeleine added her spray of red roses and yellow mimosa, bought at no small expense, to the flower piles. Then as they stood on the fringes of the crowd Jacques became aware of a greater police presence and shouts began to be heard. 'Move on, move on! No demonstrations.'

'They're either getting nervous or they've got orders to clear the streets,' Jacques said. 'I think you should make your way home now. I'll be back later.'

They both stopped to listen as a police commissioner came along going from group to group, calling that the Germans were getting angry and wanted the demonstrations ended immediately. His warnings were repeated to those at the back who could not hear. 'Go!' Jacques ordered. 'I know the students are coming after they have finished their classes – that may cause real trouble.' Madeleine nodded and walked quickly away, as units of armed German soldiers now began to patrol the Champs-Élysées.

Jacques raced as quickly as he could towards the end of the Étoile. He was in time only to be overtaken by a great crowd of students coming from the métro. They were unfurling a huge *tricolore* to form a parade. Thousands jammed the Place de l'Étoile and all sides of the high-standing Arc de Triomphe in minutes. Another group just down the hill had found and joined some war veterans. A roar suddenly came up from their ranks. '*Vive la France! À bas Pétain! À bas Hitler! Vive de Gaulle!*'

Above the deep-throated roar of the patriots Jacques thought he heard shots, but he was not sure. Then students, war veterans, patriots, men, women, linked arms and began to sing 'La Marseillaise'.

148

The impassioned strains rose from a thousand throats, rang out the ecstasy and the agony, the pride and the passion. Then came whistles and Jacques saw to his horror the doors of a cinema burst open and German soldiers pour out. They had all this time been waiting there, ready for the moment when the German commander's patience finally snapped. Not only these troops; hearing warning shouts from side streets Jacques climbed to a windowsill to see that convoys of army vehicles were closing in, dropping off machine-gun crews as they came nearer to the centre.

Before he dropped to the ground he saw the soldiers were charging into the group with the veterans. The singing faltered as the Germans ploughed into the unarmed crowds. In the mêlée Jacques heard shots and screams and as he neared the front line, he saw the rise and fall of rifle butts, savagely and mercilessly brought down on unprotected heads, young and old. A grenade exploded and someone screamed in agony. Panic now set in and those who could escape ran in all directions.

Jacques saw an old man felled and lying bleeding and unconscious on the pavement, saw his companion stoop to help him and receive a blow from the same rifle butt. He heard himself scream with rage as he hurled himself at the soldier. His kick caught the man in the small of the back; he fell dropping his rifle. Before Jacques could retrieve it someone else did and gave the fallen man a stunning blow, then ran off with the gun.

He knelt by the old man who was in danger of being trampled to death, then as the pressure of people increased he lifted him up as best he could. The old man's friend scrambled to him, holding his own bleeding head. He grabbed and tugged at Jacques's sleeve, pulling him through the circling and dodging crowd. The soldiers lashed out in all directions using both ends of their rifles as weapons. The students as well as the veterans scattered and dodged, but the man who led Jacques by the sleeve had purpose, knew where he was heading for.

He led them to a narrow passage between two restaurants, pushing his way through a red and yellow canvas blind which concealed the opening. They scurried on into a back yard full of vegetable boxes and wine crates, out through a back gate and along a cobbled entry. At the top they turned through an arched entry, then suddenly out into a street.

'Not much further,' he gasped, grinning at Jacques's bewilderment, 'been nipping in and out of these places since I was a kid.' He paused then to take a breath and inspect the hand he held to his head.

'How is it?'

'Takes more than a German to crack this old skull!' he said disdainfully and led the way on.

149

'It is not too far to where we live,' the man said. 'Can you manage him?'

Jacques nodded, not wasting breath, for even a slender old man took some carrying, but the sounds of the conflict were becoming more muffled as they went.

They came to an apartment block and the man nodded him to the doorway. 'It's here, *mon ami.*'

Jacques carried the other man inside, grateful they lived on the ground floor, and laid him on a chaise longue near the window. 'Can you get a doctor?'

'We have a friend next door,' he said and scurried off now holding a towel to his own head. Jacques gingerly explored the unconscious man for the source of the bleeding. There was a gash at the base of his neck, long, but deep only in the middle, and he had certainly been knocked out cold. The blow to his friend's head had seemed more lethal, Jacques thought, but he was still very much alive.

In moments he was back bringing with him a lady he introduced as 'Nancy, our nurse'. Then he offered to fetch bandages. Nancy greeted him as she examined her patient, who stirred as she decided his neck needed bathing and a pad. His companion returned with an ancient tin from which he took what looked like 1914–18 field dressings.

'When will you two stop playing soldiers?' Nancy rejected them out of hand while a voice from the chaise longue said huskily, 'When the Germans are defeated.'

'Oh!' she exclaimed going over to him, 'so we're not so worried about you any more. I'll look at your cousin's head first then.'

Cousins, brothers in arms, thoughts floated a little haphazardly in and out of Jacques's mind as he sat recovering, watching Nancy patch up the pair. He thought of the two Jewish brothers who had committed suicide together. These two cousins had nearly done the same. Then there was old Hector. He wondered if he was still persisting in raising the *tricolore* each morning. The courage of the old, like Madeleine, Verit, Madame Verit, often overwhelmed him.

At last satisfied that these two old soldiers would live to fight another day he took his leave. They were reluctant to let him go, fulsome in their thanks, with Nancy unexpectedly catching and kissing his hand saying how much she cared for 'these two old rascals'.

He did not want to be out on the streets too late that evening; he could guess there would still be much activity. He was torn between going home to make sure Madeleine was all right and going to Marie's to see how her friends had fared.

He decided he did not have sufficient daylight left on that November Monday to go over to the students' lodgings, so he made for home. In the distance he could still hear abnormal activity: engines, occasional shouts and once running.

He was near his home square when turning a corner he confronted a small group of German soldiers. It was too late to do more than drop his head and keep moving – try to keep moving – for he found himself confronted by a solid wall of broad-shouldered Nazi uniforms.

'So?' a voice questioned.

Heart thumping, he mumbled a good night and tried to walk around the group. His collar was immediately grabbed and he was swung off his feet. As he fell to the ground his coat fell open to reveal his shirt heavily stained with the old man's blood.

'Ah! just so! In the thick of the action were you! Well, don't worry, we will round you all up eventually.' The next moment a jackboot kicked into his side. He did not look up as the man, full of the glory of power, screamed instructions, and the toe of the boot drew back to strike again.

Without a thought he spat as much phlegm as he could muster on the highly polished leather. He felt a strange hot and searing sensation on his head and a curtain of black rolled down over his eyes.

Chapter Sixteen

Stella was alone and feeling resentful; her new role as a cross between housekeeper and Hector's assistant watchkeeper did not excite her. She felt they were all conspiring to relegate her, decommission her, confine her to barracks until after the baby was born. Ernest was the worst and she really felt fine – fat but fine – her baby could not be due until January or even early February and – the next moment she spun round in alarm as a man spoke quietly from the doorway.

'Pardon!' Edmund Chabrol said, 'I tried not to startle you.'

'Did Hector see you?' she asked, aware that one of them should have seen or heard his approach.

He smiled the tight little movement which seemed all his lips would allow. 'Oh yes, he waved from the orchard.'

'Everyone else is out.' She reached for a coffee cup but he shook his head.

'It's you I've come to see,' he told her and her heart gave a flip of concern.

'Jacques?'

He nodded.

'Tell me,' she said and sat down, hands spread on the table before her.

'He's been detained, but he's still in Paris.'

'Detained! By the ...'

'SS.'

She was for a moment too distraught, her heart pounding too loudly, to hear more. She saw Edmund's lips forming words – information she was missing – and forced herself to hear, to listen.

'No one missed him for a night and a day. His landlady ...'

'Madame Astier.'

He nodded. 'Thought he must have gone to a see a certain Madame Verit who lives with her granddaughter, a student at the Sorbonne.

The next day she went there ...'

She remembered being introduced to Verit in the square near Jacques's apartment, and being entertained by stories of his stormy relationship with his overbearing wife.

'A huge Armistice Day demonstration has led to many arrests,' Edmund was saying. 'There are many many students just missing – some detained here, some there – but one or two are now released and we know where Jacques is.'

Stella, watching him intently, saw there was something he intended: this master planner had an idea. 'And?' she prompted.

He stood up and turned his back on her, reminding her of old pictures of Napoleon, hands clasped behind his back, planning war strategies. 'This isn't a moment for niceties, there is not time. We have worked out a scheme which might save his life, but it involves you.'

'His life,' she whispered.

'Yes.' He turned to face her, his coal black eyes glittering, uncompromising. 'The longer he is in prison the greater the risks. Has Jacques ever spoken to you of Professor Thierry?'

She shook her head. Words would not form as she thought of the awful prospects he was outlining. Then she remembered hearing Jean-Paul talk of such a man, but Edmund was already going on, as always at speed.

'Professor Thierry, code name Panther, is in a position of some importance in Paris. He is desperate that Jacques should be rescued before he can be ...' He paused to make a gesture into the air. Her knowledge, imagination and fear filled the gap as he went on '... be transferred from the Paris prison to a concentration camp, which could be anywhere, Germany, Holland! But we need your help.'

'Anything,' she said urgently. 'Tell me.'

'Professor Thierry knows this particular prison and its surroundings very well indeed. There is a small hospital which adjoins it, but which has separate entrances. His assistant, a young woman, has been into that hospital and believes if a prisoner was sick enough and transferred to that hospital it might be possible for him to escape.'

'Sick enough?' she queried.

'My father can arrange that.' He paused as if to allow her to absorb these details. 'People have been allowed to take parcels for prisoners, one or two even to see their partners. If you were to go to the prison posing as Jacques's wife ...'

'My condition would be an advantage,' she said immediately.

'Well, yes!' His smile was a bit wider this time and he nodded approval of her spirit.

153

'And if it's someone Jacques knows and trusts.'

'And the authorities do *not* know, but there will be no room for errors or time for second thoughts.' He pushed his hand into his inside pocket and drew out a small folder. 'Madame,' he said, spreading a little fan of papers out, on top of which lay the necessary permit for her to cross back into the Occupied Zone, all in the name of one Madame Lamonte.

She ran a finger under her forged married name. 'Ernest will not be very happy. I feel he's putting my and Jacques's coming child into part of the gap left by Gaby.'

Edmund nodded. 'But I think he will see the sense of what Professor Thierry and I have planned,' he said. 'I'll talk to him.'

'I couldn't just go now?'

'Maurice Chaillet, Pas de Crédit as you call him, will come for you in the morning.'

'You have *everything* arranged.'

He nodded. 'It is how we will beat the Germans, planning, nibbling away at their organisations all the time.'

'You were sure I would go.'

The smile parted his lips. 'I have come to know you very well. I knew no one would stop you.'

Madame Astier was at the Gare de Lyon to meet her. Her joy at seeing the familiar face and figure, cloaked as it were by the pretence of an aunt waiting for her pregnant country niece, made it easy for them both to embrace and kiss and exclaim with delight in a most natural way.

'So the baby grows,' Madeleine nodded her approval, 'but you look tired.'

'Only from the journey I assure you, it is a long way.' If she momentarily closed her eyes she could still see the flashing expanses of the Rhone in its great valleys, vineyards, wheatfields, meadowlands, still trundling past her eyes, making her feel unsteady.

'That is good, because,' Madame paused to shake her head and to ensure that no one was near enough to overhear their conversation, 'you have no time for respite. I have to take you straight to the home of Marie Weilburg, the granddaughter of Madame Verit. There also will come the assistant of Professor Thierry who knows the hospital next to the prison. I think you will have to be strong, brave and tireless.'

'To rescue Jacques I will be,' she said, but the dragging tiredness of her body and the empty-headed stupidity which comes with extreme fatigue made her hope that there might be at least a pause before she was expected to be all the things Madeleine asked of her. She must make no mistakes – no margin for error, Edmund had said.

Arriving at the granddaughter's flat they found Madame Verit alone. Stella had expected a domineering person, large in size and manner. Instead she found a bird-thin but virile and aggressive woman eager not only to meet Jacques's girl, but to instruct her in the ways of taking clothes and food into a prison, while never labouring the lack of information about the fate of her own husband.

Stella was fed and taken to a bedroom to rest quietly until 'the mademoiselle from the museum' arrived. She took off her shoes and lay down. But once on the bed her mind was suddenly alert, racing. Any idea of a brief nap deserted her in the anticipation of what they were to attempt. No, not attempt, do! What they were to *do*. Yet it hardly seemed real. She could not imagine Jacques in a prison. The free spirit of the man, the evangelist, incarcerated? How would he look? What would they have done to him? She remembered Edmund's pause '... should be rescued before he can ...' Her mind now added 'be made to talk.'

She was sitting on the edge of the bed when barely fifteen minutes later Madame Verit came to tell her that their visitor had arrived. Stella was delighted to recognise the petite Frenchwoman who had smuggled the radio from the museum, and come looking for Maxim and the newspaper lorry.

The recognition was mutual and overwhelmingly friendly, but this woman made no secret of her surprise. 'You are,' she said, '*enceinte*, with child – we did not know this! It is a dangerous thing you will be doing. Jacques ...'

'Is the father of my child.' She shrugged, then feeling the statement sounded blunt, cold, she added, 'And I love him more than my life, or this child I do not yet know.'

The young woman caught her arm and nodded vigorously. 'Of course, I understand. But the plan must be undertaken tonight, this evening, there is not one hour to be lost. You have brought the tablets?'

Stella nodded and took the unlabelled packet from her deep dress pocket. Dr Chabrol had supplied her with hormone pills women took to lose weight, but which given to a man produce a raging fever.

Madeleine produced a corduroy jacket, trousers and underwear from her bag. 'From his apartment,' she said, placing them next to the packet.

'*Très bon!*' the young woman exclaimed, then taking a pencil and notepad from her purse went on, 'My code name you should know is "Cub", Jacques will recognise it.' She tore a page from the book and

155

began to draw a street plan. 'This is the prison.' A cross on the page. 'This is the gate where relations and visitors have to go.' A short line slanted inwards. 'Once inside you must try to see Jacques, give him the pills and tell him to take them all as soon as he gets back into his cell.' She sighed. 'We cannot risk putting the pills in the clothes because everything is searched, and often not given to the prisoners for days, weeks, if at all. Your condition may help,' she paused and shrugged, 'they may take pity on you. Perhaps you could make up some story about the doctor saying you may not survive the birth and you wish to see your husband just once more. Don't alarm him too much however.'

For a moment Stella felt hysteria threaten at the melodrama which was *not* to alarm Jacques. 'He does not know I am pregnant. So it will be some surprise for him to find that not only is he married but he is soon to be a father.'

'It may however, make him more determined to escape,' Cub asserted, with Madeleine and Madame Verit making sympathetic but positive noises of agreement.

'So will the pills make him ill enough?' Madeleine asked, looking at the slim packet.

'A raging fever.' Stella repeated what she had been told.

'The Germans will immediately be alarmed,' Cub went on. 'The conditions in the prison are ripe for some epidemic or other, they won't want to risk it spreading. Jacques will be transferred to the small hospital next to the prison. It is the routine, Germans like routine.'

Now the plans on a second piece of notepaper became more detailed. The hospital, the entrance hall, reception desk, clinics, treatment rooms, the ward for prisoners.

'How do you know all this?' Stella asked, astonished. 'Have you worked there?'

'I knew the name of a doctor who was off duty last night. I took a small black attaché case, containing a few medical magazines I stole from a library, and went all around asking for this particular doctor. I just kept saying I had been directed to the different departments. It was very easy really.'

'It was very courageous,' Madame Verit said. 'The kind of courage I know my old fellow had.'

'So it has to be tonight?'

Stella nodded, acknowledging what both women said, while wishing Madame Verit would not talk of her husband in the past tense.

'Then tomorrow morning I shall again take my briefcase. I know exactly where Jacques will be, and in my case I shall have a pair of workmen's blues. Jacques will put these on, then walk along the corridor to this utility room. The guard on this isolation unit is at the far end. From that window ...' Another neat sketch showed the utility-room window, a guttering, a first-storey roof, a dotted line from window to guttering, then up and over that roof. 'And here, in this street, another colleague will be watching. As soon as Jacques appears on the roof he will drive a lorry close to the wall. Jacques will realise he is to let himself down on to the lorry. It should take only minutes from room, to roof, to lorry. Then away, but not too fast, not speeding.'

'And you?' Stella queried.

'I should still be inside delivering a package of medical magazines for my absent doctor, creating a diversion.'

'And me? Where can I wait for him?' She glanced doubtfully at Madeleine; the apartment hardly seemed a good idea.

'There will be a big outcry, searches, swift reprisals. We'll need you and Jacques somewhere secure. My professor would prefer you to be at the museum. We can make you comfortable, and he needs to talk to Jacques as soon as possible.' She paused and looked at the two older women. 'Madame Astier, you should stay in your apartment, both of you keep out of sight for as long as you can. Do your shopping today, then stay in for as many days as possible.' Her hand described a swift exit from sight.

She rose to leave, picking up the pencilled drawings as she did so. 'You know all this?' Cub asked. Stella nodded and the pieces of paper were thrust into the burning stove.

She was surprised how much she recognised of the buildings as she approached clutching the bundle of clothes and her handbag, but with the pills carefully folded inside the double cuff of her coat. She did not have to feign the weariness as she climbed the steps, or the apprehension as she approached the blond German soldier behind the desk.

She stood silently, as instructed, until he looked up. His eyes went from her face to her 'wedding-ring' to her condition. He nodded his permission for her to speak.

'I am the wife of one of your prisoners. I have come a long way to see him – perhaps for the last time – I am not well.' She dropped her eyes downwards and added in a whisper, 'Things are not right.'

'Prisoner's name?'

'Henri Lamonte.'

'Hmm! No chance I would think. I'll give him those things if you wish.'

'Merci,' she murmured gratefully, and meekly handed over the bundle. 'If there would be any ... last chance for me.'

He tutted, then sighed. 'Sit down.' He gestured to a thin small bench behind her.

He went through to a room behind the reception office, then she heard another door being knocked and he seemed to be talking to someone in a yet more inner sanctum. She heard her situation being explained, then a crisp comment she did not catch and an abrupt hoot of humourless laughter. Was she being denied access? She prepared herself to make a more dramatic appeal.

The man came back some minutes later, accompanied by a woman officer, sturdy, strait-jacketed into her uniform, hard-faced. She did not speak to Stella, just took away her handbag and hurled it casually on to the counter, then motioned her to stand and flipped her hands to indicate Stella should raise her arms. Swiftly and intrusively she searched her body, lastly running her hands down Stella's arms. The slim packet carefully placed beneath the buttons on her cuff was not detected. She carefully controlled a sigh of relief, and to hide the emotion she reached for the handbag. The woman's fist came down hard on her hand. Stella now controlled the urge to retaliate.

'You'll get it when you come out,' the soldier said. 'Come this way. You've been granted ten minutes.'

He led her along a dark corridor with heavily barred windows one side, doors the other. Some way along he stopped, unlocked a door, ushered her in, and left her there, locking her in. She fought against a shudder which spread up from her back to her shoulders and arms. So this was what it was like to be imprisoned, at the mercy of the people with the keys and the power.

She looked carefully around. There was a desk with a chair behind it, and another chair, the one on which she sat – and there was a smell. A smell she at once recognised but could not place. She knew she had encountered this same mild stench before. Another shudder quickened across her back and shook her body with a violent spasm as she remembered. It was the smell she always associated with the sawdust strewn on the floor of the local butcher's shop; as a child she could remember drawing patterns on the floor. It had stirred this same smell of rawness, it had always reminded her that the meat being ordered came from the living animals in the fields. So had people bled here, was the questioning and the torturing done in this very room? Had Jacques sat here, where she was sitting? She turned her eyes towards the walls, all around, searching for tell-tale signs. There was she realised also another ingredient to the smell, one she had not appreciated until now – it was fear.

Two days before, Jacques had been well aware of the room's purpose

158

when he had first become conscious. He knew he was not in a cell, nor was he alone. He recognised the voice of the officer whose boots he had spat on. Not, he told himself as he lay doggo, a very clever thing to have done.

A huge hand descended on his collar and he was hauled up on to a chair, held there in the same titan's grip. The officer whose boot he had defiled came forward and spat full in his face. Jacques felt the man's spittle on his own lips; revolted, he forced himself to remain motionless.

'So! A man of steel, a Frenchman of steel!' The officer gave a brief hoot of laughter. 'We shall see.'

Jacques was aware of the nod, then saw that the original giant in uniform had a mate. A matched pair, he remembered thinking before the beating began. The force of the blows at first startled with their ferocity, but most chilling was the businesslike manner in which they were delivered. This was a job, their work; then as a blow landed with exquisite accuracy into his groin, he thought no, it was more a skill, a profession even. There was no emotion, no pity, no acknowledgement that what they dealt with was of their own kind, was human.

He had not been asked any questions. He guessed that would come later, after this softening-up process, and as he tried to absorb each new attack he remembered his own personal vow. He had sworn that if ever he found himself in such a situation, he would say nothing. Not a word.

He soon began to pray for unconsciousness, struggling against any groan or sign of pain. When he fell off the chair they kicked him about the floor like an outsize rag-doll before lifting him back to the seat.

Then the officer did begin to ask him questions, but he schooled himself not to listen, just to take the beating, just to hope for oblivion. He remembered as he fell from the chair again one of the men dragging him by the ankles, swinging him, his head hitting the wall. Nearly knocked senseless, stupid thoughts kept popping into his head. These people were not very fussy with their guests. He'd complain to the management. He'd certainly tell someone, someday.

He stared back at the officer and noticed with some satisfaction that his fury had made white spittle, like fine froth, collect in the corners of his mouth. The man came nearer and asked what sounded like the same question about the Armistice Day demonstrations. Jacques did not attempt to answer, merely shaking his head. The officer took his burning cigarette from the ashtray and stubbed it out deep into Jacques's neck. He heard and smelt his own skin burning and screamed inside his head like an animal trapped at the end of its tether. The two soldiers held him as if he were a child, as fresh cigarettes were lit, the officer inhaling

159

deeply a few times so the ends glowed, and the process was repeated in his palms.

'So, Henri Lamonte, you are a hard man!'

He heard his pseudonym hissed in his ear. It felt like a victory even as the blanket of dark red pain engulfed his vision. He was then dragged from the room; he remembered seeing the doorframe swing over his head, then as he was twisted towards a cell his leg was trapped behind the wall, and the angle at which they propelled him forward too acute. The men heaved relentlessly, and he heard his mother's voice from childhood: 'Your legs are too long, that's your trouble' and he heard a terrible crack. They had broken his leg, mid-calf somewhere.

The next sensation he remembered was of someone moistening his lips with a finger dipped into water. He licked his lips and looked up into Verit's face, but even as he opened his mouth to exclaim Verit put a finger first over his lips then over his own, then cupped his hands behind his ears. The message was clear: the Germans were listening.

It was as hard a task to disguise pleasure as pain. Old Verit was alive – haggard, thin, filthy – but alive! Then he saw that the fingers that mimed caution had no nails. He closed his eyes and groaned. 'Courage, stranger,' Verit said aloud. 'Courage!' He wiped his moistened finger again across Jacques's lips. Had they been deliberately put into the cell together to see if either would reveal anything, any information they had been unable to batter and torture from either of them? Verit had been a prisoner a long time.

'I should introduce myself, my name is Henri Lamonte.'

'Verit, everyone used to call me Old Verit.'

The two men leaned to each other, each hearing the other gasp, near to tears, swallow hard.

'I think my leg is broken,' Jacques said after some moments to regain control. 'Could you take off my shoe?'

Verit ministered to him as best he could. 'It's your shin bone, it's straight, but ... ' he raised his voice a little, 'they should send for a doctor to set it properly.' Then he bound all around the lower calf with his own longer socks.

'You take my socks,' Jacques gasped before the pain swept over him and he passed out again.

He came to briefly and saw that Verit was lying on the floor by him, watching, and as he stirred coming again to moisten his lips. 'Lie very still,' Verit advised, 'it is all you can do.'

When first light came the cell door was opened and Verit was taken away. It was a bigger torment than his leg or his burns, or his bruises,

160

not to call out to his old friend as he was led off.

Despair now set in, and as the day passed with neither food nor water brought to him and the water Verit had shared with him gone, Jacques tried to keep some control by composing reports of everything that had happened. One day he would tell the story to the world. He came near to tears when examining his leg he found it bandaged with carefully torn strips of what could only be Verit's shirt. So all the man would have was a ragged jumper. Such devotion, such kindness, he decided, far outweighed the inhumanity of his captors and this he burned to tell.

Of all his injuries his leg was the least painful, if he kept still, but on the morning of the second day he was forced upright and being dragged, and hopping as best he could, he was taken once more to the room. This time the officer sat behind the desk and he was put on the chair facing. 'Stand up!' the officer barked, his lips twisting into a smirk of enjoyment.

'You've cracked my bloody leg,' Jacques retorted – and he had broken his own vow of complete silence. It felt like a terrible defeat, a chink in his armour.

'Ah! So it has a voice. So tell us all about yourself.' He clicked his fingers and the two SS men from the day before appeared at the sound. 'Put him on his feet, to attention!'

The men lifted Jacques clear of the seat and the ground; as he landed he felt the bone move and he lurched sideways. He gritted his teeth. He did not mean to waste this pain, so he feigned unconsciousness, and the officer seemed suddenly to lose patience with him, pushing his chair back so violently it fell to the floor, administering a kick on the way out but ordering him put back in the cell.

Towards the end of the day, punctuated only by a bowl of thin soup and a crust of bread, he heard someone coming again. He prayed for the footsteps to pass by, but the key rattled in the lock and a different blond German came in. 'Come on,' he said, 'you have a visitor.'

Jacques made no attempt to rise.

'Your wife, come on man, or your last chance to see her may be gone.'

He could make nothing of this, beyond a wild feeling that it might be help of some kind. After all he did have friends in Paris. By using the wall to steady himself he hopped in front of this more tolerant German – but his heart sank as he was directed into that same room.

He clung to the doorframe as he was sent in first. There was a woman sitting on the chair before the desk, a young, pregnant, tired-looking woman. His mouth opened in astonishment as he recognised her.

161

Stella saw his lips part and was terrified what he might say, and though the soldier cautioned her to remain seated she rushed at him. 'Henri! Henri!' she said with urgent passion, 'do you not know your wife? Oh! What have they done to you?'

There was no pretence in this question. The soldier kept her at a distance as he put a hand under Jacques's arm and helped him to the chair. Then he carried the other chair so it was facing it, and in view of the grille in the door. 'Ten minutes – and I am watching,' he said as he went out and locked the door behind him.

Jacques stared at her in disbelief, not trusting himself to speak. This woman was pregnant and his wife! This woman was Stella. Then he remembered Jean-Paul's padding. She had been tutored in disguise – of course!

'How ...' he began but that question was not answerable.

Afraid of what he might ask she began her story at once. 'There may be danger with this child, complications, so they allowed me to see you before ... it is born.'

'I did not know there was such trouble.' He frowned as they sat almost knee to knee, wanting to take her into his arms, carry her away.

She wanted to agonise, to keen aloud, about his swollen leg, his bruised face, the purple weal on his neck and as she reached for his hands he winced. She turned them palm up.

'Stigmata,' he said with an attempt at a grin.

Stella glanced at the grille of the door, saw the blond head turning away a moment as the woman officer walked by, heard them talking. She swept the packet of pills from her cuff into his injured hand. 'Take them as soon as you get back to your cell,' she whispered. 'All of them. Cub has ...' The face appeared at the grille again.

'Call the baby after my father,' he said, 'I would like that.'

'I will,' she told him, adding as the blond hair disappeared again, 'Cub has everything arranged.' She looked fixedly into his eyes, begging him to understand, do as he was told. Jacques nodded and regardless of his injured palms swiftly pushed the little packet of pills under his armpit.

'How is my father?' he asked.

She nodded, terrified she might by some innocent remark give too much away. She knew nothing of Henri Lamonte, what his background was. There had not been time for this fuller briefing from Cub. 'Everyone is fine,' she said reassuringly.

'Good!' he said and looked so intensely he could feel he might almost hurt her with his gaze. He leaned forward and put his fingers on her knees, on her arm, on her cheek, then leaned forward and

162

kissed her gently on the lips. *'Je t'aime,'* he breathed, *'toujours,* for ever. Remember ...'

'Toujours,' she repeated and seeing the woman's face at the grille again knew instinctively their time was going to be curtailed. The next moment both started as the woman officer rattled a baton back and forward across the door grille.

'Time's up!' she gloated as the door banged open.

There was time only for Stella to nod at Jacques, urging him to understand that he must do as instructed. He looked back at her, they leaned forward to kiss, their lips met – and the woman stepped between them.

Stella felt her lips bruised by the solid bulk of the woman beneath the rough uniform. She exclaimed at the brutish behaviour and called out as Jacques was half led, half carried out by the soldier.

She listened to the dragging steps and wondered even if the plan with the pills worked whether Jacques would ever manage to escape from the hospital. In her mind's eye she saw the dotted line from the window, to the guttering, over the roof – then to drop on to the roof of a lorry!

'Here!' The woman indicated her bag on the reception desk, the contents strewn right across the table, the bag itself with its lining pulled out, gutted.

Chapter Seventeen

He pushed the first four pills right to the back of his tongue, holding his head up and taking half the mouthful of water from the mug. They must go first time. They didn't, they stuck to his dry throat, making him want to gag. He pushed the other four into his mouth, manoeuvred them backwards on his tongue as far as he dare without causing himself to choke, then very slowly took the rest of the water. Some of the pills went. He shoved his knuckle into his mouth and sucked, trying to produce more saliva to finish the swallow.

It left him exhausted and his throat was lined with a residue which tasted more foul by the moment. He put his thumb right into his mouth, sucked like a child and remembered Stella's 'pregnancy'. He had been both appalled and delighted by her visit. Appalled she should put herself in such danger for him, appalled to see her in that room. Her performance had amazed him, the typical young peasant wife, like Nadia on a bad day! If he had been called upon to write a critique he would have extolled her debut as an actress as astonishingly realistic.

So what to expect now? Was the plan that he should pass out, lapse gently into unconsciousness? He lay quietly awaiting developments, thinking he could argue a good case for being administered a lethal dose. If the Germans found out his real identity he certainly knew enough of the activities centred round the museum to send many people to prison or death. *If* they could make him talk? They had come near to succeeding when he saw Verit. Where was Verit now? What else had they done to him? Old, courageous Verit.

He turned his mind to the piece of paper he still held, the small square the pills had been wrapped in. Keeping an eye on the door he scrubbed it backwards and forwards over the filthy wall until it looked old and tattered, then he folded it as small as he could. He began to feel over-warm in that cold dank cell as he struggled to push the tiny

164

twist of paper into a crevice in the wall.

He lay back and pulled open the front of his shirt. His face began to burn and soon his whole body felt on fire. Before long he was sure he was dying, and a feeling of panic began to overcome him. He found it difficult to breathe, began to suck in air through his mouth. His skin began to prick with the heat, and he heard himself talking aloud. His reality became a series of scenes in which he tried to take part. He began to ramble, then he heard himself shouting. Sometimes he felt he was shouting above the noise of the presses rolling off the printed pages; sometimes giving a report to his old newspaper boss; other times he was laughing uproariously at jokes in the café which the newspapermen frequented. Then he saw Stella in her black French clothes disappearing into the distance, sucked up it seemed along some gigantic tunnel – becoming a speck in the distance. He shouted for her to wait, tried to fight his way after her.

Then he wondered if he was on the way to that room again. He was manhandled, pain shot through parts of the fever like arrows piercing his body in different places. 'St Catherine!' he shouted, seeing her tied to her wheel. There were bright lights, he felt he was moving without effort now, rushed along at a great speed. '*C'est bon*!' he shouted and laughed and laughed at all the faces that peered at him.

'*C'est bon*!' he shouted at the anxious voices, at the hurrying footsteps, at the walls collapsing with lazy underwater elegance. The rush paused, stopped, someone all in white came close, held his arm for a moment then there seemed to be some kind of moments of intense activity round him, as if they were preparing him for an operation.

He knew no more until he came round in a vastly different place. It was quiet and clean, white, a hospital ward. So what now? Where did he go from here? Cautiously he lifted his head, then dropped it back as a feeling of extreme nausea swept over him. The pills had been the means to get him transferred to this hospital ward – how long would the effects last? Very cautiously he turned his head on the pillow. He seemed to be quite alone. Gradually he raised his head a second time; there was a clock on the end wall. Eight o'clock, he glanced at the window, in the morning, so he had been here all night. He had been put into a white gown but when he lifted the sheet his leg was still bound by Verit's old shirt. He had a drip into one arm, but none of his burns or injuries had been touched.

He was just trying to lift his head a little higher from the pillow when the door opened a fraction and a slight female figure slipped inside.

'Cub!' He mouthed the word as she came swiftly to his bedside.

'Listen carefully, I may only have minutes.' As she spoke she was

165

opening the case, pulling out blue overalls. She looked at him closely. 'Are you listening, hearing what I say?' He nodded as he received a string of instructions.

'I've a broken leg,' he whispered, 'pull the trousers over my feet, then I will manage.'

For once he saw her disconcerted, but only momentarily. The sheet was off the bed, his feet rapidly threaded into the overalls and pulled swiftly up as high as she could get them, the sheet pulled back. 'You have to manage,' she told him sternly.

'The utility room, the roof, the lorry.' He nodded.

'Now!' she whispered fiercely.

Mon Dieu!' he whispered as she slipped back out of the room. He held his breath listening, waiting for her to be challenged, but nothing. So if nothing, if no guard was there to challenge, then now was the time he should go.

He heard himself whimper with pain as he sat up. He removed the drip needle from his arm, pulled off the gown and put on the loose blue workman's top. He pulled the trousers up as far as he could without standing. Cautiously he put his good leg to the ground, the room spun sickeningly so he was forced to wait before he could move again. But he knew to have any chance he had to move much quicker than this. He stood on his good leg and pulled the trousers to his waist, fastened the belt.

He gauged the distance to the door. If he fell he was sure he would not get up again. He had to hop five or six steps. He needed something to help his balance. There was a small locker on wheels next to the bed. He made a tentative push; it moved, not easily but without noise. He gauged the strength needed to propel it about halfway to the door. It did not go that far. He must take two hops to reach the locker, steady himself, then perhaps five or six to the wall near the door.

He took several deep breaths like an athlete preparing for a race. First time, he told himself, first time. He had intended to rest at the locker but the impetus he gave himself from the bed made him lurch forward so far when he reached the locker it moved, slewed away in the wrong direction. He had to go on, three, four, five lopsided, staggering hops before he stood shuddering by the doorframe.

He regained his breath, listened. Still nothing. He opened the door a nick and saw an empty corridor, a pair of swing doors some fifteen yards away and between them the two doors on his left Cub had described. The second one was his target. He edged out of the door and, leaning on the wall, he slid along until he reached the first doorway. He attempted to hop past this which he did, but his shoulder just caught the doorframe of the next room, which threw him outwards. The corridor

166

was just too wide for him to save himself, and he fell.

Even as he went down he was trying to angle himself to land quietly. Once on the floor he pulled his body into a taut circle, reached for the door handle, pulled it down, and slithered eel-like into the utility room. He curled his damn long legs around the door and with infinite care closed it behind himself – only then did he pause, listen, sit grasping his leg with both hands above the break to contain the pain.

He allowed himself the time it took for his heart to still, then with an effort lifted his mind above the level of his pain and contemplated the next barrier. The window. It was not barred, it was just an ordinary sash window – the kind that in his experience often stuck fast, defying even the effort of men and hammers.

With noiseless care he dragged himself to the window, hurled himself to his good foot and pushed. It went up so quickly, so quietly he nearly over-balanced again. That was incredible, unless it had been prepared for his getaway. Cub again. It showed also the need for speed: nothing must delay him. 'Now!' she had said.

He estimated the distance from the windowsill to the leaded gutter below and thought he should be able to lower himself nearly all the way. For once his height would be a help. He sat on the sill and, turning, began to lower himself. The burns on his palms made it agony, his fingers curled to try to relieve the grazing and slipped from the sill. He landed square on both legs and crumpled.

He lay in the guttering listening to some strange noise as wave after wave of a new fever swept over him. First he was burning up then he shivered violently. He tried to concentrate, trying to assess where he lay, what the noise was. As he looked up from the guttering towards the apex of the roof he had to climb, he saw his hands stretched in front of him, beating a kind of nervous tattoo on the tiles. He jerked them upwards, and swinging round slightly, sat in the guttering folding his arms over his stomach and leaning forward, sick, desolate, alone. 'Christ!' he muttered, the word coming out in a long whispering shudder, and his whole body succumbed to shakes.

He told himself he should be more like his father, more able to make long continuous efforts at things. 'Stick at it' had been one of his father's favourite sayings as he experimented with his apples and vines. When bad years came he would start again, breaking new ground, setting new plants. Jacques had loved his mother, but he hero-worshipped his father. He had sought always to emulate him, and always judged he had failed.

There was nothing in the world he wanted more than to farm at Cleauville – farm and write – and marry Stella. He wished Stella was pregnant, was carrying his child, then if he did not make it there

167

would be someone of his still living at Cleauville. He was sure of one thing: his father and Lucille would always look after Stella if he couldn't.

Was he really going to give up that easily? He could almost see his father's minimal shake of his head. His father's slightest disapproval hurt more keenly than his mother's effusive but swiftly forgotten reprimands.

'So!' He gritted his teeth and spread himself forward ready to belly up the roof. With no weight to support, his right knee slightly flexed so the foot did not catch the edges of the tiles, this part was easier than he thought. Suddenly the street noises seemed loud, and a pigeon which came to land on the roof gave a clatter call of alarm when it saw him.

The urge to rest was cut short as he wondered how many other windows might overlook this bit of roof. He pulled himself up to the ridge tiles, and felt exposed to the whole world. He *might* be taken for a workman – except for his bare feet.

He could see some distance up the side street to his right, and almost at once a tarpaulin-topped lorry drew forward, came on the wrong side of the road, up the footpath. He leaned forward, pulled his other leg over and began the descent.

He reached the old square guttering, but instead of it steadying him, it gave. He swung his left foot out to try to regain some control, but all that happened was that it slewed him sideways. He made the lorry top while almost as if in slow motion he saw the rest of the guttering falling into the street, heard the crash which obliterated all other sounds for a few seconds.

He scrambled more to the centre of the tarpaulin cover, pushing off a section of guttering which had come with him as the lorry drove on. Any plans to immediately recover him from the top of the lorry were obviously impossible. As they turned the corner people came running from the front of the building. He caught an involuntary glimpse of them all looking up to the roof.

With admirable control the driver changed direction several times. Jacques carefully turned until he lay crossways between the metal supports of the soft top, so it sagged and partly obscured him. He could do no more, except pray.

Chapter Eighteen

The morning light had come slowly through the windows of the high domed roof. Stella had felt it was like walking under a miniature dome of St Paul's. Completely exhausted, she had still slept only fitfully in the solitude of the great museum. She had been able to bolt herself into this weird half-office half-boudoir created by the professor and assistant in this attic, but it felt as if all the strange and fantastic items exhibited or stored below might easily take up their extraordinary secret lives, like the nursery story of the toys that came to life at night.

She was sure the hiding place had been made for the purposes of the Resistance, but she was equally sure that the bedroom end had been created by both these academics with tongue in cheek regard for the affair they were certainly having. When Stella had exclaimed at the huge bed with its carvings of cupids and swans and the drapes so artistically transforming the beams of the attic space, Cub had replied, eyes sparkling, 'We like a challenge.' That she meant her professor was quite obvious. Just as obviously she was totally enthralled by this older man, would without hesitation do anything he asked of her, certainly lay down her life to save him.

Stella had gone straight from the prison to the museum where she, Cub and the professor had had an immediate conference. They had been full of praise for her success in seeing Jacques. 'Now,' Cub declared, 'I just have to go back first thing tomorrow morning.'

'Just.' The professor gently repeated the one word and seemed to hang it quizzically in the air, like a freakish example he was displaying at a lecture. She remembered Cub had laughed.

So the morning was here and if things had gone to plan she would soon, soon, see Jacques again. The plans for their return over the demarcation boundary were already made. There were new papers for Monsieur et Madame Georges Leclerc with a home in Marseilles and

169

Georges's demobilisation papers from the army because of his injuries. The professor was nothing short of a genius when it came to planning, and Cub was just astonishingly brave and intuitive.

Soon there was a three-two knock at the door and she unbolted it to find a complete stranger. He held out a hand and bowed. 'I am the doctor,' he said as he surveyed the empty attic. 'I'm early perhaps, but I am also room service!' From behind his back the elderly man who looked, with stiff wing-collar and black tie, the cynosure of the old type of unapproachable professional, produced a paper carrier. 'Breakfast,' he announced, 'as ordered by *le professeur*.' While she poured herself coffee from the flask and bit into a huge fresh croissant, he went on. 'I am supposedly out on a difficult confinement.' He hesitated, then bowed stiffly from the waist. 'Which I trust, madame, yours will not be.'

Being addressed as a married woman and her 'condition' so openly referred to she found disconcerting. In a stupid, stubborn way she knew she still tried to ignore it was happening to her. At such a time it was an unnecessary inconvenience, which Jacques too in that prison room had apparently overlooked, or ignored.

Shortly afterwards the professor arrived. He looked unkempt in so far as one strand of his hair stood up from his slick smooth head, and he ran his hand over his chin and mouth from time to time as they waited.

'She left in good time,' he said once, to neither of them in particular.

'It is a dangerous affair,' the doctor said solemnly.

The professor consulted his pocket watch for the fourth time and decided, 'It's time our lorry arrived, I'll go downstairs.'

While they waited the doctor again went over the injuries Stella had observed and which had prompted the professor to call his medical friend.

'His leg seemed the worse, the foot looked at a slightly strange angle. He certainly couldn't put his weight on it.'

'I've brought splints, and I understand the professor has an ancient pair of crutches in the museum from when he had a ski-ing accident years ago.'

Stella indicated the crutches in one corner of the attic. The doctor, for want of something better to do, went over and tried out their sturdiness. 'They're sound enough,' he said.

They were both alerted by the sound of a swift repeat of the prearranged signal, and the professor arrived back.

'Jacques!'

He shook his head. 'The situation is confused.' The two men talked gravely of the many students arrested, most guilty of nothing more than being near the Arc de Triomphe or one of the other demonstrations. There would be much pressure for their release, the professor decided as he began to pace up and down.

'We must make provision,' he said as he turned and looked towards Stella, though whether he was seeing her or not was doubtful, 'for the unexpected.' He mused a little longer then turned to the doctor. 'Can you wait a little longer, my friend?'

'It may be better if I return, easier for me to set up a second visit to a confinement than be absent too long.'

The professor inclined his head, but asked, 'Fifteen minutes?'

Stella went back to the bed and straightened it, piling the pillows ready for their patient. She brought the crutches near to the bed. The two men passed desultory remarks, watched her, and all three of them listened intently by turns at the top of the stairs.

The doctor prepared to leave. 'I'll be back in three hours, but should there be an emergency ...'

The professor nodded. 'I know what to do,' he said then turned to Stella. 'I must see the doctor away. Stay here my dear, bolt the door again after me and wait for my knock.'

She drank the rest of the coffee, telling herself there were many things that could delay such a plan. She kept seeing pictures in her mind of the lorry being stopped and Jacques dragged from it and returned to the prison – when *surely* matters would go much worse for him.

She was to fret away much of the morning, walking the floor in stockinged feet, lying on the bed gazing at the wintry sunshine moving with the hours around the circular windows of the dome. She tried to think of someone, or something, other than Jacques, or she felt she might well run from the room in the museum to the prison, but in seconds her mind was back with him. *What had happened?* It was surely inconceivable that the professor had forgotten about her? No, that was not the answer. The answer she kept coming back to was that something quite awful had occurred.

It was nearly midday when she heard someone returning and the pre-arranged knock sounded on the door. Any questions she had intended to throw at whoever it was died on her lips as she saw the professor standing there, standing there a changed man, a deeply worried man. It was Cub, for sure something had happened to his girl.

Instead of the questions she found herself taking his arm, leading him to a chair.

'I think we must assume it has gone wrong,' he said, 'and the only news I have is ... that there is no news. We have to wait.'

171

'Is there no one we can contact? Could I go to Jacques's apartment? Madame Astier may have news.'

He held up his hands as if to calm her wild ideas. 'We must do nothing – yet, nothing hasty. If you go, then news, or Jacques arrives, what then? No, I think we must wait longer.'

'Cub?' She studied him more intently as he sat with his hands gripping his knees, the bones thin and sharp through his pinstriped trousers. 'Your young lady? Has she come back?'

Even as she asked the question she knew it was stupid. There would have been some kind of news if she had returned. 'No,' she answered her own question.

'This I find the most worrying thing,' he said. 'It is possible that the lorry, with Jacques on board, may have had to make some kind of detour, but Cub should have been back hours ago. The trouble is the whole of Paris is in a turmoil. The State Police and the Gestapo are still trying to find and arrest anyone who took part in the Armistice Day demonstrations. It is difficult to move anywhere without being stopped.'

'Do you think Cub has gone to ground somewhere instead of coming back here?'

'That is what I hope.' His face brightened a little. 'She is too impulsive, that is the problem. The other you have probably guessed.'

'You care too much about her.'

'Cub is the joy of my life.'

'And you of hers I think,' Stella said quietly, sure the professor would also have a wife and family somewhere.

'*Merci*,' he said with a brief smile, 'and so we must both wait for news of our loved ones. I have my midday radio call to make, but I should not be long. Be patient, *ma petite*.' He kissed her hand. 'We must take care of you, Jacques would never forgive me ...'

'I'm fine,' she assured him.

When he came back she did not think it was good news; he looked grim, even older than less than an hour ago. She rose slowly, needing to know, but not wanting it to be any of the dreadful scenarios she had been imagining for hours.

'I have heard from one of our agents near the demarcation line, the lorry is there – with Jacques.'

'He has escaped!'

He nodded. 'But things went wrong just as he escaped, the driver dared not risk coming to the museum. He's taken Jacques to a safe house he knew of, one we've used before to transfer our agents on to Vichy and Clermont-Ferrand. He will be taken to one of those towns.'

So Jacques was free! 'And Cub?' she asked.

'She has not been seen since she left to go to the hospital.'

'No news, we say in England, is good news,' she said wishing she knew him well enough to put an arm around him.

He nodded. 'She is so impetuous, it has been part of her charm – until France capitulated.' He shrugged ruefully. 'I just have to wait. But now you have to move quickly. I wouldn't like to trust you to the safety of the museum if Cub has been taken. It would not be long before she is recognised. We're both well known in Parisian circles and not all Paris is loyal to France. You must go to Jacques's apartment. There is so far nothing the Germans know that will connect him with that. Then in a few days you must travel back to Avignon. Here are the papers that were made out for you and Jacques. They have been altered to fit the new circumstances.'

He broke off as there was the sound of someone coming lightly up the stairs. He flung open the door before any knock was given. Cub stood there carrying a cage almost as big as herself, with two green birds inside.

'What are you doing?' the professor asked, with remarkable self-control, Stella thought.

'I got all caught up, did you hear about the guttering? Is he safe?' She directed her question to Stella as the professor still eyed the cage, the birds and the girl as if they were part of a puzzle he had yet to solve. When Stella nodded she went on. 'I made for the home of a friend,' she lifted the cage as if in proof, 'the one where I'd left Maxim's parakeets until I found somewhere permanent.'

'And have you?' the professor asked.

'I thought you could have them in your flat,' she answered, placing the huge cage on a small table.

Stella watched the emotions come and go on the man's face. He was not sure whether he wanted to spank her or bed her – probably both.

'I'm glad you're safe,' she told Cub. 'I'll never be able to thank you enough for Jacques's escape, his life.' The two women embraced and kissed.

'You take care of his baby,' Cub said.

'So now I shall take you as near as I dare to your apartment,' the professor said.

She noticed his hands shook as he started the car. 'She does not know what she puts you through,' Stella said.

'I don't intend her to,' he answered. 'She might realise how old I am!'

It was good to share a brief laugh with him before they parted. He stopped within walking distance of the apartment. 'Keep out of the way for a few days until the city quietens down, then go south.'

173

'Thanks again. Be happy, you and Cub.'

He shook his head and smiled at her. 'Make your lives count,' he said as she closed the car door, 'as is said across the Channel, no hole in corner affair for you two.'

Madeleine let her into the house after some cautious minutes. 'It's gone wrong or you wouldn't be here,' she said. 'What's happened?'

The full story was told, with the two of them gripping each other's hands. 'So Jacques is free! But the lorry has taken him direct to a safe house.' Madeleine persisted wanting to get all the facts straight in her mind. 'And you?'

'I have altered papers to travel back by train in a few days.' She opened her bag and took out the papers the professor had given her. 'He said they'd been altered. They were to be for a married couple, army demobilisation papers for the husband on the grounds of war injuries.' She was opening the papers as she spoke. 'Oh!' she exclaimed.

'What is it?' Madeleine asked.

She displayed the papers. Across the name of the man the word 'deceased' had been stamped.

Chapter Nineteen

'Pas de Crédit! Crédit!' The mechanic muttered his own nickname as he worked. It still amused him to remember how shocked Lucille had been when he suggested 'Crédit' as his Resistance call sign and she had finally realised he knew what the younger family members called him.

He had never minded. The Blair family were his, and had been his father's oldest and most respected customers. Maurice, like his father before him, had always prided himself on his good service to his paying customers; nothing was too much trouble for them.

He had established a routine for the regular radio call times. He always went off in his truck into the maquis, the local scrubland. If the Germans stopped him on the road he had a back full of metal bottle racks he was welding for whichever Resistance-friendly vineyard he was near to. Occasionally he dropped a new blob of molten metal on to a joint to make the racks appear they had just been worked on.

Hector said there were rumours of a German detector device being used in one of the Opel cars used by the officers. Maurice was cautious but determined nothing would stop him relaying what came from the Cleauville group on to London. He felt like a partner to the young, courageous – and ever restless – Jean-Paul, passing on the coded information he gathered, taking messages from England, Paris, Vichy; they were also expecting news from Clermont-Ferrand about more radio sets. Maurice had volunteered to train new operators. Two things gave him great pleasure: his increasing skill with the short-wave radio and the feeling that he now served a wider community, he served the interests of France.

Once deep in the countryside he stretched out his radio antennae either side of his truck and stood his pocket watch alongside his headphones to wait for the hour. It was so still, so solitary, only the sound of an occasional bird and the occasionally crack of a late broom

175

seedpod broke the silence. This secret, dangerous activity had given him some of his most peaceful moments since boyhood. He would never have taken time from his work to come and sit 'wasting time' in this beautiful wilderness. '*C'est la guerre*!' he breathed, watching a covey of ducks flying down towards the Camargue.

The hour came and he clamped his headphones over his beret. He sent out a sequence of 'V' signals for his English contact to home in on, then his identifying code 'CDT'. The return acknowledgment came within seconds. Then having nothing to transmit he listened out and was about to remove his handset when the receiver stuttered to life again. A message from Paris. Meticulously he transferred the sounds he heard to dots and dashes across the page, his lips moving to the rhythm of the 'dits' and 'dahs' as letter followed letter. He acknowledged receipt, then followed his routine of refolding the radio antennae, repacking his radio, rearranging his lorry's load, before returning to his cab and the more leisurely task of decoding. Today as he walked round to the driving seat, something flashed on a distant hillside like the sun catching the lens of a pair of field glasses.

It could have been many things but Maurice's knowledge told him no local should be on that hill at that time, there was no reason. If he had been watched by the Gestapo, or Pétain State Police, then he would most certainly be arrested. His truck was easily recognisable.

He roughly assessed the content of the message – 'Frère' and 'Clermont-Ferrand' featured. This could be the message Stella and all the Blair family, were waiting for, news of Jacques.

He drove his truck at its bone-shaking top speed down the track to the road, and his garage. Without pause he stripped the lorry of the radio, put it into the carrier on one of his bicycles, checked he had the code pad and was about to leave when an impulse made him turn back. He went over to his ramshackle desk and straightened his home-made 'Pas de Crédit' sign. Then he took a look all around at the tools he had inherited, made and on occasion bought; at the work he had in hand – ploughs, crop-sprayers, hand-held and wheeled, cogs and gears from presses. He sighed, shrugged, and left to cycle by back lanes towards Hector's cottage.

His first stop was near an ancient stone bridge, partly derelict, used only occasionally by shepherds and land workers. He took the radio and clambered down to the stream, then up and under the old arch where he secreted the radio in one of the many craggy niches high above any possible water level. Then he rode on towards his old friend's home. It was possible some of the family would be there, they often were. Hector's cottage was halfway house between the farm-house and the hideouts. He would decode the message properly, pass

176

it on, and make them aware that he thought he had been seen.

When he got near, he pushed the bicycle well into the bushes and reconnoitred the cottage to come in from the trees. He was approaching the door when Hector called to him. 'Come in, you old elephant! I've been listening to you this last ten minutes.'

Maurice ran his arm over his forehead, suddenly quite exhausted now he had reached some kind of safety. 'I've done worse, old friend,' he said, pulling out a chair, leaning heavily over the table. He told all that had happened.

'So you've left the lorry at your place.' Hector went through the details. 'And the radio ...'

'Under the old packhorse bridge.'

'And the message?'

'I'll finish it now.' Maurice spread out his pad and quickly decoded the whole message. '"Frère with operator Clermont-Ferrand, needs help from your end."'

'We should let Jean-Paul see this as soon as possible,' Hector said. 'He and Monsieur are at the bories. I'll signal for them, you rest, old lad. Lie on my bed for a bit. Can't have you old timers getting worn out.'

Maurice, younger than the First World War veteran by some ten years, shook a playful fist as his friend went outside to light two separate bonfires, the twin plumes of smoke the signal that those at the bories were wanted.

'Ernest,' Jean-Paul pointed across the valley, 'that looks like a fair-sized fire. Not a bonfire, or ...'

Ernest joined him on the ridge above the stone houses. 'No, and it could mean trouble, look!' He pointed in the opposite direction to where the thin twin spirals of smoke came from Hector's garden. 'We're wanted.'

The routine for return was well practised. First they discreetly scanned all the roads they could see from the ridge above the bories, then again before they reached the bottom of the valley. One of them then went ahead and if all was clear gave a low birdlike whistle, twice repeated, if the other was to follow on.

In Hector's cottage the message was quickly reported. Jean-Paul began making plans to go at once to Clermont-Ferrand. 'It will mean our radio operator, I know him, he's the contact for the man we hope is going to make us more radios.'

'Thank God to have news of him,' Ernest said.

Jean-Paul put his hand on his shoulder. 'Stella'll be relieved, even though it doesn't sound all good.'

177

'We know he had a leg injury,' Ernest said. 'We must hope there's nothing more.'

'But there is more you must know.' Pas de Crédit told them that he believed he had been observed, and how he had left his truck at home, hidden the radio and cycled to the cottage.

Jean-Paul looked at him very soberly, then at Ernest, both immediately thinking of the dense cloud of smoke, which might well be coming from the direction of the man's home and workshop.

'You must keep out of sight, until we find out if you're right,' Ernest said. 'If you have been seen we should think of getting you out.'

'Out?' Pas de Crédit exclaimed. 'Out where? No, no, I belong here. I'll hide out in the stone houses until things cool off, but there's no way I am leaving my home. I'd be ...' he gave an exaggerated gesture with his arms as he searched for the right word, 'ridiculous anywhere else.'

The two men exchanged looks, acknowledging the fact that they both knew he would never leave. 'All right,' Ernest conceded, 'Hector will look after you with supplies – but go immediately, I think, better safe than sorry.' He balled the paper with the decoded message in his hand, and dropped it into the centre of one of Hector's small bonfires as they left.

When they were out of earshot he said, 'I'll take one of the bikes and go and look at Pas de Crédit's place. Hopefully we're wrong. You have your travel plans to make, and there's Stella, would you tell her the news, be gentle, she's been very anxious.'

They parted as Ernest went to the bicycle store. Stella was coming downstairs when Jean-Paul reached the hall.

'What is it?' she asked immediately, stopping and standing gripping the banister as he stood looking up at her. 'You've heard something, a message!'

'Jacques is in Clermont-Ferrand. I have to go to fetch him.' He repeated the exact words of the radio signal.

Joy at the first words turned to speculation. 'So he's not mobile.'

'He needs help.' He went to her on the stairs, put an arm around her waist. 'Come on,' he said 'it's a shock after waiting and wondering every hour of every day, but it is good news.'

Jean-Paul's gesture of comfort made her realise again how much she missed and needed Jacques. Tears threatened, and she was glad the hall was shady as she gritted her teeth hard. 'Yes, but it is positive news. He's still alive! After all that happened in Paris I was beginning to wonder. Does his father know?' she asked.

Jean-Paul nodded and told where Ernest had gone.

'Oh! no!' She was appalled. 'We mustn't let them get old Pas de Crédit, he's part of our lives, our childhood.' She felt it would be like some final act of injustice if anything happened to their old friend. 'I think of him as a kind of uncle. He's just part of Cleauville and Avignon, and life here.'

He nodded. 'But if,' he paused calculating, 'if the worst did happen and he was picked up, we must be prepared. You still have your papers ...'

'Showing me as a war widow? Yes.'

'This is the role to keep to now. It will cover your baby and mean you can stay here at the farm as housekeeper, with Hector, caretakers for the duration of the war. It just leaves Ernest and myself to hide out in the case of real trouble.'

'There will be Jacques,' she reminded him.

'Oh! we have some remarkable hiding places!' He grinned and kissed her on the forehead. 'I'm off to see Edmund now to let him know what's happening and arrange to fetch this young man's father.' He patted her lightly on the stomach.

'*His* father?'

'Oh yes, I have it from the ultimate authority, Nadia. She says she knows it is a boy because you are carrying it so high.' He mimicked her broad, intensely confidential tones when she talked of 'family things'. '"Boys are carried nearer the heart!"'

She raised her eyebrows at him, but understood why Lucille loved him to the exclusion of Philip. It was a rare man who could lighten your heart at such times.

'But of course,' he went on, 'you love us all, us boys, that is why.' He planted another kiss on her forehead. '*À bientôt*! Don't worry!'

She was pleased not to be on her own too long; the need to tell and talk was overwhelming. She counted the minutes until Lucille returned from the hospital, almost pouncing on her the moment she returned.

'So Jean-Paul will be off again,' Lucille suddenly realised in the middle of the rejoicing.

Stella knew that each time, each parting devastated Lucille. 'Yes, but with luck *then* we should all be together again.' She gave a passing acknowledgement to her brother, Philip, who wavered at the edge of her conscience like a pale peripheral ghost.

'Perhaps even for Christmas. Yes, we must think of that.' Lucille pulled her nursing apron straight in a businesslike manner.

'I've been so afraid,' Stella said. 'Ever since that lorry whisked him out of Paris, we've heard nothing. Being in that awful prison just for a short time, and seeing him there, made me realise how people can

179

disappear without trace, how evil people can be in such utter control.'

'Stop it, now,' Nurse Lucille ordered. 'In fact stop it both of us. My chap is going to fetch your chap, and together we will be!'

'Yes.' The two friends grinned and tried to embrace.

'This young man is getting a nuisance, I'll be so pleased to get back to a normal shape.'

'It's wonderful that Jacques's baby is going to be born here, at our home.'

'Even if it is under a false name.'

'We'll know the truth, that's all that matters, and if Jacques *and* Jean-Paul ...' Lucille broke off. 'We'll be aunt and uncle, do you realise that!'

Stella wondered what her father would say if he knew of his coming grandchild, out of wedlock, and Jean-Paul spoken of as uncle when he was not even part of the family. Conventions were also war victims.

They heard someone coming through the courtyard. Ernest hurried in, pale, his forehead beaded with perspiration. 'You've heard about Jacques?' he asked.

They both did no more than nod, his distraught manner making it obvious there was much else on his mind.

'They've burned down Pas de Crédit's house and garage,' he said. 'I didn't get too close, but the locals said the Germans went in, ransacked the place from top to bottom, stripped his truck.'

'Looking for the radio,' Stella said.

Ernest nodded. 'Then they up-ended a petrol can and threw down a match. They stood and watched, wouldn't let anyone near to try to put it out, not even locals with machinery in there for repair. One man was knocked down with a rifle butt when he tried to intervene, but more significantly the officer was apparently heard to say, "He won't need a home or a business where he's going."'

'So is he at the hideout?' Stella asked.

'Yes. I called at the cottage. There's no one there, so Hector's looking out for him. But there's his bicycle in the scrub. I think that should be retrieved without delay. Brought here I would think, just put among our bicycles, no one will know.'

'I'll go and get it,' Lucille offered. 'It's probably one I've ridden before anyway. And *you* should go and hide at the bories,' she told her father.

'No, I'll go up in the stable roof. That's secure enough, unless they burn us out. And that would be over my dead body anyway,' Ernest told his daughter, adding, 'If you'll get the bike it'll be one less clue hanging about.'

Lucille changed quickly into slacks and blouse, also calculating that by leaving now she should be back in time to see Jean-Paul before he left once more for the occupied sector. She felt physically sick at the thought of the danger he placed himself in. She hated the look of anticipation and excitement which so quickly came over him when another mission was being planned. She dreaded the moment when his eyes showed that his mind was already ahead dealing with the problems to come, so unaware of the fleeting moment, in a way already gone, already lost to her.

If ever he was lost – did not return, she knew she would not want to go on living. He was her life, her future, she wanted nothing else. She supposed it was an unhealthy and unwise conclusion to come to in wartime.

Hurrying to Hector's cottage she remembered an old man she had helped nurse in England. His wife was continually at his bedside until the end. The next day they were shocked to hear that the old lady had taken her own life in the night. At the time Lucille had believed it a mortal sin; now she began to understand.

She reached Hector's cottage and found it still deserted. She started to look for the bicycle either side of the paths through the woods. Then she heard someone coming, carelessly, noisily. She was surprised when it was Hector, hopping and hobbling along at a great speed with the help of the single crutch he used on uneven ground. He gestured urgently as soon as he saw her.

'What is it?'

'Aaah!' he exhaled in a great ragged exclamation. 'Maurice! We were going up to the bories when he saw smoke, and he is sure it is his place, that the Germans are burning it down ...'

'He's right,' she interrupted. 'My father's been to look. They have fired it and are keeping everyone away while it burns.'

'God Almighty!' He looked round desperately as if for a remedy. 'He's gone crashing down the hillside like a bloody old mountain goat. There was no way I could stop him – and the thing is he's carrying my gun and a belt of ammunition.'

'Where's his bicycle?' she demanded. 'I could still overtake him if I had that.'

'But ...'

'If I get in his way he won't just shoot me to get past,' she said. 'Come on!'

They found the bicycle well hidden under a bush. She rode off immediately, weaving to avoid holes and boulders back to the path and down towards the road. 'Appeal to his responsibilities to his customers and friends!' Hector shouted after her.

181

She was surprised not to overtake him well before she came in sight of his house and garage – or where they had been. A huge pall of black smoke hung above the spot, gathering still under the grey sky. A car some distance ahead of her stopped and the unmistakable figure of Pas de Crédit climbed out.

The car turned abruptly away along a side road but Pas de Crédit walked resolutely straight on towards his garage. She pushed the pedals as fast as she could and shouted his name, but he either did not, or could not, hear – or ignored her.

She could soon see there was little left of the old lean-to workshop and his house, ramshackle always, but his home, his livelihood. Her heart felt torn with alarm for the little bull-necked man walked straight on towards the group of German soldiers and their officer who looked as if they were just getting ready to leave the scene. One idly kicked a piece of shingling that had fallen clear of the flames back into the fire.

Lucille saw Pas de Crédit raise the gun and fire. She stood frozen with disbelief as the soldier dropped. There was complete confusion among the group of men. Pas de Crédit fired again; several fell injured, screaming. For a moment the officer also seemed too incredulous to do anything. Pas de Crédit stood in the centre of the road and reloaded the gun, pulling the cartridges from the belt around his shoulder. Two of the soldiers began running towards him shouting orders. He raised his gun again and fired at point-blank range into the first of the soldiers, while behind them the officer at last screamed an order. Several rifles fired at the same time. Pas de Crédit half spun round, stumbled, then with a supreme effort of will she saw him very deliberately fire the second barrel towards the officer. More and more shots were fired. Lucille heard her own cries as Pas de Crédit's body jerked and jumped as the bullets thudded into it. It was over.

But no! Not over. She watched appalled as the officer, gripping his own shoulder where he had been hit, kicked the body over and fired his revolver straight into the face, twice. She saw one of his men turn away. She too turned and very slowly walked away. It did not occur to her to get back on to the bicycle. For a long way she just pushed it. Her mind was numb with shock and disbelief. It was only when she stumbled and nearly got pulled over that she realised she was walking with Pas de Crédit's bicycle – one of those she had borrowed from the garage when she and Stella had first returned. When she did finally get back on, she stood on the pedals to ride ever faster and faster as if she might somehow out-distance the evil she had just witnessed.

Hector saw her turn the corner into the farm drive as if all the devils of hell were after her. He rushed forward to catch her handle-bars as he saw she was coming too fast, at too sharp an angle to negotiate the curve.

The back wheel skidded away from under her and she saw the flag-pole describe a wild arc in the sky. She fell as if in slow motion with time to wonder if he might insist on running up his black flag to half-mast for his old friend.

'I ...' she began then stood aghast at what she had to tell.

'What is it? What's happened? Did you stop him?'

'I ... no ... he'd had a lift in a car.' She leaned back on his fence, then slid down to a crouch and told him what she had seen.

'You're sure he is dead?' Hector asked grimly.

She struggled to tell him about the last shots full into his face and head, but Hector gripped her shoulder. 'Don't try to go on, I under-stand. We shall take revenge, old friend,' he promised, looking into the distance. Then he asked, 'And what about his body?'

She suddenly felt very remiss for abandoning the dead Pas de Crédit.

'I'll go, I shall see about everything. Tell the farm not to worry, I shall see to it all. They may not let anyone move him tonight, they like to make examples.' He reached a hand down to her. She was surprised by his strength, the way he had cushioned her fall and now pulled her to her feet. 'You must go quickly and tell them.'

She nodded. He heaved up the bicycle and held the handlebars while she mounted. She felt so tender towards this old soldier, who like Pas de Crédit was, had been, so much part of their lives. 'Take care, old friend, when you go to the village,' she said, 'we can't afford to ever lose you.'

He looked up, surprised, his dark old eyes vulnerable, for once without the aggression which made him a survivor.

She put the bicycle under several others in the store and hurried towards the house, then slowed as she heard Jean-Paul's voice.

'Edmund says I should leave at once, there's to be a real clamp-down on the area. The Boche know we have a radio and are determined to find it.' There was the movement of plates and glasses, then he said, 'He's given me a quick route and I'm going in the Wolseley tonight, to a safe house near the demarcation line ...'

She stepped in at the door and saw how she must look mirrored on their faces. Her father rose from the table but then stood quite still and all three just silently stared at her.

'What's happened? Lucille!' Stella demanded.

'Did you get the bicycle?' her father asked.

Jean-Paul came forward quietly as one might approach someone unstable, on the verge of violence, or breakdown, and led her to a chair, held her hand. She looked around at them all. Such a fragile thing, life, she thought, it could be snuffed out in a moment.

'Pas de Crédit – the Germans have shot him.' She heard herself give a strange strangled laugh. 'They didn't have much choice really.'

What she did not remember to tell, they asked, quietly, not rushing her but needing to know, needing to put things in order, see the sequence.

'I think,' she said after a time and with what she thought was great rationality, 'we should all go to England.'

'There's Jacques,' Stella reminded her.

'I mean after that.' She looked at Jean-Paul in an agony of loyalty pulling several ways at once. 'After that.'

Her father stood up and moved away.

'Father?' she queried.

'I shall never leave,' he said. 'This is my home.'

'Like Pas de Crédit then!' She was suddenly so angry. 'He died for his home, for bricks and sheds, and ramshackle old places that could have been rebuilt.'

'I shall stay with your mother,' he said with quiet but determined dignity.

She remembered what he had said about Cleauville being burned down, 'over my dead body'.

'Then you will probably join her – and I'll have neither mother nor father.'

'Lucille! Don't,' Stella pleaded. 'Please stop.'

She clapped her hands over her ears and then echoing in her mind she could hear the sounds of the shots, the clatter of Pas de Crédit's gun as he fell, and deeply etched on her memory were the moving pictures.

She felt Jean-Paul half lifting her to her feet. 'Come and help me,' he said taking her arm, drawing her out of the house, away by themselves. 'It helps to keep busy,' he added as he led the way to the barn.

He took her into the barn by the side of his Wolseley and held her tight, not speaking, not moving, just holding her. For a time she tried to resist, almost wrestled against him, angry because they were by the car, not wanting his departure, another loss on top of Pas de Crédit's stupid valour!

'For God's sake!' she moaned, rocking her head against Jean-Paul's shoulder. 'I can't take this.'

'Listen!' he said almost roughly. 'I know what a man looks like when his body jumps around when he is shot many times. I know what it looks like when a man is blown to pieces.'

'I – don't – want – to – know!' She spaced the words out like drum beats.

184

'When we were defending the canal from La Bassée to St Omer,' he told her anyway, 'we didn't have enough anti-tank weapons to cover all the crossing places the tanks were using. In the gaps were men digging holes.' He paused as if gathering his own strength to go on remembering. 'Men who have seen the worst action never talk about it. No one wants to relive the worst moments of their lives.' He paused. 'Some men are never the same again.'

She was still, not alone with the horrors now, eyes closed, head pressed hard into his shoulder.

'*Ma petite*, I would like more than anything in the world to stay with you, to love you, to hold you while you sleep, to keep all harm from you.'

She remembered him comforting her out here before when she had been still shocked from the suicide of the Jewish brothers. 'You're always looking after me,' she said.

'It must be what I'm about then.' He stooped to add low in her neck, 'what I am for.'

She closed her eyes and just let herself relax, sink into and know the feeling of being in his arms, how their bodies pressed together, how comforting he was to her, as now, one hand cradled the back of her head, as if he held a baby, while the other pressed her close as only a true lover did.

'I shall always love you,' she said, and meant for ever, eternity, but perhaps she was learning not to burden people too much with extremes. 'Come on,' she added, 'let's get this car dusted off again. Don't want my fruit buyer running about in any old thing.'

Much later the two girls were alone in the farmhouse. Ernest had agreed to sleep in the stable hideout. Lucille and Stella both had their false papers and stories ready if the Germans paid them a visit.

'Do you think there will be reprisals?' Stella asked.

'Yes.' Lucille had dropped all pretence when Jean-Paul had left.

'I could wish the next two days away,' Stella ventured.

'I could wish today had never happened.'

Chapter Twenty

'So, madame, what has been so carefully covered in this barn?' The German officer pointed his highly polished jackboot at the folded tarpaulin removed from the Wolseley.

Stella, having answered what she thought were all the German officer's questions in the house, now found herself trailing around behind him and his three men as they searched the outhouses and barns.

'It was the large wheeled crop-sprayer,' she told him, 'but I understand my employer has lost this in a fire. It had gone in for repair and . . .'

'Quite!' he snapped, impatiently gesturing his men on as they emerged from a circuit of the empty barn. Then as if looking for some other line of attack he asked, 'Your accent, madame, it is not of this area?'

'I spent some time in Switzerland as a child,' she began on a kind of automatic reflex of lying as she watched the men enter the stable-block. Ernest had kept to the hiding place since Jean-Paul had left and they had heard these visits and interrogations – and arrests – had begun in the area. 'With an aunt, my mother was ill for some time after . . .'

He turned away, had heard enough and she was wise enough not to elaborate on any lie he had accepted. 'The old man,' he said and there was a new note in his voice as if here he knew he was on safer ground. 'He I presume knew the mechanic who did the repairs for the farm?'

'I understand they have both lived here all their lives, never been away until . . .'

'So where is Hector Lafont now?'

'Monsieur Lafont is in charge of the whole farm.' She spread her arms, as she saw the men move from the stables to the next block of outhouses. 'He'll be working somewhere.'

186

'He is a patriot, I gather.'

'He fought in the 1914–18 war if that's what you mean.'

'Perhaps!' he said, at once sneering at her, yet she saw in his eyes he was assessing her as a possible worthwhile conquest, even though she was heavily pregnant. 'Your husband is dead, I understand.'

She merely nodded, keeping her head down as might befit a grieving widow, not trusting herself to look at him, or speak, in case she lost control and said what was on the end of her tongue: 'Mind your own bloody business you unctuous German pig!'

'Tell Lafont we'll be back, to watch himself and to burn that French flag he has stowed away in his cottage. The old France is dead, Liberty, equality and fraternity have given way to family, work and the Fatherland.'

She stood and watched them go, consoling herself with the thought that if they had searched Hector's cottage and found only the *tricolore* then Hector had done a good job hiding everything else that he had made and had over the years which would have shown precisely what he felt about Hitler and the fascists. It had always seemed to her littered with maps and anti-German material.

She heard a faint noise behind her and knew Ernest was coming down from his hiding place.

'So is it over,' Ernest asked from the shadows, 'have they gone?'

'For now, I was worried when they went into the stables.'

'That lot! They'll never find that hideout. I've made a secure place there, though I say it myself.'

She turned and smiled at him. Whenever they were alone these days they seemed quite naturally to fall into English idioms, indulging each other in hackneyed phrases and ironic humour. She took his arm and leaned on it as he patted her hand and said, 'It'll be good to see Jacques.'

'Won't it just! And he could be quite near now, this is the third day.'

'Edmund has people out watching the roads, ready to stop the Wolseley if it looks likely to run into any of these patrols.' He suddenly stretched and shuddered at the same time. 'Oh! A ghost must have walked over my grave,' he said with a shaky laugh.

She looked at him with some concern; he looked tired, a tired old man. 'Come on,' she said, 'let me make you some real English tea, and we'll go into the sitting room and just sit and drink it.'

'You have a deal,' he said, 'provided we talk about Avonside and the river before the war, our old green and pleasant land.'

She was spooning some of their precious store of remaining tea into Gaby's best china teapot when there was the sound of a car, stopping at the front of the house she thought. She stood for a moment riveted to the spot – if this was the Germans back ... Ernest was in the sitting room, she was standing before a tray laden with two cups and saucers. She sped to the front of the house to see Ernest rushing from the sitting room to the front door. 'They're here!' he shouted.

'Who?' she heard herself say. Then over his shoulder she caught a glimpse of the Wolseley and Jean-Paul getting out.

'My boy!' she heard Ernest call.

'Oh they're here!' she repeated and ran stumbling towards the car. Ernest drew back from his handshake as she did so. 'Here's our man, Stella,' he said. It sounded like an introduction, and she felt his hand briefly touch her shoulder in a passing disconcerting gesture of comfort.

In the back lay a blanket-wrapped man. 'Jacques?' The query in her voice was there before she could stop it. Had he been in a hospital ward she knew she would have walked past him.

'Hi!' He held out a hand.

'Jacques, my darling, thank God you're safe.' She fought back the tears, understanding his father's brief touch of sympathy now. Everything about this man, even the look in his eyes, spoke of someone desperately ill.

'This is a shock,' he said as if speaking for her.

'Yes.' She clambered into the car, half kneeling in the seat-well so she could reach up and kiss his cheek; she felt the angular bone of his chin hard against her cheek. She took his hand, so thin, so cold, kissing it several times as if to reassure him that even though she had not recognised him nothing had changed between them.

'It is a shock, Pas de Crédit and everything. But what happened to you after Paris? I mean *you*,' he emphasised. 'I didn't know you were really ... ' he shook his head with bemused amazement.

'He thought I had padded you up when you went to the prison,' Jean-Paul said.

'Oh!' She felt suddenly clumsy, enormous and near to tears because of his obvious illness, and on top of that tongue-tied.

He squeezed her hand and waved Jean-Paul away. 'Ah! I understand,' Jean-Paul joked as he walked away from the car with Ernest, 'only wanted on voyage!'

'You're not sorry, are you, sorry it happened?' She shook her head at him and smiled. His face, his pale gaunt face lit up with an answering smile. 'I think it's wonderful. I love you so much, Stella.'

'And I love you, but you need looking after.' It was the mildest way she could think of to voice her concern.

'I'm in your hands,' it was nearly a grin he managed, 'I'm all yours.'

'There's a bit less of you than there was,' she said, noticing that Jean-Paul had taken Jacques's father a little way from the car. While Jean-Paul talked rapidly and with much gesturing, Ernest stood very still listening, head down, then he nodded. Jacques immediately went off towards the bicycle store and Ernest came back towards the car.

'What have you decided to do?' Stella asked.

Ernest leaned into the car and looked at his son. 'Apparently it took three to get you into the car, and it played havoc with the leg.' Jacques did not answer but grimaced. 'Jean-Paul is going to cycle to the village to ask the good doctor's advice. It might be safe to drive you straight down to his surgery, we've just had a visit from the Germans, with any luck they'll be finished with their house visits for today. Their commander likes to get up to the château in the early evening. He's formed an attachment with our widowed countess, and she always was a baggage anyway.'

'What about tea in the car then?' Stella asked. 'Your father and I were just going to indulge in English tea. Would you like some?'

Jacques nodded.

'Stay where you are, I'll get it,' Ernest said and as he went back to the house Jean-Paul rode quickly away. She noticed that no one said, or called after him, 'Take care,' and probably no one ever would again. 'Taking care' had become a matter of survival, a constant way of life.

'Sit by me, don't kneel down there.' Jacques patted the seat alongside his legs.

'I don't want to hurt you.'

'I've spent all these months apart from you, seeing you once in a prison cell, not knowing anything about ...' he fretted, almost feverishly she thought, 'about what I'd done to you, what you were going through. For God's sake I thought you were playing a part set up by Jean-Paul! For God's sake!'

'All right,' she said, manoeuvring to sit as gently as she could on the edge of the seat. She put her hand up to his forehead, found it burning hot. 'Stay quiet, we're together now, and that's a miracle, when you think ...'

'I know I'll never forget what you risked for me.' He gripped her hand tightly, so she could feel every bone in his hand. 'You're so brave,' he said, 'about everything.'

'It was Cub and the professor who set the whole thing up ...'

'Of course, Cub, the professor, the driver and his mate – everyone – but you! *Formidable*!'

She felt him grow very still as he thought of all those who had risked so much. 'I saw Verit in prison.' Then his hand moved slowly and with infinite gentleness over her stomach. At that precise moment

189

the baby kicked and he started, called out, his hand leaping away.

'It moved!' he exclaimed. 'I felt it move!'

'Alive and kicking,' she said, 'our baby.'

'Our baby? *Our baby*!' He looked more alarmed than she had ever seen him before and he kept repeating the same words, so many times she wondered if he was delirious. 'Our baby!' Then after a few moments looking first at her then down to the bump again he very tentatively lifted his hand and hovered over it.

'For goodness sake,' she said, caught his hand and put it firmly over the lump.

'I can't feel anything now,' he said.

'No, you've probably frightened it to death.'

'*Mon Dieu*!'

'It is a joke,' she said, seeing his expression.

'You shouldn't have come to that prison when you are having a baby, my baby, risking it ...'

'I wasn't going to risk it not having a father.'

His hand now explored the extent of the swelling, marvelling, approving. 'And my father, how did he take the news?'

'He drank our health, and his coming grandson's health, in the farm's best vintage, some he laid down the year you were born.'

'Everyone knew about my baby before me! When did you first know?' he asked suddenly suspicious, trying to do sums.

'I wasn't really sure until after I left Paris last time. It was Madeleine really ...'

'Paris,' he mused, his look saying much more, saying: We were happy in Paris in spite of everything.

'It'll be like that again, in the spring, when we're both back to normal,' she whispered. But though she was trying very hard the morbid stench inside the car, which must be coming from his injured leg, was frightening, bringing doom-laden words like septicaemia and gangrene to her mind. She tried to push them away, but found herself hoping the doctor would be contacted very quickly indeed. Neither did Jacques seem to remember he had mentioned Verit – was everything just hope and delusion she wondered.

Ernest came carring out a tray, questioning whether his son was hungry. She was suddenly alarmed in case he said yes; if he needed an anaesthetic, an operation, eating would not be advisable. But he shook his head and took no more than a sip of tea.

Ernest was pacing out his anxiety in front of the house when they saw Jean-Paul cycling back at top speed.

'We're to drive him to the doctor's house now. Lucille has finished at the hospital and will be waiting for us at the house.'

'You've seen Lucille?' Stella asked as Ernest took charge of the bicycle.

He nodded. 'You'll stay here,' he said as he opened the back door of the car for her to get out.

'I'm coming with you,' she insisted.

'It would be better if you stayed here ...'

'It can be better, wiser, what you will. I am not parting with Jacques so soon. I am coming with him. Ernest must obviously stay here, but I'll sit in the front with you.'

'I don't want to waste time, the doctor's eager to get Jacques into his house while there are no patrols round about. You just never know when they may pass through again.'

'Off we go then,' Stella said as she transferred out of the back seat.

Jean-Paul shrugged at Ernest as if to say, Well, I did try.

They drove to the side door of Dr Chabrol's house where two men and Lucille were waiting just inside the walled garden with a stretcher. Lucille greeted her brother warmly, kissing him as she reached in to begin unwinding the blankets so he could be lifted. 'You look terrible,' she told him.

'Spoken like a true sister,' he said, gritting his teeth and closing his eyes, trying not to make any sound as the process of lifting and passing him from the car to the stretcher began.

Stella went ahead and opened doors. He was taken to a small room looking out on to the rear garden. The room where for as many years as Stella could remember Dr Chabrol, and his father before him, had conducted their surgeries and minor operations. There was a small flat couch, to which Jacques was lifted.

'The doctor has asked me to take off whatever dressing you have on your leg,' Lucille said, 'and he will be here quite soon – but he's been invited to go up to the château to see the countess, the German commander's girlfriend. He feels it would hardly be politic to refuse. He must keep on good terms to be allowed to keep the hospital going, and while the countess gets her goodies we get a few extra supplies – and information.'

'So while the son runs the Resistance, the father flirts with the *Kommandant* and his French baggage.'

Stella thought that sounded much more like the old Jacques, but found herself nauseated by the smell which became stronger as Lucille unwound the bandages from the leg. She would have been glad to stand back, but Jacques suddenly waved her forward. 'I was going to to tell you,' he said, 'Verit's alive, they put him in my cell. He tore up his shirt to bandage my leg when it was first broken. I wanted to keep some of the strips to send to his wife, but they were

191

burned when I was in Clermont-Ferrand.'

'Not surprised if they smelt like these,' Lucille said and seeing Stella's face sent her to Dr Chabrol's kitchen for hot water.

'We're back to the sore feet routine, I know,' she pretended to grumble but going towards the kitchen she met the doctor coming in. 'He's here, doctor, in the surgery.'

'Good! Good! Let's go and have a look at him then.'

He shook Jacques warmly by the hand, lifting his free hand to feel his patient's forehead. 'I hope we're going to have time for some good talks when we've got you well.'

'Ah!' he exclaimed when he saw the leg. 'This should have been X-rayed and operated on immediately. It is not a simple break, as you must know.' Jacques closed his eyes as the doctor's fingers explored the separate pieces of his shin bone. 'And there is an infection, which is what is sending your temperature up.' He put a thermometer under Jacques's tongue. 'And other injuries?' he asked. Jacques opened his palms; one was healed but the other was red and festering. He also pointed to his neck.

'When did you last eat and drink?'

'Yesterday sometime, I think, I didn't want anything,' he said. 'A sip of tea when I arrived at home.'

'No more than moistening your lips,' Stella added.

'Lucille, could you act as my anaesthetist? I'd like to clean the leg and set it immediately.'

'Of course,' she said.

'Finish what you are doing then scrub up,' he said then taking Stella's arm he propelled her before him out of the surgery. 'I want you to go back with Jean-Paul and prepare a place where Jacques can be nursed – possibly for a long time. You're going to need your strength not just for his baby, but for him.' He walked her on through the house, giving her no chance to interrupt. 'Had he been his own self I've no doubt he could cope with this leg and infection without too much trouble, but you can see he is not himself. It has all been neglected. He will need powerful incentives to get well.'

'But he will get well?'

'I'll do my very best on that score, but your part afterwards will perhaps be even more important – and,' he said with finality, 'the sooner that Wolseley is removed from the side of my house the better.'

Chapter Twenty-One

It all took much longer than even Dr Chabrol had expected. The leg had tried to heal but at such an angle that the decision had to be made to rebreak the fragile strings that linked the two sections of bone. He took time to place these alongside the bone as he reset it hoping they would grow in, strengthen it, speed the rebuilding process.

As he neared the end of the operation he glanced at his surgery clock. The limousine from the château, always prompt, would arrive in half an hour. He told Lucille this as they worked on the final cleaning up and stitching. He saw how large her eyes grew above her mask. He wondered if these nurses knew how attractive they were to young doctors, how irresistible.

'You may have to complete the plastering,' he told her, 'I'll show you exactly what to do. The aftercare you're happy about?'

She nodded, eyes trusting, though full of concern for her brother, very aware that the operation had been complex.

'Moving him will be a problem, but I suggest we forget that until I return from the château. My wife will stay on the ward through the night and until Nadia comes in tomorrow, so you can forget the ward for the time being, make Jacques your priority.'

He glanced at the clock again and wondered at his own role in this strange time. Law-abiding to the point of prudishness, he was now practically a self-appointed double-agent: going to dine with a countess (whom his father had brought into the world), who had grown up a spoilt troublesome brat, and an eager German collaborator so her good times and way of life could continue. Knowing where the local commander was at such times was a great bonus to Edmund Chabrol's Resistance group.

The price the countess paid was acute hypochondria. Though at forty she was probably at the peak of her mature physical beauty, the doctor knew it was her waning youth that constantly worried her. The

193

petals would begin to fade and droop and her life when the Germans were driven from France (and he would not allow himself doubts on that outcome) would most certainly be permanently blighted.

Lucille, in contrast, though living through perilous and heart-rending days, blossomed every time this Jean-Paul came into sight. If life was fair she should have long life, and many children, and live in peace on her mother's family's land. He smiled under his mask. This was what France was about, this was what he, his wife and son worked for.

He eased his aching shoulders for a moment, then dressed the burn on Jacques's hand, while supervising Lucille on the final careful plastering of the leg. Then both started violently as the door of the surgery was rapped sharply. Dr Chabrol opened it quickly, it was a smart German soldier, the chauffeur who drove for the countess's admirer.

He pulled down his mask, 'Ah! Come in! Come in! I'm a little late, a rather large stitching job.' He gambled on the usual reaction.

'I'll wait outside for you, sir.'

'As you wish, I'll not be long.' He turned back to Lucille before he closed the surgery door behind himself. 'You can finish off, nurse?' The big grey eyes looked fixedly at him, and ignored the chauffeur as she nodded. Jean-Paul, he thought, was a lucky man.

At the château he found what was the usual situation. Colonel Wilhelm Voss-Beker was making sure the countess fully appreciated the range of gifts of food, chocolates and a flat box full of tissue paper and lacy lingerie he had brought her, payment for which he would no doubt extract later.

The countess was being playfully encouraged to eat some of the chocolate truffles – just before dinner, the doctor noted. In fact the luxury food items which arrived regularly at the château, and which were apparently freely available at expensive pro-German restaurants in Paris and Vichy, had probably more to do with the countess's migraines and abdominal troubles than anything else.

It was also apparent to the doctor that the colonel was having what might be for him a final fling away from home. His family were of the old German army élite, men who swore personal allegiance to the Kaiser, and treated everyone else as inferiors to be soundly punished if they offended. The glamorous countess, probably nearly twenty years his junior, obviously fascinated him.

This particular evening he had come well provisioned with wine and a tall stone bottle of Dutch gin, confiscated no doubt, and both these and the truffles were being consumed with a greedy and sensual rapidity the doctor found revolting. Quite why he had been requested to come when there seemed to be no other guests expected, and he was obviously surplus to the couple's enjoyment, was not so far evident.

He rather expected that before the meal began the countess might summon him for a private consultation, but as the meal of pâté, fish, chicken and desserts progressed it became obvious that it was the colonel who was going to proposition him, 'man to man', for the countess withdrew after the meal, leaving them with the brandy.

He watched dispassionately as the tanned distinguished-looking officer, his hair more grey than blond, poured himself another brandy and tossed it back with no change of expression, or hint of enjoyment. The colonel then cleared his throat and began an oblique dissertation about his affection for the French countess, but his duty to the Fatherland, and his family. The phrase 'men of the world' was repeated and the doctor at last understood what he was being asked to do.

He sat staring at his hands, white-knuckled, and as the colonel saw the situation was well understood, he was silent, waiting, but still Dr Chabrol did not speak. Waiting was a ploy he had used for years with patients; experience had shown him there was always more to be gained by listening, though now the beating of his own heart made him almost unable to hear the German.

The colonel leaned forward in a confidential manner and began with promises of supplies for his household, and following a disparaging glance from the doctor, medicines and supplies for the village hospital.

'I am a Catholic,' the doctor said very quietly.

The colonel clenched his fist on the table, suddenly impatient. 'And I am an officer of the Third Reich, the country France has surrendered to.'

'Our country, not our souls,' he spoke slowly and he hoped his voice was firm for inside he shook with emotional rage. 'What you ask I consider a mortal sin.'

'For those who do not co-operate,' threat now took over the colonel's voice, 'there will be reprisals. Five people, perhaps ten, will be shot for every German killed.'

The doctor raised his eyebrows at the colonel, now flushed with fury and drink. 'The countess's child would be a German.'

'*Nein*! *Nein*! I have my children! This is a different thing altogether,' he blustered. 'Before – what I was talking about before was that garage proprietor's random shooting of our men.'

'As they fired his property,' the doctor said, thinking the colonel managed to make 'garage proprietor' sound like the lowest, meanest occupation in the world.

'Quite! Quite! He should not have interfered. Now the whole area will be stirred up! I have extra troops on the way here even now!'

195

'More work for you,' the doctor prompted. Here was information Edmund would be anxious to have.

'Indeed! This is why I need this other matter settled.' He waved a swift dismissive hand.

'When are these other troops coming exactly?' The doctor posed the question without emphasis, but hung on the answer.

'In exactly,' he paused to consult his wristwatch, 'five hours and twenty minutes. When they will immediately go to every house not already meticulously searched – even yours Dr Chabrol, we must not make exceptions or the populace will think you are a collaborator!'

'In the middle of the night?' the doctor queried.

'Oh! yes, Herr Doctor, birds come home to roost at night!' The colonel rose and strode a little unsteadily up and down before the baroque fireplace, but the information included in the crass attempt at bullying engaged Dr Chabrol with another problem.

Jacques might not be recognised immediately as an escaped prisoner, but his presence would be questioned, his papers demanded. The doctor had a duty to his own wife and son. Edmund's activities must be screened from scrutiny – and his own tiny hospital ward preserved. He must leave the château as soon as possible and ensure Jacques was moved to a secure hiding place. Five hours and twenty minutes. He glanced covertly at the huge ormolu clock on the mantelpiece: to be exact five hours, twelve minutes. To defeat the Germans they would have to learn to be as precise, calculating, and as devious as the enemy were.

He became aware that the colonel had stopped pacing and was looking fixedly at him. Dr Chabrol cleared his throat but was not averse to keeping this elderly Romeo on a razor's edge. He also realised with something of a constitutional shock that he was not averse to leaving a doubt in this man's mind. If he revealed at once his total unwillingness to abort any baby, even an unwanted German bastard conceived in a welter of obscene over-indulgence, his usefulness to the Resistance was over. He needed time. 'What you have said has shocked me,' he said. 'I feel I need to go home to think this out. Perhaps we might meet again in say two or three days.'

'Two or three days! I think you misread the situation.' The German obviously did not relish either the less than positive answer or the delay. He leaned on the overmantel, staring into the fire, his head lowered on his forearm, fists hard clenched. After a few moments the colonel made a low grunt of decision, and straightened slowly. Watching, the doctor was reminded of a snake rising up, positioning itself ready to strike.

The colonel came to attention, clicked his heels and bowed. 'I *will* arrange to visit you,' he said shortly, 'after which I expect you will be ready to come back here – when, of course, the procedure can be carried out. I shall inform the countess that you had urgent matters to attend to and asked to be excused.'

It was the doctor's turn to bow as he was shown out. He tried not to think of the moral trap which seemed to be closing around him and to forget the revulsion that overcame him at the colonel's words 'the procedure', which still rang coldly in his brain.

His son came to greet him in the hall. 'I heard the car – you're early, has the countess taken to her bed?' he quipped. Then he saw his father's face clearly. 'What's happened?'

Lucille too heard and came through from the surgery.

The doctor held up a hand to check his son while he enquired quickly about his patient.

'He came round, was very sick. He's dozing again now.'

He told them both of the influx of new troops and the approaching searches, but not about his moral impasse.

'The farm's already been visited, Stella dealt with them, we should move Jacques there at once,' Lucille said.

'I don't think we have much choice but to move him, unfortunately,' the doctor agreed, another aspect of good medical practice weighing on his conscience.

'I'll get our car,' Edmund said.

'The Wolseley's bigger,' Lucille said.

'Jean-Paul's taken the Wolseley to a new hiding place, miles away,' Edmund replied on his way out to their garage.

Lucille thought briefly of the joy of also being miles away with Jean-Paul, in another country, England preferably, then turned to listen to what the doctor was saying.

'We'd better get our patient as well prepared for the journey as we can.' The doctor led the way to his surgery, thinking his son never seemed to take much in the way of time to make decisions.

He had been disappointed when Edmund had chosen not to follow two generations of Chabrols into the medical profession, but at least it didn't involve the boy in all this moral addition and subtraction. Figures were, he supposed, usually either right or wrong.

Jacques was told what was happening, but his half-glazed eyes and his unquestioning acquiescence as they carefully strapped his legs together before lifting him made it obvious that he was still only hazily aware of reality. It became more obvious that he was unfit to travel as he was loaded into the back of the Citroen. He laughed obligingly when spoken to and groaned when moved.

Lucille crouched in the back trying to keep her brother as

197

comfortable as possible. She knew the note of the doctor's car would be recognised by most locals who were awake. They would merely wonder who was ill, or perhaps in difficulties in childbirth.

Stella heard its approach with more concern. Heart thumping, she was downstairs and at the door in her dressing-gown, well before Hector had risen from his couch in the nearby office.

It was the doctor who reassured, Edmund who explained about the coming troops and new searches.

'Jean-Paul has the radio up at the bories,' Hector said, 'it'll be safe enough there.'

'Hector?' Jacques suddenly questioned, as if he had just become aware of where he was. 'Is that Hector?'

His sister reassured him, relieved to see he was more alert. 'The night air's reviving him,' she said.

'Will you take him into his own bedroom?' Stella asked.

'If he's found we'll all be interned,' Edmund said matter-of-factly. 'Prison or labour camp at best.'

'So in my hidey-hole above the stables,' Ernest decided. 'We can all rest easier if he's up there with me.'

'And if the Germans do come again, they'll find exactly what they found before,' Stella said as she nodded agreement, 'but how will we do it?'

'Let's get him into the stable and solve it stage by stage,' Edmund said, then he paused listening intently as the sound of several heavy lorries came from the main road.

'The German troops,' Lucille noted, 'but that's earlier than we thought.'

'They'll need time to form up and get instructions,' Edmund said scornfully. 'But we shouldn't waste any time all getting back to where we should be.'

Edmund held beneath Jacques's arms, while Ernest and the doctor between them carried and supported his lower half and the weight of the plastered leg. Once out of the car, the distance to the stables and the stairs up to the stable bedroom were accomplished without too much difficulty. Jacques was lain on the bed while a two-section ladder was pulled out from its hiding place behind the huge old chest of drawers, and put together. Ernest climbed up to a trapdoor, well concealed among the corner beams, and opened it.

'The only way you'll get him up there is on someone's back,' Hector said.

'That's if he could hold on,' Lucille said, 'and he can't.'

'If I bend over he could ride on my back.' Edmund demonstrated. 'I could come behind and support his legs ...'

'Tie his hands together?' Edmund speculated, 'then loop them over my head.'

'No!' Stella interrupted, 'take him up on the chair. Bind him to it, have ropes up in the loft, his father underneath, then pull and push the chair up the slope of the ladder, like a sledge!' Eagerly she demonstrated how, tipped backwards, the chair would ride up the ladder.

'Genius!' Edmund said, snatching a long leading rein from a hook. 'Here's the rope.'

'We can use a sheet to secure him to the chair,' Lucille said, pulling one free.

'I'll be up the top with Edmund to help pull,' Stella said from halfway up the ladder.

Edmund grinned at his father in the light of the lantern. 'Bit late to protest,' he said as the young woman in flowing satin dressing-gown disappeared through the trapdoor.

Dr Chabrol shook his head, but he had seen more foolhardy acts by heavily pregnant farmers' wives over the years, and this young Englishwoman was making the best of her unplanned pregnancy.

With infinite care it was achieved. 'Compliments to the master of works,' Edmund gasped, well out of breath as Jacques's head appeared through the trapdoor. There was a moment of awkwardness as the chair reached the full extent of the ladder. 'Take the weight, you two below,' Edmund ordered, 'and stand clear, Stella!' With an effort of will, more than strength, he hauled the chair the final millimetres through the trapdoor and across on to the wooden flooring.

'Oh! he's passed out,' Stella called as Jacques sat slumped into the chair, only the swaddling sheet holding him upright. She lifted his legs, for the final heave had struck the plastered foot on the floor. Lucille and the doctor clambered rapidly up into the loft. Stella helped them untie the sheeting strips and Jacques was carried to the bed. He was lain carefully down, his leg carefully placed, and his breathing monitored.

There was a general easing of tension as he moaned slightly, moved his head, then opened his eyes. 'Lie still,' Stella told him, 'you're safe now. All you have to do is get well.'

Lucille moved quickly, almost too abruptly, as if the statement gave her cause for unease. The doctor too began to move around again. He took a bottle of pills from his pocket and put them into Ernest's hand, instructing him to give his son two as soon as he recovered sufficiently. 'Then two every four hours if he needs them. They'll ease the pain. You've got plenty of water up here?'

'Yes, I've everything we need,' Ernest said, anxious they should go.

Stella went to the bed, kissed Jacques gently on the forehead. 'I don't want to leave you,' she said, 'but I must in case the Germans do come again.'

'I'll take good care of him,' Ernest reassured her as she lingered.

'Go,' Jacques added in a hoarse whisper and lifting a shaky hand to his lips he blew her a kiss.

Ernest saw her safely down into the stable bedroom, then pulled the ladder up into the loft. 'Rest well,' he called softly as he closed the trapdoor.

She had not heard the car drive away, nor was she prepared to see Lucille still there.

'They don't need me until the morning, I'll go then,' Lucille said. Her papers as Lucille Cleauville, living on Cleauville Farm, but choosing to nurse in Dr Chabrol's hospital had been accepted both by the State Police and the German colonel, so this was no problem.

Stella suddenly realised she was cold, and shivered slightly. Lucille put her arm about her. 'Go in,' she said. 'Hector's gone to bed and I'm going up to Jean-Paul.'

'But, you can't ... you ...'

'I could go to our bories blindfold, you know that.'

'It'll take you hours!'

'Forty-four minutes, Jacques and I have often timed it. He once did it in twenty-nine! I just need to be with Jean, while I can, and he needs to know what's happening. I think he ought not to make the morning radio calls with all these extra troops about.' She gave Stella a quick kiss on the cheek. 'You are cold. Go in, rest while you can, tomorrow Jacques will need you.'

Stella wanted to protest, thinking what foolhardiness, what a ridiculous thing to do, then she pushed the torch into her friend's hand. Like brother, like sister, she thought, remembering the effort Jacques had just made to blow her a kiss.

She stood listening, aware that the sky was lightening; she could see the blackness of buildings against dark grey. Suddenly her shivering became a frame-shaking shudder. She remembered what Ernest had said about someone walking over his grave, and though he and Jacques were nearby she had never felt so alone.

Chapter Twenty-Two

The path was so well known to her that she could almost visualise every rock, every pothole. She walked some twenty metres along the farm drive, then struck up into the fields, leaving Hector's cottage on her left, through the spinney, up to the scrubland beyond. Here the path narrowed then petered out, leaving a confusion of passable ways, where animals, or the rains, had driven clear spaces between dense bushes and boulders.

Lucille could have found her way to the medieval bories by any one of a dozen paths. It was one of this hiding place's advantages – that and the fact the bories were rumoured to be haunted, a story which the Blair children had helped cultivate at every opportunity, eager to keep the place to themselves.

She crouched low as she came to the highest point, aware that even in this dark grey light she might be spotted on the skyline by some sharp-eyed German, or collaborator. She knew of quite a few, less elevated than the countess, who were making themselves as comfortable as they could under the Vichy regime.

The ancient drystone shelters lay some five hundred metres deeper into the scrubland, but now she must be cautious. She wondered if there was some signal she should give of her approach? She mustn't just blunder in, she should try to identify herself to Jean-Paul.

Nearer the bories the scrub had grown thicker than she remembered it. Several times the wild broom was so long and strong it threatened to entangle her legs as she cautiously pushed through. She made for where several olive trees of great antiquity stood in a group. Reaching the first of their huge trunks, sculpted by eight or nine hundred years of growth into caricatures of grim trees in fairy stories, she wondered if she might venture to call, or briefly shine her torch. She ruled out the light, for that would give no clue to her identity. Perhaps she could go a little closer and call, gently; she could say her own name – that would be best.

If she delayed too long it would be daylight and almost time for her to go back. She moved on to the next gnarled trunk, as she had done in many a game of hide and seek, but the next moment froze as a low voice almost in her ear ordered, 'Don't move!'

'Jean?' she gasped. 'It's me.'

'Lucille?' his voice was hard, censorious. 'What's happened? What are you doing up here in the middle of the night? I could have ... dealt with you in a very nasty way.'

'Jean, I needed to see you.' She gripped his sleeve, alarmed by the harshness of his challenge. 'How did you know I was here?'

'You've been through several tripwires. But are *you* sure you've not been followed?'

'Quite sure, all the action is the other side of the village.' When she would have said more he shushed her, took her hand and led her towards the stone shelters.

'Come on, mind your head.' He had to bend nearly double to lead the way into the most complete borie, which Lucille and the others as children had always called 'the chieftain's hut'. The low entrance was like that of an igloo, a small arched passage-like doorway. She knew it all as intimately as she knew her way across the hillsides. Inside this borie there were two separate rooms, one leading at right angles from the other, so it was possible to have a low light in the second room and no glimmer be visible until one turned the corner. As he led the way she saw there was an oil lamp, its circular wick glowing. It made a wonder of the beehive shape over them, a work of art of the stones carefully keyed together, skilfully graded from bottom to top. These shelters, guarded by the strange group of ancient olive trees, had always given this place a special significance to Lucille, who had never let it be known that she more than half believed the stories of it being haunted.

She was drawn to the tiny bamboo table where the lamp stood. It felt so strange to see furniture in this place; all it had ever held before was her dolls' tea-set, set out on the dusty floor. She recognised all the things: the table, a chair, the lamp, a pile of goatskins and a dark bearskin rug on a camp bed, all were from the farm. Her mother had used this table last summer for drinks near her couch. She rested a hand on it – and told him about the troops, and about Jacques. 'He's so ill, worse than Stella realises, his resistance to infection must be so low – then having to move him.'

'Is there anything more that can be done?' His voice echoed with low but theatrical intensity in the inverted stone bowl. 'Anything I can do, or get for him? Another doctor? A specialist?'

'It's more general care and just the will to go on.'

'But surely he has that! Stella and his baby coming.'

'He's so tired, so thin. I think it was seeing those two in such trouble that made me need to see you so urgently, reassure myself that *you* are ...' She broke off. 'That nothing's happened to you.'

'I'm fine,' he told her.

'I think you ought not to make the radio calls in the morning, in case it gives you away.'

'Did Edmund suggest that?'

'No,' she admitted, 'I just thought it probably wasn't wise.'

'Whereas crashing up a hillside in the dark, and nearly being garotted is!'

'No ...' she began, but he lifted his hand still holding the coiled circles of thin wire.

Instinctively she put up a hand to her neck. 'But after Pas de Crédit ...' she persisted.

'His truck probably gave him away. It seemed a good idea at the time.'

'So did coming here,' she answered. In the light of the lantern his shadow was thrown up and right over the rounded roof, and beneath his high cheek bones the hollows were dramatically deep. He could only stand upright in the very middle of the room. She shook her head at him.

'What is it?' He raised the wire before pushing it into his jacket pocket. 'I couldn't know it was one of my foolhardy followers.'

'One?' She tutted at herself for even making the query. 'No, it's you! Look at you! Are you always in fancy dress?'

He spread his arms and looked down at his black baggy trousers tucked into black boots, a blue blouson shirt and a black jacket, a bandolier across his chest and a large black beret pulled down at a rakish angle. 'So?' he exclaimed. 'This is what this year's partisan is wearing!'

'Why can't you be ...'

'What, a nurse! Like you.' He pulled her towards him and spread her coat to reveal her white overall.

'No, sort of ... ordinary? I feel if you were more ordinary, more everyday, I would have more claim to you.'

'You ridiculous, beautiful girl, come here.' He threw off the bandolier, then his hat, his jacket and opened his arms to her. 'How's that!'

She shook her head at him again.

'Not enough?' He pulled off his shirt and stood just in trousers and boots, looking amazingly virile, like a matinée idol.

203

'No!' she pleaded. 'Just stop! Stop fooling, stop acting, I get so afraid for you.'

'No,' he ordered, 'you must never be afraid. Never. Dismiss it from your mind, young woman! I'm doing it again, fooling around,' he said repentantly, then added more quietly, 'but you should also know that sometimes I think if I stop acting, or fooling, I'll disappear, stop existing. There sometimes doesn't seem to be much of me under all these acts.'

She suddenly remembered what Madeleine had said when he had come to the Parisian apartment and made so light of taking a convoy to the front line. 'It's how some men have to deal with things, make light, make jokes.' She also remembered her saying that he should not be going to war at all, he should be on the stage.

Lucille felt such a flood of tender love and concern for him. 'Oh, you exist.' She wanted to tell him he existed for her so much she had to force herself to find space in her brain for other things. She put her arms around his naked torso, running them up his back. 'You feel quite warm.'

'I am warm, and I am sure I exist when you are with me. I feel more alive, even immortal, that I could live forever when you're here. I feel more of everything,' he lowered his voice to a new intense register, 'more needing you, wanting to make love to you.' He gestured towards the skins and fur. 'They are wonderful to lie in. Eskimos you know ...'

'I know!' She pretended to censure this new line of nonsense.

He began to slip her coat from off her shoulders. 'I could,' he said, 'throw all the skins on the floor and be in them much before you. I've a whole lot more than a head start.'

'You fool,' she whispered endearingly as he unbuttoned her overall and that joined her coat on the floor. 'You tender, wonderful fool.' She unfastened his leather belt.

He kissed her lips, her cheek, her neck and unzipped her skirt. She stepped out of it and unbuttoned his trousers. 'I need to take two things off you, to my one,' he whispered nibbling her earlobe, 'that's only fair.' The bite made her squirm hard up against him and the pace of undressing increased. She would have led him to the pile of skins and fur, but he made her pause. 'Let me look at you,' he said.

She stood tall, then on an impulse threw her arms back and thrust her face up to where the small chimney looked out on the lightening sky. She felt as if they both stood on a narrow band of time which ran back to man's dawn – and forward – but she could not know for how long. She only knew that now had a significance beyond war and worldly fears and ambitions and was very important indeed. She heard

204

him gasp, then felt herself lifted up, and up. She spread her legs around him and he slowly lowered her on to himself.

On the furs afterwards she lay replete in his arms. 'I think the nicest time is afterwards.'

'Do you?' He made the words sound like satire.

'Don't you?'

He laughed softly in this throat and rolled over towards her again.

Chapter Twenty-Three

It was still cold as Stella came from the stables for the second time, though the rim of the sun was visible above the horizon. Her name was called and she turned to see Lucille hurrying towards her. The rising light caught her friend's blonde hair, giving it a bright halo, which Stella thought went very well with the general glow of happiness about her.

'How's things?' Lucille asked, then as if she felt that sounded too frivolous she added, 'with Jacques? What kind of night has he had?'

'His father said he took some water through the night, but he doesn't want anything now, to eat or drink.'

'Early days after an op. Did he sleep? You didn't,' Lucille judged, 'you look exhausted.'

'While you look positively radiant!'

'*Pardon*!' She was aware of the sin of private joy and general worry.

'Don't be silly. Make hay, as they say, while the sun shines on your particular meadow. But come and see Jacques, I'm anxious to know what you think about him.'

'You've only just climbed down. I'll go, then come back and make us both breakfast. *Go and sit down*!' Lucille ordered.

She called to her father as she climbed into the second of their hiding places she had been in during the last few hours. This one, she reflected, was certainly warmer, with its wooden rafters and floor – wood and worry though – while the other one had been a kind of seventh heaven in stone.

'Hi!' she greeted her father and more gently her brother who lay awake but very still.

'How are you feeling?' she asked. She felt his forehead, which was hot but slightly damp. She lifted the sheet to look at and discreetly smell his leg. It was a technique that had proved an invaluable guide who to treat first when so many arrived with ulcerated legs and neglected wounds wrapped in multifarious collections of bandages. She was relieved to find all seemed normal. 'So how are you?'

'Exhausted,' he said as he attempted to smile.

'It's your body telling you it needs the rest.'

'I'm not arguing.' He closed his eyes again.

'Have you had breakfast?' she asked her father. He, she thought, looked more rested than Stella.

'Stella's going to take over from me in a while.'

'So, what do you think? Should the doctor come?' Stella asked when she went back to the kitchen.

'I don't think there's anything more he can do,' Lucille began then seeing her friend's alarm added, 'I mean it's just rest and care that's needed now, just time.'

'You really think that?'

'I do,' she said firmly, doubtful that there was anything more the doctor had in his store of medicines he could prescribe.

'I thought he looked so much worse this morning,' Stella persisted. 'Will you tell Dr Chabrol that?'

'Yes, of course, I shall give him a full report. He's a good doctor you know – in all ways.'

'I do know, of course I do.'

'Get dressed, have your breakfast then go up and sit by Jacques, you'll be happier where you can see each other. But don't let him talk too much, you know what he's like. Just have a quiet time together. Jean-Paul will be here later.'

'Thanks.' She was so weary she was grateful to be told exactly what she should do.

'You must remember that moving Jacques last night was bound to take a big toll on his strength. I'll be back about three and Jean-Paul said he would look in. Don't worry!'

Stella thought Jacques was asleep when she relieved Ernest, but when his father had gone and she had settled in a chair next to the bed he turned his face towards her. 'You mustn't keep climbing that ladder.'

'It's good exercise and I am getting better at the trapdoor; turn slightly to the left and I'm through with no trouble at all.'

'You'll be glad when it's all over,' he said, spreading a languid arm in her direction.

She took his hand. 'I shall be glad when you're better.'

'We haven't really talked since you came to the prison ...'

'Later,' she said, 'I'm under strict instructions not to let you talk too much. "Sister" Lucille says we both have to rest.'

'I only have to close my eyes and I'm asleep,' he told her.

'Right, we'll both do that.' Her own eyes ached with fatigue and now she was comfortable by his side she could feel sleep ready to claim her.

When she awoke she was quiet for a time watching him. The rest had made her feel ready for almost anything. Jacques woke soon after, but he wanted only a drink of water.

She was becoming more and more concerned the longer he fasted and would drink nothing but water. Taking over from Ernest again just after midday she thought Jacques still slept but then realised he was breathing more rapidly, through his mouth, and before long sucking at the air in ragged gasps. She spoke to him, gently at first, then more urgently.

'What is it?' Jean-Paul appeared through the trapdoor. 'I was just on my way up.'

'I think he's unconscious,' she began then a faint rambling moan came from the bed. 'I can't wake him properly!'

Jean-Paul stooped over the bed, called Jacques's name several times with low urgency. 'I'll see if I can contact the doctor,' he said.

'Be very careful,' she warned. And very quick, she added silently.

'I thought he was still sleeping,' she agonised to herself as she poured water into a bowl, squeezed out a flannel, then placed it on his forehead. The doctor had mentioned infection; so had Lucille. It must be taking him over, swamping his system. She began to pray for the second time in two days for the doctor to hurry.

Jean-Paul had only been gone only a short time when she was startled as Jacques suddenly cried out in alarm. 'Mind! For God's sake!' His voice rose almost to terror. 'Stella!'

'What is it?' she cried out, equally alarmed.

He lifted his arms as if fending something off, calling her name over and over again. Her own voice was panic-stricken as she rushed to the trapdoor. Ernest was there immediately reassuring her, 'Yes, yes, I heard him. I was coming to tell you, Lucille's just cycling down the drive. I'll get her.'

Stella tried to calm Jacques, whose eyes were open now, but he was seeing some terror which threatened her for he kept calling her name in the most anguished way.

'Is the doctor coming?' she demanded as Lucille arrived. 'Did Jean-Paul bring the message?'

'Yes, yes, but it wasn't easy. They've spent the morning ransacking Dr Chabrol's house *and* upset the hospital, and gone to Nadia and Claude's house! It's as if there was some personal spite against the doctor! He'll come as soon as he can, but there's so much activity it's frightening.'

'What can we do?' Stella agonised as Jacques again called out, nothing intelligible this time, just a great alarmed shout.

Lucille lifted the sheet. 'His leg seems all right.' Then she felt her brother's head, pulse, and in answer to Stella's repeated question she said, 'Fetch me all the blankets you can find, and more drinking water. We mustn't let him dehydrate.'

'What is it, what's happened to him? I thought he was just asleep.'

Lucille, lacking a stethoscope, put her ear down to Jacques's chest. 'It could be pneumonia.'

'I knew it was something bad.' Stella stood aghast, hand over her mouth.

'Go and help Father find blankets,' Lucille ordered and as they went, she called after them, 'Bring some brandy, Pa.'

When they returned Lucille piled the blankets on her brother right up to his chin and instructed Stella not to let him throw them off. 'We must try to break the fever,' she said. 'I think a little brandy in the water will help, and we must make sure he drinks every twenty minutes.'

It became something of a strenuous task as Jacques began to fight to free himself of the suffocating heat of the blankets. Stella wondered if they were doing the right thing as the spoon was knocked from her hand, but Lucille showed her the best way to hold his jaw to force the liquid into his mouth.

'What if he chokes?'

'He won't! He must drink,' Lucille told them. 'But if you'll go on doing as I've said, force him to drink and force him to keep the blankets on tight, I'll cycle back to the hospital. The doctor may have something like sulphapyridine tablets. I don't know, everything is in awfully short supply.' She paused at the top of the ladder as Jacques again pushed out his arms. 'Don't be soft with him Stella, push his arms down! He must be kept as warm as possible, and the drinks are vital.'

Her father nodded at her. 'You go, between us we'll manage.'

Two floors below she found Jean-Paul waiting for her; he stooped to kiss her quickly on the cheek. 'I could hear Jacques shouting,' he said.

'He's delirious. If the Germans arrive he'd have to be kept quiet, and I don't think those two would manage it.'

'I'll go up to Ernest. Stella should be in the house.'

'Edmund thinks his father has offended the colonel personally, so it could be a risk even having the doctor here.'

'But he's so careful, so precise.' Jean-Paul shook his head.

'There's something.' Lucille was sure. 'The way the colonel and his lackeys acted in the hospital and in the house was despicable. Madame Chabrol was in tears when I left. They've deliberately

209

smashed family china and pictures, destroyed photographs. It wasn't just in passing, but deliberately searching out things as if to be as hurtful as possible. Jeannette Chabrol said her husband just stood stony-faced until they had gone. Then he went back to his patients – accompanied by a sergeant.'

'The doctor's been cultivating the colonel for information ever since the liaison with the countess began,' Jean-Paul told her. 'Edmund even said he thought the colonel enjoyed his father's company!'

'The relationship has soured,' Lucille said succinctly. 'And when I left the colonel was enquiring where Nadia lived!'

'So is it anyone connected with the hospital or the doctor they are persecuting?' he wondered. 'If so it does mean they could come here anytime.'

'They've already searched here,' she was saying when they both heard the sound of an approaching car. 'The doctor's if I'm not much mistaken,' she added as she ran outside. 'Yes!' she called back and ran to greet him, while Jean-Paul went to tell Ernest and Stella.

She stopped mid-stride as the sound of more vehicles reached her, one or two at least. 'I think the colonel's following you with his men,' she said.

He plunged a hand into his pocket and pushed a bottle of tablets into her hands. 'Tell them to crush them and give as I've written on the bottle. Then get the ladder up and you come back to me. I'll be in the kitchen.'

There was no time to question, only to trust.

She pushed the tablets at Jean-Paul. 'I heard,' he said and ran to the stable, where he began to pull the large door to before she reminded him, 'Stella should be down here.' He left the door ajar and disappeared. Lucille turned but did not run to the kitchen for the troop carriers, led by the colonel's limousine, had already turned into the drive. She did not want to alert them to anything that was causing her to hurry.

'They're almost here,' she told the doctor, who was sitting at the table, looking as weary as it was possible for a man to look and still be on his feet.

'I've no time to explain anything, just trust me and follow my lead,' he said as they heard the first of the trucks stop outside. 'Sit down,' he added.

They sat listening to sounds that had become all too familiar: troops jumping down from trucks, the shuffle of boots, the clatter of rifles as a sergeant ordered them to fall into ranks, then the voice of a more educated man, an officer, then silence. They listened more intently and then they heard Stella's voice.

'Can I help you, colonel?'

The doctor rose and went to the door.

'Ah! so you have the good doctor here, how lucky you are to have his services. Do you have a particular problem? Apart from the obvious.' The sergeant shuffled a foot and the colonel glared at him.

'I am here to collect my nurse,' Dr Chabrol told him.

'Ah! yes, we're here to visit your nurse too. We have visited your other assistants' homes.'

'I heard,' the doctor said. 'I'm here to collect my nurse on the way up to the château.'

'Aaah!' The colonel nodded at him as if approving of a man who had finally seen sense.

'We will accompany you,' the colonel said, 'we don't want you to be delayed any further.'

When the sergeant queried whether they should search the farm, the colonel turned on him with all the fury of the Kaiser's old military aristocracy. 'Load your men and accompany me – and speak when you are spoken to.'

Lucille and the doctor headed for the doctor's car, but the colonel insisted Lucille travel with him, while the sergeant accompanied the doctor to the château.

Once there the men were deployed outside the servants' quarters. The young countess came, speaking only in private to the colonel, merely commenting to the doctor and his nurse in passing that she had expected them 'hours and hours ago'.

Lucille did as she had been told, followed the doctor's lead, but he led so hesitantly she became more and more concerned. Finally in a sideroom off the countess's bedroom she had the opportunity to ask what they were going to do.

'Can't you guess?' he retorted almost roughly and suddenly she understood. She knew why the doctor's house and the small hospital ward had been targeted, why Nadia's home. It had been anyone connected with the doctor.

'You refused the first time,' she whispered.

He bent his head over his bag of instruments. She caught and gripped his hand. 'Now you have no choice.'

'If it were just myself ...'

'It isn't,' she said grimly, knowing the price they would all pay if the colonel was thwarted. It amounted to an unwanted foetus versus the lives of her family and friends.

He had on his gown and his eyes sought hers. She nodded urgently at him, but he looked like one bereaved, like a man deprived of all he had previously held dear.

Chapter Twenty-Four

Ernest showed them how to crush the tablets by nesting two spoons together and pressing hard, though the resulting powder floated stubbornly when stirred into a little water. He pinched Jacques's jaw to force his mouth open, then efficiently spooned in the mixture and closed his mouth. As his son fought Ernest pinched his nose, cutting off his air supply, to make him gasp and swallow. It was an ordeal Stella watched in anguished admiration. A lesson in caring parenthood?

'Could you do that?' he asked, the very question she was wondering about.

'Yes,' she said firmly, if it was part of the cure she could. Jean-Paul nodded.

'If only he would begin to sweat,' Ernest said, pushing the blankets back up around his chin.

'Oh!' Stella exclaimed quietly as she suddenly remembered an old lady who lived in Avonside who used to specialise in making cotton wool-padded jackets for pneumonia patients. She became recognised for her skill at sandwiching the wool between thin layers of material; requests came from all around. Stella could remember them exactly. They had wrapover fronts with ties, so the patient couldn't throw them off.

She explained to the two men who were looking at her with some concern after her exclamation.

'It sounds like a good idea,' Ernest said. 'Could you do it?'

'But where would you get the cotton wool?' Jean-Paul asked.

'I couldn't of course, but there might be an old quilt I could cut up.'

'Cut up whatever you like,' Ernest said. 'And it would be a good idea for you to be in the house if the colonel and his men come back, hopefully with Lucille and the doctor ...' He broke off then asked

212

with angry concern, 'What the hell do you think he's taken Lucille off to do?'

'The colonel's manner changed, from ...' Stella paused to think. 'Well, I would say he was definitely getting his way about something.'

Jean-Paul laid a hand on Ernest's shoulder. 'Whatever, we can trust Dr Chabrol to look after Lucille.'

'Of course, of course!' Ernest shook his head in remorse, trying to fight off the morbid fear that had momentarily come over him, a sudden fear of losing all his family: Gaby gone; Jacques desperately ill, and Lucille taken off with a gang of rampaging Germans and Pétainist police. Then he watched as Stella came forward to replace the blankets yet again, he saw *her* desperate concern, her love – and she had the extra burden of the child she was carrying. He reached over and held his hands on the covers. 'I do think this jacket thing is a good idea.'

'It shouldn't take me too long,' she said, remembering the old treadle sewing machine in the old nursery.

She hurried to the house feeling she had something positive to do for Jacques. She found Hector getting out cutlery, setting as many places as he could around the table. 'No one's eaten properly since yesterday,' he said, 'that won't keep the garrison going.' He paused to ask, 'How is he?'

After she had told him the old man reassured her that the doctor would certainly be back to take a proper look at Jacques.

'You think so?'

'*Oui*, but of course, and he too won't have eaten. We must keep these people going.' He looked at her speculatively.

'If you'll peel some potatoes, we could do chips, eggs and bacon for everyone in turn, but first ...' She went on to tell him of the jacket.

'A gamgee,' he said to her amazement as she recalled that was what they had been called.

'How did you know?'

'Lived a bit longer than you,' he said, balancing himself to lift potatoes into a bowl for paring. 'There was an English nurse in the last war who was making one for a local lass, she had a tiny premature baby that needed coddling.'

'Did it live?'

'I wasn't conscious long enough to find out once they took my leg off.'

'Hector, are we going to win?'

'Good fights for longer than evil.'

213

'Prevails in the end you mean,' she said.

'That's it my lass.' He nodded to her and took his heavy bowl of vegetables to the sink. 'The secret is to keep busy – I'll peel while you sew your gamgee.'

She found a blue quilt in a chest, and one of Jacques's shirts. Laying the shirt on the quilt she cut out a much larger edition of the back with the sleeves included, then cut two individual pieces for the front allowing a generous wrapover each side. Without pause, but wishing she had taken a more genuine interest in school needlework lessons, she took it to the sewing room.

When she had only to sew on the tapes, she took it downstairs to talk to Hector as she worked, and he put before her the meal he had cooked for the two of them. She had eaten at least something and was finishing the last tape when she heard the doctor's car returning. She and Hector were at the door in time to see the doctor and Lucille get out. They both looked tense, the doctor looked ill and stumbled as he crossed towards them. Behind him Lucille shook her head as the first question trembled to their lips.

'Come and sit down, monsieur.' Hector brought coffee and poured some brandy from a second bottle Ernest had left on the table. The doctor took both.

'Are you cooking?' Lucille nodded towards the pan of potatoes as if to draw attention away from a sight neither had seen before, the doctor's hands shaking so much the drinks slopped over.

'Bacon, egg and chips for anyone who wants them,' Hector replied, noisily repositioning the pan on the draining board.

'Marvellous!' Lucille said but her voice lacked any enthusiasm. 'I must be hungry. I can't remember when I last had a meal.'

'Will you have a look at Jacques?' Stella asked.

'Of course.' It was the doctor who spoke and rose.

He greeted Ernest and Jean-Paul; Ernest was immediately all concern for his old friend. He enquired of Lucille with a frown over the doctor's back as he bent over the bed, but she shook her head and shrugged her lack of information.

Lifting his stethoscope from Jacques's chest the doctor confirmed what Lucille had said. 'But everything you are doing is right. Just careful, careful nursing to break his temperature. Carry on as you have begun.'

Stella displayed the jacket and he declared it excellent. He and Ernest put it on the patient. 'He won't be able to throw that off! Excellent!' he repeated as Stella tied the tapes. 'Now you, my dear, must give him the will to get better. The will is more important than any medicine.'

214

The doctor refused to stay for anything to eat. 'I must go home. I shall have no peace until I know all that's happened to Nadia, she can be fiery, and it does no good with these people.' He paused and sighed. 'And I must help Jeannette.' He looked around at them all. 'I think you can be assured that the colonel and his men will certainly not be back tonight, hopefully not for some time.'

Lucille thought he was probably right. She remembered the aftermath of the abortion with a clarity which she thought would probably never leave her. The colonel had seen them out with the words, 'We shall not be troubling you again, doctor.'

'Or those who work with me I hope,' the doctor had said stonily, 'they do not deserve your attentions.'

The colonel had smiled and bowed acquiescence. 'From me you have nothing to fear, from those who come after me ...,' He shrugged.

'You are leaving?' the doctor had asked and Lucille had thought he sounded as if he had been deceived.

'I am to go to Vichy,' the colonel had said. 'There are those in the new French government who apparently need a firm hand.' He laughed uproariously and Lucille had wondered if he was a little drunk – but it was after they had driven away from the château that the worst moments came.

The doctor had suddenly stopped the car. He had grasped the steering wheel in a vice-like grip and begun to shake until he was in the grip of the most violent ague. She had called out to him, tried to release his hands from the steering wheel, but he had been quite outside the reach of ordinary measures. She had loosened his collar and taking a pad from the medical bag put it between his teeth to stop him biting his tongue. She had talked to him reassuringly all the time and waited for the fit to pass.

When the shaking had stopped, his hands too gradually relaxed. He gave a deep shuddering sigh and his hands fell into his lap. He closed his eyes and leaned back in his seat. She had watched him closely but was silent, giving him time, waiting until some vestige of colour returned to his face. Eventually he had turned and looked at her.

'I ask you not to tell anyone of this,' he had said.

'Has it happened before?'

He shook his head. 'But when you act contrary to the most fundamental morals of your whole life and upbringing, you must expect reaction.'

'You had no choice.'

He shook his head but offered no argument.

'Do you feel all right now?'

'I can carry on,' he had said, and reached forward and started the car.

But could he forgive himself? She watched him now as Jean-Paul questioned him. She thought that either Jeannette or Edmund should know of the moral trauma he was suffering.

'But they can't have found the radio,' Jean-Paul was saying.

'No and they're moving much further south, searching the farms and properties that way. They think the car Pas de Crédit had a lift in came from Marseilles.'

'*Oui*,' Jean-Paul agreed. 'It is what Edmund wanted them to believe.'

For a moment the doctor's expression lightened. 'He's cleverer than I realised,' he said.

Ernest and Stella took turns at Jacques's bedside through the night. His father was always there at the time the tablets had to be given.

Midnight tipped down to two a.m. and she remembered all the old adages about this being the time when life was at its lowest ebb. She began to talk most earnestly to Jacques, restraining his arms so he could not accidentally strike her as he raved and she spoke close into his ear.

She held his hand on his child, said how he or she would grow up knowing and loving Cleauville as they had done. 'You and your father will teach him or her about the vines – perhaps we'll produce a famous wine, have our names on the bottles, which will go all over the world! Hector must teach him all the work of the *vigneron* tending the vines in the fields, then his speciality of expert *décanteur* from cask to bottle, and you must be overseer, dreamer, writer, business-man. You see you have to get well,' she told him. 'There is no way after all this I want to give birth to a fatherless child. It is not reason-able!' In her voice she heard echoes of her own father. She talked on and wondered what the war was doing to him, to 'Redhead One'.

She watched closely, waiting for every indrawn breath, agonised that they were so shallow, so quick, sounding like nothing more than meagre sips at life.

She glanced at the clock, twenty minutes past two. She felt she had been talking for hours. She spooned the weak brandy water between his lips again. He lay turning his head from side to side like a frac-tious child.

'Oh! God!' she prayed, 'please let me keep him.'

'These conditions don't change all that quickly,' Lucille had told her.

Tears suddenly began to flood down her face, a hot steady

unlooked-for stream. She brushed them away angrily, since they helped nothing. She cast about in her mind for what might help. She padded around the loft, eight strides one way, ten the other, then going back to the bed she could neither hear nor see his breathing, and he was still – so still.

She felt her own heart miss several beats, leaving her breathless. She knelt by the bed to listen, her ear almost to his mouth. There was a breath, another, and the breathing was slower, deeper. Her hand trembled as she stretched it out and almost fearfully put it on his forehead. It was moist. The fever was breaking. She took a cup of plain water and spooned some between his lips. He swallowed quite naturally several times, then sighed slightly and turned his head away from her. She fetched the lamp, held it up above him to make sure she was not making a mistake. But the change in him was so obvious, it did not need a doctor to say that this sleep was natural, a calm healing sleep.

She turned down the lamp and went back to the bed, lay her head on the pillow by his, holding his hand.

Ernest's earlier state of alarm swept over him again as climbing once more to the loft he saw Stella slumped over against his son. He moved quickly to the bed to lay an exploratory hand on her shoulder when stooping lower the sound of regular rhythmic breathing stopped him. The early morning light was sufficient for him to see that they were both in a deep natural sleep. He put his hand on his son's brow and felt a damp coolness. He looked at the two, heads close, Stella clasping Jacques's hand. Children, he thought, only children playing at being grown up.

He lowered himself to his knees next to Stella and head in hands silently thanked his God.

Chapter Twenty-Five

'Sign he's really improving,' Ernest said as his son cursed roundly and forcibly about his leg.

'Bloody thing never will hold my weight!'

'Time is what you need!' Lucille shouted back at him. 'Time and patience!'

Ernest grinned at Stella's solemn face. 'Come on,' he said, 'leave them to it. We always used to say when you started shouting at them you'd stopped worrying about 'em.' He took her arm and walked her out into the Boxing Day sunshine.

She walked sedately, like a ship in full sail, she thought, leaving brother and sister to deal with the disputed matter of using crutches. Days, weeks of slow, slow recovery had been followed with disappointment for Jacques when his leg remained so weak as to be incapable of supporting any weight.

She also wondered if they had not fallen into a very false sense of security. Yesterday, Christmas Day had been a wonderful time, often nostalgic when her thoughts had gone to her father and brother, and she knew Ernest had often thought of Gaby, but Jean-Paul had been amazing. After a meal of wild duck supplied by Nadia's husband, they had sat long at the table with Jean-Paul plying Hector with wine and getting the old boy to expound on the quality of each bottle. The amazing thing was the more he drank the more qualities he was able to find in each glass. Lucille had thought he should have no more, but Hector winked at Stella and she had known it was all an act for their amusement. It would, she guessed, take an awful lot of wine to bemuse Hector's senses.

Then everyone helped clear the table and do the washing-up, with everyone getting in each other's way, Lucille flipping her brother with the soaking end of a teatowel. 'Paaa!' he wailed like a child, 'look at her, look what she's doing to me!'

218

'That's it!' Jean-Paul had declared, 'we'll play charades! I am so good at charades, it will be a treat for you all!' He had cringed under a barrage of wet teatowels – but they had played the game. Jean-Paul picked the sides.

'Jacques has a crutch and two legs, so he counts two, so Victor and Jacques and I will take on ... let's see. Stella and Hector must be on the same side because,' he had paused before going on outrageously, 'because the bit he has missing Stella makes up for, so that's fair! So we're against Lucille, Stella, Hector and Ernest.'

It had become even more outrageous as Jean-Paul's team had illustrated 'Mein Kampf' in a tableau of mining and all-female camp cabaret, which much to their chagrin Hector had guessed very quickly. Hector was also the star in their acting out of the title of the carol 'God Rest Ye Merry Gentlemen', which he had only vaguely heard of, but played the 'merry gentleman' with realistic verve. Victor looked bemused; it was his first experience of charades.

The evening had ended with them drinking a solemn toast to 'absent friends and loved ones,' in the best quality brandy Ernest could find. Ernest slept in his study, Hector on the bed settee in the hall, like two elderly watchdogs. The couples had gone upstairs tacitly to share double rooms.

Almost as if Ernest's mind was running along the same lines he said, 'I wish we could see the two of you married.'

'Difficult when we have to have names publicly posted up,' Stella said with a smile, 'but we will, after the war.'

'Yes,' he said, 'after the war.'

They walked on in silence but the mention of the war had banished the feeling of euphoria that had been so much part of the day before. She wondered if the false sense of security had begun after Colonel Wilhelm Voss-Beker had left the area. Since that time Cleauville had seen nothing of either his replacement, troops or State Police.

Victor and Jean-Paul were both sceptical, suspicious, for though they had made two more successful runs to the Spanish border with British and Polish airmen, news coming from other areas of occupied and unoccupied France was bad. There were reports of those caught harbouring escapees being shot, of English internees being actively hunted out, rounded up and sent to labour camps in Germany. Spies, Resistance workers, were being tracked down, their trials were transitory, the executions swift.

Shortly after the removal of the colonel to his new post, news came that over thirty mayors and town councils all over the Unoccupied Zone were being forcibly removed from office because of their unwillingness to follow the orders of the Nazi-ordered Vichy government.

The war news too was all of German successes, but packed inside a replacement car exhaust delivered to the village from Clermont-Ferrand had come a Resistance news-sheet telling how the Royal Air Force was turning the tide and inflicting very heavy casualties on the bombers which were taking part in the day and night attacks on London. Two mass day and night raids on London and the south of England had resulted in the loss of a hundred and seventy-five German planes; nearly half of those which flew over England's coastline in that twenty-four hours never returned. The invasion that had been expected in September or October had it seemed been put off because Hitler had not managed to smash the might or the spirit of the Royal Air Force.

They had painstakingly copied out the news-sheet, to which Ernest added extracts of Winston Churchill's rousing words declaring that England would *never* surrender and that if its Commonwealth and Empire lasted a thousand years men would look back and say 'this was their finest hour'. The copies were dropped secretly through people's letterboxes.

'After the war,' Stella mused as they walked on arm in arm. 'How long will that be?'

'If America would get off the fence not so long!' Ernest said vehemently. 'Churchill's dropped enough hints, told them that if Britain fails the whole world, *including* the United States will fall, as he put it, into a new dark age.'

She smiled at the rolling deep resonance he unconsciously assumed when he spoke of Churchill.

They had strolled nearly to the end of the drive when the sound of a horse and cart reached them, unusual for such a day. 'We're not expecting anyone, are we?' Ernest asked.

'No, best get of sight until we know who it is.'

'Will you be all right?' he asked as he moved away from the drive into the trees.

'Fine,' she said, 'go on.'

She walked slowly on towards the roadway. The cart drew level, then into the drive. The man hailed her and she was both surprised and perturbed to realise it was the old man who had come upon herself and Jacques in the olive grove, who had called God to witness their sin.

He let the horse come close to her before he finally reined in, and peered at her with his narrow foxy eyes. Would he recognise her again – with short black hair and the clothes of a young French matron? If he did, he might have cause to think his judgement had been right.

'You'll be the widow who's supposedly running the Cleauville place,' he said. 'What's happened to the son of the house, journalist in Paris wasn't he?'

Relieved for herself, she was now full of apprehension for Jacques and did not answer. She hadn't liked the old man much on their first encounter, and liked him a whole lot less now.

'And the daughter,' his mouth curved to a sneer, 'everyone knows she's nursing in the village and calling herself Cleauville. Do they know she's half English I wonder?'

She felt herself breathing quicker. By 'they' she presumed he meant the puppet Vichy government, but still she did not answer him. She remembered how persistent he had been before, pursuing Jacques and herself from field to road to car, never letting up his attack. She wasn't sure where matters would lead if she began to answer him back.

'He grunted to himself. 'Do they know the land's owned by an Englishman? Confiscated, that's what it should be, the whole lot of it.'

'It is owned by one of the oldest families in France, a family which gave its name to the area!' she heard herself saying.

He leaned over her from the cart and demanded, 'How did you come here?'

'I came here to work for the Cleauville family,' she told him. 'What are *you* doing here?'

She took a firm hold of the reins under the old horse's muzzle and when he did not answer she began to push the horse's back in the direction of the road.

'You wait, young woman!' he told her and scrambled down from his cart. 'I'm here for a purpose, I need to see your land manager, *if* there is one.'

'You'll come another day then, not during the Christmas holiday. What's so important?'

'I've come about this idea of work sharing on the land, pooling land and labour, the State think it is a good idea.'

'The State?'

'The Vichy government.'

'Ah! Marshal Pétain!' She did not make the mistake of saying anything against the new State of France, but before her look he had the grace to drop his eyes. 'But you see we have our own *loyal* men and women who will come from the village to work when we need them.'

'I need to see your man,' he persisted.

'What's this then?' Hector came unexpectedly from the copse

221

behind his cottage carrying a bundle of kindling which he dropped by his doorstep. 'What part of the world are you putting right today, Monsieur Marsan?' Marsan took a step back as the belligerent veteran bore rapidly down on him alternately using and waving his crutch.

'It's about men to work on the land, a rota. I've been told to organise a rota.'

'Men to work on the land! Whose land? Yours? You've never paid a man to work on your land in your life. You'd sooner work your wife into the ground. Don't come here with such stories. What do you really want? Whose pay are you in?' Hector came right up to the man and pushed his belligerent moustached face close. 'Because there's one thing that's sure, you're not here unless there is something in it for Monsieur Marsan!'

'It costs nothing to collaborate, active collaboration the Marshal says, not passive! Active!'

'You may find that's not true in the end,' Hector muttered, 'there's always a price to be paid. Now clear off and mind your own affairs.'

'I'll have to put you down as having no men on the farm ...'

'You put me down as estate manager,' Hector told him, 'and Cleauville down as not needing help of any kind, from you, or your rota. Just don't try any dirty tricks! I've known you too long! I'm ready, ready to take on such as you, Marsan, anytime.'

'It won't be just me,' the man promised as he climbed back on to his cart. 'I told you collaboration costs nothing, but obstruction – *resistance* –' he fell on the word as if it was an inspiration, '*resistance* can be very expensive!'

'Let him go.' Stella put her hand on Hector's arm as he would have gone forward again when Marsan gave his old horse a fair crack on the rump with a hefty stick. 'He likes to have the last word.'

'*You* know him?'

'I've encountered him once or twice before.'

'He's *always* trouble, he's not here for nothing. He's up to something.'

'Do you think he's working for the police or the Germans? He said land might be pooled.'

'Did he! The bugger! That's his game!' Hector exclaimed. 'He thinks with the men out of the way there's a chance for him to do a bit of annexing of his own. A lot of his holding is bound about by ours.' He tutted. 'I wish I had thought of that when he was here and warned him off. Bloody collaborator!'

'Perhaps we could get Nadia's husband to have a stroll around a few of our fields with his hunting-gun of an evening.'

Hector grinned at her, that big naughty broken-toothed smile that gladdened her heart. 'If the bugger as much as puts a toe on our land we'll shoot it off!'

When Ernest rejoined them, he was furious. 'Gaby's land is our sacred trust, there's no way any German, or any thieving Frenchman, is going to get their hands on an inch of it!'

'That's right!' Hector forcibly endorsed.

They had another visitor when she and Ernest got back. Edmund had come by the field path and was alight with news. His eyes shone and he could not sit still, but first of all he brought gifts of baby clothes his mother had knitted. Nadia had also sent cotton nightdresses handmade and embroidered by her. Then he came to his news.

'We are going to get an airdrop!' he told them, his fists clenched with excitement.

'What of?' Jean-Paul wanted to know.

'No, it will be a who. It's because of the possibility of Clermont-Ferrand being a source of short-wave radios.'

'But I don't see ...' Ernest began, then asked, 'Where's he coming from?'

'England!'

Stella watched amazed as the men all got more and more excited. She tried to think of the right word to describe Edmund's mood. Triumphalist was the nearest she could get.

'I hope the man comes direct from de Gaulle! I hope we're going to get some overall plans about our resistance, our fight. I think we've been chosen because we've sent in early reports about possible airdropping or landing zones.'

'So he's going to ...' Jacques began.

'Parachute in!'

'No,' Jacques persisted, 'I mean is he bringing us instructions, or what?'

'I don't know, yet. We've just got to wait for the signal to come through for his arrival. Then we'll go to the place, meet him and bring him perhaps first to here, or wherever is safest.'

'So how soon could this be?' Lucille wanted to know.

'They may choose a full moon,' he said, 'and the plane could come up from the south over the Camargue, that would be a good idea ...'

'But this is just speculation isn't it?' Lucille tried to pin him down, puncture his excitement, be realistic. 'A full moon, this month? Next month?'

'That is not what is important,' Jacques interrupted. 'What's important is that we're being recognised. They know they have a growing force of people here in France wanting to help, waiting to fight.'

'That's it!' Edmund exclaimed. 'That's exactly it.'

'Think,' Jacques lectured, 'if we could recruit say just half the population of France, and every one did some small act of sabotage, think of the disruption. The cut telephone wires, dirt in petrol tanks ...'

'Machinery tooled just a thousandth of an inch out,' Victor added with satisfaction.

'Men shot, women widowed!' Lucille butted in. 'I'm for the Resistance, you know that, but let's keep a sense of proportion. Let's deal with what we know, or think might happen here today, or tomorrow – not when the next moon's full. Let's deal with the problems we have.' She looked so directly at Edmund that he was at last sobered.

'You mean my father, don't you,' he stated. 'He won't tell me whether he's ill or ...'

'Just tortured by his conscience. I think he's borne the burden on his own too long, he's making himself ill and wretched. The only thing that has held me back from saying anything before is he asked me not to, and even when it is told I am not sure it will help him. But at least you will all understand.'

She told the story of the countess's abortion.

Edmund held his head in his hands. '*C'est terrible*, for my father it is terrible.'

'He took the life of a German bastard to save all of us,' Lucille said, 'have no doubt that if he had not done it, the colonel would have taken all kinds of revenge on us. He would have searched and rooted us out unmercifully. We would probably none of us be here.'

There was silence. Stella watched her friend. It was the first time she had ever known her to break a confidence. That too had cost her dear and she rallied to her support. 'We've all remarked about his changed appearance, and wondered if he were ill, or just grossly overworked. Is there any need for him to be told that we know?' she asked. 'We could perhaps help by just making the right remarks in general conversation.'

Edmund laughed and Ernest shook his head. 'He is too wily a bird to be fooled by that. I think it is better Lucille tells him that she has confided in us.'

'But perhaps best of all would be if he and Jeannette could be invited here – say this evening for supper and we could *show* him our mutual understanding and support,' Jacques said, 'there are surely enough things being done in a clandestine way. In this way we can be open, honest, share his trauma – and celebrate his devotion to his family and to France. What about that!'

Stella might have accused *him* of triumphalism if she had not thought it was such a good idea and Lucille hadn't looked so relieved.

'There would still be no need for anyone beyond our group to know,' she said.

'No, quite,' Ernest agreed solemnly.

Edmund pondered for a moment or two then decided, 'If this is what has been haunting my father all these weeks then it must be good to bring it into the open, lance the boil as he himself would say, let the poison out.'

So that evening the doctor and Jeannette accepted the unexpected Boxing Day supper invitation. Stella and Lucille prepared as lavish a cold collation as they could muster, adding a hot soup. Ernest again raided his store of wines and brandies, and when the meal was finished, Edmund as arranged rose to his feet and lifted his glass.

'I have a toast to propose, but first I need to say some things that may surprise some of you, perhaps one thing that will surprise all of you. When I was quite a small boy I went with my father to a service during which he read a piece about being a doctor. I can't remember many of the words but I know it asked for the wisdom never to put a doctor's learning before his common sense and always to strive for the greater good.' He paused and Stella glanced at his father who was now sitting ramrod-straight, attentive to every word. 'I have always known my father always chose to strive for the greater good ...'

Stella swallowed hard as she saw the doctor realise what was being implied; she saw his hand go across and grip Jeannette's. His wife's bewilderment made it obvious she had no knowledge of what had happened.

'He has ...' Edmund was saying, 'been such a shining example to me, I want to tell him now, in front of all our dearest friends, that it is for this reason that after the war I shall be quitting the world of figures and enrolling in a medical academy. I only hope I can be half as good a man and doctor as my father. My father! Dr Chabrol!' He lifted his glass and everyone else rose to their feet and shouted 'Dr Chabrol!'

'But I don't quite understand,' Jeannette began. 'Has this something to do with the spite the colonel showed to our house, the hospital and poor Nadia's home?'

Dr Chabrol rose slowly to his feet as the others sat down. He lifted his glass, unsteadily circling it around the company before sipping. 'You all,' he paused to tip a reproving finger lightly in Lucille's direction 'know my secret except the most important person in my life.' Still standing before the company he told Jeannette how against all his principles he had aborted the countess's child.

Jeannette grew pale and looked up at her husband as he still stood by her side, pilloried it seemed by his own admission. 'Not you ...'

225

she whispered. 'I ...' Then she straightened up and said with vehemence, 'I hope you smacked her bottom at the same time, she's needed it for years!'

There was a second's silence in which they all watched the doctor; he gave a gasp that was half laugh, half relief. It freed them all to clap and cheer. Edmund went to his father and took him in his arms, when he was questioned about his medical ambitions. The doctor was obviously delighted.

Stella felt a very tentative invitation had became a most successful evening, a one-to-remember event, and with luck the turning point for Dr Chabrol, not to forget, but to be able to live more comfortably with what he had done.

In the following weeks it was noted that his appearance and vigour improved with dramatic rapidity. 'The mind has more influence on your health than your body I think,' Jacques commented.

'Really!' Lucille said. 'Seen no sign of that when you've been going on about your leg.'

'It'll be better in time to help receive this parachutist,' Jean-Paul hazarded.

'You bet!'

'Whenever that might be.'

It was the morning of 18 February 1941 when Stella realised that the next arrival would not be the parachutist.

Chapter Twenty-Six

The first grumbling ache came well before dawn, but it was not until she was up and had breakfast that Stella realised the pain low in her back was the beginning of labour. Nadia had warned her that first babies were never quick. 'Stay on your feet as long as you can,' she had advised, 'it hurts more when they get you on a bed.'

So until midday she told no one, then as there began to be a pattern to the pain, a regularity which shortened from twenty minutes, to ten to eight, then it seemed too quickly to five, she told Jacques. He regarded her with a look between joy and terror, put his hand under her arm and insisted she sit down while he telephoned for Dr Chabrol.

'Nadia was obviously right,' she muttered as she found even sitting far more unsatisfactory than walking around and got up again.

'Go upstairs if you want to walk around,' Jacques instructed her while still waiting for a reply to the doctor's telephone. 'We don't want any accidents downstairs.'

'It's as much your accident as mine,' she retorted, knowing the antagonism she suddenly felt towards him was unfair. He had been so attentive, so concerned, meeting her whims almost before she had them, calming her occasional and uncharacteristic fears about the future. Ever since the New Year when he was able to move with just a stick he had done everything he could, even practised riding a bicycle in case he needed to when the time came. Only his impatient nature occasionally got the better of him as he complained, 'All I do is wait for things to happen these days!'

'I know,' she had commiserated, 'no parachutist or anything.'

'No baby, or anything.' Then they had both laughed.

She now felt a moment of panic when she heard him say, 'Oh! So he's where?'

'Of all places!' he exclaimed, 'he's at Marsan's place, the wife has

227

had some kind of accident. Lucille's gone with him. I'll find my father then go over there.'

'You can't! You don't want him of all people to see you.' Her reasoning was spoiled by the fact that she had to hang on to the newel post as another pain overtook her.

'Don't worry, I'll find some way of attracting his or Lucille's attention, but I'll find my father first. Stay where you are.' Before she could protest again he was away limping across to the bicycle store so quickly he had forgotten his walking stick.

She sighed. Did he mean stay where she was, or go upstairs? It began to make sense that she should be upstairs, but she found hauling herself up step by step by the banisters was in fact agony. It also occurred to her that until Ernest came she was alone. So keep walking around, she told herself, come on, no slacking – and time the pains. She carried the alarm clock around with her: every five minutes and getting much stronger.

It seemed hours and hours before Ernest arrived and gave her a tot of brandy, 'Always helped Gaby,' he said. It made her feel sick, but she thought stoically that even that helped take her mind off the pain. Should it be this painful? It was a natural function, wasn't it? But she did remember how cows bellowed pitifully when they had their calves. In fact she felt if she could lift her head and give vent to a stentorian bellow it might help a lot, but just at that moment Jacques returned and he looked as if he might well pass out if she so much as whimpered.

She was in the end much relieved when she heard the doctor's car and Lucille come running upstairs first. She ushered her into the bedroom they had specially prepared for the birth. 'Just let me walk around, she begged, 'until I really need to lie down. Please,' she begged hanging on to the chest of drawers, then the windowsill, then the doorframe, repeating the plea at every stop, with Lucille following her around. Then the doctor was heard coming upstairs talking to Jacques, who was firmly sent back downstairs by his sister.

Soon the nature of the pains changed dramatically and she was glad to do as she was told, to pant and push, hold her breath, push, pant, keep going – 'doing fine' – everything seemed to reach her through a daze of unreality. She knew she wanted to tell the doctor something, something she had thought of earlier and now couldn't remember.

The day was waning when at last it came back to her. 'It must be born today,' she told him between pains, 'the eighteenth.' Vaguely she heard him say they must all do their best, then before the next pain hit her she shouted the reason at him. 'It's my Irish grandmother's birthday!'

228

'We'll make it,' the doctor assured her. 'Now we want a great effort.'

She made it.

'Now pant and wait!' he shouted at her, 'now one last push!'

She felt something hot and wet by her leg, she felt the pains disappear like magic, then there was the cry of the newborn, Lucille scooped up the bundle and wrapped it in a towel to put in her arms. 'I've got a nephew,' she said.

Stella looked at the tiny scrap of dependent baby, totally amazed at this brand new individual.

'So are you going to call him Sean or Paddy?' the doctor asked and when she frowned he reminded her that she had wanted him born on her Irish grandmother's birthday. 'We just made it – five minutes to midnight on the 18th of February.'

'That's wonderful, a good omen,' she said, enclosing the tiny tremulous exploring fist in hers. 'No, this is Billy. William Ernest Blair, or he will be when his parents make an honest boy of him.'

'Hello Billy,' Dr Chabrol said, 'we'll just tidy you up, then the proud father can come and see his son.' He looked about to say more but stopped himself. 'Time enough later for instructions,' he said and after a few minutes he opened the bedroom door. 'Come on, young man, you've a perfect healthy son. Congratulations!'

Jacques looked first at Stella lying back exhausted but happy. He kissed her cheek and asked if she was all right? 'I'm fine,' she said then nodding down to the swaddled baby she held, asked, 'What do you think of him, our son?'

He just looked for a long, long, moment, then very gently took the baby into his arms. He stood so still just regarding his child it was as if some silent communication was going on between them, and when he spoke his voice was thick with emotion. 'God help me never to let you down,' he said, then glancing at Stella he added, 'you know I feel sure we've met before, I'm sure we know all about each other.'

Stella was reminded of the hours of crisis in the loft when she had put his hand on his unborn child. He was right, they had met before. His son had helped persuade him to recover, to stay. She knew it was fanciful and perhaps she would never tell anyone, but she felt it was true.

'Born on my Grandmother Kenney's birthday,' she told him.

'My, so you'll have all those fairies and leprechanuns on your side too.' He peered at the top of the baby's head. 'Are you going to have red hair too I wonder?'

Ernest tapped at the open door hesitantly, and Stella waved him in. He came to her bed, stooped and kissed her. 'All right, my love?' he asked.

She nodded. 'What do you think to young William Ernest Blair?'

'Really?' he queried the name with a broad smile. 'Named for your grandpas! Wonderful!'

'Jacques and I decided ages ago.' A girl would have been Gabrielle Kathleen, but she did not tell him that. She watched silently, smiling as he intervened between Jacques and Lucille who wanted to wash and dress her nephew. He took the baby into his arms and held him with the comfortable expertise lacking in Jacques's anxious clasp.

'Well, young man, I've a lot to show you.' There was an astonished gasp as the newborn baby struggled to open his eyes as if he must see this person who was talking to him. 'Just so,' Ernest told him, 'we've not a moment to waste.' He carried him to the window. 'In a week or two I'll take you to see your first vines growing on your family's land.'

It was only days later that Dr Chabrol came again to the matter that had so concerned him since just before Billy's birth. He declared his patients blooming then going thoughtfully back to the kitchen he lingered. Hector and Ernest were there, and Jacques, hearing their voices, came through from the office where he was helping to sort out a backlog of farm business.

The doctor sat down, accepted a cup of coffee from Hector and reminded them that on the day Billy was born he had been called to the home of Marsan. 'I was switching a bad wrist wound which Madame Marsan said she had done with a sickle, while cutting hay from a stack. When Jacques arrived ...'

'She became very agitated,' Jacques remembered, 'and pleaded with me to go at once, before her husband came back.'

'I believe that woman cut her own wrist sufficiently seriously so that I had to be sent for – and she chose a time when her husband was in town. She wanted to tell me that Marsan is actively collaborating with the Germans. He told her it's what Marshal Pétain has said everyone should do – which is true of course. But she says the Germans have made him promises of great rewards of land ... whose land you can well imagine.'

'His wife was a comely girl, until he got his hands on her,' Hector commented unexpectedly, 'but if he thinks he's also getting Cleauville land!'

'He's clearing the field where you grew melons last year.' The doctor dropped the bombshell into the pause.

'What! My field by the river?' Ernest exclaimed, jumping to his feet, at the same time as Hector, who used more explicit language as to the man's parentage.

'The field that lies nearest his house, the one his side of the river,'

Jacques said as if visualising the situation.

'Wait!' the doctor told the other two. 'Sit down and think!'

'Yes,' Jacques agreed. 'He's doing this as some kind of bait, something to draw us out of hiding. If he is in contact with the authorities, it would be a tasty dish to hand them . . .' He looked at the doctor who went on for him.

'An Englishman, an Englishwoman, a half English son and daughter – and Billy. No one would then deny him numerous hectares of your land.'

'Not while I'm around,' Hector growled. 'I'll get Claude and his gun . . .'

'The point is the land won't matter too much if you've no one to inherit,' said the doctor as he looked pointedly at Ernest. 'To be blunt I think you should – we should – make every effort to get Stella, her baby, Jacques and Lucille out of France as soon as possible.'

Jacques was silent for a moment. 'You're thinking of this plane that's supposed to be coming from England.' He paused again. 'The girls and the baby should go if there's any chance.'

'Edmund is sure there will be. The man will definitely be airlifted out, though it will probably be from further north.' The doctor went on urgently, 'I think time is short. The news coming from Vichy is that this area is getting a new commander, a man anxious to do well, and with a stated intention of sweeping France clean of Jews and anti-German activists.'

'A new broom,' Ernest mused, 'we have a saying a new broom sweeps clean.' He turned to his son. 'You could do a lot of good in England. You could write openly there, let the British, the world, know what's happening here, that the biggest percentage of the French population still wants to fight.' He leaned forward to urge, 'Take my grandson to safety. If there's a chance to get out, it's only common sense to go. Stella could take the boy to her father's home, and you could all come back after the war.'

'Stella could go,' Jacques answered quietly, then looked fiercely back at his father and asked, 'What about Jean-Paul, Victor, Nadia and Claude? It would not seem right or fair.'

'They are all French, they don't risk automatic internment. I wouldn't like to see you *recaught*,' his father said deliberately to remind him of the trauma.

'And,' Chabrol added tersely, 'fairness, morality, are not things we should consider – or so you told me – when we're fighting a megalomaniac.'

'Hitler will eventually take too big a bite, invade Russia and then . . .' Jacques began on another tack.

231

The doctor was clearly startled by such a proposition. 'They signed a Russo-German pact in 1939,' he said in spite of his supposedly anti-fair, anti-moralistic stance.

Hector raised a gnarled brown finger to endorse Jacques's remark. 'If you'd read his book you'd know that Hitler regards the Urals, Siberia and the Ukraine as the fuel for German's new prosperity and expansion. How else is he going to get that without invading!'

'Stella won't go without you,' Ernest interrupted, not allowing his son to wriggle out of the real issue. 'She has to be told to prepare herself to go.'

'We must pray nothing happens in the meantime,' the doctor said, rising, 'and I must get off on my round.'

'I was thinking,' Hector said, 'if we do nothing about Marsan on our land, won't *that* look suspicious?'

'That's true,' Ernest said, 'we can't just let him get away with it.'

'I could get Claude with his gun, we'll have a walk over there.' Hector glanced at his employer, then added 'Two guns would be better.' Without a word Ernest handed over the key to the hidden gun cupboard.

'Telephone my house,' the doctor suggested. 'Nadia will be there, she'll run across and tell Claude to come.'

'The most sobering thing is that Marsan suspects,' Jacques said. 'He must feel he has a good chance of flushing us out some time.'

'And he has,' Dr Chabrol said. 'He's a neighbour, and good as you all are at keeping watch and hiding, sooner or later ... that's why I think you should go at the first opportunity. You'll be more effective in England!'

It was a very sober two men who returned later that evening. Hector and Claude had indeed found Marsan on the land.

'He only began working when he glimpsed us coming,' Hector told them. 'He kind of turned his back and began swinging away with a scythe as soon as we appeared on the horizon. He didn't really know who we were. I only realised what he was actually doing when we got right over to him.'

'He'd laid a trap for us,' Claude contributed. 'For somebody anyway.'

'What happened?' Jacques wanted to know.

'He let us get right over to him, never turned round. Just stood hacking away at a few old stems.'

'Then when we were on top of him, he straightened up and called out – but in surprise – because he hadn't expected to see Claude. I reckon he thought it was either of you two, a tall figure you see. Then, as we collar him and ask what the hell he thinks he's doing, from round the back of the bushes near the river come four German soldiers, a policeman and an officer.'

'They tell us to drop our guns and put our hands up. The officer goes over to Marsan, who takes him aside and obviously explains that we are not who he was hoping for. The officer was not too pleased, he stomped about a bit while he was talking to Marsan, then called his sergeant over, gave him some instructions, then strode off with Marsan towards his place.'

'The sergeant examined our papers, and told us to be careful what we were doing and confiscated our guns. We told them they were for duck shooting, and vermin, but ...' Hector shrugged, apologising for the loss of Ernest's gun.

'The sergeant told us to keep away from that area in future, that it would be for our own good,' Claude said, 'he didn't seem too bad a chap, said he was sorry about our hunting guns.'

It was some weeks later as Hitler committed Germany to fighting not in Russia but in Greece and Yugoslavia that Jacques watched his father carry Billy around in the field next to the house. He and Stella stood together, his arm about her shoulders, and he repeated all that the doctor had said. 'We are risking Billy,' he concluded, 'every day more. I think you should take him back to England.'

She turned to look at him. 'Edmund came today while you were with Jean-Paul. He told me exactly what he and his father thought – and what *your* father thinks. Why haven't you told me before, discussed it with me?'

'It was seeing you with Billy, I just wanted you to have some time ... I don't know, some peace, just a short time without the war spoiling it all.' He stopped and dropped his hands, confessing, 'I asked them not to tell you until we knew when the plane was coming, I thought that was time enough.'

'The plane is coming the next full moon, in five days' time, but it will be a parachute drop in, and a landing to go out – just ten days later – but from further north. Edmund asked me to tell you.'

'Oh!'

'We take Billy out together,' she told him, 'or I don't go.'

Chapter Twenty-Seven

The moonlight seemed to flatten the wide watery fields and yet make huge unfamiliar shapes out of well-known groups of trees along the banks of the Rhone tributary. Jacques and Jean-Paul, lying under bushes on the riverside, from time to time held their breaths afraid they might miss the first sound of the plane which would drop their VIP from London. Edmund was at the far side of the water meadow. Jacques discreetly shone the flashlight on to his wristwatch. Two o'clock in the morning, death-time he'd heard it called. The plane could be here anytime; the plan was to wait from one until four.

'Listen!' A theatrical cue from Jean-Paul along the bank. A low rumble became the sound of an engine, a heavy plane, not the small Lysander they might have expected. The noise grew, the plane was already coming in low. From across the field a light flashed from Edmund and immediately the other two switched on their lights forming for a few brief moments a triangle of beams which met in the air over the centre of the dropping zone. The noise became louder and louder until it seemed deafening.

Jacques recognised a British Armstrong-Whitley bomber swooping low over the French countryside. The moon was so bright he could even see something hanging out of the bomb bay. Then he recognised a man's legs. He wondered for a moment if the pilot was too low. The pilot perhaps had the same idea for he circled the lights, came in again from the south slightly higher and the next moment something hurtled from the plane, falling, falling, then jerked back upwards as the parachute opened. Above the bomber waggled its wings, climbed steeply and was away disappearing to the north, leaving the land to silence, to the parachutist.

The chute looked most extraordinarily white and conspicuous in the sky; from Jacques's angle it occasionally swung across and obscured the moon. Anyone, he thought, who parachuted into enemy territory

234

deserved a medal before they ever came to earth – provided they made it.

It was a perfect pinpoint landing. If the man had trained for a flying circus he could not have landed with more precision and on his feet. Well before the three had reached him, he had released himself from his harness and was gathering up the chute. Of medium height, stocky, he gave a feeling of strength and capability as he stood there already dressed in a suit of clothes any middle-class man in the area might have worn.

Jean-Paul introduced himself, Edmund, then Jacques as he came limping last across the field to him. 'Raymond Malin,' the new arrival answered with a nod of appreciation as Jean-Paul took over his parachute, allowing him to take a trilby hat from his pocket, knock it back into shape and place it over hair that shone silver

'You have a little way to walk,' Jacques told him. 'We're taking you to a hideout for the remainder of the night.'

'Fine, we can talk there presumably.'

They found Raymond Malin had an air of authority about him. His questions when they reached the borie were crisp, clear and brief. They noted his habit of peering directly at the person he addressed, but once the answer began to come he looked down as if the more to concentrate on every bit of information imparted.

After a time, he put his hand in his pocket and handed round cigarettes, French cigarettes. He saw them looking, and at last really smiled. 'Nothing left to chance my friends! Now I must tell you a little of my mission I have been asked to look into organising, co-ordinating and setting up an order of control for the units and men in this southern area. Linked with this I have a particular assignment for Jacques, if he'll take it. It has been obvious to London for some time that there are several factions here in France which could hamper rather than help the formation of a cohesive opposition. We need someone to come to London who as well as being involved with the Resistance knows the social structures, the political parties, particularly the role of the Communists in France ...'

Jacques felt himself breathing quicker, two divergent thoughts in his mind. He could do this, and do this well – but was he being set up, was this a way Edmund, his father, or even Stella's father in London had manufactured to persuade him to leave?'

'This latter,' Raymond Malin was saying 'has particular importance as Hitler is massing his troops on the Russian border.'

Jacques gasped, his inner reservations momentarily forgotten. 'The fool,' he rejoiced, 'the glorious vain fool!'

'Right!' Raymond approved. 'Now is the time we – England and you here in France – must think of the day we will strike back, and strike back with a united force.'

'I have to ask,' Jacques began, 'though I do know the divisions that have plagued France for years, *and* can see the importance of this assignment, why me? I mean it seems so coincidental when I am being urged by everyone to take my son and his mother out of the country – now this offer comes.'

'The one came about because of the other,' Raymond said. 'Because of the request to fly certain imperilled people out, you were investigated and found to be just the person we need at this time. There's no mystery, no collusion, you are just fortunate that I know both Professor Thierry in Paris and a certain man in London who goes under the name of "Redhead". I think he thought he was going to be your father-in-law – but if you have a son ...'

'He is,' Jacques admitting, half scowling, half grinning, 'he just doesn't know he's a grandfather yet!'

'He will be meeting the plane when you land in England,' Raymond dropped the information delicately.

'Good God!'

'Damned if you do, damned if you don't,' Edmund ventured and they all enjoyed Jacques's embarrassment before plans were made for Raymond's concentrated programme, but before they parted he gave Jacques a piece of paper.

'This is the rendezvous for twelve days' time. If I am not there the plane will come back the next night – and the next – for three nights. If I am there the first night and you are not the plane will not return. And absolutely no luggage, there'll not be room.'

'I understand.'

'Jean-Paul too will know the rendezvous point, he will be there with me. Edmund will not, I want him here at the centre of his operations all the time, with Victor as his legs. So if I need a companion-guide, or whatever, it will be Jean-Paul. I suggest, Jacques, that if there is any material you might need to gather before you return to London then this is the time to do it.'

'What is it?' Stella was to ask later in the day when Jean-Paul had already left with their visitor.

'I feel as if I've just been back to school. That chap must be a head-master of somewhere like Gordonstoun I should think. The amount he knew about us was extraordinary, and he listens so intently.'

'Why he knows so much then.' She laughed as she knelt against Billy, who was lying on the floor. She was dangling one of Jacques's old teething-rings over him. Ernest had rediscovered a box full of old

236

baby and toddlerhood delights in the attic. 'So you've been put in your place?'

'Well, I've been told where my place is,' he said quietly.

She put the ring in the baby's fingers, then sat back on her haunches and regarded him with the utmost seriousness. 'And where is that?'

He told her first about the assignment, then handed her the piece of paper.

'And?' she queried, wanting no more doubts about this.

'We'll be there,' he answered.

She got to her feet and went to him, held him tight. 'I know what it's costing you, leaving your father and Cleauville, but I'm sure it's the right decision.' She turned and they both looked down at Billy who was now juggling with the silver soldier attached to the bone ring.

'I do know it is.'

'And Lucille?'

'She doesn't know yet but Jean-Paul won't come back here. He's gone with Malin and will meet us at the landing place ...'

'And fly out with us?'

He nodded.

'Then Lucille'll come!' She felt a real lift of excitement at the prospect of all four of them going to England together.

'I think they want to brief him as a possible courier.'

'In and out of France you mean?' She tried to imagine what that would do to Lucille, on top of having to leave her father.

'She'll prefer to come,' he said, seeing her doubts. 'She'll see him some of the time.'

Spoken like a true *brother*, she thought, but there was something else she needed them to think about.

'Jacques, we couldn't leave your father here just with Hector, why don't we ask Nadia and Claude if they'd come and live here? Then with Hector keeping up his night-time patrols, they would be here in the daytime, and we wouldn't feel we'd abandoned him – not quite so much.'

'Hector's life would be a lot easier with someone else in the house,' he agreed. 'He could go back to his cottage more or less permanently, I know he'd prefer that.'

She looked at the paper again before Jacques put a match to it. 'There's only twelve days. So that means we should probably leave here ... when?'

'Allow two days for travelling and making sure we have the right location.' He told her what Malin had said about the procedure if he was there the first night. 'They will just go, no second chance for us if we're not there.'

Stella stooped and picked up Billy, who had dropped the ring on to his face, making him pucker as if about to cry. The pick-up diverted him and he smiled and wriggled. 'You,' she told him 'are a little charmer.'

'And your English grandpa is going to be at the airport when we land.' He watched her closely, appreciating the indrawn breath, the range of emotions she was experiencing, just as he had done earlier.

'Oh!'

'I think that's what I said.' He pulled the two of them into his arms. 'Doesn't matter how old you are, there's still a feeling of "Who's been naughty then?"'

'I know it will be all right when he gets over the shock,' she said. 'It's just . . .'

'Who could not love little Billy.' He put a finger gently into his son's side and the baby collapsed over it wriggling. 'Why, you're ticklish!' he exclaimed and did it again to make sure. 'Don't let the girls know,' he whispered in Billy's ear, 'they'll make your life hell.'

'If your pa agrees about Nadia and Claude, I'll walk over and ask them right away.'

As Stella pushed Lucille's old baby carriage towards the village that late May day she had a strange feeling of *déjà vu* brought on by the tall pink candles of flowers on the chestnut trees. Paris had been in flower when she and Lucille had arrived there last May.

Only a year? She felt the time must be longer, or was it that she had travelled so far in such a short time? She looked at Billy, who was watching the fringes of the pram canopy with wide blue eyes fringed by long black lashes. She had travelled from girl, to woman, to mother – that was surely the most significant journey of any woman's life.

But there were not just chestnut blossoms here. Life was burgeoning in Cleauville, wild iris (flags, the old people called them at Avonside), white, blue, purple, and abundant purple-pink tamarisk boughs and rambling roses, pink, red, yellow were blooming in the gardens, growing over the houses. Where was her heart, she wondered, in England or here, the home of her son?

Her thoughts were disturbed as rather late she heard a vehicle and before she had time to turn a sleek open-topped limousine slid by her. She glimpsed an officer in the back, one arm resting along the seat, the other lifting a cigarette in a long fashionable holder, a small moustached man. The new broom they had been expecting? She did not like the look of him. A premonition of some impending disaster this man might augur pushed reminiscence and pleasant speculation aside and she hurried on.

At Nadia's house she found Claude and Nadia both talking of troops they had heard were going up to the château to be stationed there.

'Surely not.' Stella doubted the truth of this rumour. 'Though it was always easier to keep track of the old colonel when he was engaged with the countess!'

'Well, if she can get goodies she won't care which German it is,' Nadia judged, then turned her whole attention to Billy. She swept the baby up into her arms, cooed and carried him under Claude's nose. 'They make good babies those two, don't they!'

Stella laughed at Claude's embarrassment. 'Makes it sound like a receipe for a gâteau, or something, doesn't she?' she said to Claude who looked as if he might leave if they were going to have baby or woman's talk. 'But I've come to ask you both something,' she went on, and as she began to tell the reason for the visit Claude sat down and Nadia was very quiet.

'So, you're going home, back to England,' Nadia stated and there was an ambiguity in her voice, a not-knowing if she was glad or jealous they had a way out. Then she tutted as if at herself, caught both Billy's hands in hers. 'You should all have gone before. My Claude has always said sooner or later you'd all be found and put in camps.'

Claude cleared his throat before making his points about the suggestion. 'Nadia's worked hard to make this place a home, and to put it to rights after the raid. If we leave it to live at Cleauville we may find it's gone, been relet or confiscated when you come back.'

'Ernest was concerned you should know that he would see Dr Uhabrol and through him pay the rent on your house for the time you live at the farm, plus wages for you both as caretakers there.'

'So he will stay there in hiding?' Nadia asked.

'Yes, he won't leave – and of course this puts you in danger if he were found ...'

'They have good places,' Claude told his wife, 'and with just him there it should be easy. It'd be our war effort, our chance to hoodwink old Marsan *and* the Germans,' he said darkly, then looking at Nadia nodded his agreement.

'All right,' she said, 'when do you want us to come?'

'We leave in twelve days ...'

'So soon.' She lifted the baby and he smiled obligingly. 'Yes, young Cleauville, the sooner you're safe away for the duration the better.'

It had been decided to give Lucille the letter Jean-Paul had left for her, before telling her of the arrangements that had all been made so quickly since the parachutist had landed.

239

'Gone?' she asked, taking the letter. 'When? Where?'

'With the man from London, he's . . .'

'Read the letter,' Jacques said, 'then we'll fill you in with anything you don't understand.'

'Thanks!' she almost snatched the letter from her brother and went up to her room. Once there the momentum of disappointment and anger left her. She sat on the bed, put the letter on the table and sat looking at it for a time. Why did she have the feeling that this was all bad news? Why had he just gone? Slowly she lifted the envelope, slid her finger under the sealed flap and stopped, closing her eyes, overwhelmed by the feeling that she was already bereft. 'Stupid,' she told herself and quickly slit the envelope and forced herself to open out the single page.

My darling Lucille

Time only to write a quick note before we are away on a packed itinerary, but we will all meet again quite soon. The others will explain what is happening.

The important thing is to say that I love you more than life – and you still haven't told me the story of the paper boat! Marry me, Lucille, let's have a double wedding as soon as possible.

Your loving Jean

Torn between tears, anger and happiness she raced downstairs to confront her brother. 'So what have you done? What have you arranged? Without me!'

'Here, now, come on,' her father ordered with a paternal gesture of calming. 'Let's all sit down and talk about this like adults. It sounded more like summer holiday quarrels and tantrums, did that.'

The remark made them all feel like children; Jacques winked at Stella as they sat down. Lucille remaining standing, aggressive, pacing about a bit as the story of the man from London was told, turning her back when the airlift details were given. Throwing Jean-Paul's letter on the table when she realised she would not see him again until they all travelled to a field near Lyons to meet a British plane to take them to England. She picked the letter up again, looked at it as if every word written on it were incomprehensible.

Then her father explained that Nadia and Claude were going to move into the farm for the duration of the war, 'Until you all come back.'

'If any of us come back,' Lucille said. 'If any of us even get to this

240

'...' she shook the letter, 'landing place.' Then she turned on them all, hurt, inconsolable. 'Everyone knows all about this, don't they! Nadia, Claude, Edmund, Dr Chabrol, his wife. I can see now why they were being so ... sort of sympathetic before I left. Everyone knew but me!'

'It was just the way it happened,' Jacques said. 'Jean-Paul had to go straight away to help this chap from London.'

'Oh! so "this chap from London" couldn't wait a few hours.'

'No,' Jacques said with the utmost certainty, 'you'll have to accept there was not time.'

'I ...' she began then ran from the room.

'I'll go,' Stella said.

In the bedroom Lucille sat with Jean-Paul's letter on the edge of her bedside table, the curtain threatening to blow it off. Stella went and sat by her side, put her arm around the stiff tense shoulders. For a moment there was resistance, then the letter fell to the floor and Lucille turned into her friend's shoulder and sobbed.

'Is it leaving your father?' Stella asked, for Jean-Paul's possible future role had not been mentioned.

Chapter Twenty-Eight

'No luggage.' Stella wasn't sure they didn't all repeat this to themselves many times over the next few days. Anything they took for the two days en route would presumably have to be left behind, but there were some things ... Only that morning Ernest had come from the bottling store carrying the two last bottles of the wine he had laid down the day Jacques was born.

'I wish I could send your father these,' he said wistfully. Stella had taken one from him and told him they would drink the other when they all came back. He had gone off happy at that, while she packed and repacked essential Billy things around the wine. She knew it was ridiculous, but it was also so symbolic she could not refuse, or leave it behind.

She devised a canvas bag she could sling over her shoulder; with clothes packed around the bottle and a shawl folded on top she could also use it as part carrier for Billy. She was feeding Billy herself, but a bottle of sterile water and fruit juice and other essentials would be shared between pockets. One small suitcase was to suffice for all of them until they reached the landing strip, when this would be abandoned.

It would, she acknowledged privately, be a relief to be off. Time spent with Ernest was becoming overwhelmingly nostalgic and emotional; not that he deliberately made it so, but every turn and corner held memories for them all. Everyone wanted there to be many more good times to come. Everyone knew there was the chance that this could be their final parting, when so many hazards assailed their futures.

Lucille came home from her work at the hospital three days before they were due to leave and told them that the doctor felt she should not risk coming from the farm to the village any more. 'He says the soldiers and police are moving back this way. They are even questioning the schoolchildren. They think some who come in from

242

outlying farms are carrying extra food in their lunchboxes, and leaving it in the woods for hidden Resistance workers and escaping soldiers.'

'The other side of Avignon the children are doing just that,' Ernest confirmed.

'The doctor and Jeannette send their love and say God speed, they won't risk coming again or it might draw attention here.' Lucille paused and drew a letter from her pocket. 'He gave me this at the last moment, told me that I must take it to England with me.' She turned it over. 'It's not sealed.'

'Read it then!' Jacques urged. 'Let's all hear it!'

This letter also was one page, not much longer in content than Jean-Paul's. She scanned the page then exclaimed, 'Oh! It's a kind of reference.' She looked up in surprise. 'A glowing reference, about my excellence as a nurse, my "ability to learn techniques that were beyond the normal call of a nurse's duties, and carry them out successfully. Reliable, capable, hard working, quite exceptional."'

'What a lovely thing to think of doing,' Stella exclaimed, 'that is certainly something to take, to be proud of.'

'It could help you back into a good nursing post,' Jacques told her. 'Well done, little sister!'

'You were always the doctor when we played nurses and doctors,' Stella remembered, 'perhaps you might even study and become a doctor. Why not!'

'Why not?' Ernest echoed. 'That would be wonderful. Yes, when you come back I'll have my own doctor, my own estate manager, and Billy to lead me by the hand and talk to me in my dotage.'

The when-you-go and when-you-come-back syndrome seemed inescapable and it was almost a relief to see Hector coming across the courtyard to the kitchen. 'This looks important,' Jacques said casually, watching the rate at which the crutch, the peg-leg and the foot came to their door.

'You have to go now,' he told them and when they stood staring at him, he waved his crutch at them. 'The police and the German officer are at Marsan's farm ready to encircle and raid this place. They've learned something, or one of you's been seen. Madame Marsan is at my cottage– she's risked her life to come and tell me.'

At that moment the telephone rang. Jacques picked it up, listened, but did not speak. 'We have to go up to the borie now, this second, just grab Billy and come. Pa, you come too.' When Ernest hesitated he cried, 'You can come back later for God's sake. Come on! That was Edmund: the Germans are on their way here from the village.'

Lucille stuffed her letter into her pocket. 'I'll help you with Billy.'

The inertia, that moment when limbs seemed paralysed by disbelief, was swept aside as the two of them ran upstairs. 'Take that little case,' Stella said as she slipped the canvas bag she had been experimenting with over her head, pushed a shawl on the top then picked up Billy and balanced him there. Lucille nodded and they ran back downstairs. Jacques was holding the door open, Ernest and Hector stood outside.

'*Au revoir* my dear old friend,' she said to Hector. 'Take care!'

He nodded and gestured her on her way. Lucille paused and pushed something into his hand, kissed his cheek and ran after her brother as he limped rapidly after Stella and Ernest.

He walked out to watch as they ran into the wood behind his cottage, away out of sight. He had done all he could. He opened his hand. The child had given him her Bible and rosary, and tangled with the rosary a fine chain containing a St Christopher pendant. The patron saint of travellers. She had surely intended to take that with her. It upset him to find it enmeshed with the carved ivory beads.

Once they were well out of sight of the road, they slowed the pace. Stella looked anxiously down at Billy, but he seemed quite content with the movement and the sight of the bushes going by. 'You are a good boy,' she breathed, but when they came to the borie he certainly did not like that. 'I'll take him outside,' Ernest said, 'you all rest while you can.'

Carefully Ernest carried his grandson around the medieval complex of houses. 'I dare say babies were born here, and boys played here,' he told him, 'and when you're older I guess your pa and your Auntie Lucille will bring you here to show you this place. It'll perhaps mean more to you than just a playground, which it was to them. It will be the beginning of an important journey for you, so perhaps it will have a special significance.' He smiled as the boy's eyes wavered, then closed. 'There,' he said with a smile, 'it was all so important your grandpa's talked you to sleep.'

He found a boulder in the middle of the stone houses and sat for a long time cradling the boy – a secret hour, having him to himself. He did not form into words his wishes, his hopes, the knowledge of what was shortly to come. He let his mind drift, expand to the infinities of time this ancient place held, the echoes of lives long, long, forgotten – and Billy's still to come. He experienced that strange selflessness of being one with everything, every stone, every blade of grass, part of the land, the sea, the sky, as if his present life were already cast off and his breath returning like a sigh to the wind.

The evening and the night came and they were glad there was food and a lamp up there. Stella fed Billy, but he would not be put down inside. She propped herself up on the skins so he could stay in her

244

arms. The two men took turns on guard, and the intricate system of tripwires were all set and checked. They spent much time listening, but they were too far away to hear any activity at the farm or village, unless as Jacques said there was 'gun fire or heavier stuff'.

At first light Jacques saw Edmund approaching. He skirted the trip-wires. 'All safe?' Edmund asked.

'And you?' Ernest asked, coming from the low doorway.

'It's been very touch and go,' Edmund admitted. 'Hector's all right. They searched the farm, the house, the outbuildings all again, still didn't find the loft. Our new colonel is an arrogant and ignorant young upstart, eager to make a mark, and so far he's done nothing! He's frustrated and nasty. I'm also not sure about the Marsan place. He may still have men there, I'm not sure, no one can get near, but he acts like a man with a card still up his sleeve.'

'You knew Madame Marsan had been to warn Hector?'

'There's still more to this than we know,' Edmund acknowledged, then went on. 'I've arranged for you to be picked up near Alès. You'll have to set off right away, because you've a long trek over the hills. I've made you a route.'

'One of your famous routes,' Stella could not resist saying as he produced a piece of paper and they grouped round him.

'This is probably the most important you will ever have,' he told her as he pointed out the footpaths they must follow. Next the trek went across scrubland up over the tops, then down to a small road leading to Alès. 'The man who will pick up you is absolutely reliable. His name is Berol. He'll take you to an old schoolhouse, been disused for years, and from there you'll be picked up and taken to Lyons.'

'Who picks us up from Alès?' Jacques asked.

'That Berol will tell you. Once you get to Lyons I'm not sure where you'll be taken there either, but I understand the place is a rabbit warren of hiding places. All the old houses have interjoining attics, they apparently go for kilometres!'

He held out his hand, which Jacques was a little slow in taking. 'You're leaving now?' he asked.

'No, you are, my friend, you are. Until we meet again.'

Stella wished a hymn sung in school assemblies had not echoed in her mind. 'Until we me ... e ... t at Jesu's feet.'

They assembled their few goods in a kind of scramble then stood watching and waiting as the goodbyes were said, curiously like saying farewell to one's hosts after a formal party, first to Edmund, then Ernest.

Jacques gave him a back-patting hug and Stella heard him murmur, 'God help me be as good a father as you.'

'Better I would think,' Ernest said, gripping his forearms as they parted with a kind of bracing gesture and a nod of approval.

Lucille held her father in a tight embrace for so long that Edmund took her hand and gently pulled her away. 'Jean-Paul's waiting for you,' he told her, and her father nodded and smiled reassuringly.

'Off you go,' he said, then he added, 'I wonder how big you'll all be next time I see you.'

'Oh! Pa!' The exclamation was half laugh, half cry. It was what he had always said when he and Gaby had seen them off after their holidays.

'This one will have grown.' Ernest touched the baby's cheek, then leaned and kissed Stella, whispering to her, 'God speed back to Blighty, now don't let them delay any more. Off you go.'

Striking upwards through the maquis the little party was soon out of sight. Edmund took Ernest's arm and was about to speak when there was a faint metallic rattle, then another. They both stood as if frozen, both knew what it could be, but needed confirmation. It came. A definite rattle of the tins at the end of one of the tripwires. Not an animal, not the breeze, a person.

Both were aware that they must act quickly, but this time it was Ernest who took control. He indicated to Edmund that he should take a path at right angles to the direction the others had taken and also away from the farm. He gestured 'Go'! Edmund queried the older man's intentions with a questioning nod. Ernest gave him a thumbs up, repeating the 'go' instruction more urgently.

Edmund gave him a salute, their hands met in a final clasp, then he was away, quickly, bent double, running with all the speed of a young fit man. Ernest moved back into the shadow of the borie so that if Edmund looked round he would be out of sight.

Then he went back inside the shelter and removing a small stone in the inner wall drew out a revolver and ammunition wrapped in oiled cloth. He had taken it there when Gaby had first died – a last escape. Now it had a better purpose. He had left it concealed when the hiding place had been furnished. His one regret was that there was obviously no time to hide the radio.

Above his head the tripwires began to orchestrate. What he needed to do was to create time for those escaping; every minute would be valuable. He assessed the advantages he had – a gun, knowledge of the area, the shelter he was in, the fact that as the tripwires had only become active after the party had left, and were the ones coming closer and closer to him, he could assume that no one had seen the others leave. He must keep those approaching interested in him for as long as possible.

246

Another advantage was what Edmund had told them of the new German officer: arrogant, eager for results – so probably easy to convince he was about to earn himself honours.

Suddenly Ernest knew what he would do. If he couldn't save the radio he would make it work for them until the end. Moving with resolve now he placed the headphones as near to the doorway as he could, then positioned himself so he could reach the morse key and cover the way into the inner chamber.

He mouthed a kind of silent prayer as the tripwire triggering the alarm nearest 'the chieftain's hut' began to sound. 'I don't know, Gaby, if there's anything after this. I do know you're not here like you used to be, and if you're not there either, well nothing matters too much. Help give that son and daughter – and grandson – of ours a head start, that's all I ask.'

Very deliberately he began to tap out a series of meaningless dits and dahs – and suddenly the tinkling alarms, the covert scrapes and snaps of twigs stopped. He could imagine them listening; the noise from the headphones must have been riveting in the stillness. He bet they couldn't believe their luck. Not only had they found the radio, they were about to catch an operator red-handed. 'You're also about to catch more than you bargained for,' he silently promised.

His hand began to ache. God, they were cautious. What was taking them so long? The delay was however just what he wanted. Perhaps they were taking down what he was sending, They would have fun trying to decode it!

He lifted his hand from the key to listen more intently. There was someone near the entrance, or inside it, the unmistakable sound of a boot being edged over stone echoed. He gave two more notes on the radio to encourage them.

He paused again and heard a man's voice, harsh, whispering, but unquestionably ordering. More covert noises. Some poor sod being ordered in here, he thought. But the next moment something dropped down through the chimney almost at his feet.

It could only be one thing. He pounced on it and threw it out into the other chamber. It exploded outside and there were screams and curses. Then he heard a noise on the roof. Another grenade? He waited two seconds then fired the handgun up through the chimney. There was a slither and a crash outside. Whoever had been up there had fallen off.

Regrouping now, he thought, ready for the next move. What next? He began clicking the key again, that should keep them interested and infuriate them. The new commander badly wanted to capture the radio.

He knew he must be near the end. In a final gesture he aimed his pistol at the doorway with one hand and with the other he tapped out a message no one in the world would ever understand but him. 'Dah-dah-dit, dit-dah, dah-dit-dit-dit, dah-dit-dah-dah,' her name and then the beginning of the message, 'dit-dit, dit-dah-dit-dit ...' But the word love was never completed as a German soldier with a machine gun stepped through into the inner chamber.

The shots sounded like the echoing outraged cries of hundreds of old ghosts as he and Ernest died together.

Chapter Twenty-Nine

Their heavy breathing as they topped the first rise, then rapidly began the skidding descent on loose scree, made Stella unsure whether she had heard shots. She paused for a moment, as did the others; they exchanged glances then hurried on. There wasn't much time for coherent thought as she struggled to keep Billy safe in his homemade sling, for going down was worse than climbing. Even the baby looked alarmed as she struggled to stay upright, throwing out his arms as if he too needed to balance. She was terrified she might fall and bump his head or crush one of his flailing arms.

Lucille was in front carrying the case, Jacques was at the back. He had his stick to help, but on uneven ground his leg was not up to this kind of punishment. Stella was aware he was struggling, his limp was becoming more and more pronounced. She turned to ask if he wanted to stop a moment, but he shook his head determinedly. 'Time to rest when we get to the road.'

Lucille, after having to be pulled away from her father, now seemed to have the man at the other end of the journey in her sights. She pressed on at a pace Stella and Jacques found hard to match.

Even so as soon as they emerged on the Alès road and looked about to find their bearings, an elderly man, as sinewy, withered and black as an old vine led a horse and cart from the gates of a solitary vineyard. 'Berol,' he announced and immediately took the case from Lucille and put it into the cart, then helped Stella to climb aboard with the baby, clucking and winking at the boy's wide-eyed attention. He motioned Jacques on to the front seat with him. 'It's not far,' he told them. 'You will find everything you need – for the baby too – in the old schoolhouse. You will be safe there and tomorrow a greengrocery van will call for you at six o'clock, no later, no sooner.'

'Do we need to know his name?' Jacques asked.

The man shook his head. 'You'll know when the time comes,' he told them.

Berol dropped them at an ancient schoolhouse half hidden by trees and briars, with not another building in sight. It looked as if no one had been inside its front porch or opened the double front doors for a hundred years or more.

Berol gestured them to go round the back, and having helped them alight, warned them to stay out of sight and waved them goodbye.

Billy was getting fretful, hungry, tired and uncomfortable. Leaving the other two debating the look of the place, Stella carried him round the side and to the back where a smaller door was accessible, or at least there were no creepers or bushes obscuring it. She pressed down the latch and pushed tentatively. It did not yield easily, its timbers had sagged on their hinges and resisted, but the door did open.

The room she found herself in had been a cloakroom; there were a few pegs still askew on the walls. It was dusty, full of dead leaves and had certainly not been prepared for anyone. Disconsolate, she wandered through into the former classroom, where not even a chair or an old desk remained to sit on to feed Billy, then through into a room which she supposed had been the head teacher's room – and here were the promised things. It felt like walking into Aladdin's cave. She fell on a pile of old but meticulously clean nappies like one reaching Mecca. She could have wept with joy. Here was a stove and water, and food and beds. She suddenly thought of Pierre, still working for the cause in his home town of Marseilles. He had taken such trouble doing such things as washing socks for the refugees. Now she knew how much it must have been appreciated. She ran back to tell the others. Edmund and his contacts had done them proud. His instructions must have been detailed and precise – as they would have been of course – and the attention given to them had been meticulous.

The essentials done for Billy, even his soiled nappy washed, their night in the schoolhouse in Alès was one of total emotional and physical exhaustion. Stella tried to recall the exact noise they had heard far behind them. Shots? Explosions? The twists and turns of the ways they had taken made even the direction from which the sounds had come uncertain. For a long time her mind went over the events and she heard the others give occasional sighs, their minds too active for sleep, their bodies too exhausted to move.

Then the next thing she knew was that someone was gently squeezing her hand. She looked up to see Jacques standing above her holding a cup. 'Coffee,' he said. 'It's five thirty.'

The greengrocery van was there at six, arriving Jacques thought as if the driver had waited along the road to arrive on the dot as arranged.

'*Bonjour*!' A trousered young woman greeted them as she opened the back doors and began pulling out crates of melons, cabbages, apples, carrots as if she was a hefty male instead of a slim young girl. 'This is where you have to be.' She indicated seats set up deep inside the vehicle. 'But this little one won't like it in there.' She made a rapid decision. 'You have papers?' she asked Stella.

'Yes, a war widow.'

'*Bon*! Sit alongside me, you are on your way to Lyons to see your uncle who is also a greengrocer.' She pointed to the name on the side of the van, 'That's him!' As Stella memorised the name, 'M. de Gex, Alès and Lyons', Jacques and Lucille climbed into the back and the crates and sacks of fruit and vegetables were piled in front of them. 'I go to one or two farms on the way to pick up produce,' she explained, 'we work on a kind of commune basis, all produce sold and prices pooled. It seems to work well, and the authorities are used to seeing our van all over the area. I by the way am called Jenny.'

They made four more calls, then arrived at a farm situated on the rich pastureland around Lyons. The farm had a huge herd of pale cream Charolais cattle. Here Jenny de Gex announced, 'This is my last call, I pick up a private supply of butter and cheese for the de Gex families back in Alès. I won't be long.'

A woman who could have been a much old sister to Jenny came bustling out to meet her. It was immediately obvious to Stella that there was something wrong. Jenny turned her back on her van and moved a step or two further away as the anxious conversation continued. Stella turned her head and called to those in the back. 'Something's wrong I think ...'

The older woman spread her hands as if to say what else could she do and after a moment's thought Jenny nodded and the two of them came back towards the van.

'There is a change of plan,' Jenny told them, 'I have to leave you here with my aunt, Agnès de Gex.' She tried to allay their alarm with a jolly, 'Lucky for you we're a large family with many uncles and aunts!' She helped them into the house and picked up the packages of butter and cheese waiting for her. '*Bon voyage*!' Her aunt went with her to the van and watching them Jacques wondered what had gone wrong as again the two of them became involved in a short but intense conversation. Then they kissed and Jenny left.

'So,' Agnès said as she returned, 'you will be my guests for tonight.'

'What has happened, madame?' Lucille asked.

'This I can't tell you. All I have had is a brief message from my husband to keep you here tonight. I know no details of where you go from here. Georges, my husband, doesn't tell me; he says it is better that way.'

She showed them to two bedrooms in the back of the house and left them to settle in. 'Now what would you like to eat later? Do you all like pork, or would you prefer chicken?' She was more confident, more businesslike, as she asked. This was her real domain.

'We are very glad of whatever you have,' Jacques said, 'a choice rather overwhelms us in the circumstances.'

'Nonsense, nothing is too good for you who want to fight on for France. My father and two of my uncles died fighting Germany in the last war. Anything I can do to help is a privilege – so pork or chicken? The porkis dead and hung, the chicken soon can be.' They all decided on pork. She left them to settle into their rooms but called back, 'The chicken would have been no trouble.'

'It makes me feel very humble,' Stella said, 'giving us what are obviously guest rooms and offering a choice of menu. I mean it's just beyond the call, isn't it.'

No Georges appeared for dinner, and his wife did not mention him, but they were aware of her many anxious glances at the clock.

'Is there no way to find out what has happened?' Lucille asked.

'He will come, he never lets anyone down!' It was an automatic reassurance, to which she added sombrely, 'Sometimes arrangements have to be changed.'

'Often?' Jacques prompted, all hanging on her answer.

'No, but he'll be here, I know, and,' she rose briskly from the table as if she wished to finish both meal and speculation, 'I'll call you early in the morning.'

'How early?' Lucille asked.

'I shall call you at six,' she told them, refused offers to help wash up. 'No, you rest, while you can.' Stella felt she wanted to be left alone to worry by herself.

'So do we fly out tomorrow night?' Jacques pondered as he and Stella prepared to spend the night in a large civilised double bed with Billy fast asleep in a Moses basket.

'She's terribly anxious,' Stella said, 'trying to put a good face on it – but definitely worried. I don't think anything like this has happened before. She certainly expected him before dinner, she set him a place.'

She looked over to where Jacques lay relaxed, hands behind his head, thinking, probably composing.

'When you think of how we've been passed so quickly from place to place, hand to hand, there's a lot of organisation already been done, more than even I realised. A lot of people risking their lives, a network of bravery.' He turned to her. 'My first headline, "A Network of Bravery", what d'you think?'

'Great.' She climbed on the bed and bent to kiss him. 'We're going to make it, aren't we.'

'If this last chap turns up, I really think we are.'

There was a discreet knock on their door.

Lucille came in looking anxious. 'I'm not happy,' she said, 'it all seems to have gone wrong. Where's her husband? I mean will they get us there on time? And I was wondering if *we didn't* get there on time would Jean-Paul still fly out with that Malin?'

This begged a certain answer, but when neither of them said anything she persisted with, 'What do you think? Would he, or wouldn't he?'

'Yes I think he would go. He's been asked to act as a courier, he would feel it his duty,' Jacques told her.

There was a short silence, then his sister demanded to know *exactly* what he meant. When she had listened to Jean-Paul's possible role as a spy moving between the two countries she rose and went to the window overlooking the lush green pastures, the great creamy white herds of cows like pale ghosts in the night. 'I wouldn't have left Pa if I'd known this,' she said. 'I think you should have told me. This is not fair.' Her voice and passion rose as she continued. 'I could eat my heart out as well at home as in England. You two could have come without me.'

'Pa wanted you to come,' Jacques reminded her. 'He wanted you to be safe.'

'I wanted *him* to be safe, but he wouldn't come with us!'

'He also needed to stay for your mother's sake, for her land,' Stella said quietly. 'It's a sacred trust to him.'

'I do know that,' Lucille admitted, 'but I just can't bear to think of Jean-Paul ...' Her hand described a rapid going to and fro.

'There may be other work ...' Stella began trying to find some comfort for her, and failing, as Lucille interrupted.

'Oh he'll volunteer for everything, particularly the most dangerous work!'

'Well one thing is very certain,' Jacques said, '*you* can't go back now.'

'No,' she said after a few seconds' thought, 'no.' She turned and left their bedroom.

Stella heard a noise in the night and rose to look at Billy, but he was fast asleep. She tiptoed to the window and looked out. A man

253

with a rifle was walking across the yard, then she heard a door open and the light from the kitchen shone out. The farmer's wife stepped out to meet the man. She caught his arm as if enormously thankful to see him. In the moonlight Stella saw his hand grip and hold hers as they went together into the house.

Stella returned to her bed. At least Georges was back, but something in the way he had gripped his wife's hand, instead of giving it just a reassuring pat, convinced Stella that something serious, or at least significant, had happened. She wondered if they might be called immediately to move on. She lay awake for much of the rest of the hours of the night and was up and had fed Billy when Agnès came to their bedroom door with coffee. 'Breakfast is ready for you downstairs.' Her face was solemn, no greeting smile, though when she saw Billy was up and ready she carried him downstairs, with the words, 'Come and meet my man.'

Downstairs they found a man who looked some years older than his wife, and as if he had slept in his clothes and had not shaved.

He shook their hands, then they all sat down to breakfast. 'Things have gone – well,' he looked up and smiled tiredly, 'wrong. In the same day we have had twelve members of our group arrested, two of our safe houses have gone. We do not know how much more information the Germans will have by now.'

They were all silent, the implications dire, the danger for them all extreme. 'But,' he went on, 'there is at least some good news for you, your two fellow travellers were prevented from falling into the trap the Germans tried to spring, and we transferred them to the pick-up place last night.'

'You mean,' Lucille asked, 'you mean the two men who are flying out with us are ...'

'They are hidden near the landing place, yes. Hungry and tired, much earlier than they planned, but there.'

'When do we go to join them?'

'As soon as we've breakfasted we'll be off,' he said, allowing himself a brief smile as he added, 'The taller, younger, of the men was asking much the same question about you.'

As they ate, and he did so like a man with hardly the energy to put the food into his mouth, he told them a little more of the problems that had beset this particular mission from the outset. 'Your two men were nearly picked up in Clermont-Ferrand. It's almost as if the Germans knew something of this man from England. They've been snapping at his heels several times. Last night was closest of all.' He paused to drink strong black coffee. 'They'll be expecting a plane to come to pick him up. But I don't think they have any idea where.

We've laid a false trail, we've even got some men the opposite side of the château, clearing fields of stones, and tree felling, as if they were preparing for a plane landing. So we must hope for the best.'

When they were ready to leave Agnès handed them a huge package of food and container of milk. 'You'll have all day,' she told them, 'and the other two won't have eaten since yesterday.'

A truck was to complete their journey to the landing site. Stella felt it was strange to be travelling in this kind of vehicle, with its tarpaulin-covered back and solid cab. It was just like those they had travelled alongside when they had first motored from Paris in a line of refugees – trucks with mattress tied on cab-tops as an extra precaution against the German dive bombers machine-gunning the stream of fleeing civilians.

She wondered if Lucille too had this strange feeling of having come full circle. Looking across at her, Stella did not think she was *remembering* anything, she was just anticipating reaching Jean-Paul.

It was nearly midday when Georges stopped his truck on a hilltop for them to see their destination. They overlooked a beautiful stretch of countryside, with the Château Allier, whose land it was, standing high the other side of a huge valley. A perfect setting with vineyards on the slopes up to the château and flat pastureland beneath. '*Magnifique!*' Stella breathed.

'Ideal for a landing,' Jacques judged, 'and the weather looks set fine. All should be well.'

'And we know we'll be going out together as soon as the plane arrives,' Stella said and was somewhat taken aback by the brilliant smile Lucille gave her. She glanced at Jacques, whose smug look as good as said, told you so!

'There is a small shelter in those trees, which was a hide for hunters.' Georges pointed to a dense group of birch and oak trees near the edge of the château's western plain. 'You'll soon be there.'

They unloaded from the truck on to the road and Georges asked them to forgive him for not walking further with them. They all dismissed such an idea.

'You have done more than enough my friend,' Jacques told him. 'Go back to your wife, Georges, we shall never forget either of you!'

'Godspeed!' Stella added.

They began the short walk through the wood towards the hide, but they had not gone far when Lucille dropped her case and ran to a man she had glimpsed coming towards them.

'Not Livingstone, I presume!' Jacques quipped, stooping to pick up the case.

When finally their long embrace was ended, Jean-Paul came smiling to greet them. '*Mon ami*!' he greeted Jacques and the two friends hugged and slapped each other on the back. Stella too was kissed and embraced. Jean-Paul stooped and took Billy into his arms. 'A handbag is no place for my nephew,' he told him, 'even though your name is Ernest!'

The seriousness of their situation dissolved into abandoned laughter.

'Is this a private party,' Malin came from the shelter to ask, 'or can any passerby who hears join in?'

'*Touché*!' Jacques admitted but told him the joke – it lost in the telling, but the food they had brought made up for the indiscretion.

'Never tasted anything so wonderful!' Raymond Malin exclaimed, biting into slices from a great crusty loaf packed with cold pork and oniony stuffing. Jean-Paul ate with one hand, the other holding Lucille's.

When they had eaten the elation of meeting gave way to more reflection about the mission. Malin was well pleased with the results, though 'It's been no tea party! I'd have been a goner several times if it were not for Jean-Paul here, and it's certainly shown me what the people of France are capable of. The risks they run! And last night the price some of them pay. I also know the kind of equipment the Resistance groups need as well as money.'

Stella, who had not slept much the night before, closed her eyes as the others talked. Lucille reached over and took Billy. 'Jean-Paul and I'll walk him a little outside, we'll keep good watch.' As they left the setting sun outlined the three of them in the doorway, just as the early morning sun had done when Lucille had come down from her night at the borie with Jean-Paul. Stella felt herself smile and fall from rational thought into sleep.

When she awoke they began making final preparations for their flight. There were maps from Channel coast agents, some codenames and contacts. It was decided to share the information between them all, so that if there was any mishap only a fraction of the information would be lost. As they were doing this Stella saw Jean-Paul pull off the signet ring he wore and slip it on to Lucille's engagement finger. It was too big, but as they waited Lucille spent some time winding strands of wool from a jumper that was being left behind through the ring to make it a safe fit.

As the night came, the moon rose higher and higher in the sky, so the panorama of the plain was as clear as if in daylight. Only the colours were different: the grass was deep blue-green as if a dew hung just above it; the firs were darkest aquamarine, while the birch trees played games with the moon, their leaves like fish as they moved in the silver light.

Grouped at the edge of the trees, they were all listening intently. The screech of a hunting owl came clear, sharp and sinister, but nothing more. There had been vehicles on the road earlier but now complete and utter silence fell, a listening silence, into which came a sound which Stella at first took to be a motorcycle on the road, then as the engine noise increased she realised that there was a black shape no bigger than an owl silhouetted against the moon. It rapidly grew larger. Beside her Raymond Malin flashed a series of long and short lights from his torch. Lights on the Lysander switched on and off in response, and the plane swooped low, the noise lessening as it throttled back to land. Lower, lower, they watched it sweep down, the band of sky under its wings getting narrower and narrower. Then it touched down, its grace suddenly gone as it rattled and bumped across the field. As she watched it ran to the end of the field where they were and turned, ready for the take-off.

'Now!' Jacques said and they set off towards the plane at a run. She saw the rear cockpit thrown open ready to receive them. She reached the plane first, thrust Billy in, then herself, then Lucille, Malin, then ... lights blazed from all around the field, and vehicles with sirens screaming came towards them.

'Christ!' she heard the pilot say. 'We gotta go, folks!'

There were shots.

'Come on!' Malin screamed from his position in the doorway and the plane began to rev up. The headlights were coming nearer, closing in. There were more shots and someone cried out, 'My God! No!' The next moment Malin had jumped from the plane with the order to the two girls, 'Stay there!' He was back in seconds, dragging another man with him. Even as he was in the plane and the other man still outside, they began to move. Malin leaned far out, heaved on the arm of a man and pulled him in as the plane gathered speed. Jacques. He was inside and closing the door when Lucille hurled herself towards him. 'Jean! Where's Jean!'

'Shot,' Malin said, pushing her back as he struggled to secure the cockpit. 'He's dead, my dear, they got him in the head.' He finally secured the door and turned to look. 'He wouldn't have known anything about it,' he added.

'We must go back!' Lucille shouted, trying to reach the door fastener as the plane raced across the field.

Jacques tried to hold her and contain her violence as they were thrown about, Stella trying to keep Billy from harm in the crowded space.

The plane reached the end of the field, seeming to meet other vehicle lights head on. The lights were surely too near, the aircraft not fast enough – the aircraft half faltered – then it lifted clear, the bumping of the wheels ceased and only Lucille cried out in agony to be taken back.

'You've left him? How could you!' She flailed at her brother's chest and face with her fists, so Malin was forced to help.

'Listen, m'dear,' he said clearly, 'he was dead before he hit the ground, before we were all in the plane, before we took off. If we had gone back it would have been for his body, we would have all been caught or killed on the spot for nothing. There's other people to think of, there's this baby.'

Lucille put her hand over her mouth and drew her knees up close and stared into space. Jacques took her other hand and against her will held it tight, held it until she stopped fighting him and suddenly turned into his shoulder, but now she did not cry, did not speak, did not move. 'He was my best friend,' Jacques said.

'Is there anyone else I can get for you when we land?' Malin asked Stella, as brother comforted sister.

'If my father's going to be there he'll arrange everything for us ... everything that can be done.' Just, she thought, as he had done when they had travelled into France.

They had travelled to France with Lucille griefstricken about her mother, now they returned with Lucille bereaved, she thought, in emotional terms, widowed. Stella glanced at the hand with which Lucille covered her head, seeming to try to shield it from any further blow. The left hand, with Jean-Paul's ring on.

Billy reached up to touch her face, poking his fingers into her mouth as she hung her head close to him. She felt overburdened with good things compared with her friend. She had vowed long ago that she would do all she could to help; now she made the same vow again, though it would she knew take longer. But there would be others alongside her. Jacques, her father. Philip? She had no idea where he was.

The plane began to make its descent, to an England as moonlit as the France they had left behind. Stella felt that this was the end of the most important journey she would ever make in life. It had in all ways sealed their futures, for better or for worse.

Epilogue

Stella and Jacques were married six months later, with Raymond Malin as their best man. Stella's father, handsome in the uniform of lieutenant-colonel, was accompanied by his wife-to-be, a fellow officer in the communications and decoding section of the secret service.

Philip, after the evacuation of Dunkirk, had gone on into the Middle East war zone. Taken prisoner at Tobruk, he was one of those exchanged for Italian prisoners. He returned home with amoebic dysentery which left him with utter suicidal depression. He told Lucille that all that had stopped him committing suicide was that he was too weak to climb over the hospital balcony railings, and that Stella had told him Lucille was finally coming to see him.

He recovered and less than six months later formed part of the D Day invasions. On his return he and Lucille were married. They made their home in England, where Philip became a barrister in his father's chambers.

Stella and Jacques returned to Cleauville after the war. Claude and Nadia, and general enmity against Monsieur Marsan, had managed to keep the land intact, though much neglected. Claude and Nadia stayed on in Hector's cottage. The old soldier had lived long enough to see Germany beaten. He had died peacefully in his sleep, his table covered with a set of maps bestrewn with homemade flags showing the last phases of the war, and on his flagpole his *tricolore* had been flying.

Stella and Jacques had three more children, two more boys and finally Gabrielle Kathleen. Jacques wrote, his injured leg, which was a problem all his life, propped up on a padded stool under his desk. He became an expert writer about wines and their districts, and as Billy grew old enough to take on some of the organisation work of the vineyard began to experiment with fiction.

Victor stayed on in Cleauville, and it was thanks to him and the de Gex family that Jean-Paul's body was brought back to Cleauville and entombed nearby.

Lucille and Philip came every spring to Cleauville, usually as the years went by in May when the temperature suited them, and they would, the four of them, walk by the river, the two men in front and the women dawdling, hanging on each other's arms, behind. It often seemed little short of a miracle to Stella that the four of them could walk this last part of their journey still together.